WORLD DIVER

HAYLIE HANSON

WORLD DIVER

THE LUMINAUT TRILOGY

BOOK ONE

HAYLIE HANSON

To every person who's ever felt like

a square peg forced to fit a round hole,

this story is for you.

Let your Light shine.

CHAPTER ONE

I'M GOING TO CATCH a big one, I can feel it.

Holding my breath, I lay flat on my surfboard, feeling the rhythm of the tide beneath me. Anticipation tugs inside my chest, like the ocean pulling me into its ebb and flow.

Water begins to rise just behind my board, and I paddle fast, angling my board slightly ahead of the building wave. I won't let this chance to ride a monster slip through my fingers, not after a whole afternoon of losing waves to summertime tourists clogging up the swells, or more experienced surfers dropping in when I've clearly got the right of way.

This one is all mine.

"Get it, Callie!" The excited whoop of my best friend, Will, echoes behind me.

A smile forms on my lips around ragged breaths, and I swim faster. The wave starts to crest, and my arms shovel the salty spray like long, spindly paddles. I won't miss this wave. I'll ride it all the way to the break.

As soon as the giant wave peaks, I hop to my feet and drop in. Water barrels under the nose of my board and I zip away, fast as a rocket cutting through the swell. Salty droplets cling to my lashes and an ecstatic laugh escapes, ringing through the air over the crash of roaring water.

Will and a few other local surfers cheer me on.

"Yeah, Callie!"

"Way to go!"

The rush of the wind and stinging spray nips my face, blowing my hair away from my neck. I pull up the nose of my board, spiraling into a quick, spinning turn. Will might call me a show-off, but he'll be secretly jealous he didn't catch my wave.

All too soon my ride is over, and my board slows in the flats. That's the thing about waves—all that hard work for a ride that lasts about thirty seconds, and then, poof, the wave is gone, little more than a ripple against the shore. But while they last, they're the most fun I've ever had.

I kick out of my ride and hop off my board into the icy Pacific, basking in the bluer-than-blue California sky and the brilliantly white August sun.

"Dude, Callie, that was awesome!" Will rushes up, trudging through the knee-deep water, dragging his board behind him.

"Did you see the whole thing?" I grin and pull my heavy board out of the surf, walking next to Will toward the shore. He flips his mop of floppy hair out of his face in one swift motion, his eyes dancing in the sunlight.

"Yeah, it was totally sick!" A smirk turns up the edges of his mouth. "You didn't have to crank that turn, though. You make the rest of us look bad."

I laugh again, the sea breeze tearing the sound away. "You need to rise to my level. I'm not going to suck just to make you feel better about yourself."

"Whatever." Will rolls his eyes, but smiles anyway.

Will Avila has been my best friend since the first day of kindergarten. He's like another brother, only we don't fight and I'd rather hang out with him than my three real brothers. He even looks like he could be my brother. We have the same smattering of freckles on our cheeks, almost the exact same shade of golden brown hair, large brown eyes, and olive skin, and nearly identical bow-shaped mouths. The only difference is I'm long, lean, and lanky, whereas Will is short, bordering on stocky. Will knows me better than anyone in the whole world — which is more than I can say for everybody else in my life.

We deposit our boards on the beach, then unzip our wetsuits and peel them off like orange rinds, flopping onto the white, sugar-fine sand in our bathing suits while the sun dries our soaked skin and hair.

"I think you like showing off in front of all the big-league Verona Beach surfers." A teasing grin lurks around the edges of Will's mouth. "Don't let it go to your head, because I've got all kinds of embarrassing stories about your early epic fails, Calliope James."

"I asked you not to call me that in public, Wipeout Will." Will is notorious in the Verona Beach surf community for his hardcore bail-outs. Seriously, arms and legs flying everywhere like a confused pelican. It's hilarious.

"Your name is not that big of a deal," Will counters.

"It is, too! Some lurker from school could hear you and my life would be over." Eh, a touch dramatic. Whatever.

"I know you don't like being called Calliope, but I think it's awesome." Will nudges me with his elbow. "Don't you remember reading *The Odyssey* freshman year? Calliope was a muse. Even the gods were in love with her."

"The only thing I remember about *The Odyssey* is that it bored me to death. Besides, my parents didn't name me after ancient Greek poetry. They aren't hipster." I whip my hair over my shoulder, wringing out the salt water before it becomes a frizzy mess. Tiny droplets turn the white sand tan. "I'm named after my

Great-Grandma Cal on Dad's side."

"At least your mom and dad didn't have you as an afterthought right before they retired." Will scowls. "Mine only wanted a kid to take antiquing with them. Or caddy golf clubs. Take your pick."

"At least *yours* aren't in your face about college morning, noon, and night." I roll my eyes just thinking about it.

"College? Seriously?" Will makes a face like he just stepped on a sea cucumber, or something equally slimy and gross. "Did they forget you've got two more years of high school?"

"Dad says I've got to start thinking about my future," I summarize the lecture I've heard daily. All. Summer. Long. "I'm aimless, and have no motivation, and no college will take me with my mediocre grades and lack of extracurriculars. He wants me to play sports, like Jase, get straight As, like Ryan, and learn every musical instrument in the orchestra, like Tyler." I tick off the list of my brothers' accomplishments on my fingers as I rattle them off.

Will shoots a smirk my way. "Not the last one. You tried to learn flute in 7th grade, and you were so terrible, he begged you to quit."

"That's true," I say. "I thought he was going to take a screwdriver to his eardrums."

Will laughs. I smile, to humor him, but I don't laugh. It's not a very funny subject for me. There are five kids in my family, and I'm the only one who isn't talented at anything. Jase has been king of the soccer field since before he started high school, Ryan is a certified genius (Mom had him tested), Tyler is a modern-day Mozart, and Olivia, the three-year-old, is adorable and sweet, and does modeling for one of the boutique children's clothing shops in town.

And then there's me: stuck-in-the-middle Callie James

Actually, I'm not entirely incompetent. I'm getting really good at robotics, and I've practiced coding all summer. Not that Dad would care about robotics, or anything else I love that he has no point of reference for, but at least it's something I can say I'm good at. Also, I've never been lost. I just *know* how to get places without looking at a map. Mom would get lost going to the grocery store if not for me. I'm basically a human GPS with fantastic night vision—Dad says I move like a cat in the dark. They're useful skills, but not exactly talents, especially compared to my prodigy siblings.

"Looks like the weather's about to get gnarly." Will frowns at the dark clouds rolling in from the north. As if on cue, the wind picks up, snapping the California state flag against the pole. My damp hair blows against my cheeks until it sticks to my skin.

"Dad said there's going to be a storm this afternoon." I watch the sun begin to fade behind thunderclouds. "I bet he'll dock the boat at the marina early. He always brings clients back early when there's a storm."

Dad runs a sport fishing charter, and never plays around with bad weather. If there's even a chance of rough seas, he hightails it back to port, stat. He never wants me to surf when there's a predicted storm, either. I usually ignore him.

"That's smart," Will observes. He stands, and a strong gust whips his hair away from his forehead. "We should make like your dad and bail."

"Why? It's not storming yet."

I cast a hungry glance across the building waves. They're intensifying rapidly, but it's nothing Will and I can't handle. Well, nothing *I* can't handle.

"You want to surf in that?" Will arches a brow. "You've got a death wish."

"The masses of tourists taking lessons are leaving." I gesture at the churning water, where surf instructors call out to their students to make for the beach. "More waves for us, right?"

"No way." Will shakes his head firmly.

"Scaredy-cat," I tease.

"Text me later if you're alive." Will heaves his board under his arm. His eyes hold a querying look. "Is Jase coming to pick you up?"

"Yeah, at three."

"He's still hogging the car?"

"What was your first clue?" A scowl wrinkles my forehead. "He took it early this morning to go to soccer camp and meet his new girlfriend, Jen, for lunch—and pretty much takes it all the time without consulting me, regardless."

Mom and Dad allow the unfair monopolization because he's super-star athlete Jason James, and "soccer will get your brother a college scholarship, surfing won't." Athletic skills equal car privileges in my family, and since you can't varsity letter in surfing at Verona Beach High, any activity I want to drive to is automatically superseded by Jase.

By "activities," of course, I mean going to the beach to surf, and sometimes Starbucks. It's not like I actually *do* anything. But it's the principle of car-sharing, right?

"I'm taking off. Don't drown, okay?" Will calls over his shoulder, his surfboard cutting a trail through the sand as he plods toward the parking lot.

"See ya, Will!" I wave goodbye, then slip back into my wetsuit. Now that the tourists have cleared out, it's my turn to ride a few awesome barrels.

I jog into the surf, water splashing all the way up to my face. Once the water reaches my thighs, I launch my board and stretch out on the deck. Forceful waves push me back every time they break. It's laborious work, and I'm getting pretty raked over, but it's worth it. See, Mom and Dad? I *can* work hard for things I really want. Just not stellar grades and varsity sports.

At last, I paddle past the edge of the pier. There's something impossibly wondrous about looking back at the beach and the tiny, dollhouse hotels, nothing surrounding me but endless ocean. The feeling of being free and alive washes over me, settling deep into the calm place inside my soul—a comforting peace I can't find anywhere but out here. A feeling like I belong.

Not many surfers remain in the waves, maybe two or three guys known for being extra gutsy. I guess it isn't just tourists who are spooked by the impending storm. All the waves to myself? No complaints here.

"Hey, Callie!" One of the local surfers, Derek, calls to me from a couple yards out.

I wave my arm high. "Derek! What's up?"

"You better head back, things are about to get dicey." Derek straddles his board and points to the blackening sky overhead.

I smile brightly. "It's cool, I'll be careful!"

Derek looks incredulous, but shrugs, turning away. He stretches out on his board and surfs the next wave, hightailing it up the beach to the safety of the parking lot.

I catch two amazing waves early, but the surf is rapidly getting rough. Waves break violently all around, forcing me to bail in deep, dark waters. A strong rip pulls my board out toward the wildness of the windy sea, dragging me farther and farther from the safety of the shallows no matter how hard I swim against it. I'm the only surfer left in the water, and even I can admit when waves start to get sketchy.

"One more," I tell myself. "One more, and I'll go."

BOOM CLAP

A deafening roar as the thunderclouds above my head rumble and quake, smashing into each other, shaking the sky. White, electric light flashes terrifyingly close, and I scream, heart pounding out of my chest.

Lightning on the ocean—instant electrocution.

Will was right. Surfing alone in the storm is going to kill me. He'll never let me live it down. Except, I'll already be dead. Have a good laugh about it, Will. Make sure everyone at my funeral knows you told me so.

I cower atop my board, breath sticking around a sob. Getting struck by lightning is a pretty fast way to go, isn't it? Sudden and immediate death. Maybe I won't even register the pain.

But nothing happens. I crane my head to look for the strike I'm sure I saw and heard. What I find instead takes my breath away.

"Whoa."

No crackling sparks of electricity, no popping tendrils reaching into space. The light before my eyes doesn't connect to the gloomy clouds gathering just a hundred yards out to sea, or split the fabric of the air. No, this light spirals from the water itself, stretching toward the sky like a glimmering, golden beam of pure brilliance. It is the most beautiful thing I've ever seen.

CRASH BAM

A rogue wave slams into me, dragging me under, my board spiraling out of control as the leash yanks my ankle painfully back and forth. The sea tosses me about, little more than a mermaid rag doll in the strong current that reels me in like a fishing line toward impenetrable depths.

You suck sometimes, ocean.

At long last, my face crests the surface. Gulp after gulp of salty air floods my lungs before another wave breaks over my head, taking me down deep with the undertow. Okay, fun's over. I have *got* to get to shore. Swimming with all my might, fighting the push and pull of the storm surge, I heave my upper body onto my board. I'm paddling against the crest of a behemoth swell when something catches my eye. Something — odd.

Just past the edge of the pier, where the mysterious light rose from the surface of the water, there's a *thing* stuck to the seabed. And it's *glowing*.

"What the…"

Laying flat on the deck of my board, I paddle out closer to get a better look. Whatever it is, it's clearly visible, despite the murky water. From the seabed, the glowing thing brightens, begins to pulse, and a strange, almost magnetic feeling of need overwhelms every sense, every fiber of my blood and bone. The longer I look at the glow, the deeper I fall under its magic spell.

Callie… Callie… It's as if the glowing thing calls me, begs me to take it, urges me to dive deep. To lose myself in its unknown, strange brilliance.

Let's back up for a moment and assess: this is the point where most people would decide it's a weird, bioluminescent fish or a piece of equipment that fell off a boat. They would surf back to shore and wait for their brother to come get them. Because safety, and not-dying.

But I'm not most people. I'm… impetuous? Impervious? Whatever word Mom uses to describe my stupidity — because what I'm about to do is incredibly, entirely, and absolutely stupid.

I plunge headfirst into the raging water.

My lungs burn, my body pleads for air. The pounding in my head and ears creeps toward my eyes, and I blink against black spots, then white flashes. A rip current drags me farther and farther out, but I can't leave the thing. The glow is so entrancing, so — hypnotic. One last reach, struggling against my board leash, and my fingers wrap around my prize.

I suck in breath after desperate breath the second my lips bob above the water, clutching the glowing thing close to my chest. It feels light, cool, and smooth against my palm, like it's made of air, water, and solid matter all at once. About a foot long and narrow, cylindrical, and yet not truly formed. Somehow, it's… sticky? No. Not exactly. More like magnetic, as if it's somehow bonded to me. The thing molds itself into my hand, nestling against every crevice of my fingers. Wiping stinging saltwater from my eyes, I hold it up and out of the surf, getting a better look.

Whir – zum.

The object starts to vibrate in my hand, pulsing energy through my entire body, cutting to my core. Muscles and veins become unsettled, warmth and burning power ripping through them. The glow manifests brighter and brighter until it blazes like star-fire. Light dances white, gold, every spectrum of color, spinning through my field of vision until light is all I can see, all I can comprehend.

Birds scatter. The air grows silent. The water calms, becomes a glassy mirror despite the violence of the oncoming storm. All around me a gentle ripple spreads, growing more and more intense until the ripple builds into a violent rumble, like an underwater freight train charging toward the surface. Toward me.

"Ah!"

I shriek, shoving the glowing thing under the surface of the water, and will my hands to open, to drop the thing onto the seabed. But my fingers only tighten, moving apart from my consciousness. It slips even further into the curve of my hand, almost like it *knows* it belongs there.

Did anyone see it? Shallow, raspy breaths pant hard against my lips as I scan the horizon for other surfers, tourists strolling the beach or the pier. But everyone has taken shelter from the storm. Nobody lingers, not even the gulls.

Unzipping the neck of my wetsuit, I shove the glowing object inside, next to my skin. Immediately, the blinding light fades. The waves grow weaker, more predictable. Even the current, which had been so strong just minutes before, seems subdued, and the sky overhead opens with gentle rain.

But the glowing rod still hums, still pulses.

Everything about my discovery feels dangerous, wild, and untamed — as treacherous as the storm that tried to carry me out to sea. There's nothing safe about it, nothing subdued. It is raw power made manifest, and I should be terrified. A rational person would immediately begin coming up with ways to get rid of it for good.

And yet, somehow, in ways I can't explain, it all feels like *me*. Like the feeling I get when I'm waiting for a wave to crest, to take me on the most spectacular ride, or the sensation of freedom, peace, and belonging I get when I'm sitting alone in the midst of the blue deep, breathing clean air and drinking in sunlight. The rod feels like that, too. It's as if the power in the rod and something deep in my soul are inextricably one and the same.

Whatever this thing is, it's *mine*. And it's coming home with me.

CHAPTER TWO

"YOU'RE LATE, LOSER!"

Jase waits in the parking lot with an absolutely murderous scowl on his face as he shouts at me from the driver's side window of our beat-up Camry. Nice to see you, too, Jase.

"Sorry, lost track of time." I secure my surfboard to the roof rack with bungee cords the best I can in the onslaught of pounding rain, then hop in the passenger side, combing my tangled hair with shaking fingers. Can Jase hear the rod in my wetsuit, humming away?

"'I lost track of time,'" Jase affects his ditzy-girl voice, the one he uses to make fun of me. "You're an idiot for surfing in that, by the way." My brother nods toward the crashing waves beyond the abandoned beach. "Mom and Dad will kill you when they find out."

He doesn't hear the rod. Whew. "I was fine," I assure him. "It's just a little rain."

Definitely not going to mention the sparkling light column spiraling from the ocean, or the freaky, glowing rod thing I'm taking home. The rod that's still pulsing softly against the skin of my back as I lean into the seat. The rod I almost drowned trying to retrieve, that wormed its way through my skin and into being the second I touched it—that rod.

"A little rain? Dad's already home, and Mom's wedding was postponed," Jase shoots me a sideways glance. "There was a huge lightning strike when I was driving to get you. Didn't you see it?"

"Yeah, I saw it."

It wasn't actually lightning, but trying to explain a light phenomenon spouting from the depths of sea to Jase would be like explaining the theory of relativity to a bored first-grader. Jase has zero tolerance for anything that can't be summarized in two or three words.

"You didn't take that as a hint to get out of the water and come wait for me? You're even more of an idiot than I thought."

I start to seethe as Jase puts the car in gear and we pull out of the parking lot. I'm really not in the mood to be interrogated and called names, not when I've got a possibly-deadly glow stick of unknown origin hidden in my wetsuit.

"Lighten up," I snap. "You don't like me in your business. Stay out of mine."

"I'm just worried about you dying, is all," Jase retorts, his dark eyes narrowing. "Why are you so ticked-off?"

"I'm PMS-ing right now."

It's a lie, but all I need to say to get Jase off my back. Immediately, his face wrinkles into a look of pure disgust, like I just served him a plate of rotted fish guts.

"Majorly TMI, Callie."

We don't say another word as we drive away from the empty beach.

The second we get home, I dump my surfboard in the garage and slip past the kitchen. First order of business: hide the rod somewhere safe. Ideally, somewhere my family will never find it—ever. Maybe I can sneak into my room without Mom or Dad catching sight of me. A few tiptoes along the hallway, into the foyer, and I'm almost free and clear. I just have to cross the living room, and I'll be—

"Hey, Callie, how was your hot surfing date with Will?"

Great, I've been spotted. Ryan and Tyler, my younger brothers, sprawl out on the floor, engrossed in a video game. Their skinny limbs resemble starfish on a rock. Neither of them bothers to look away from the television as I dart across the living room toward the hall. I swear Ryan has eyes in the back of his head. Must be a genius thing.

"It wasn't a date, Ryan."

"Seriously, Callie? You're the densest person alive," Ryan snarks over his shoulder, never once tearing his eyes away from the blood-spurting video game zombies he's slaying. "Is he your boyfriend yet?"

Ryan's asinine question irritates me. "I don't like Will like that, and he doesn't like me like that, either."

"Can't you like him just a little bit?"

Ryan keeps pushing the issue—probably because he can't see my expression, which grows more lethal with every passing second. My brothers give me a hard time about Will pretty much constantly, and it's *not* appreciated.

"I've always wanted a rich relative," Ryan goes on. "Nepotism has perks. Vacation condos in Puerto Vallarta, private planes, Porsches."

"Shut up and play your game, Ryan."

"I'm telling you, Callie, you need to get in on the Avila money." Ryan decapitates another zombie. "We'd all be set for life. It's not like we can count on Jase. There are rocks smarter than Jase."

I purse my lips. It's so rude the way Ryan talks about Will's family. I mean, yeah, they're one of the wealthiest families in Verona Beach, and their house at the top of the hill has ocean views from all the windows, even in the bathrooms, and it has three gigantic balconies. So what? Will doesn't act rich. He's not a snob, he's cool. Just not dateable. I mean, not to me.

Goes to show how little my brothers actually know me.

"You'd better stop teasing me about Will," I threaten Ryan, "because if you don't, Old Man Ormandi will come get you in your sleep."

Ryan snorts a laugh when I name-drop Verona Beach's local boogeyman, but Tyler tears his attention away from the game to stare, gape-mouthed and bug-eyed. He's eleven, young enough to believe in urban legends.

"Callie, don't say that!" Tyler cries. "Saying his name three times will summon him!"

I remember the grade-school myths all too well. Leaning forward, I cup my hands around my mouth to whisper ominously. "Old Man Ormandi, Old Man Ormandi, Old Man Ormandi!"

"Stop it!" Tyler yells.

"Dude, Tyler, did Jase tell you what happened when he egged Old Man Ormandi's house two Halloweens ago?" Ryan turns his head just enough that I can see his wicked smile. "He said a pair of glowing yellow eyes stared at him from the front window and followed him down the street."

"Was it yellow eyes?" I tilt my head. "I could have sworn it was fires starting themselves behind all the curtains."

Tyler's face pales white as a sheet. "You better be joking, Callie."

"When a pair of glowing eyes sets your room on fire tonight, let me know, okay?"

Tyler chucks a throw pillow at my face, and I sprint to my room, laughter ringing down the hall.

Okay, time to figure out what this rod is, and, most importantly, where to hide it in the meantime. I unzip my wetsuit slowly, careful not to let the rod fall to the floor, and ease it away from my skin. As soon as it's in my palm, the rod sticks itself to me, and the glow intensifies. The pulsing becomes a tremulous whir, so powerful it numbs my hand.

"Ow!" The rod crashes to the rug, and I shake out my hand to ease the painful tingles. Except...

Except my fingers are glowing—brilliant, shimmering, and golden.

"Oh, no." My heart thumps out of my chest when I hold my fingers in front of my eyes. The strange, wild power and all-consuming energy I'd felt when I grasped the rod in the surf cries to break free, trapped in my incandescent hands. Swirls of light, little more than threads, manifest in thin air from my fingertips—remarkably solid and near-sentient, dancing and twirling around each other as they explore my room, my hair, my face.

Stop glowing. Go away. Be normal.

As quick as the glowing in my hands appeared, it begins to fade—as if obeying direct orders from my unspoken plea. The power retreats through my hands and arms, settling against my heart until all is silent, dormant, trapped.

What *is* this thing I found? Why does it surge light inside me and all around, turning my hands into neon torches? If it can manifest unnamed power through my entire body, make the ocean freak out in the middle of a storm surge, and shoot a beam of light into the sky, who knows what else it can do?

I'll google it later. The internet knows everything, right?

"Callie? Are you home?"

Just what I didn't need—Mom barging in, unannounced.

I throw open my closet, pulse pounding in my ears as Mom's footsteps approach my bedroom door. Frantic, I scour through my secret robotics nest of motherboards, motors, wheels, and claw clamps, desperate for something to hide the rod. In the very back, there's a shoebox from a pair of boots I got last Christmas. Not ideal long term, but for present purposes, it works. I dump the boots out of the box, shoving the glowing rod wrapped in my beach towel inside just as my door creaks open.

"Gah! Mom!" I drop the shoebox. It crashes to the floor, but by some miracle, it doesn't open. I leap in front of it the second Mom peeks her head in.

"Callie?" Mom scowls at the box, then at me. "What's going on?"

"Uh, nothing important." I wasn't hiding anything from you, Mom. Especially not some otherworldly, glowing, rod-thing I found in the ocean.

"Why is that shoebox in the middle of your room?"

I slide the box into my closet with my foot and shut the door. "No reason. Trying on my boots."

"In August?" Mom looks skeptical. I just stare at her, like, really awkwardly.

Mom clears her throat and tucks a piece of her hair behind her ear. "So, how was the surf? You and Will were out of the water by the time the storm hit, weren't you? I worry about you surfing when the weather turns. Dad hates you surfing in rough water, too. It changes so suddenly, the worst can happen any second."

"It was great, really awesome." I force a smile around grinding teeth. "Nothing out of the ordinary at all. We were out of the water in plenty of time."

More lies. But Mom seems to have forgotten about the weirdness with the shoebox, so score one for Callie.

"That's a relief. Get changed and come help me with recipe testing. I'm trying some new things I might want to put on the catering menu, since my wedding was postponed."

Mom softly closes the door, and I release a rattled breath.

Close call. After changing out of my wet bikini into regular clothes, I check the rod in the shoebox one more time.

It's still humming. And vibrating. Delicate strands of physical, floating light peek through the fibers of my towel, reaching for me like disembodied fingers. They tickle my skin, glittering specks of glowing gold erupting along the backs of my hands. I should be absolutely horrified by the rod, by everything it can do—but I'm not. I don't know which part I find most unbelievable: the rod itself and the power it contains, or my total fascination with it.

A different kind of vibration buzzes in my pocket. I've got a text. Will.

> Hey, are you alive?

I chew my lip, debating whether or not to tell Will about the glowing rod. No, I'm not going to tell him. Not yet. It feels a little deceitful, because Will and I tell each other everything, and we've never had secrets between us. But it won't be a secret forever. I'll come clean once I can figure out what the glowing rod is. *If* I can figure out what it is. I text back.

> No, I'm dead.

My phone buzzes again a split second later.

> Lol, very funny. Glad you made it back okay. See you tomorrow.

I don't send a reply. Instead, I shove my phone in my pocket and check my hands one more time. No glowing. No power surge. No golden flecks. Just regular, suntanned Callie hands.

I close my closet door and march down the hall.

Mom and Dad chat in the kitchen with Jase about his soccer club schedule when I round the corner and don my apron. Mom hands me a chef's knife and a bunch of tomatoes for *bacalhau no forno*, which is salted cod with tomatoes and potatoes, and we eat it weekly at home. Why Mom wants to put a rustic, Portuguese fish recipe on her fancy, French-inspired catering menu, I don't know, but I also don't care enough to question it. I get to work dicing in silence. Maybe Dad won't notice my presence and I can go the rest of the day without a sermon, because this has been an unsettling enough afternoon without—

"Hey, Cal, did you finalize your school schedule this week?"

Never mind. Dad can't go twenty-four hours without a lecture, it seems. I bristle instantly. "I'm all set with the required classes. English, US History, Chemistry, Algebra II." The same answer I gave him yesterday. And the day before that.

Hopefully, he'll sense my impatience regarding this particular topic and drop it. Dad and I used to be really close, but lately, all he wants to talk about is school, or extracurriculars—and my disappointing lack of participation in them. Which has made things incredibly tense between us.

"Junior year is a big year," Dad goes on, oblivious. "You've got to start prepping for college."

I purse my lips, focusing on the tomatoes, their juice dripping across the cutting board. "Yeah, I know."

Jase turns eighteen in September and is going to be a senior. *Why don't you talk to him about college, Dad?* Like Will said, I've got two more years to figure out my future.

"What about your electives?" Dad persists.

Tomato seeds stick to the chipping nail polish on my fingernails. "I'm not signed up for those yet."

In the corner of my eye, I see Dad give his head a jerking shake—something he only does when he's really frustrated. I recoil inside, the weight of his disapproval hitting my stomach like a leaden brick.

"Calliope James." Dad says my full name. Not my middle name, that's reserved for Mom when she's about to ground me. But Dad only calls me Calliope when I'm letting him down.

Deep breath — salvage the damage. "I think I'm going to sign up for robotics."

It's the first time I've brought up my super-nerdy, super-secret interest to my family, and I'm not certain how they'll react. Not even Will knows the extent of my growing fascination with robotics — he thinks the YouTube videos I stay up late watching are random vlogs, not teaching myself coding. But Dad perks up.

"Oh, yeah? What's that all about?"

"You work with little machines and things," I explain, tearing my gaze away from the tomatoes at the prospect of rare parental approval. "The class gets to design and build their own robots throughout the year, and program them to have different functions."

"That sounds like a lot of fun!" Mom smiles offhandedly as she arranges sliced potatoes and onions into a baking dish. A small, semi-distracted gesture, but it makes me almost giddy after Dad's stinging disappointment.

"It is a lot of fun." I set aside my chef's knife and add the diced tomatoes to the dish with the onions. "At the end of the semester, they build an arena in the parking lot for everyone to show off their robots, and —"

"News flash, Callie, that class has a huge waiting list," Jase interrupts. "You would have had to sign up back in May if you wanted to get in."

"I got an A in Design and Technology last year, so I got put at the top of the waitlist," I counter. "My counselor called Thursday and said there's an open spot in the class, but I have to let her know Monday or she's moving down the wait list."

"That's great. I think you should take it." Dad *almost* looks proud. "It's been ages since you've shown interest in anything other than surfing with Will Avila. STEM classes look great on college applications, too." He sips a cup of coffee, and I can practically see the 'how do I get my lazy, deadbeat daughter to take an interest in life' wheels spinning around in his brain. "What about sports? Maybe volleyball? I always thought you'd be great at volleyball."

I knew the sports conversation was coming. It always does. "Dad, I'm not very good at sports." Except for surfing, which Dad considers a waste of time and not a real sport.

"She's right," Jase adds. Thanks for nothing, Jase. "Besides, she's too old to start as a junior."

"Not necessarily." Dad sets the coffee mug he's been nursing on the table. "There were a couple guys on the baseball team with me that didn't start playing until they were juniors. Colleges like varsity sports."

I lean into the corner of the counter, as if pressing against it with all my strength will allow me to turn invisible. "Yes, you like to remind me. A lot."

"Because it's true." Dad frowns, stern, and I take a deep breath, steeling myself for inevitable flaying.

"You can't go through life like a perpetual beach bum, Callie. All you want to do is surf, or waste time at the beach with your friends. You're going to be seventeen in four short months. You need a purpose, a direction. People have to grow up and make choices about what they're meant to do in life. Figure out what your choice will be, before life makes it for you."

"I'll do robotics." My voice barely registers as a whisper over the booming fury of the storm outside the kitchen window. "And I'll try out for volleyball."

"Good." Dad nods like he's satisfied. "That's my girl."

Bitterness lingers in my mouth, and a lump in my throat makes it hard to speak, but that's probably for the best. The less I say around Dad lately, the more we get along. Better to be ignored than for him to realize I'll never be any of the things that are important to him.

A huge thunderclap rattles the walls, and the house shudders before going black. Olivia shrieks, scurrying into the kitchen to find Mom, who simultaneously comforts Livvy while griping about her ruined fish. Ryan and Tyler groan about their stalled game, and Dad grumbles about having to check the circuit breaker.

"Callie!" Mom cries. "Flashlights, quick!"

Having a perfect sense of direction and preternaturally good night vision makes me the favorite child in thunderstorms. I head down the darkened hall toward the supply closet, grabbing three flashlights and a few candles before heading back to the kitchen.

"Callie?" Mom whirls all around at the sound of my footsteps. "Is that you?"

"Yep." I click one of the flashlights, light streaming across the darkened room. "Here. I got the supplies."

Mom smiles, the flashlight reflecting off Olivia's tear stained cheeks. "Thanks, honey. We can always count on you in the dark, can't we, Livvy?"

"Big sissy!" Livvy reaches for me, smiling.

"Little sissy!" I'm wrapped in too-tight three-year-old hugs and sloppy kisses. At least Livvy likes me for me.

Just as Mom starts to light the candles, the lights flicker back on.

"Fixed it!" Dad yells from the basement. Ryan and Tyler cheer as the television crackles back to life. Mom turns her attention back to her recipe, Jase glues himself to his phone, texting ferociously, and Livvy begs to be let down so she can play. I'm ignored.

Now would be the perfect time to escape to my room. The last thing I want is Dad continuing his lecture on how I'm a horrible good-for-nothing who will never amount to anything in life.

The worst part is, Dad's not entirely wrong about me. I *am* aimless. Thinking about my future, my purpose—my *destiny*, to borrow a super-dramatic turn of phrase—makes me feel like I've got an itch I can't scratch, as if the answers I'm seeking about who I am and what I'm meant to do are just out of reach, dangling like the proverbial carrot I'll never be able to snatch. But I'm only sixteen—*almost* seventeen, as Dad likes to point out, but still—isn't that normal?

All the books, TV shows, and movies say it's normal, anyway.

I sigh a really big, angsty, teenage sigh and flop down on my bed, fully embracing the obnoxious sixteen-year-old Dad says I am. If the shoe fits, as they say. The sky outside my windows looms black with clouds, the ocean peeking around the hills and rooftops even blacker. Appropriate. My world feels pretty bleak at the moment.

Inside my closet, the rod gently hums. I go to it, pulling the shoe box toward me. Light sparks, swirling from the corners of the towel. I sense its call, begging me to pick it up and cradle it in my hands. Like it wants to comfort me in my sadness.

I run my fingers over the towel, and the light attaches itself to my skin, turning my suntan into burnished gold mixed with diamonds. I let the power take hold, the light soak deep inside, and suddenly, I feel... clarity. Peace. A sense of belonging and home I don't feel in my own house—not even in the surf with my board.

Another rumble of thunder, and for a split second, my room goes black. Multiple power outages in the space of an hour.

Storms suck.

As I yell down the hall for Dad to check the circuit breaker again, an eerie cold creeps across my skin. The rod whirs to the point of pain as the darkness surrounding me takes on an almost tangible quality, like a swirling mist through space, before the lights flicker to life and the balmy warmth of August returns. The rod calms, settles into its familiar hum as soon as the shadows flee.

Well, that was creepy.

As I tuck the rod away inside my closet, goosebumps from the flash of icy chill rise like pebbles along the skin of my arms.

CHAPTER THREE

"OKAY, LET'S GOOGLE this thing. Glowing rod."

I type the words into the search engine on my phone while I lounge on the hood of my car, waiting for my friends to arrive on the first day of school. Jase already ditched me for his popular clique, who are way too cool to acknowledge my presence. Whatever.

I scroll through the websites that pop up, looking for anything remotely scientific. But the results I'm getting are...

"Ew. Ew! OH MY GOSH EW!"

Who *are* these icky internet people?

"Callie!"

I stow my phone in my pocket. Isabella Hernandez, one of my two best girlfriends, rushes toward me, arms outstretched for a hug. She's trailed by Emily Sawyer, the third member of our girl gang. Will hangs back with a sour look on his face. I leap off my car to embrace Izzy and Em in a tight friend-wich.

"Is it true you're going out for volleyball?"

Em certainly didn't waste any time confirming the rumors, because Em is a literal bloodhound for the smell of gossip. It's eight o'clock in the morning on the first day of school, and word of my volleyball ambitions are traveling around Verona Beach

High School. Great. Why can't my peers forget about being in each other's business for five seconds?

"Of course it's true, Will told you." Izzy faces Emily with a small look of triumph, and Emily flips her bouncy, blonde curls over her shoulder.

"Well, you know, Callie hates sports, so I feel justified in having doubts."

"Would you both chill out?" I heave the heavy gym bag on my shoulder. "I'm only going out for a sport to get my dad off my back. It's a requirement to pad my college resume."

"That's *so* not cool." Izzy falls in step beside me as we make our way to our lockers. "Surfing is totally a sport."

"Not according to my parents." I roll my eyes behind my sunglasses.

"I can't believe they're so down on surfing." Emily catches up to Izzy and me. "You could be sneaking out to party every weekend."

"You're getting me confused with Jase." My girlfriends laugh.

"I don't think any of this is funny," Will growls, agitated. We all turn to stare at him. He's scowling. Well, no, *pouting* is the correct word. I'm so irritated with him I can hardly look at his mopey face.

"Callie isn't one of those stuck-up sports girls, and that's what makes her cool." Will glares at me. "Why do you have to be just like everyone else?"

"Hey, Will, drop it, okay?" I shoot over my shoulder.

This isn't the first time Will has voiced his opinion on the subject of me trying out for volleyball, and—surprise—he isn't very happy about it. He's been texting me non-stop for a solid week about quitting before tryouts and sticking it to my dad, that I'll break my ankle and won't be able to surf, and I probably won't make the team, anyway, so I should just forget it. He was even texting at five-thirty this morning, a whole hour before I'd normally wake up. Supposedly, he's 'concerned about me,' because the volleyball players are "snobby and popular," and I'm— I don't know, but not snobby and popular, I guess.

"Lighten up," Izzy tells Will. "She's obviously being coerced by unreasonable parental demands." We arrive at our lockers, and she opens hers, setting up her locker mirror. "Do you guys have your schedules yet?"

"Got mine yesterday." I whip my schedule out of my backpack. Emily reads it around my shoulder.

"I didn't know you were taking robotics, Callie." Em's blue-green eyes meet mine with a strange look. "Isn't that kinda nerdy?"

Izzy snorts. "Majorly nerdy."

"Imagine all the mouth-breathing," Emily adds with a laugh.

"Maybe Callie likes geek boys," Izzy teases. "The odds are in her favor."

Embarrassment blazes across my face. Yeah, robotics is a huge geek class at our school. But who cares? I'm not a geek. Or a nerd. I mean, I don't think I am. Everyone's allowed a fringe interest— mine just happens to be robotics.

"Actually, this could be to our advantage." Izzy fixes her hair in her mirror. "Callie can build a robot to sneak into the teacher's lounge and steal the answer key for all the chemistry tests. Then, we'll all pass. No studying required."

"I'll get right on it, Izzy," I joke.

"Yeah, Callie's gonna need all the help she can get this year, especially since the volleyball team will be taking up her free time," Will snarls, shoving his backpack into his locker.

"Will." I give him a warning stare. He sticks his chin out stubbornly.

The bell for our first period rings, and I stuff my sports bag into my locker.

"What do you guys have first period?" Izzy asks.

"English with Evans." I fold my schedule and shoulder my backpack.

"Oh, me, too!" Emily smiles brightly, and claps her hands.

"Wait, you guys have English together?" Izzy heaves a groan after a glance at her schedule. "I've got Algebra II with Harmon. I'm changing my schedule. Like, today."

Izzy heads for the math wing, and Emily, Will, and I walk toward the humanities building. It's just past the main quad, which is my favorite part of the whole school— picnic tables, benches, a wide lawn for studying and games, and a perfect view of the Pacific. I pause, looking toward the ocean, breathing the smell deep into my lungs.

"You're slowing us down, Callie, we're gonna be late," Will sneers. "I thought ace volleyball players had to be fast, or else."

Okay, that's it. I've had it. I grab Will's forearm, squeezing so hard his eyes pop. "Go on, Em," I call. "We'll catch up."

Emily nods, giving Will a you-royally-screwed-up look, and heads into the humanities building. Once she's gone, I whirl on my best friend. I haven't been this mad at Will since middle school when he told me my braces looked like tangled up barbed wire in front of my eighth-grade crush. He and his friends stared at me right as I was picking bits of tuna fish sandwich out of the aforementioned braces.

"*What* is your problem?" I snap. Will tries to wriggle away, so I dig my fingernails in even harder.

"Ouch, Callie, that hurts!"

"Yeah, well, you're being awful about this volleyball thing, and it's hurting my feelings." I release him, and he rubs his arm. "Knock it off. Got it?"

"Or what?" Will retorts.

"Or I'll—never surf with you ever again." My threat is hollow, and Will rolls his eyes.

"Yeah, sure, whatever," he grouches. "It's not like you're going to have time to go surfing with me anyway, not if you go out for volleyball."

I pause, staring at his mopey face, and it dawns on me—the reason Will is mad has nothing to do with volleyball.

"Is that what you're worried about?" My voice softens. "That you're going to lose your surfing buddy?"

"Not just my surfing buddy." Will shrugs, glancing at his feet. "We always do things together. We do our homework together, we hang out, we get coffee or food and mess around town."

"I'm still going to do all those things with you, Will. I promise."

"Are you sure?" He's guarded—he'll hardly hold my gaze.

"Will, I need you." I put a hand on his shoulder, imploring him. "Who else is going to boost my self-esteem and make me feel like the best surfer in the world? Who else hardcore wipes out every single time? You, Will Avila."

The corners of Will's lips quirk, his eyes gleam, and, at last, a huge laugh escapes. I laugh, too. All is forgiven.

"Come on." Will throws a playful arm around my shoulder. "You're gonna make us late for first period. I mean it this time."

We scoot into class seconds before the late bell rings.

I can tell right away English is going to be a good class. My teacher, Mr. Evans, starts off by explaining our theme for the year is following your dreams. We'll read novels about characters overcoming obstacles to realize their potential, and view films and study true stories about kids who overcame the odds to become successful.

Our first assignment is to research a career field we would describe as our dream job and write a report to present to the class.

Mr. Evans gives us the last fifteen minutes to brainstorm in small groups. Emily, Will, and I push our desks together.

"I think I want to be a teacher." Emily takes out her Chromebook and begins typing. "Like, kindergarten or first grade. What about you, Will?"

"I don't know." Will shrugs, really noncommittal. "Maybe business or something?"

"What about you, Callie?" Emily glances at me.

I haven't thought much about my future career, which I figure is completely normal—even if my parents think I'm a slacker for not having a twenty-year plan *right now*. I don't think about much beyond next weekend. But I like engineering-type stuff: designing, building, and fixing things, especially robots. I almost tell Emily mechanical engineering.

Then, I remember the glowing rod, the light and the power, the hold it has on me every time I'm in its presence. How I found it in the storm, just beyond the end of the pier, stuck to the bottom of the ocean...

"Uh—oceanography."

"Really?" Will can't hide his surprise. "I thought for sure you'd say something to do with your robotics class."

Don't make me change my mind, Will. "Yeah, I mean, I like robots, but I also love the ocean."

"Robotics would be cooler," Will persists.

He's right, it would. I'd have a lot more fun researching robotics, too. But this is the perfect opportunity to figure out what the glowing rod in my closet might be, since googling has been massively unhelpful and gross. Spending the next three weeks researching the ocean ought to give me *some* clue about its origins, right?

"Okay, oceanography for Callie." Emily types some more.

Sounds like I've got a lot of reading ahead of me.

"Well? Did you suck?"

My first volleyball practice just ended, and all Jase wants to know is if I sucked. Typical, Jase.

"Hi, little sister, how was your first day of school? Oh, it was wonderful, big brother, thanks for asking."

I can't see him roll his eyes behind his sunglasses, but I know Jase's eye-rolling-face well. "Cool it with the snark, Callie."

My brother puts the car in drive, and we exit the parking lot. Jase's soccer club practices at the sports park across the street from the school, since the high school season doesn't start until the winter. Usually, I catch a ride home with Will, but since Jase and I are both doing sports, we're driving home together this semester. Yippee.

"Seriously, how did you do?"

"Okay, I think." I wipe some residual sweat off my forehead. "The coaches seemed pretty certain I'd at least make JV, so Dad will be happy."

"Sweet."

Jase and I drive in silence a ways, until I remember my project. "Hey, can you swing by the library really quick?"

"Why?" Jase and libraries—well, reading in general—are like oil and water. There is no love lost there.

"It's for an English project," I answer. "I have to use at least two books as resources."

Jase huffs through his nose, obviously annoyed. "You've got homework already? It's the first day of school. Who's your teacher?"

I take a sip of water from my sports bottle before answering. "Evans."

"Evans," Jase mutters. "That guy is a tyrant."

I glance his way. "Did you have him last year?"

"No, I had Heller," my brother replies. "She was cool. But you know Caleb Rodriguez, right? He's our fullback. Anyway, Evans almost failed him last year for no good reason."

Now I'm the one rolling my eyes behind my sunglasses. "Let me guess, he only forgot to turn in three papers and bombed a test, but that's no good reason to fail somebody, right?"

"He didn't *bomb* the test, he got a D." Jase scowls. "And he didn't turn in two papers. Not three."

"How do you and your friends even function, Jase?" Honestly, Mom and Dad think *I'm* the slacker kid?

"All I'm saying is Evans shows no mercy."

I nod, agreeing. "Right, got it. So, now you understand why I need to go to the library and start researching my project ASAP. It's due in three weeks."

Jase hangs a sharp right, taking a detour to the Verona Beach Library. As far as city libraries go, it's minuscule — the high school library is twice the size. Developers snapping up real estate for ocean-view condo complexes didn't leave a lot of room for a decent-sized library, I guess.

"Are you coming?" I glance at Jase. He nearly gags on his chewing gum.

"No way, I'm waiting in the car." Jase's hatred for libraries and the "nerds" who haunt them is too great to risk a public appearance.

"Suit yourself." I shoulder my backpack and open the door.

"You've got ten minutes," Jase calls out the window as I approach the library entrance.

"Ten minutes!" I whirl, pushing my sunglasses down my nose, and fix Jase with a pointed look. "That's not enough time. I need fifteen, at least."

My brother remains unmoved. "I'm starving. If you aren't

done in ten minutes, I'm ditching you. You can walk home."

"Oh my gosh, Jase, you are *not* seriously—"

"Nine minutes, fifty-eight seconds," Jase interrupts, tapping the remainder of my time into his phone's stopwatch. "Time's ticking."

"You're terrible." I spin around and duck inside.

The librarian at the front counter is a longtime local, a nice lady I remember from childhood library visits. She's making small talk with an old man in a windbreaker and sunglasses when I approach.

"Excuse me." The librarian turns at the sound of my voice, and the old man falls silent. "Can you tell me where the books on ocean science are located?"

"Non-fiction is to the left," she replies. "Row H, Section 2."

I flash a grin. "Thanks." As I turn to go, the old man's voice stops me.

"Good luck. The reference section is abysmal."

I glance over my shoulder, giving him a once-over. His eyes are hidden by the sunglasses, and he's got a Cal Bears baseball cap pulled low over his forehead, obscuring his face. Regardless, I haven't seen him before. But then, I don't visit the library much, and geriatrics aren't my crowd. The librarian tsk's her tongue at his remark, muttering something about reference books not being in high demand for preschool story hour or book clubs.

"Thanks for the heads up." I rush off in search of Row H, Section 2. I've only got seven minutes left, and I have no doubt Jase will make good on his promise to drive off without me.

I snatch a few books from the shelf, anything with "ocean" in the title. I don't know if these books will shed light on the glowing rod in my closet, but I've got to start somewhere.

Five minutes left. Time to check out. I go back through the shelves one last time, searching the titles for something, *anything* about strange ocean phenomena. Or, more specifically, light-emitting, pulsing rods stuck to the seabed.

"O'Brien, O'Neill, Ormandi..." I read the names of the authors aloud as I scan the book spines. That name makes me stop. "Ormandi."

Dr. Richard Ormandi. As in, Old Man Ormandi? The boogeyman wrote a book? That's about as believable as Jase getting straight As, or Ryan becoming a basketball star.

"Rare Oceanic Phenomena: A Scientist's Explanation for the Unexplainable," I read the title of his book aloud. "The unexplainable..."

I pull the book from the shelf. It's old, with a cracking spine and yellowed edges. I thumb through the first couple of pages. Black and white photos accompany a distinct moldy paper smell. Yep, ancient. But maybe it'll be useful. After all, it's about the unexplainable.

Three minutes. I toss the book by Old Man Ormandi on top of my stack and rush to the check-out desk. The old guy with the sunglasses is gone, and the librarian scans my books. I scurry back to the car, books precariously balanced in my arms, just as the stopwatch on Jase's phone beeps.

"Perfect timing, for once." My brother pockets his phone, glancing at the books in my lap, then at me. "Ocean phenomena? Are you sure this isn't for science?"

"We're supposed to research our dream job and write a report." I pull the door shut.

"Dream job? That sounds like some Mr. Evans bullcrap. Isn't everybody's dream job to be a professional athlete or YouTuber? I mean, that's what I'd write a report on."

Yes, Mom and Dad. I'm definitely the kid with the lack of realistic goals and expectations for my future.

Jase backs out of the driveway onto the street, and we drive up the hill toward home. Old Man Ormandi's book watches me the entire way.

CHAPTER FOUR

"... *ST. ELMO'S FIRE is a weather phenomenon in which a luminous plasma is created by a coronal discharge, often during a thunderstorm at sea. St. Elmo's fire can appear blueish or violet in color, and is usually accompanied by a hissing or buzzing sound...*"

"Hmm... St. Elmo's fire..." I *did* find the rod during a storm at sea, although it isn't remotely close to blue-violet color. Still, it's a lead. I write this new information in my notebook. Could the glowing rod be nothing more than a type of plasma? Maybe the part where plasma makes your fingers sparkle comes later in the book.

I'm learning some pretty cool facts about the ocean—things I never would have known had I not chosen to research the rod for my project. For example, algae bloom can cause the tide to turn blood red, rivers and lakes of brine can stretch for miles across the sea floor, and bioluminescent plankton can cause waves to glow bright, neon blue. Absolutely zero about humming, glowing, pulsating rods that make your skin glow, and your body surge with inhuman power.

And also, *super* bone dry. I'm sure some people find page after page of technical figures thrilling. Ryan, probably.

"Okay, boogeyman, let's see what you've got to say." I pick

Old Man Ormandi's book from my stack, cracking the delicate spine. "Chapter One: Maelstroms."

At least Old Man Ormandi's writing style is slightly more interesting than some of these other scientists-turned-nonfiction-writers. The guy can wax poetic about an underwater vortex, that's for sure. But I'm mentally wiped, and the smell of lasagna wafts down the hall from the oven, making my mouth water. Maelstroms can wait until tomorrow. I snap the book closed, tossing it aside.

On the back cover, a washed-out photo stares at me—Dr. Richard Ormandi. I've never seen a picture of him, and confirmation he exists as a real person, not some phantom threat lurking around dark, creepy corners, is jarring. His brown hair is slightly off-kilter, and deep-set, piercing black eyes glint observantly in his angular face. He'd been surprisingly young and not-nerdish for a college professor, more like a co-ed just starting his major.

Definitely nothing like a boogeyman, either.

Beneath his picture, there's a typical 'about the author' paragraph. "Dr. Richard Ormandi received his Ph.D. in Marine Science from the University of California at Berkeley, and began his career researching deep ocean phenomena at Verona Beach State University," I read aloud. "Dr. Ormandi teaches oceanography and marine science at Verona Beach State University, where he is currently head of the ocean science department. He resides in Verona Beach, California, with his wife and son."

With his wife and son? Nobody ever said anything about Old Man Ormandi having a family. Maybe this Dr. Ormandi, Richard Ormandi, is not the same person as Old Man Ormandi. A brother, or a cousin, or something.

A soft tap on my door startles me.

"Callie?" It's Dad.

"Come in," I announce.

"Whatcha reading?" Dad steps into my room, nodding at the books on my bed.

"Ocean science." I begin stacking my books and notepapers. "It's for a school project."

"Well, I don't want to interrupt your studying. Just came to tell you dinner was ready." Dad starts to shut my door.

The sight of Old Man Ormandi's book sitting on my stack nags me. My questions about the boogeyman—maybe Dad has some answers. He was alive when this book was written, at the very least.

"Hey, Dad?"

"What's up, kiddo?" Dad turns, regarding me quizzically.

I hand him the book I've been reading. "Is this the same Old Man Ormandi who lives out by the cliffs?"

"Yeah, that's him." He runs his hand over the picture, shaking his head. "Geez, I haven't seen him since...."

I scowl, tilting my chin. "Since what?"

"Never mind." Dad shakes his head and hands me the book. Any shock he might have felt at seeing Old Man Ormandi's picture is long gone.

"So, what happened to him?" I go on. "Dr. Ormandi, I mean. It sounds like he used to be a really smart guy. A college professor, even. It says he has a wife and a son, too. Do you know them? Dr. Ormandi and his family?"

Dad's weatherbeaten skin draws tight around his cheek-bones as his hazel eyes fall to the book in my hands. The heavy silence seeping from his pores and filling my room is so thick I could reach out and touch it.

"Dr. Ormandi had a son." I don't like the way Dad says *had.* "His name was Nate."

Neither of my parents ever mentioned Old Man Ormandi's son. You'd think it would have come up at least once, considering how often my siblings and I tease each other about the boogeyman. "Seriously? What happened to him?"

"Nate died when he was in high school." Dad's face twists into a sad grimace. "He was the star of the baseball team, one of the best catchers in the state. Smart as a fox, too. He'd just accepted a full ride athletic scholarship to Cal—we all swore we'd see him in the majors one day." Dad halts, taking a rattled breath. "So much potential, and then it was just gone. The whole town was in shock."

I sink into my bed, staring at Dr. Ormandi's smiling face on the back of his book. He looked perfectly confident, as though his life hadn't yet been touched by tragedy, and blissfully unaware of his child's fate.

"Losing Nate was extremely hard on Richard." Dad sighs heavily. "His wife died of cancer, I think, or something horrible like that. Nate was all he had. He was a kind man. Very shy, and always wore sunglasses, even in the rain. Odd duck, in a way, but kind."

I search Dad's sun-damaged face. "Is that why he became a hermit?"

Dad sits on the edge of my bed next to me. "Richard retired from his professorship after the accident and went into seclusion. Honestly, I don't blame him. His life was just one blow after another, you know?"

My stomach churns, sick with guilt. I've never egged Old Man Ormandi's house like some of the other kids at school, but how many times have I called him the boogeyman, and used him to tease and scare my younger siblings? If both his wife and son died tragically, he has a valid reason for being a recluse. He definitely doesn't deserve abuse from local teenagers.

"Well, that's enough tragic talk." Dad puts his hand on my shoulder, squeezing it tight. "Come on, it's Italian night, lasagna is calling. And Mom made chocolate cheesecake for dessert."

I stand to follow him into the kitchen, but stop in my doorway. "Dad?"

He faces me expectantly. "Yeah, Cal?"

"How did Nate die?"

Dad shakes his head, a look of far off memory filling his eyes. "A boating accident. There was a storm that day — a really violent one. It came on so fast. His skiff was lost at sea and he drowned." He blinks hard and turns away. "Anyway, that's what the Coast Guard and the coroner said. They never found him."

I know I should drop it. This is clearly a topic Dad does *not* want to talk about. Boating and fishing are Dad's favorite things in the entire world — he built his entire business around them. But the same kind of accident that killed Nate Ormandi could easily befall Dad if he made one wrong move. No wonder Dad has a reputation for being the most cautious sport fisherman in Verona Beach, with an internal weather radar better than any meteorologist.

"Why would Nate keep sailing during a storm instead of coming back to port?" One last question. Hopefully, one last answer.

"He was trying to find something…" Dad trails off. "Rumors swirled around — you know, small-town gossip. Something about him tracking a light shooting into the sky from the middle of the ocean." He shrugs his shoulders, as though shucking off the heaviness of the past to come fully back to the present. "People make up the weirdest stuff, don't they? I mean, who ever heard of something so off the wall?"

I've heard of light shooting from the ocean into the sky. The glowing rod I'm hiding can do just that.

I hang back in my door frame, glancing at my closet before I follow Dad out of the room. Did Nate Ormandi die trying to find something like the rod in my closet?

The whirring grows a little louder, almost like the rod *knows* I'm watching it. Not great optics, glowing rod. The suspicion that my discovery—and the power it contains—might be dangerous grows by the minute.

"You coming, Cal?" Dad calls over his shoulder, halfway down the hall.

"Yeah, on my way!"

I close my bedroom door, more determined than ever to find out the truth.

Nate's easy to find online—you can find anything on the internet, even old sports articles (what you can't find are answers about magic glowing rods, but details). His image leaps from my screen so vividly it's as if he's here in my room, sitting beside me on the floor.

"Nathaniel Ormandi. There you are." The first article is about graduating seniors receiving full-ride scholarships to California colleges and universities. I rattle off his impressive list of accomplishments. "Varsity baseball, Academic All-American, California Scholastic Federation, National Honor Society." Dad said he was smart. No joke.

Also, strikingly handsome. A carefree mop of dark, wavy hair swooped off to the side of his forehead, with magnetic dark eyes and a wide, dimpled smile stretching across his face, lighting it up with megawatt intensity.

I find another article featuring the Verona Beach High varsity baseball team on their way to state championships. Sure enough, Nate's front and center in the picture, wearing catcher's gear over his uniform. He was really tall for a catcher—Dad and Jase would argue a guy like that should play first base. But the article notes Nate was the best all-around defensive player in the league.

"Buff arms," I note. A weird thing to notice about a dead guy, but hey, they're obvious. And buff.

I scroll rapidly, bypassing archived newspaper snippets, hoping to find more pictures of Nate. One article about a state-wide chemistry award stands out, featuring Nate in the VBHS science lab. Even showing off his prize-winning experiment, there's a distracted air about him, as if his mind is a thousand miles away. It's a look I know all too well—his eyes swim with a strange juxtaposition of emotions, lost and drifting, but un-nerveingly clear and focused. I might not know him, never will know him, but I *know* he wants something. Desperately. And he'll do anything to get it. I know because I've felt it, too. The sense there's something missing, something you're meant to be doing, but the answer remains forever out of reach.

Too bad he didn't live to find whatever it is he's seeking.

The very last article is Nate's obituary: a stark, black-and-white rendering of Nate's senior picture with very little info, as though whoever wrote it was in too much grief and denial to believe such a brilliant light could've been snuffed out.

Nathaniel Laszlo Ormandi, the obituary reads. *Son of Richard Ormandi and the late Mariasol Zaira-Ormandi. Lost at sea May 28th.*

"Lost at sea…" Suddenly, a strange presence comes over me, like somebody is standing right behind me. I can feel their breath on my neck, their body close to mine, but instead of the warmth of a fellow human, I just feel—cold. Emotionless cold, almost sinister in its intent, lurks behind my back like a creeping ghost. The tiny hairs on my skin stand up straight, and my pulse jackhammers in my ears as I whirl around.

Nobody's there. I'm all alone.

The presence evaporates, and I breathe deep, heartbeat

slowing to a normal pace. "Weird…"

I pocket my phone and scurry out of my room before any lingering trace of the ghostly presence follows me down the hall.

CHAPTER FIVE

"JASE, I'M TAKING the car to the cemetery."

My brother eyes me with the same look of horror he'd had on his face last week when I asked him to stop by the pharmacy so I could buy tampons. "Why?"

"I want to take Grandpa some flowers," I explain. *And try to find Nate Ormandi's grave...*

"Which grandpa?" Jase hits back with another question.

"Grandpa Georgie, Dad's dad," I tell him with a strange look. "Avo Estevao lives in Ventura, we just saw him last Thanksgiving."

"Oh, yeah. Is it the anniversary of his death, or what?" For somebody who doesn't like people in his business, Jase sure has a lot of nosy questions.

"I was just thinking about him." Actually, I've been thinking about Nate Ormandi since I spent the better part of an hour last night stalking his pictures in old newspaper articles online. "How he'd always come over and play with us when Mom and Dad went on a date, or take us to the beach to look for shells and dead starfish."

"He was a cool grandpa," Jase agrees. "How long are you gonna be there?"

"Not long. I already picked some flowers from Mom's garden." I hold up the bouquet of zinnias clutched at my side.

Jase stands, pulling a cap low on his forehead. "I think I'll go with you. I haven't seen Grandpa in a while."

"Um, sure." I try not to grit my teeth when I smile. "That would be awesome." I'm totally lying. Jase tagging along is going to seriously wreck my snooping plans, but what am I going to say? No, super popular big brother, don't come out in public with me because I want to spy on the grave of a dead guy we don't even know.

Not happening.

I spend the car ride thinking of ways to ditch Jase. My brother spends the car ride reminiscing about Grandpa Georgie buying him his first soccer ball and teaching him corner kicks in the backyard. Any other time, it would be an awesome bonding moment for me and Jase, but right now he's getting in the way of my morbid curiosity.

Why can't Jase ever be cool when I actually need him to be?

When we pull up to the section of the cemetery where Grandpa Georgie is buried, Jase follows me to his headstone, still going on about watching Premier League with Grandpa on weekends. Just as we're approaching the big coastal oak in front of Grandpa's plot, Jase's girlfriend, Jen, texts. I'm not a huge fan of Jen—I think she's fake-nice to me because she's dating Jase—but I could kiss her for blowing up Jase's phone.

"I gotta text Jen." Jase motions for me to go on, retreating to the car. I jog up to Grandpa's grave.

"Hi, Grandpa Georgie." I lay my flowers on top of the head-stone. "Look, I'm sorry I can't spend more time with you, but I'm on a mission. I know you understand. I'll come back soon. And I'll bring more flowers. I promise."

I weave up, down, and all through the cemetery, hoping

Nate's grave might be close by. I haven't got a lot of time. Jase will find a way to end his conversation sooner than later, especially if Jen is angry about something. Stalking the rows, I scan the names on the graves. I spy a large granite stone a few rows up, "Ormandi" etched on the front, surrounded by dahlias and fresh-cut sunflowers.

"Nathaniel 'Nate' Ormandi," I murmur, reading the inscription. "Beloved son and friend."

My heart sinks. Even though I know how Nate's story ends, to see the written confirmation of his death on cold, white granite is a tragic shock. At least he seems to be remembered by someone. The flowers in the sconces by his headstone are fresh and bright, and arranged with visible care.

Sadness overwhelms me, heavy with the finality of it all. I reach out to touch the smooth, polished granite, fingertips tracing the letters of his name.

"*Callie…*"

The world around me disappears from sight, a violent tug at the base of my spine dragging me backward — down, down down, until I'm enveloped in blackness. The sun shines beyond my grasp, beyond my sight. I sense it's there, but so far from everything around me it's as if warmth and light never existed at all. Swirling darkness surrounds me instead, a veil between the world I know and a world completely unseen ripped in two, tangling me tight in the middle of both.

It is bleak here. There's anger. Despair. Dread. Fear. Hate. Power and rage embodied in a terrible black fog moving in and out of my body like swirling, phantasmic tentacles, all at once making me itch for violence and yet terrified of the consequences.

And I'm cold. So, so cold.

The ghost-like presence from last night returns, stronger now, tangible and terrifying. It reaches for me, spectral fingers brushing the tips of my hair. My blood turns to ice in my veins, and I spin all around, searching for the phantom. What I catch sight of is a flash of disembodied white hair and mysterious black eyes.

"*Calliope James....*"

A jolt like a lightning strike surges through me, and I'm thrown to the ground. I sit up, blinking, breathing hard. The sun glows bright and brilliant, flooding my icy skin. Birds chirp in the coastal oak, and the faint, distant crash of waves echoes up the hills from the cliffs below.

"What just happened?" Frantically spinning all around, I look for the *thing*, the presence, the foggy black tentacles that made my world go dark. But there's nothing.

One last time, I turn and look at Nate's grave. The dahlias are dead, putrid and decaying, the sunflowers reduced to dust. Brown, bone-dry grass surrounds the grave, withering before my eyes. Just seconds ago, everything bloomed, alive and bursting with color. I stand, taking a closer look at the pattern etched into the dead grass.

Tentacles.

I don't think I've ever run away from something so fast in my life.

Rushing back to Grandpa's headstone, I will my body to stop shaking and resume some level of calm. Jase has already been a pest with the questions today. I am not in the mood to be given the third degree. Clenching my hands into fists, I breathe, in-out-in-out. *Calm, Callie. Just be calm.*

Soon, my brother joins me at my side. If he notices the trembling, he doesn't say anything.

"How was Jen?" Small talk. Yes, good. Small talk is normal.

"Fine." He shrugs. "How's Grandpa?"

"Still dead," I answer.

Jase snorts a laugh. "Did you think he turned into a zombie, or what?"

He's tense. Maybe he and Jen are in a fight. Either way, he's not paying attention to me.

"Are you ready to go home?" I ask my brother.

"Yeah," Jase replies. "I think Jen's gonna text back in a few minutes...."

They're definitely in a fight. Sure enough, Jase's cell phone buzzes like a furious bee the entire ride home. He sighs, tells me to tell Mom he'll be inside for dinner in a minute, and starts texting. Thanks, Jen—your timing is impeccable. Really, I mean it.

I shout Jase's message to Mom before sprinting for my room, slumping into a ball on the floor once I reach its safety. Whatever happened back at the cemetery has me majorly freaked out. Like, I-see-dead-people freaked out. I close my eyes, desperate to make sense of this.

"It was nothing. I imagined everything. There isn't any alternate realm of darkness and ghosts. There's here, there's now. That's it."

Obviously the shadowy phantoms, and the cold, anger, and fear were all in my head. I must have temporarily blacked out. The flowers and grass were already dying, I just didn't notice. I'm probably dehydrated and stressed, and not sleeping well enough. Visions of black despair and unearthly voices calling my name, scorching tentacle patterns into the grass, aren't real life.

Sunlight, buttery and golden, streams through the blinds when I open my eyes. The rod hums softly behind my closet door, like it sensed my presence and decided to say hi. Except it can't, because it's an inanimate object, and inanimate objects developing sentience is just silly fantasy stuff.

But then, the humming intensifies until whirring, pulsing energy reaches through the wood and nails to my very being. I am filled with everything inside the rod all at once, overwhelmed with wild freedom and violence and peace and terror. A horrific whir of sound, a freight train speeding through my room, deafens me to anything else. The rod has never been like this before— like it would break out of my closet prison and fly away if it only got the chance. Reverberation shakes the closet door, rattling up the walls and across the ceiling.

Lights in my lamp and ceiling fan flicker once, twice, and a haunting chill manifests just over my shoulder. I gulp for air, an exhale sticking in my throat. I'm drowning in fear and confusion, splintering with despair. Any positive feelings in my soul are replaced with shadow.

I catch sight of myself in the mirror. Just behind my hair, a black silhouette materializes, tentacle arms reaching out to caress my cheek, my hair, the nape of my neck.

Pop. Every lightbulb in my room bursts, glass shattering, flying everywhere. My whole room goes black as icy breath tickles my skin.

A voice, otherworldly and ominous, whispers inches from my ear. "Hey there, beautiful."

I don't stick around to come face-to-face with the phantom. I bolt out of my room as fast as I can.

With terror-stricken desperation, I switch on every light in the living room before flinging myself across the couch, pulling a throw blanket over my head. As silently as I can, I cry into a pillow, muffling my horrified screams.

The rod did this. It's the only explanation—the rod freaked out, and seconds later, something like a ghostly apparition appears behind me, whispering. *Physically speaking to me.* I have never been more petrified in my entire life.

What if the rod is responsible for everything else, too? If this rod is the thing Nate was looking for when he died, is it somehow responsible for the storm he drowned in? Will it cause another storm, stronger than the last, and try to kill me, too? Or will the ghosts and phantoms the rod makes manifest kill me first?

I shudder, swallowing the urge to vomit.

All I know is the glowing rod is going back where it belongs — the fathomless bottom of the ocean. I will throw it into the depths the first chance I get. And I will never think about it again.

CHAPTER SIX

"HEY, CALLIE! Want to go surfing this weekend?"

"Gah, Will!" I leap so high my head slams into the top of my locker. Spinning on my heel, I peg Will with a glare. "You can't startle me like that!"

To say I've been jumpy since my real-life paranormal encounter is an understatement.

"Sorry." Will isn't sorry. "Anyway, like I was saying, we should go surfing this weekend. What do you think?"

"I have to work a wedding with my mom on Saturday." He forgets some of us have to do actual work for our spending cash.

"What about Sunday?" Will persists.

"Sunday might be okay," I reply, heading toward the gym. The final bell rang five minutes ago, and I need to get changed for a volleyball game. Will trails after me.

"Your mom isn't making you work on Sunday, too, is she?"

"No, but I need to work on my robotics project," I remind my best friend.

"Is that going to take you all day?" Will's expression is eager, expectant. I stop in my tracks and heave a sigh.

"It won't, but between volleyball, homework, and weddings with Mom, I haven't had time to work on robotics, and I need to."

I haven't had time to ditch the glowing rod, either, but Will doesn't know anything about the rod. It's strange, keeping a secret from Will, but there isn't any use telling him about something I'm going to dump in the sea the first chance I get. *Definitely* not going to mention the glowing hands and ghostly stuff. It would only make him high-strung and anxious for nothing.

Will scowls, his forehead wrinkling. "Yeah, and because of JV volleyball and you suddenly caring about your grades, I've hardly seen you, and we haven't surfed together in forever."

"Not *forever*." I can't believe Will picked this exact moment to whine about surfing. I have a game, a glowing rod to ditch, and creepy goings-on to eliminate as soon as possible. Surfing is not on the radar.

"Whatever, it's been too long." Will's brown eyes look like a sad little puppy who just wants a cuddle. "I miss you, Callie. I miss surfing with you."

I know Will misses surfing with me. I miss surfing with him, too. He just picked a horrible time to talk about it. "Look, I'm going to be late for warm up. But I promise I'll work on my robotics project tonight so I can go surfing with you on Sunday. Deal?"

Will smiles. "Deal."

My robotics project is something I can show off to my family, unlike the killer glowing rod hidden in my closet. I pull my chihuahua-sized, boxy creation from my duffel bag as soon as I get home, and get right to work. Ryan and Tyler's geek radar ramps up to level eleven at the sight of my robot's parts strewn all over the table, and they clamor to join me in the kitchen.

"What does your robot do? Shoot flames?" Ryan inspects the hand torch I brought home from class for the weekend while Tyler absentmindedly twirls loose screws.

"It doesn't do anything yet, but that torch does, so be careful or you'll burn your eyebrows off." I pick up the screwdriver and one of the screws Tyler's messing with. "Next week we're going to start working on coding and setting up the internal components for the different functions. Right now I'm just assembling all the guts, making sure everything is in the right place."

"Geez, they say I'm the nerd around here," Ryan observes.

"Hey, it's wheelbase looks like one of my RC cars." Tyler picks up my robot and frowns. "Did you—"

"Don't worry about it, Tyler." I snatch the robot and tighten all the screws on the contested wheelbase. "What if I let you name it?"

"Okay, that's fine, then," Tyler agrees.

"I'm really proud of you for building a robot all by yourself, Callie," Mom speaks up from the corner of the kitchen. She's doing last minute prep for her wedding tomorrow, and the kitchen smells of beurre blanc and grilled salmon.

"What's this thing for?" Ryan picks up a rectangular box with two black knobs in the center.

"It's the head, see? The knobs are his eyes. They've got tiny LED lights inside, and they'll signal when the robot's switched on and off." I adjust the head onto the neck base. "The neck is rigged with a small wheel and motor so the robot will be able to turn his head once he's programmed."

Ryan looks impressed. "Nice. This is a legit robot."

"It's way cool," Tyler says.

I place the motherboard inside the robot's body—useless until I can program it in the upcoming weeks—and screw the side panel in place over the electronics. My creation is finished, for now.

"There, done," I announce with a smile.

My robot is pretty cute, if I do say so myself. It's small, a little bigger than a remote-controlled car, with a metal body attached to the wheelbase, a neck housing a tiny, rotating motor, two spindly metal arms complete with two-fingered pincer hands, and a rectangular head with beady black eyes. I give its head a pat.

"Is your robot a boy or a girl?" Tyler asks. I shrug.

"It's neither, it's a robot. Why?"

"You said I could name it, so I want to know if I can pick a boy name, or a girl name," Tyler elaborates.

"Pick anything you like." I smile at my little brother. "After all, you have naming rights."

"Okay." Tyler inspects the robot closely before he sets it on the table. "Nemo. His name is Nemo."

Ryan looks at Tyler like he can't believe he was born into *this* family of idiots. "Nemo is a fish, genius."

"Callie said I could name it, and I like Nemo," Tyler replies.

"I like Nemo, too," I agree. My little brother beams. "Nemo it is."

"I christen Callie's robot Nemo." Ryan grandly touches a butter knife to each of the robot's tiny shoulders like he's bestowing a knighthood.

"You didn't christen him anything, I did," Tyler argues.

Dad comes sauntering in the front door before a full-blown fight can erupt. Dad has good timing sometimes.

"Hi there, family!" he greets us. "Who wants to go fishing to-morrow morning?"

"Don't you have clients, Ted?" Mom glances over her shoulder at Dad. "You don't usually get a weekend off this time of year."

"I *had* a client, a guy and his young sons, but he got the stomach flu and his kids aren't old enough to go deep sea fishing by themselves." Dad hangs his cap on the hook by the door and joins us at the table. He straightens his sandy blonde hair with his fingers, brushing it off of his suntanned forehead. "I haven't taken any of my kids fishing in a while. Who wants to go?"

"I can't, I get seasick." Tyler performs a disgusting reenactment of himself barfing all over the kitchen table, complete with sound effects.

"I have a Mathletes competition tomorrow morning," Ryan chimes in.

"Jase's club team has a soccer tournament," Mom speaks for my older brother.

"I'll go!" Fishing trip, just me and Dad, none of my siblings around to pester me, spy, and ask questions? Sounds like the perfect opportunity to toss the glowing rod back in the ocean where it belongs. Plus, you know, bond with Dad and stuff.

"I knew I could count on you, Cal." Dad cuffs my shoulder.

"Callie is working at the Flores-Stevenson wedding tomorrow." Mom fixes Dad with a stern glare, the kind that means he knows better than to steal her labor force.

"It'll just be a quick trip along the coast and some fishing," Dad assures Mom. "I'll have her back by noon. I promise."

"Noon at the *very* latest," Mom reiterates. "We've got to be in the hotel ballroom by one to start prepping."

"Yes, Sofie. Noon at the very latest." Dad turns to me. "We'll have to leave by 6:30. Can you be up and ready that early?"

"Yeah, sure!" I grin.

"That's my girl." Dad notices my robot sitting on the table and picks him up. "What's this? Did you make this?"

"Yeah, it's my first project for robotics class," I answer. "He's not functional yet, but he's fully assembled."

"I named him Nemo!" Tyler pipes up.

"This is great!" Dad beams, and my heart swells. "Really neat stuff, Cal. Nice job!"

I'm so happy I could dance. Mom and Dad are proud of me

for something—truly proud, not faking. Most importantly, I've got the perfect excuse to get rid of the glowing rod for good. I'll toss it into the ocean when Dad and I are out on the boat tomorrow. It'll never hum, or vibrate, or make my hands glow, or fill my room with phantoms ever again.

This weekend really can't get any better.

Saturday morning dawns clear as a bell, with calm water and pink-hued skies as far as the eye can see. A strong breeze blows my hair away from my neck as I breathe in the salty sea air. It's the freshest, cleanest smell in the world. Rhythmic rocking of gentle waves against the boat mingles with the piercing cries of seagulls as we sail away from the marina.

"Great morning for fishing, huh, Cal?" Dad calls from the helm.

I turn and smile at him. "It's amazing."

"Not a cloud in sight," Dad goes on. "Too bad about my client, but at least we get to have some fun, right?"

Dad comes around to stern, where I sit in the raised chair his clients use to reel in huge tuna and swordfish. He leans against the gunwale, looking out across the endless stretch of sea. Sunlight sparkles brilliantly golden above our heads, making the water shimmer like deep, mesmerizing blue crystal. Cotton ball waves butt a narrow strip of tawny beach in the distance. Further down the shoreline, rocky cliffs rise into the sky, craggy spires climbing to meet each other until they gently crest into sloping, green hills. Verona Beach has got to be the prettiest spot in California.

"This is the best feeling in the world." I can't tell if Dad's talking to himself, or to me. Either way, I agree with him. "It's so calm out here. So peaceful."

"I love it, too." I nudge Dad with my foot. "Maybe I can take over the fishing business when you retire."

Dad shakes his head, meeting my eyes with a serious look in his own. "I love this boat and I love what I do, but I work my fingers to the bone every day. I'm constantly sunburned, my back always hurts, and the carpal tunnel is ruining my wrists. It's as harsh and unforgiving out here as it is beautiful. I don't want this life for you."

What about the life I want for myself? Dad doesn't seem too concerned with that. But then, I don't know what kind of life I want any more than Dad does. The thought of maintaining a commercial boat and running a sport fishing charter doesn't thrill me, but I don't want my future dictated, either.

Dad fiddles with a rusty nut and bolt that's come loose on a piece of railing. "I can fix that," I offer. "Next time we come fishing, I'll bring my torch from robotics class. I'm getting pretty good with it."

"I'd rather you use that torch to make your robots," Dad tells me with a grin. "It's a much better use of your time."

Typical Dad, telling me what's best to do with *my* future, *my* time. I thought this was going to be fun, just Dad and me fishing with no mention of everything about me that disappoints him. Maybe I was wrong.

"If I build a Mars rover one day, I'll name it after you," I joke, trying to lighten the mood. "Martian Ted."

"That would make me the proudest guy that ever had a robot named after him." Dad smiles as wide as the brim of his cap before catching sight of something and going still. A tern dips and dives near the boat, angling a tasty catch. "I think we'll break out the rods. The birds seem to think something's biting down there. Might be a school of rockfish."

Potential lecture averted. Whew. I turn around in my chair as Dad makes his way to the starboard storage closet where he keeps fishing supplies. "Do you need some help?"

"No, no, I got it." Dad grins. "You sit tight. I've got some coffee in a thermos if you want any. I'll just be a minute."

A minute is all I need.

I reach under the chair and snatch my backpack. The rod lies nestled inside, still wrapped in my old beach towel, waiting to be thrown back into the sea. With a hop, my feet hit the deck, and I move to the very edge of the stern.

"Goodbye, glowing rod," I mutter. In the blink of an eye, this nightmarish headache I've been dealing with for the world's longest month will be over. I can forget all about the rod and its power—its tangible, swirling light, and magnetic hold over me. I'll never again worry about its cryptic connection to Old Man Ormandi and his dead son. Could it kill me, too, and everyone I love? Who cares! In five seconds, I won't have to think about it ever again!

I whip the rod out of my backpack, still wrapped in the towel, and lift it high over my head, cranking my arm back to lob it as far as I can.

As soon as the rod is in my hand, it starts being freaky. Because of course it does.

The rod hangs in midair, ready to be thrown, pulsing and whirring as loud as a Coast Guard chopper. Seriously, how does Dad not hear this? Or see it? Dazzling light burns brighter than a dying star on the brink of explosion, piercing the fabric of the beach towel. My limbs quiver, the rod sending shockwaves through my whole body. It attaches itself to my nerves, my tendons and muscles, filling even my blood cells with light.

The ocean cresting mildly against the sides of the boat ceases all motion, transforming into a flat, smooth mirror. Gulls and terns scatter like flies. Power surges through me, unbound and free. Wild freedom mixes with perfect, calm clarity, like the feeling of my surfboard dropping into the most epic wave imaginable, leaving me otherworldly and shaken. Every fiber of my being and soul entangles with the rod. Light flows within me and out, and I don't want to let go.

"Just do it, Callie." I grit my teeth, resolved to ditch this thing. It's dangerous. The longer I hold it, the more dangerous it might become. Dangerous enough to kill me.

Before I can follow through and toss the rod back into the sea for good, the ocean starts to swirl. What begins as a small ripple beneath the boat becomes a whirling, churning vortex in a matter of seconds, snatching the boat and pulling us under.

Dad and I are going to die.

"Callie!" Dad shouts frantically. "A whirlpool! Hang on!"

Dad guns the boat's motor, using all his strength to turn the wheel. I leap back, away from the edge of the stern as the water beneath me opens, revealing a bottomless pit with no end—just deep, all-consuming dark stretching into infinity. I shove the rod, towel and all, into my backpack and dive into the chair. The boat shudders, sinking further. I claw desperately for anything anchored and solid—anything to keep me afloat.

"I don't want to die." I press myself into the leather and metal, begging for a miracle. "Please, not like this. Please."

Dad's boat creaks and groans under the strain. We're losing our grip on the sun, the chasm below consuming every last trace of the world above. I close my eyes against tears and plead once more, hoping against hope.

"*Please.*"

As quick as the whirlpool formed, it's gone. The water calms, sloshing around the boat. We rock, unsteady, on choppy swells before the ocean smooths into placidity. Birds return as though they'd never abandoned us, resuming their predatory circling in hopes of a dropped chip or fish carcass. Cautiously, I ease myself away from the chair. Had the whirlpool really happened? Or had I imagined it?

"Callie!" Dad rushes toward me. Fear sharpens his hazel eyes, and his suntanned, freckled face is deathly pale. "Are you alright?"

"What just—what was that?" I stammer. Dad shakes his head.

"A whirlpool. It came on so fast... I've never seen anything like it."

Dad can't hide how spooked he is. He trembles uncontrollably despite his efforts to appear stoic and self-assured. Dad never gets scared—what just happened must have been really, truly horrifying for Dad to lose his cool.

Reality slams into me like a Mack truck. I imagined nothing. Every terrifying second of the whirlpool sucking us to our deaths was real—and it's all the rod's fault.

A sob breaks from my lips, tears streaming down my cheeks. "I want to go home."

Dad puts his arms around me, giving me a squeeze. His arms shake. "You got it, Cal." I try to hug him back, but I'm so weak I can barely move.

We hightail it back to the marina as quick as a flash.

CHAPTER SEVEN

I BOLT FOR my room the second Dad and I get home. Mom's voice carries down the hall from the kitchen, filled with surprise that Dad and I are back so early. Dad's hushed tones float over Mom's questions, but I don't stick around to eavesdrop on their conversation. I don't need to hear whatever story Dad's telling Mom about what happened on the boat. I lived every terrible bit of it.

I lock myself in my room, throwing my backpack into the corner. A sticky, stubborn lump chokes my throat as I slump against the door, a wall of tears cascading down my cheeks.

Whirrrr. Somehow, the rod rolls across the floor, flooding my room with light.

"Oh, no! Not again!"

Growling through my teeth, I shove the rod inside my backpack as quick as I can. Maybe I hadn't zipped it up properly, or maybe the power in the rod magically opened my backpack, because magic is a jerk like that. I don't care. All I care about is never looking at the stupid rod as long as I live. I throw it into my closet, building a mountain of jackets, shoes, hoodies, and my old stuffed animals on top until the pulsing hum is silenced.

Slamming my closet as dramatically as I can, I sink onto the floor, erupting in a mess of frightened sobs. My hands tremble, surging with power after holding the rod twice in quick succession. It's not just my fingertips that glow this time. Shimmering, golden brilliance stretches past my wrists, bursting from my skin like miniature extensions of the rod itself.

Have they been glowing this whole time? Did Dad see?

"Stop glowing!" I shove my hands into my pockets, burying my face into the soft, comforting fabric of my hoodie, choking on sobs. "Why is this happening to me?"

At the sound of my voice, a gentle tap on my shoulder. I freeze, still as a stone and downright horror-struck.

I'm all alone in my room. Nobody is here to tap my shoulder.

Another tap. My heart booms like a bass drum as I sit up and turn around.

Nemo, my robotics project, looks up at me, tilting his motionless, rectangular, robot face like a cat. The lights I installed in his knobby eyes blink to life, and he throws his little metal arms around my leg. Like he's *hugging me.*

I open my mouth to scream, but no sound comes out. Instead, I leap as far as I can, staring at the robot in utter terror. It—Nemo, I guess I ought to call it—wheels joyously after me, his metal arms waving in the air as though we're playing tag.

"Go away! Shoo! Leave me alone!"

I jump onto my bed and press my body as far into the wall as I can. Nemo shimmies up the comforter after me, undeterred. He's chasing me—like being scared spitless of him is a huge, hilarious game.

Nemo rounds the edge of my bed and tumbles to his side with a plop. His arms flail wildly, like a sea turtle on its back, and I take the opportunity to do the only logical thing one can do when faced with an inanimate object suddenly brought to life by the glowing rod hidden in one's closet: I run away. Like, really fast.

"Oh, Callie!"

Mom stands a foot from my door when I fling it open, a worried frown creasing the faint lines on her forehead.

Quick as a flash, I pull the door closed and shove my hands against my back. There's no way she can see Nemo and my neon fingers. She'd probably call the cops, or the paramedics. Like that would help this situation.

"Uh, hi, Mom! So nice to see you!" I'm too enthusiastic. Mom sees through it in a nanosecond.

"I wanted to check on you," Mom says. "Dad told me about the scare you had on the boat today."

I nod emphatically. "Oh, yes, the whirlpool. It was scary. No good. Definitely not. Good. Bad, I mean. Er, not that it was good. It was definitely very, very bad."

Mom's eyebrows inch together, making a deep furrow. "You seem frazzled."

"Well, yes, I *am* very frazzled, and so you would also be frazzled, if you had had the thing with the boat in the whirlpool and the other stuff."

Mom nods slowly, eyeing me like I'm going nuts. "Do you feel well enough to work the wedding today? I can call around and try to find another server."

"No!" There's no way I'm locking myself in my room with my suddenly-very-much-alive robotics project all afternoon. "I'm okay. I can go with you."

"Are you sure?" Mom shifts on her feet. "I can find somebody to cover, really. I'm more worried about how you're feeling. You don't look well at all. You're pale and clammy."

"I promise I'm fine." I will myself to sound as normal as possible. Mom almost looks convinced.

Scratch scratch scratch. Tiny metal claws rake against my door. Stupid Nemo.

"What was that?" Mom tries to reach around me for the door handle, but I block her.

"It was, uh, my, um, fingers." I scratch my door with my nails, making a similar sound to the one Nemo made. Mom eases up, but there's a firm, don't-argue-with-me look on her face.

"You're way too tense to work. I'm making an executive decision. You're staying home to rest." Mom gives a nod, as if agreeing with herself for making the right call. "Tea will calm you down. I'll call you when it's ready."

I want to argue that I'm fine, and beg her to change her mind so I don't have to be alone in my room with the robot all day. But Mom's stubborn when her mind is made up. It's just going to be a waste of energy.

"Thanks, Mom." I force a smile, and she leans in for a rare hug. Mom isn't a hugger. Dad, yeah, but Mom … I may get a hug once a year on my birthday. I must *really* look scared sick.

"You being safe and well is more important than helping me cater a wedding. Now go and rest."

I duck into my room as Mom retreats down the hall. Nemo has managed to get off my bed, and he wiggles and spins all around before racing toward me at lightning speed to hug my ankle. I slip down the door, sitting next to him.

"So, the glowing rod makes robots come to life, in addition to the killer whirlpools," I observe, then check my fingers. Regular human skin. "At least my hands are back to normal."

Nemo looks up at me, the lights in his eyes blinking twice before he hugs me again. He seems pretty happy I didn't panic and run away from him.

"What am I going to do with you?"

Nemo crawls into my lap, snuggling down against my thigh, and whirs the motor in his neck. It sounds like a purr. When I gingerly pat the top of his head, the whirring gets louder, even more contented. He's definitely purring.

"I have a robot cat." I scratch Nemo's head, and he nuzzles me. "This could be kind of awesome."

"Totally awesome. I wish I'd had a robot cat when I was alive."

Just when I think this morning can't get any worse, a ghost appears in my room.

Not a lurking, icy presence. Not a tentacle-shaped phantom of darkness. A literal, physical, fully-present manifestation of a person long since dead.

Nate Ormandi sits at my desk, his arms crossed behind his head and his legs stretched out casually in front of him like he's lounging beside a pool. He looks exactly as he did in his pictures—handsome, vibrant, and eternally seventeen. Faded black jeans rip at his knees above scuffed, old school Converse, and a black hoodie stretches across his broad, baseball player chest. His dark, wavy hair swishes off to the side, creeping ever closer to his forehead as it takes on a mind of its own. Piercing black eyes fix themselves on me.

Every last molecule of blood drains from my face in a swift motion, a waterfall crashing toward the pit of my stomach. If I wasn't already sitting on the floor, I'd fall. Air sticks in my lungs and throat, my vision blurs, my ears swim. Somehow, miraculously, my tongue forms words.

"Why—what are you—how—I—"

"I'm sorry, did I frighten you?" He spins back and forth in my desk chair, a charming smile parting his lips. "I didn't mean to. I should introduce myself. Hi, I'm Nate, and I'm dead."

"How is this possible?" Words tumble out with my breath, and it's all I can do to keep my breakfast down, let alone stop my heart from beating out of my chest. "You're not real. You can't be."

"Don't believe in ghosts, huh?" Nate quirks a brow, his smile morphing into something sardonic. "I didn't either. And yet, here we are."

He doesn't look like my mental picture of a ghost. There's no ethereal aura surrounding his being. No floating, wispy tail in place of legs. No pasty white, shimmering skin. No see-through bits. He looks as real as me, as solid in matter and space as me. Like I could reach out and touch him, if I wasn't so afraid of what I'd discover.

And yet, there's something "off" about him. Something not entirely human. Maybe it's the darkness of his eyes, or the way a chill fills the room with his presence. A shiver creeps over my skin despite the sunny warmth of the mid-September morning.

Nemo climbs out of my lap and whizzes toward Nate, swatting at his leg with spindly arms.

"Hey, dude, that tickles." Nate laughs at my robot. "You're going to cause a whole lot of trouble, aren't you?"

Nemo looks at Nate, blinking, before losing interest and flailing about with one of my rubber flip-flops instead.

"Why are you in my room and why can I see you?" My blunt question draws the ghost's attention.

"Honestly? No clue." Nate's eyes transfix me with their sharpness and unnerving color. "But I think—maybe—it has something to do with you snooping around my grave. I sensed you there, and then, bam, I'm here. Like a Bill and Ted time warp."

The things I saw when I blacked out at the cemetery—the tentacle phantoms, the feeling of being trapped in a land of shadows and death. Did crossing over to the dark realm unleash Nate's ghost? Is this nightmare ever going to end? Because seriously, I'm *so over it*.

"You're implying the reason you're here, sitting at my desk and talking to me, is because of something I did?" I raise a brow, staring him down. "I thought you said you had no clue."

"No implications—reasonable conjecture!" Nate tosses his hands in the air. "I just manifested in your room after being dead as a doornail. I was hoping *you* could tell *me* why I'm here. Maybe you're deep into some paranormal, ghost-summoning weirdness."

I cross my arms and glare. "Absolutely not. I don't know why you're here any more than you."

Nate's smile once again lights his features. His teeth are really straight. And white. And… perfect.

"See? We've already got something in common." He gives my chair another spin, watching me with a bemused grin. "What's your name, by the way? Girl I Get To Haunt?"

"No." I snort, rolling my eyes. "It's Callie."

"Callie." Something about his voice sounds familiar, like I've heard it somewhere before. In a dream, maybe, or a memory buried deep, freshly unearthed. "I'd say it's a pleasure to meet you in person, but I'm not exactly a person anymore."

A knock on the door, and Nate and I both turn, staring. His eyes crackle with amusement as I dive to lock it.

"Callie?" Mom jiggles the handle. "Are you okay?"

"Fine, Mom!" My voice is about three octaves too high, so obviously not fine. Who can be fine with a dead guy smirking from their desk?

"Are you talking to somebody?" Mom's muffled voice reaches my ears. "Why is your door locked?"

"Are you going to tell her I'm here?" Nate hisses.

"What was that?" Mom asks.

"Nobody—er, nothing!" I shoot Nate—Nate's ghost? whatever—a scathing look. "I'm fine. Everything's fine. I wasn't talking to anyone. I was, um, watching videos on my phone. I didn't realize my door was locked. Sorry."

"I just came to say your tea is ready. It's in the kitchen when you want it."

"Thanks, Mom."

Mom's footsteps grow faint as she pads down the hall.

"Close one," Nate observes. "What do you think would freak her out more? The ghost thing, or the living robot thing?"

"Is there a point to you being here, or can you evaporate back to the afterlife already?" I pull Nemo out of my flip-flop crate. He scrambles to gather all of my rubber shoes into his arms at once.

"I can, but you haven't figured out your robot problem," Nate replies. "I thought I'd make a suggestion."

I pluck a flip-flop from Nemo's surprisingly strong grasp. "Which is?"

"I think—just a hunch, mind you—my dad might have some answers about your… conundrum." Nate smiles when Nemo growls at me, stretching his entire body as far as he can toward the flip-flop in my hands.

"You want me to become a total outcast at school by going to see Old Man Ormandi?" I scoff. "No offense, but your dad is a shut-in weirdo whose place may or may not be totally haunted."

"No offense, but you're talking to a ghost, and a robot-cat-dog is trying to eat your shoe," Nate counters. "Explain again who's the haunted house weirdo in this scenario."

I mean, he's got a point.

"So you're telling me I ought to just waltz on up to his door and—"

I'm talking to thin air. Nate has vanished.

Let's recap my current situation, and the rest of my terrible, horrible, no good, very bad day. There are a few things I know for certain: The rod can make whirlpools. The rod can make robots come to life. Its light can pierce my skin, worm its way into my soul, and makes my hands glow—a phenomenon that's getting worse every time I touch it.

Oh, manifest phantoms in my room, and summon ghosts. Actual dead people.

This is going to absolutely decimate my social life if I'm caught, but desperate times call for desperate measures.

"Nemo," I tell my robot, "it's time to pay a visit to the boogeyman."

CHAPTER EIGHT

"REASON NUMBER 758 why you should not do this: he could be a murderer. He could lock you in a dungeon and torture you before he turns you into a skin suit. Wait, are those two reasons? No, I'm going to say it's one."

It's been twenty minutes since I parked my car a block from the boogeyman's house. Everyone at Verona Beach High knows where he lives, because his house is a common target to prank on Halloween—a whitewashed beach cottage in a quiet, pleasant little neighborhood, full of wide streets lined with bungalow-style houses overlooking the ocean from the rolling hills atop the cliffs.

It's always the quiet ones you have to watch out for. According to true-crime podcasts, anyway.

Nemo punches my thigh from inside my backpack, whirring the motor in his neck angrily. He looks and sounds like an angry cat stuffed in a burlap bag.

"Hey, chill out." I give my backpack a shove. Nemo only punches harder.

"And reason number 1,001 why I *should* do this…"

Okay, this is it. The reasons for my covert mission outnumber my reasons for burying my head in the sand and forgetting everything about the rod, Nemo, the whirlpool, my glowing hands, the shadow tentacles, and Nate Ormandi's ghost appearing in my room.

Plus, I lied to Will about eating some bad shellfish and being too sick to surf, then practically got into a fist fight with Jase to get the car on a Sunday. My ruined surfing plans and hard-won car victory cannot go to waste. Now, or never.

I pull a cap low on my forehead, grab the boogeyman's book, and shoulder my wriggling backpack as I glance up and down the street. I mean, I want answers, but I don't want to be spotted by any of my judgmental peers, either. I would never live this down. They'd have to carve it on my headstone, even. *"Here lies Calliope James, the loser who visited the boogeyman. Cause of death: eternal shame and embarrassment."*

Luckily, the street remains quiet. Only a middle-aged man mowing his lawn is out and about, and he's too busy rocking his head to whatever tunes he's got in his headphones to notice me. So far, so good.

As soon as I knock on the old man's door, I want to turn around and run away as fast as I can. And yet, something keeps me rooted to the doorstep. Maybe it's my obsession to know what the glowing rod is—why it makes killer whirlpools form in a blink, why it made Nemo come to life, what's up with my glowworm fingers.

But, really, it's probably just plain, old, paralyzing fear.

I wait for what feels like a long time, but nobody answers the door. No sound of footsteps, no hushed voice on the other side. Maybe he's not home, even though a dust-covered station wagon that looks like it hasn't been driven in decades sits in the carport.

"Who's there?" At long last, a voice reaches my ears beyond the closed door.

"Dr. Richard Ormandi?" I hope he can hear me through the barrier of wood and nails. I don't want to yell, because, like I said,

I'll be totally ostracized at school and pretty much forever.

"Yes, who is it?" The voice growls, cranky and impatient.

"My name is Callie James. Can I ask you a few questions?"

The sound of the deadbolts clicking unlocked serves as my answer. Seconds later, the door swings open.

In front of me stands an old man, gray-haired and wrinkled, with tissue-paper skin and splotchy, withered hands. Despite his visible age, his eyes glint sharply — piercing, clear, and black, just like Nate's. They're the eyes of someone much younger, not a man who appears to be at least eighty.

"If your questions pertain to whether or not I'll press charges should you egg my house, you'll find I'm not in close contact with local law enforcement," Dr. Ormandi sneers, glaring at me down his nose. "Although, I'd ask you to do me the courtesy of closing my door before you commence with your vandalism."

"I'm not here to egg your house." I swallow hard to keep my voice from shaking. "I just want to talk to you, if you can spare a minute of your time."

"No." Dr. Ormandi grabs the knob to pull the door closed in my face. I snatch his book from behind my back as quick as I can, holding it up for him to see. The door stops halfway, and Dr. Ormandi's intimidating stare finds mine.

"You're the same Richard Ormandi that wrote this book, aren't you?"

The old man narrows his coal-colored eyes. "I am."

"I want to ask you a few questions about some of the things you wrote." I gulp, wetting my parched throat.

Dr. Ormandi opens the door and faces me head on. His eyes flit across my face before coming to rest on the book in my hands. He's sizing me up. Big time. I hold my breath, hoping he won't turn me away.

"Where did you get that?" He nods his chin toward the book.

"The library. I read it for a report I did on oceanography."

Dr. Ormandi eases. At least, his hackles are no longer raised like a wolf on the defensive. He stares at me a long moment, as if trying to place something about my face. "What did you say your name was?"

"Calliope James. Er, Callie. My dad is Ted James." I tilt my chin. "He went to Verona Beach State, maybe you had him in class?"

Dr. Ormandi remains silent and expressionless. He doesn't even seem to breathe as he continues to stare without blinking, more a statue of an old man standing in a doorway than a living human being.

"Ted James, yes. Took my Intro to Ocean Science class for elective credit." Dr. Ormandi speaks at last. He steps aside, clearing a narrow opening for me to enter. "All right, come inside and ask me your questions."

I slip through the door, and he closes it behind me. Everything about the house is seventies retro, and darkened by light-blocking curtains. But it's neat, and cozy. A leather loveseat and recliner face a vintage, wood-burning stove. There's a small table beside the recliner with a lamp and Nate's senior picture resting on top, and in the corner, a TV with a few more pictures of Nate scattered around it—Nate in a Cal Bears cap leaning against the railing on the Golden Gate Bridge, Nate wearing a button down shirt and tie to accept a science award, Nate in dirty catcher's gear, hoisting a trophy. Floor-to-ceiling bookshelves line the far wall, and beyond, an archway to a tiny kitchen painted yellow. Even the front yard had been spic and span—tidy flower beds, manicured grass, and neat green shutters flanking the bay windows.

"Have a seat, if you please," Dr. Ormandi says, gesturing to the loveseat beside the stove. "We can commence with the interrogation. Would you like some tea?"

"No, thank you."

He creaks and pops into the recliner, groaning against his aging joints as he settles in. He seems totally normal for an old guy living alone — rooms full of books and pictures of his late son, but no signs of being a hermit boogeyman with a haunted house. No newspaper clippings attached by a spider web of strings to internet conspiracy theory articles, no floating specters down creepy hallways, and definitely no yellow-eyed monsters. The only "odd" observations are sets of iron bars covering the front windows, which isn't uncommon on the cliffs, where the wind can be fierce, and a dusty, spider-infested old car.

Dr. Ormandi catches me watching him, and fixes me with that piercing stare of his. "Any particular reason you're eyeing me so suspiciously?"

"Everybody says you're some kind of spooky old hermit," I answer. "But you don't look like it." The old man barks a laugh.

"You've known me all of three seconds and you've already determined I'm not a hermit?" He clicks his tongue. "You must have remarkable powers of perception, Calliope."

"Callie," I correct him. "So, are you? A spooky hermit?"

"Is this what you came to ask me?" Dr. Ormandi's eyes become like two pieces of onyx, gleaming angrily. "Whether or not the schoolyard rumors are true?"

"No, that's not what I came to ask you."

"Very good." The old man's expressive eyes lose their edge. "Now, what did you want to know about my book?"

Excellent segue. I've practiced my line of questioning with Nemo all night, trying to come up with the best way to begin asking about the rod. My robot approved every question, clapping his little metal hands enthusiastically each time I opened my mouth. I have a feeling Dr. Ormandi won't be as easy to please.

"You, um, wrote a chapter on whirlpools, or, um, maelstroms," I stammer, clearing my throat and licking my lips to wet them. My whole mouth feels like cotton.

"Yes, what about them?" Dr. Ormandi sets his chin on his fist.

"Well, um, my dad and I had something very frightening happen yesterday," I reply. "We were out in his boat—he runs a sport fishing charter, did you know?"

"I'd heard of it." Dr. Ormandi looks a bit peevish, like he wants me to hurry up and get to the point already.

"Anyway, we were out on the boat, and suddenly, out of nowhere, this giant whirlpool—maelstrom, whatever—forms and starts to drag us under." My shoulders quake at the memory. "We could have died."

"That's scientifically impossible." Dr. Ormandi switches on professor-mode real quick for a guy who's been retired five forevers. "Whirlpools do not form suddenly. Your father would have been able to see the formation and sail carefully around it, or, more sagely, turn his boat the opposite direction. He was either not paying attention, or what you experienced was not, in fact, a whirlpool."

"No." I shake my head. "It was a whirlpool."

"This is my field, I have a Ph.D. in oceanography." Dr. Ormandi looks just as stubborn as Mom when I'm trying to argue with her. "It could not have been a whirlpool. The circumstances you describe do not match what we know of the formation of underwater vortexes."

I huff angrily and purse my lips. This isn't going as planned. "Okay, so maybe it wasn't a whirlpool, but *something* started to suck my dad's boat underwater. And I know what caused it."

"You do, do you?" Dr. Ormandi raises a silvery brow. "Then why risk becoming a social pariah with your fellow teens by showing up at my doorstep under the purported guise of wanting to ask questions about my old book?"

I really should bail. I don't have to sit here and be talked down to like this, no matter what kind of answers Nate's ghost promised.

"You know what, you're right. Maybe this was a bad idea." Maybe I'll come back and egg his house — that'd show him. I stand and grab my backpack, but Dr. Ormandi holds up a hand.

"No, no, please, stay." He seems genuinely contrite. "Forgive my awkward social skills. I was never good at conversing with people I'm unfamiliar with, and that did not change with old age. I'm happy to answer any questions you have. Truly, I am."

My backpack starts wiggling the moment I retake my spot on the loveseat. Nemo wants out. I kick him softly with my foot, startling Dr. Ormandi.

"Did your backpack just—"

"Yes, it did," I cut him off. "And the reason has to do with my next question." I open my backpack, push Nemo down with my hand so he can't jump out, and retrieve the rod. Nemo whirs his wheels angrily when I zip him back up, and starts punching at the corners of the fabric. Dr. Ormandi looks equally curious and horrified.

"What is going on here?"

"The thing that caused the whirlpool that almost killed my dad and me is *this*." I hold the rod out toward him. "I was hoping you could tell me what it is."

The rod bursts with light, rays and streams peeking through the edges of the towel as I inch it away. When it finally drops to the floor, gorgeous white and gold light, sparkling with tiny prisms, fills the room, causing spectrums of color to dance over the books, pictures, and weary furniture. It's staggeringly beautiful. And yet, it's terrible and frightening.

"This… this isn't possible."

Dr. Ormandi has risen from his chair to his full height, his fists clenched at his sides while his entire frame rattles with uncon-trollable tremors. His eyes are *glowing*. They blaze golden, lit up like ultra-watt Christmas lights in his face as he stares at the rod, mesmerized and furious all at once. I shriek, backing away from him, and trip over my backpack.

Okay, so *this* is why people started all those rumors.

"Put that thing away," he snaps. "You have no idea what you're dealing with."

I throw my beach towel over the rod, and the light begins to fade. Nemo takes the opportunity to zoom out of my backpack and rush Dr. Ormandi, his arms spinning in circles like little nunchucks. He whizzes right up to Dr. Ormandi and batters the old man's ankle. It probably stings a bit, I'm sure.

"What in the world..." Dr. Ormandi regards Nemo with an intense fascination, as though his eyes are deceiving him.

"Oh, and by the way, that also happened yesterday." I snap my fingers, getting my robot's attention. "Nemo, enough. Leave his ankle alone. Get over here."

Nemo growls at Dr. Ormandi by whirring the little motor in his neck, then rolls toward me, clinging to my side when I pick him up. Dr. Ormandi gapes at me and Nemo. At least his eyes have faded back to their normal black.

"This is incredible." He takes a tentative step. Nemo growls again, so the old man backs off. "When was it animated? Just yesterday? It already has an incredibly strong bond with you. I've never heard of a mech forming a connection with a human so fast."

"A what?" I scowl. "What's a mech? And, hey, news flash, your eyes were glowing just now. Want to tell me what's up with that?"

Dr. Ormandi smirks, an expression remarkably like Nate's. "Your hands are glowing. Want to tell me what's up with *that*?"

I look at my hands, clutching Nemo tightly. He's right. Fan-freaking-tastic neon fingers, bursting with tendrils of touchable, solid light.

Dr. Ormandi bores into me with yet another piercing stare, except this time, he's not suspicious. He's tired. Ancient under the weight of his weariness. For the first time since we met, he looks his age.

"This interview has taken a rather unexpected turn," he observes.

"Yeah, no joke."

"Please, sit down." He gestures toward the loveseat, then catches himself. "Actually, it would be best if you put the Light Core in your backpack first."

"Light Core?" I glance at the object in question, its light snaking between the fibers of my beach towel, still pulsing and humming like something out of a sci-fi movie. "You mean the killer glowing rod?"

"It won't kill you. Probably."

Probably? For real? "You aren't doing a super spectacular job of convincing me it *won't* kill me. Just FYI."

"It is safer if it is completely out of our presence, where it cannot sense us," Dr. Ormandi explains. "Please put it away, and then sit."

Where *it* can't sense us. Well, that sounds petrifying. But I do as he asks. I wrap the rod in the towel and zip it up in my backpack before returning to my spot on the loveseat. Nemo wheels around the living room, happy to explore his new surroundings.

"Given that you possess Earth's Light Core, I retract my previous statement about whirlpools and their formation," Dr. Ormandi says. I sit back and cross my arms over my chest, smiling triumphantly.

"Oh, you do, do you? Suddenly the teenager without the fancy Ph.D. isn't as full of crap as she once was."

"My statement wasn't entirely false." Dr. Ormandi's eyes resume their flinty state. "The instantaneous formation of an underwater vortex in the way you described is scientifically impossible. However, the object in your possession throws every scientific rulebook out the window."

"Oh, gee, ya think?" I deadpan. "Which object are you referring to? The glow stick of doom, or my robotics project that suddenly thinks it's an attack dog?"

To my surprise, Dr. Ormandi grins. "Both, obviously." The grin fades into a measured stare, his coal-black eyes latching onto mine with an iron grip. "Why did you come to me? Why seek me out? How did you know I would have an answer for you?"

"Because, I—" It's probably not the best time to mention tracking down his dead son at the cemetery, or the fact Nate's ghost appeared in my room and suggested I pay his dad a visit. I need the least stalkery, not-creepy way of telling the truth. "When I found out about the accident Nate had on his skiff, how he died because he was trying to find something that shoots beams of light from the ocean into the sky, I thought, what if this is the same thing? The thing that almost killed my dad and me could be the reason…"

I can't bring myself to say "the reason Nate died," but I don't have to. Dr. Ormandi's expression contorts around deep pain and grief, and he closes his eyes, squeezing tight.

"Yes, you are correct." His shoulders slump, and when he opens his eyes, the incredibly weary look returns. "The hunt for the Light Core is the reason Nate went sailing the day the storm took his life."

A sorrowful silence settles over us. The only sound in the house is the faint, ticking clock coming from the kitchen.

"I'm so sorry," I whisper at last.

"It has been many long years." Dr. Ormandi flicks his hand through the air, swatting the sadness away as if it were little more than a buzzing mosquito. "Let's discuss the Light Core in your backpack. How did you manage to find it?"

Back to business. I straighten in my seat. "Remember that huge storm in August? Well, I went surfing that day, and the rod—er, Light Core—was stuck to the sea bed about a hundred yards out from shore. I dove for it, and I brought it home. Ever since, it's been doing some massively weird stuff."

"Such as?" Dr. Ormandi motions for me to go on.

"You mean other than the killer whirlpool, turning my fingers into glow sticks, and making my robotics project come to life?"

"Yes, other than that. We'll address those in a moment."

"Every time I touch it, look at it, have *anything* to do with it, it starts to…" I search for the right word. "React to me, I guess. It hums louder, it pulses and vibrates, and it gets so bright it almost blinds me. And if I take it out of the towel and touch it, it starts to worm its way inside me. That sounds strange, I know, but it's like the light penetrates my skin and attaches itself to my entire being."

"Remarkably, that does not sound strange."

There's a large crash in the corner, and I hop to my feet, whirling around. Nemo is busy pulling all of the old man's scientific textbooks from the bookshelves. I point my index finger at him in a way that reminds me a little too much of Mom.

"Nemo! No! Bad boy!"

At the sound of my angry voice, my robot hangs his head, his arms drooping, and wheels his way toward me. I pick him up and set him at my hip.

"I'm sorry." I turn my attention back to Dr. Ormandi.

"It's quite alright," Dr. Ormandi assures me. "Let's switch

gears for a moment and talk about the formation of the whirlpool, and what happened to this little fellow."

"Nemo," I remind the doctor of my robot's name. He gives a swift nod.

"Yes, Nemo. Now, please tell me exactly what happened when the whirlpool formed. I assume you had the Light Core with you?"

"Yes, I did." I set Nemo on the ground and offer him a wadded up ball of paper from my backpack. He tosses and retrieves it like a kid playing catch with himself. "I brought it with me when Dad and I left to go fishing so I could throw it back in the ocean." Dr. Ormandi gives a start, an appalled look on his face like I just said I was going to drop a diamond ring in a pig trough. "But the second I took it out of my backpack and held it in my hands, the whirlpool started to form and suck us underwater."

"I see." Dr. Ormandi watches me, his face settling into something more thoughtful as he considers me and my tale. "And Nemo?"

"After we got home that morning, the rod — Light Core — accidentally fell out of my backpack. I jumped on it as fast as I could, but it had already made Nemo come to life. I don't know how, but it did. And the glowing in my hands was the worst it's ever been. It was all the way up my arms, almost to my elbows. I had to act like a huge weirdo to hide it from my mom." I pause for breath, meeting his eyes. "Can you please tell me what, exactly, I'm dealing with here? Aliens? Secret government weapon stuff?"

The corners of Dr. Ormandi's eyes start to crinkle. "Nothing like that."

"Why did the Light Core make your eyes glow?" Questions bubble from my lips like a geyser. "Are you a mutant? Can I meet the rest of the X-Men?"

The amusement in Dr. Ormandi's eyes spreads to his mouth, and he smiles. "I wish I could tell you I'm secretly a superhero, but I'm not. I'm a Seer. And you, I suspect, are a Luminaut."

I don't know what kind of answer I'm expecting, but it's definitely not that one.

"Um. What?"

"A Luminaut." Dr. Ormandi stands suddenly, with startling swiftness. "I think I'm going to make tea after all. Would you like some?"

"Sure, why not?" When in Rome.

"Milk? Sugar?"

"Both, please."

Dr. Ormandi retreats to the kitchen. Nemo looks up at me, and I look down at him. I shrug my shoulders, and my robot shrugs his, too. A few minutes later, a tea kettle bubbles and whistles. The old man returns with two steaming, fragrant cups.

"All right. Luminauts." Dr. Ormandi lowers himself into his chair. "A Luminaut is a human who has the ability to harness and control the power within a Light Core. They are Light-sensitive beings, and will be drawn to Light wherever it can be found. In other humans, desired objects or destinations, electricity, all manner of things. They latch onto Light, and manipulate and use its power as if it were their own."

"Why do you think I'm one of those Luminaut things?" I sip my tea.

"Had you been a typical human, you would have been able to throw the Light Core back in the sea without forming an interdimensional water gateway — what you erroneously called a whirlpool." Dr. Ormandi sets his cup and saucer on the coffee table, leaning on his knees. "Neither would it physically manifest in your body — in your case, your hands. The Core would glow, but its Light would be mild and benign. It would not attach itself to you, and you would not feel its power. It would not do any of the 'massively weird stuff' you so eloquently described."

"So the Light Core is magic," I surmise. "And you think I'm a light wizard who can make whirlpools, and inanimate objects come to life with my special glowing hands." I grin wryly. "I could make a killing doing this show in Vegas."

"That's a very childish way of seeing this." Dr. Ormandi snorts impatiently, retrieving his cup from the table. "The Light Core is a power source of immense energy, enough to rip the very fabric of space and reality, and you have the ability to control it. You're hardly a party performer or a circus clown." He's so flustered he gulps his tea too fast, and it makes him choke a little. "And —" cough, cough, " — the Light Core does not animate every object it encounters. Just mechs. Or, sentient mechanical lifeforms, but for short, they are called mechs."

"So that's what Nemo's become." A quick glance at my robot, rolling around in the pile of confetti he's made out of the paper ball. "A mech."

"Yes."

"You said *they*." I frown, confused. "Are there more mechs? Living robots?"

"Indeed." Dr. Ormandi takes another sip of tea. He's calmer. No choking. "I have one in my basement."

"Shut up! No way!" I laugh in spite of myself.

"Why would I make a point of bringing it up if I were lying about such a thing?" Dr. Ormandi sets his teacup aside. "Shall I introduce you to him?"

"Yeah, bring him up, Nemo would love a playmate."

The old man shakes his head. "That isn't possible. We must go down to him."

I instantly tense, and Nemo begins growling. Dr. Ormandi cocks his head, a question in his eyes as he looks between me and

Nemo.

"What have I done this time?"

"I just met you an hour ago, and you've got a known reputation for being scary." I shrink away from Dr. Ormandi, edging closer to the door in case I have to bolt at a moment's notice. "I'm not going to follow you into your creepy murder dungeon to see some imaginary robot."

Dr. Ormandi rolls his eyes. "You watch far too much television. I'm not a serial killer, and, despite claims to the contrary made by local youths, I'm very much of sound mind." Dr. Ormandi goes into his kitchen. He opens a door that I would have otherwise said was a pantry, and stands aside.

"If you won't go down, perhaps he'll come close enough for you to see him from the top of the stairs." The old man sweeps his hand toward the open door. "Is that a fair compromise?"

"Yes, that's fair." Better than the alternative, anyway.

I snatch Nemo and move into the kitchen, standing in front of the door. Before me, a narrow staircase materializes, leading downward into impenetrable darkness.

"Spoiler alert, there's nothing down there."

Dr. Ormandi holds a finger to his lips. "Shhh."

At the sound of my voice, faint footfalls, heavy and leaden, echo all around the stairs. The footsteps rumble toward us, sunshine-yellow walls and cabinet doors shaking with every creaking step as cups and plates clatter all around. Groaning and scraping, like metal being bent against its will, fill the house and reverberate through my ears.

"He heard you." Dr. Ormandi catches my eye.

"Who heard me?"

Another smirk-smile. "The Diver."

"*The what?*"

Below, out of the darkness, a gigantic metal dome appears,

quaking the foundation of the entire house as it comes to a deafening halt. I wait, watching the faint outline of the dome against the surrounding dark. Breath leaves my lungs in short gasps, palms sweating furiously.

Zurrrrmmm. A surge of crackling electricity as a pair of glowing eyes blink to life.

And they're staring right at me.

I scream, jumping backward, and hit my head on Dr. Ormandi's kitchen cabinets. Stars dance back and forth across my vision, and I can barely register the now-do-you-believe-me look in his black eyes.

"Calliope James. May I introduce the World Diver?"

CHAPTER NINE

SOMETIMES IN LIFE, you're faced with a scenario in which you should politely excuse yourself and ditch the whole thing. It's just easier for your typical, mundane teenage existence. There's a lot to be said sometimes for sticking your fingers in your ears and singing la-la-la-I'm-ignoring-everything at the top of your lungs.

Case in point: when I saw the Light Core glowing on the seabed, I should have hauled surfboard back to shore. Forget diving for it, much less carting it home and squirreling it away in my closet. Now, as I'm peeking through the darkness into Dr. Ormandi's basement to look at the World Diver, I know I should leave his house for good.

I can hide Nemo in a special room with a secret passcode lock so only I can get in and out. I'll wear gloves all the time, because, you know, randomly glowing hands. I'll just say I've got a thing about germs. And I'll bury the Light Core in a steel safe in the backyard while I learn to dodge tentacle phantoms in the shadows.

Other than those little oddities, my life will be normal.

But when have I ever been "normal" — whatever that is. Not since I was, like, two, probably.

"Well?" Dr. Ormandi's voice floats in my ears. I rub the back of my head where I'd slammed into the cabinet.

"Well, what?"

Dr. Ormandi grins. "Aren't you going to go say hello?"

"I've never been inside your basement, and there's a giant robot down there," I retort. "You go first. I'll follow you."

"I'm old and rheumatic," Dr. Ormandi warns. "I don't take these stairs very quickly. And there are many of them."

I carefully plod down the steps after him, clutching Nemo to my thundering heart. Dr. Ormandi isn't kidding, there are fifty bajillion steps. Okay, overstatement—let's just go with *a lot*. We descend a narrow flight until we hit a landing, then zig-zag down a very rickety, swaying, metal staircase that feels more like a glorified ladder. At long last, my feet hit solid ground. And there, standing before me, is the World Diver.

"Whoa."

The robot is fifty feet tall, at least, and housed in what looks like an underground hangar. Several jet airplanes could fit comfortably inside, and blinking strings of incandescent bulbs hang on strings of wire along the perimeter, giving the hollowed out cavern a perpetual twilight glow.

The Diver himself is enormous, covered in rust and grime— the copper and brass of his cogs and gears made dull by age and neglect. But, surprisingly, I'm not intimidated by him, or scared. He feels instantly familiar, and I can sense his emotions right away. Which, in all honesty, ought to be terrifying. What kind of robot has emotions, much less ones that worm their way into my consciousness? Who in their right mind would make a sentient robot, anyway? Did Dr. Ormandi build him? Is he an evil mad scientist, bent on taking over the world with his monstrous robot?

And yet, the Diver is happy, peaceful. Like he's being reunited with a long-lost friend. If he could hug me without crushing every bone in my body, I feel like he would. Basically, he's a big old teddy bear in a robot suit. Definitely not a humanity-obliterating domination machine. He bends at the waist to inspect me closer, which makes an absolutely deafening creak. The earthen walls shake and crackle with the effort it takes for him to lower his hand for me to climb onto.

"Go on," Dr. Ormandi encourages me. "He won't harm you. In fact, I think he likes you very much."

I whirl on the old man, instantly wary. "You seriously think I'm going to hop onto his hand and fly fifty feet in the air to stare at his face? Saying hi is one thing, taking a potential death-ride is another."

The Diver gently nudges his fingertips toward my gut, urging me to climb into his palm. Nemo swats at the Diver, shooing him away with a growl, but I stuff him into my hoodie to keep him still. The Diver's eagerness and curiosity are palpable, and I feel them as strongly as I feel my own hesitation and fear. I look at the robot's face. It's shining with urgency.

"Okay, fine, but don't you dare drop me," I tell the Diver, hopping over his rust-encrusted fingers into his palm. I doubt he understands me, but hey, better to lay my ground rules from the get go, right? The giant robot is not allowed to drop the human girl. End of story.

Instantly, my body rushes through the cold air, being lifted like an elevator up, up, up until I come to an abrupt stop. Before me is the colossal head of the Diver. The round eyes in the dome of his face shine softly golden as they regard me. If he'd had a mouth, he would have smiled.

"H-hello," I murmur. The Diver radiates contentment, a feeling of being safe and secure. All of my nerves and jitters vanish at his steady calm, and I reach out, grazing my fingertips against the smooth, metal surface of the robot's face.

"What do you think?" Dr. Ormandi calls.

"He's... warm." I turn around, almost too fast. The Diver moves his hand along with me so I don't take a nose dive to the ground—as if he knows the next dumb move I'm going to make even before I do. "Why is he warm? This basement is freezing."

"Warmth is life," Dr. Ormandi answers. "He is not alive like you and me, but he is sentient. Self-aware. Surely you've sensed his emotions."

"Yeah, he feels all the things." I turn to face the Diver once more. "Can you understand me?" To my surprise, the robot nods. Dr. Ormandi's soft chuckle echoes all around the dimly-lit basement-hangar.

"Of course he can understand you. You may tell him to put you down, if you wish. He will obey you."

"Can you put me down, please?" I ask the giant robot.

Away I whoosh, coming to a halt inches from the dirt floor. The Diver's hip and knee joints creak and crack with age and decay, and he loses some nuts and bolts in the act of bending. I step off his palm, and the Diver lowers himself to the ground with an exhausted-sounding thud.

"He's kind of an old guy, isn't he?" I pat the Diver's cobweb covered foot, then face Dr. Ormandi. "How long has he been down here?"

"He is indeed very old." Dr. Ormandi makes his way to an old office chair, the swivel kind, and sits down. "Millenia old, in fact—the last of his kind in existence. But he has only been trapped in his underground cage for about fifty years, when all is said and done."

"Why is he locked up? And how did you even *get* him down here? What is this place? It's huge!" My brain is not fully functional right now, except for questions, questions, and more questions.

"Ah, the curiosity of youth," Dr. Ormandi laughs. "This place is my laboratory. We are far underground, below the city sewer system, even. It was hollowed out over the course of several decades, with the Diver's help. That was before this neighborhood became the residential subdivision it is now. By the time the town spread out and reached us, this laboratory was finished, but the Diver was trapped inside."

"This place is awesome." I scan the massive space, the ceiling almost seventy-five feet above me, twinkling little lights stretching into the farthest corner and back. "I'm seriously impressed."

I set Nemo down to explore, and take a closer look around now that my eyes have adjusted to the dim light. Dr. Ormandi's chair sits beside a worktable, littered with charts, pencils, and notebooks. Oceanic maps are plastered along the walls, with push pins and red and black circles and x's marking different locations. There's even an old, early-nineties computer plugged into the wall, and a record player next to it.

"You get electricity and the internet down here." I observe with a grin. "How's the cell signal?"

"I do not use a cell phone and my wireless access is… nonexistent. That's because I have not bought a computer in several decades." Dr. Ormandi spins the seat around. "This laboratory is set up to run on hydroelectricity. The city has no knowledge of it."

Even more impressive. "How'd you swing that?"

"Mariasol—my late wife—was rather gifted with electrical systems. She created several turbines underwater near the cliffs to harness the power of the waves and currents. She was even working on creating an exit tunnel and watertight door so the Diver could be free of this decrepit hole. However, she passed away before it was complete." Dr. Ormandi makes a gesture toward the darkness at the back of the lab. "You can see the remnants of it in the corner over there."

Sure enough, there's a deep gash in the earthen walls on the very far side of the basement.

"Was your wife an electrical engineer?" I take a seat beside the Diver's foot. I don't know why, but I feel comfortable sitting next to him—even though he could squish me like a bug. He feels comfortable sitting next to me, too. In fact, he's happy as a clam.

"Yes, she was," Dr. Ormandi answers. "But, more importantly, she was my Luminaut."

I cock my head. "Your wife was a light wizard? The thing you think I am?"

"Stop calling it a light wizard," Dr. Ormandi growls in a very irritated way.

"Luminaut. Sorry." I fiddle with a loose rusted gear on the old robot's ankle. It's so corroded it falls off in my fingers, practically disintegrating as I twirl it around my palm. "So the Diver is old, busted, and locked up." I glance upwards. "Sorry, big guy, that sucks."

The robot looks down, his orb-like eyes shimmering just like my fingers whenever I touch the Light Core, and gives me a gentle pat on the back. It's surprising something so huge can be so careful with something relatively tiny and delicate. In a way, it's... adorable. Not in the hyper-baby-kitten way Nemo is adorable, but in a huge, cuddle-monster way. Dr. Ormandi smiles at the gesture.

"He's very glad to have a new friend," the old man tells me. "And, potentially, a new Luminaut."

That word again, as if it means something I instinctively ought to know. I touch the Diver's foot, my fingers absorbing his warmth. "What's the deal with the World Diver and Luminauts? Why can I feel what he's feeling?"

Nemo whizzes up mid-question with a new plaything—a

pencil nub he found on the ground somewhere. He shakes it, like a toddler showing off a favorite toy. I give his head a pat, and he whizzes away, enthralled. If my little friend notices the absolutely ginormous robot next to me — or cares much — he doesn't show it.

"Much like yourself and Nemo, Luminauts and World Divers are connected to one another by their inner Light." Dr. Ormandi watches Nemo play with the nub before giving me his full attention. "Once the Diver has found his Luminaut, they will be bonded for the rest of that Luminaut's life. Luminauts are the pilots of the World Diver, navigating gateways through the multiverse to hunt for the hidden Light Cores."

"Excuse me." I blink hard. Did he just say what I think he said? "Uh, what multiverse? Do you mean, like, other planets? The Diver is a space traveler?"

"No, no, nothing like that." Dr. Ormandi swishes his hand through the air, batting my ridiculous notions away. "Other worlds. Realities entirely separate from our own, populated by their own peoples and cultures, with rich histories. *Not aliens.*"

Dr. Ormandi saw me open my mouth and anticipated my next question. He's good. "So, are there a lot of Light Cores hidden in the multiverse? Are they like buried pirate treasure? Because I could really dig being a light pirate."

"A light pirate is a closer approximation than a light wizard." Dr. Ormandi rolls his eyes when he says *light wizard*. "Each world in the multiverse has a hidden Light Core. And they must be found."

"Why? Why do Luminauts need to find the hidden Light Cores? How do they find gateways to travel to the other worlds in the first place? And you still never told me what a Seer is, by the way. Is that why your eyes did the weird glowing thing upstairs?" So many questions. A lava flow of questions, erupting from my mouth.

"You have a great number of queries, and I will not answer them today." Weariness overtakes to the old man's features, and he slumps a little in his chair. "But, if you wish to know the answers, you may come back and visit us another time."

I scowl, chewing my lip. I'd wanted answers about the Light Core, and I'd gotten my wish, but this whole 'paying the boogeyman a visit' thing has opened up a serious can of worms.

Luminauts, Seers, gateways through the multiverse... he could be making this stuff up. Maybe all his talk of Light superpowers and other worlds are just stories he's told himself to cope with the tragedy he faced. Maybe I'm better off forgetting him, Nate's ghost, and everything else that happened because of the Light Core.

And yet, I'm sitting next to a sentient robot that's three stories tall. One who acknowledges me, who picks me up and pets me, who wants to be my friend. I have a powerful, mystical, legendary Light in my backpack that creates whirlpools from nothing and makes robots come to life. *That* part is very real. What if the other stuff is real, too?

"Listen, I don't know if I believe any of this," I admit. "I'm even less certain I'm a light wiz—erm, a Luminaut. But I really like the World Diver, and I'd be happy to help fix him up a bit, if I can. I'm taking a robotics class at school this year, and I'm getting pretty good with my hand torch. I could at least help him move his joints more easily. Will you answer my questions if I come back and work on repairing him?"

Dr. Ormandi grins. "One question per visit. Perhaps two, if I'm feeling generous."

"That's kind of stingy," I counter. The old man's grin becomes a smile.

"My castle, my rules." He holds out his hand for me to shake. "A visit to the Diver in exchange for a question answered. Do we have an agreement?"

"Yeah, sure." I stand up and shake his hand. "I don't know when I'll be able to come back, because I have to share a car with my older brother and we basically get into a cage match every time I want to use it, but I promise I'll visit again as soon as possible."

"Excellent." Dr. Ormandi seems pleased with our deal. "The Diver and I will look forward to it."

I call for Nemo, and he wheels to my side in an instant. "Can I ask a couple teensy questions before I go? Since, technically, the one question rule isn't in effect until the next visit."

"You may." Dr. Ormandi gives me a nod of consent.

"What should I do with the Light Core? And Nemo? And my glowing hands?"

"If you keep the Light Core hidden and away from the ocean, it will not harm you," Dr. Ormandi replies succinctly. "I would resist the urge to touch it or interact with it. The more the Light comes into contact with you, the more you will begin to physically manifest it, hence the glowing fingers and hands. So leave it wrapped in your towel, at least until you have learned how to control your powers. Which I will not address now. Another question for another time."

I smile. "You're getting good at picking up when I'm going to interrupt you with a question, aren't you?"

"Indeed. You can be rather predictable." A shadow of a laugh brightens the old man's face. "With regards to Nemo—" he glances at my robot, who growls and punches as I try to stuff him into my backpack "—I would begin training him immediately. You seem to have taught him a few commands, but he will need to learn a good deal more restraint if he's supposed to pass for a typical robotics project."

"Sounds like I've got a lot of work ahead of me." I shoulder my backpack, trying to ignore Nemo's jabs, which are stabby and sharp in the middle of my shoulder blades. The first thing I'm going to teach him is how to be less of a pill in my backpack.

"I believe you'll find yourself more than capable of the task ahead of you." Dr. Ormandi grins. "Good luck."

"Thanks." I turn and make for the intimidatingly steep staircase up to his house. "I'll see you again as soon as I can, Dr. Ormandi. You, too, Diver."

The Diver glows with happiness, a faint sheen flashing over the dull metal of his frame. I smile at the robot's domed face before beginning my climb up the rickety steps.

"Goodbye, Callie," Dr. Ormandi calls over his shoulder. "Meeting you today was... interesting, to say the least."

"Yeah, same." Interesting doesn't even begin to cover it.

I climb the stairs, and shut the basement door behind me.

CHAPTER
TEN

"OKAY, WEDNESDAY NIGHT is free, but I have a lot of algebra I need to get caught up on, so I should do that instead. Thursday I've got volleyball practice and a study group. Friday I have a game. Saturday Mom's got me doing a wedding."

Figuring out when I can sneak off with the car, go see the World Diver, and start work on the rusty old bucket of bolts would be a lot easier if I wasn't so involved in extracurriculars and keeping up my grades. Thanks, superpowers and sentient robots, perfect timing.

"What about Sunday…" I scroll through my calendar on my phone, looking at the day in question. "Sunday could work, but Jase will probably fight me. Again."

Speaking of my big brother, I've been sitting on the benches outside the gym waiting for Jase for the better part of half an hour. Sometimes soccer club runs a bit later than my volleyball practice because they're going over new plays, but this is getting ridiculous. Just as I'm tapping out a very strongly worded "where the crap are you" text, he roars into the parking lot and screeches to a halt in front of me. But he isn't alone. There's another passenger in the front seat, and it's not his girlfriend, Jen.

It's Zack Mendes.

A moment of sheer, unadulterated panic overtakes me. Zack Mendes is one of the most popular guys in my junior class. He plays soccer on Jase's club team, and he runs with Jase's beach bonfire crowd. I think we have spoken two words to each other since freshman year, and now, I'm going to have to sit in the same car as him, covered in sweat with no makeup. Also, I probably smell. I pretend to wipe my brow so I can take a sniff of my armpits. Kinda funky.

I could slaughter Jase for not telling me about this. I swear, Jase is the worst.

Shouldering my bag, I pop my sunglasses over my glistening (and not in a good way) face and make my way to the Camry. Why Zack is in my car with Jase is a mystery, but I'm sure it will be explained. It better be.

"We're taking Zack home," Jase announces once I hop in the back seat. Zack has taken my spot up front.

"Obviously," I deadpan. Zack turns and grins.

"Hi, Callie." He knows my name? Fascinating. "You want to switch seats? I'm probably in your spot."

A nice gesture, and not one I expected. For one of Jase's friends, Zack seems halfway perceptive. Although, Jase is about as obtuse as a brick wall, so that's not a huge compliment or anything.

"It's okay, thanks, Zack." I grin, too.

"My car is in the shop, so Jase offered me a ride. Some trouble with the transmission." Zack gives an embarrassed shrug—about his car or being seen with me, I'm not certain. "My car's not the newest."

"Have you gotten a load of the piece of junk you're riding in?" I inch my sunglasses down my nose, giving Zack a look over the rim. He laughs.

"Don't talk smack about my car, Callie," Jase warns.

"It's my car, too, and it *is* a piece of junk," I retort neatly. "But at least it runs, which is more than we can say for Zack's car."

Zack laughs again. I can't tell if he actually thinks I'm funny or if he's humoring me because I'm Jase's sister. Probably the latter.

Zack and Jase talk soccer the rest of the drive to Zack's house, ignoring me in the back seat. At least nobody comments on how badly I may-or-may-not smell, or the state of my sweat-soaked hair. Light Cores, ghosts, and sentient robots have entirely upended my existence without the added joy of rumors regarding my body odor.

Jase drops Zack off in front of his house and speeds away before I can switch to my usual seat up front. "Once around the park and home, James," I joke. Jase isn't amused.

"Ha ha, very funny," he mutters.

"It *is* funny, and it was rude of you not to let me move up front when we dropped Zack off." I cross my arms over my chest. "How long are we going to be giving him rides home?"

"Why does it matter?" Jase responds with a defensive question.

"Because I want to know how long I'm going to be relegated to the back seat of my own car like a kindergartner." I push my sunglasses to the top of my head and fix Jase with my best scowl. "You didn't tell me we were taking Zack home. If I'd offered to drive one of my friends home without texting you first, you'd be livid. This isn't just *your* car, Jase, it's mine, too. As much as you like to think you have sole ownership and driving rights, you don't. The least you could have done was send me a text. It takes five seconds of your time."

Jase takes a deep breath, and his shoulders drop. "Okay, I'm sorry. I should have texted. I didn't think you'd mind."

An apology is more than I expected from Jase, so I guess I

should be satisfied. But I'm still annoyed.

"Oh, by the way," Jase speaks up. "There's gonna be a bonfire down on the beach Friday, and I'm taking the car to—"

"Ugh, you are impossible, Jase," I groan.

"Why? What big plans do you have? A date with Will?"

My face burns, and I lean forward in my seat, flicking the back of Jase's ear. "I don't have a date, and even if I did, the last person it would be with is Will. But leading with 'I'm gonna be greedy about the car Friday night' after our last conversation isn't the best plan you ever had."

"Don't flick my ear, that hurts." Jase's narrowed eyes meet mine in the rearview mirror. I set my jaw.

"Yeah, well, I'm not sorry."

"Okay, then, Calliope," Jase uses my full name, which he knows I hate. I glare daggers at the back of his head. "Do you want the car Friday night?"

"Thank you for asking, but no," I reply. "I have a game and Dad is taking me."

"Wow, there's a shocker. Callie James being a kiss-up daddy's girl." Jase snickers. "I know you hate sports, and you don't give a crap about your grades, so why are you trying so hard now? You think it'll make Dad see you as anything other than a total failure? Just accept that you're the family loser already."

Okay, that's it. I lean forward to give Jase a piece of my mind when an absolutely brilliant idea strikes. I don't hit gold often, but when I do, it's solid. I lean back in my seat, smug in the knowledge that I'm about to play my trump card.

"You can have the car this Friday," I begin, "but it's mine every Sunday. All day. No arguing, no negotiating. Every. Sunday."

Jase smirks. "Yeah, like that's gonna happen."

I feign interest in my chipped fingernails, shrugging. "Then I guess I'll have to tell Mom and Dad that you're already flunking Civics."

Jase's eyes pop. He swallows hard. I can hear his Adam's apple bob up and down in his throat. "How do you know that?"

"I heard your dear, sweet girlfriend, Jen Jarvis, talking about it yesterday in chemistry. Really loudly." I look up, batting my eyes at Jase. "Oh, did you forget she's in my chemistry class?" Clearly, Jase had. "It's unfortunate Mom and Dad will restrict your driving privileges to nothing but school and soccer practice once they find out. Bye-bye bonfire night."

Do I feel a little bad about blackmailing Jase? Sure. I mean, I know he struggles in school. When we were younger and thick as thieves, I used to help him with his remedial math and reading. But then Jase morphed into a self-entitled snob who acts like he's too good for anyone's help, mine or otherwise.

"You suck, Callie," Jase growls under his breath. He's fuming, but I've won. The car is mine every Sunday. World Diver, here I come.

"Come on, Jase, it's not so bad," I gloat. "Now you've got a whole day every weekend to study Civics!"

We don't say another word the rest of the way home.

"Okay, I've got my hand torch, my buffing cloths, rust remover, gloves, goggles—what else do I need?"

My first Sunday of exclusive car rights has come, and I'm reveling in the freedom. Jase whined all morning, and even offered to take me to Starbucks and buy my favorite frap in hopes I'd change my mind, but I turned him down flat. I'm antsy to see the Diver and get to work on his gnarly leg and hip joints. I don't know how much good I'll be able to do, but more than anything I think the old robot appreciates my company. And, if I'm being honest, I like him, too.

Nemo whizzes up to me with a ball of paper. He officially switched from my flip-flops to paper a day or two ago—equally awful toys for vastly different reasons.

"You want to fetch?" I take the paper ball and toss it into the corner. "Go fetch, boy!"

Nemo scurries away, and I focus on packing supplies in my duffel bag.

"Going somewhere?"

I shriek, bumping against my closet door. The handle digs into my spine as Nate Ormandi's laughing eyes find mine.

"Can you announce your presence in a less ghostly way?" I rub my back where the handle just assaulted it.

"Well, I *am* a ghost." He reclines on my bed this time, elbow propping up his head as he watches me intently. Instead of the hoodie, he's wearing a black t-shirt with ripped black jeans. He must have a thing for black. I mean, it looks awesome on him, with all that dark, wavy hair spilling across his perfect—never mind.

"Get off my bed," I command.

A gleam lights his eyes. "Why?"

"Because I sleep there and I don't want your ghost cooties infecting it," I retort. "I mean, the whole 'ghost appearing in my room' thing is weird enough without you invading my private space."

"As you wish." Nate vanishes in a blink, reappearing at my desk. "Is this better?"

"Nothing about this situation is 'better,'" I mutter, picking up Nemo. He's enthralled enough with the paper ball that he hardly notices me stuffing him inside the duffel bag. "I should probably call a priest or a pastor to come cleanse this place and get rid of you. Isn't the number one rule of ghosts that it's a bad idea to commune with the dead?"

"I don't know the rules, I haven't been a ghost very long." Nate fiddles with my earbuds. "Maybe you could explain the rules — girl who spies on dead people for kicks."

I narrow my eyes. "Is the sole purpose of these hauntings to scare the living daylights out of me before turning into an unreasonably irritating apparition? Because if so, you're very effective."

"I'm not irritating, I'm delightfully clever and funny." Nate flashes a jaunty smile. "Besides, I like talking to you. You're the first human I've interacted with since becoming fish food. The company where I'm from is pretty dead in the water." A pause, and he holds back a laugh. "Dead in the water, get it?"

I roll my eyes. "You're punny. That's cute."

"Glad you think so." Another smile, this one borderline flirtatious. *Kick-thump* goes my heart against my ribs before Nate turns his attention to the earbuds in his palm. "Is this really how people listen to music nowadays? How can you hear anything with these?"

I lean against my closet, crossing my arms. "So why are you here this time? Or do you enjoy watching me crack my spine in half whenever you show up?"

Nate snorts. "Your spine isn't in half, you're standing up and walking around. I died before I finished anatomy, but I know —"

"Focus. The point. Getting to it." I swear, he's as bad about scientifically accurate tangents as Dr. Ormandi.

"My greater purpose in haunting you is helping you figure out your robot situation. You don't seem to have anybody but me who knows the truth about your little project-turned-pet. Sometimes a girl needs a confidential ghost friend. You need me, so I'm here." Nate glances my way. "Was your visit with my dad helpful?"

"How do you know I went?" I raise a brow.

"A hunch." His eyes flash. "A ghostly hunch." He tries to wrap the earbud cord around his ears. "Anyway, did you talk about anything important?"

"The buds go inside your ears, not around them." I come close, shivering at the deathly chill surrounding him (ghost thing, probably), and snatch the cord out of his grasp. He stands, facing me, watching with interest as I demonstrate with my own ears.

Holy Hotness, Batman, those arms! I can make out every single muscle in his—I mean, um, he's tall.

"Interesting." A look of understanding lights Nate's features, and he pops the buds in his ears and looks around. "Where's your cassette player? Or are you one of those cool girls who has a CD player?"

Cassettes? CDs? The nineties called and want their tech back, Nate.

"My parents are the only people I know who still listen to CDs." I make a face. "We have music on our phones now."

"The phone?" Nate's eyes get big and excited when I show him my music app. "This is awesome! What's the sound quality like? Nothing is better than vinyl, but anything's better than cassette. Do you have vinyl, by the way? If you do, I'll love you forever."

I'll love you forever—kick-thump.

Stop it, internal hot-guy radar. Said hot-guy is *not* hot, because he's dead. I scroll through my phone and put on a song for him. His smile stretches as wide as his earlobes.

"Wow, check out the rad stereo effect." He bobs his head. "You've got good taste in music. Who is this? Somebody I'd know?"

"I thought you wanted me to tell you about your dad and the

World Diver?"

"Hm? Oh, yeah. Go on, I'm listening." He's not listening, he's bopping his chin and drumming out a beat with his index fingers on my desk, his wavy shock of hair bouncing against his forehead in time with the rhythm.

"What we talked about was… interesting." I shoot him a humorless glance. "It would have been helpful of you to warn me your dad has a fifty-foot tall, self-aware robot in his basement, and is a Seer with freaky, glowing-eye powers."

Another roguish smile. "Where's the fun in that?"

That smile—charming and broad, taking up such an embarrassing amount of my mental real estate. A cat-like slyness dances around the edges, a hint he's got a secret or two up his sleeve. It draws me in like a moth to a flame, whispering of danger and heartbreak, and yet, I can't help but fall deeper under its spell.

Stop it, Callie, he's a ghost. Not hot, not charming, no cute smile. In real life, he's a pile of bones at the bottom of the sea. There. That puts it into perspective.

"So, I'm assuming you were initially wigged out by the giant, sentient mech and the Seer's Eye, then got used to my dad's superpowers, and…" Nate trails off, motioning for me to go on.

"And then he talked to me about Luminauts and Seers and the multiverse," I reply. "Which, I'm assuming, you know about."

"Given that my mom was a Luminaut and my dad a Seer, to say I'm familiar with the Lore is an understatement," Nate deadpans. "Anything else?"

A casual shrug. "He thinks I'm a Luminaut, but—"

"Really?" Nate's eyes pop. He takes my earbuds out of his ears, setting them and my phone aside. "Why?"

Another shrug, this one more indifferent than my first. "Because I found Earth's Light Core, and—"

"You found the Light Core?"

I didn't think it was possible for Nate's eyes to get bigger, but they do. And blacker. I know what ravenous looks like, and the glint in Nate's eyes is like a wolf on the prowl. And in a very real moment of horror, I'm reminded he's a ghost, and I'm a human, and there's a strong probability he might cause me harm—I've seen enough scary movies to know when I ought to be terrified.

"Hunting Earth's Light Core killed me." Nate's voice lowers, sharp as a razor's edge as he comes even closer. The benign chill around his presence becomes an icy blast, slamming into me with every word. "Even my mom couldn't find the Light Core, and she searched for decades." Nate's immensely black eyes flit toward my duffel bag. "Is it in there? Can I see it?"

I back away from him, as far into the corner as I can go, clutching my bag tight to my thundering heart. "No, it's hidden. Somewhere else." Hopefully, he can't hear the Light Core whirring under the piles of clothes and shoes in my closet—or my pulse. "Your dad advised me to keep it that way. Whenever I touch it, bad things happen."

Nate steps away, the iciness thawing, his eyes fading into their normal color and shape. "Yeah, well, bad things happen around Luminauts in general," he murmurs. I tilt my chin and frown.

"What do you mean?" I'm still wary when I step away from my corner, cautiously close to him once more.

"Exactly how much Lore did my dad tell you?" Nate asks with a pointed stare. "Because there's a lot he likes to leave out."

A tap on my door. I whip my head toward the jiggling knob, then turn to warn Nate to make himself scarce. But he's already gone.

Will swings my door wide, leaning on his arm against the frame as he pushes his sunglasses to the top of his head. He's beach-ready in his flip-flops and board shorts, twirling his car keys around a finger. An eager smile lights his face.

"Hey, Callie, ready to go surfing?"

"Oh!"

I totally forgot I made surfing plans with Will since I ditched him for Dr. Ormandi and the World Diver last weekend. The way Will's smile fades at the corners when he eyes my yoga leggings, t-shirt, and Nikes, he knows I forgot, too. "Why aren't you ready to go?"

I open my mouth, reeling for an excuse. "Listen, Will, I, uh, I have to do robotics stuff." It's unsettling how easily I spin lies nowadays. "I'm sorry, but it's important. Our whole class tries to help each other on their projects, and if I bail on them, I'll never live it down."

"But we've had this planned since Monday!" Will protests, disappointment clouding his eyes. He steps into my room and looks around. "Were you talking to somebody just now? I heard your voice."

"I was confirming our meeting plans with my classmates." Actually, Will, I was chatting with the ghost of the boogeyman's son who's been invading my room since I found this magical Light Core, and went spying on his grave for no discernible reason.

Will scowls. "I could swear I heard a guy's voice, too."

"Listen, Will, I'm so sorry I have to ditch you today." I take his shoulders and face him head on, deflecting any further questions. "I promise — like, pinky-promise-times-a-million — I will surf with you next weekend. Look, I'm putting it in my phone right now." A few clicks and the date is set on my calendar. I hold up the screen to show my best friend. "See? Surfing date with Will. Right there. No canceling last minute."

"But, Callie, we—"

"I gotta run, I'm already late." I give Will a big hug, then rush out of my room. "You can shut my door for me, right? Have fun, catch some good waves! Try not to suck!"

Will hangs back in the doorway, shoulders slouched deject-edly, as I round the corner of the hallway and bound out the front door.

CHAPTER ELEVEN

"CALLIE!"

Dr. Ormandi grins, more than a little surprised to see me on his doorstep. His eyes that look just like Nate's—or is it the other way around?—grow round in his withering, wrinkled face. "I wasn't expecting you back so soon."

"My brother is failing Civics, so I've got the car every Sunday now." I step into his house, and he closes the door softly while I make myself at home, hanging my cap and jacket on his hook by the door.

"I don't understand how those two things are inherently related, but I'm pleased to see you nonetheless," Dr. Ormandi replies. "Would you like some tea?"

"Nah, I'm more of a coffee person. But thanks anyway." I make my way into the kitchen and call over my shoulder, "I'm going to go see the World Diver now."

The sound of Dr. Ormandi's hoarse chuckle meets my ears when I open the basement door. "You don't dawdle, do you?"

"Not when I've got an enormous, banged-up robot to fix."

The second I begin my descent into the basement lab, the Diver creaks toward me with excitement. If his mangled joints allowed him to run, he would. The brilliantly glowing eyes inside his domed head find me, and he hobbles as close as he can to the rickety staircase.

"Hey, Diver." I grin, holding onto the railing for dear life as a particularly loose set of stairs sways beneath my feet. "Have a good week? Probably not, since you're trapped in this basement by yourself. That's got to be boring."

The World Diver can't speak, but he clearly agrees with me, because his eyes glow bright. I carefully finish my descent, testing each step before putting my weight on it. Taking a thirty-foot dive to a solid dirt floor would be the epitome of not-good. The robot eases his body to the ground with a metallic groan, losing bits and bobs in the process.

"Let's get to work." I unload my duffel bag, including Nemo, who immediately wheels toward the Diver and tosses his gnarled, well-loved paper ball at the giant robot's hand. When the Diver doesn't pick it up and throw it, Nemo growls, scratching at the Diver's fingers with his little claws.

"Nemo, be polite," I chide. "The Diver doesn't want to play with you."

The Diver warms, amused by Nemo's frustration and insistence on being acknowledged. He glows with curiosity as Nemo begins to whirl around, inspecting the metal pieces that fell from the Diver before tossing them aside when he discovers they aren't paper.

"Nemo is kind of on a perpetual sugar high." I climb onto the ancient robot's leg, fixing the propane canister to my hand torch. "He'll chill out soon. I hope. Anyway, do you have a name?"

No response. But it's hard to talk without a mouth.

"Can I guess?" No response again. "Um… Thomas? George? Hank?"

The Diver shakes his head. But he appreciates my attempt.

This guy has been around since forever and traveled to other worlds; why would he have an old-school, American, grandpa name? I try a different approach. "Can I give you a name? How about Robby? Robby the Robot, that's pretty cool right?"

The Diver shakes his head again. His eyes dim in a way that feels like glaring, and his being radiates disgust.

"Wow, okay, that's a no," I surmise. "Iron Man?" No. "Marvin? Max?" No and no. "Voltron?" Hard no.

"Just 'Diver' then?" The Diver glows with contentment. He pats my back, his happiness filling my heart as strong and gooey-warm as if it were my own. I slip my hands into the gloves and fix my goggles over my eyes, flashing Diver a smile.

"Okay, Diver. Let's see what we can do about these knees."

I don't hear Dr. Ormandi coming down the stairs over the sound of my torch, but when I take a break and look up, he's sitting in the swivel chair, watching me work. A smile brightens his curmudgeonly face.

"It's good the Diver is getting some attention," Dr. Ormandi nods toward the torch in my hand. "He's been neglected for far too long."

"I was trying to figure out his name." I push my goggles to the top of my head. "I suggested Robby but he hated it."

"If he ever had a name, it's been lost to time and memory, and likely only exists in a language that hasn't been spoken in eons," Dr. Ormandi replies.

"He just wants to be called Diver." Diver pats me again at the sound of his name. He shines with affection and peace—like the feeling you get on Christmas when all your family is close and just basking in each other's presence.

"That sounds about right." Dr. Ormandi grins. "So, you are already communicating with him?"

"Communicating?" I scowl. "He's not saying anything. But I can sense how he feels about things, and he hated all my name suggestions. Can he actually talk?"

"No, not as you or I can," Dr. Ormandi answers. "Mariasol described it as a strange bit of telepathy. And before you ask—" I pause, mouth gaping like a goldfish, "—no, Luminauts cannot read minds, it is a process that only works on the Diver, and, to an extent, other mechs."

Well, nuts. Knowing exactly what people wanted me to say or do at any given moment would take care of so many of my problems.

"Does Diver communicate with you, too?" I take my gloves off and set them at my side.

Dr. Ormandi's eyes take on a sad look. "Unfortunately not. Seers cannot control or command the Diver the way a Luminaut can."

"So you can't boss this guy around?" I nod toward Diver.

"No." Dr. Ormandi's lips quirk; almost a grin. "He will come to me if I call him, or pick me up if I ask. But that is his desire for my companionship. He gets quite lonely."

"You mentioned Diver is old, but exactly how old? What can you tell me about ancient Luminauts?" Seems like the perfect way to try and understand a bit of the Lore, which Nate dropped some heavy-handed hints I ought to ask more about.

"It remains unknown precisely how old mechs like the World Diver actually are, but he has very likely existed since before recorded history." College professor mode, commenced. "Ancient Luminauts would have piloted him in their travels with Seers to protect and defend people with the Light."

"Ancient Luminauts were protectors?" I search the old man's face for a sign he's concealing anything. He's placid.

"Indeed." Dr. Ormandi nods firmly. "It was their call and purpose."

"But they were human, so they couldn't have all been good,

right?" I tread cautiously, keeping my face neutral and innocent. "I'd assume some of them became corrupt."

"Luminauts are beings who embody the Light," Dr. Ormandi gives me a strange look. "Why would they fall into corruption?"

"For example, if I'm a Luminaut, like you say I am, I'm totally not a goody-goody saint," I elaborate. "Ask my mom and dad how completely flawed and self-centered I can be. They'll give you an earful, trust me."

Dr. Ormandi nods succinctly. "Yes, I see what you're getting at," he replies. "That's not what I meant. Luminauts have human emotions and shortcomings like anyone else, but one hallmark of a Luminaut is the powerful, protective nature of their inner Light. Perhaps you've felt this yourself."

"I don't know, I haven't been in too many scenarios where I've had to be protective." I give a shrug. "The whole reason I tried to toss the Light Core back into the ocean was to protect my family. And I protect Nemo by hiding him. But I feel like anybody would do that."

"One day you may find yourself in a situation where you are forced to act as a true Luminaut would." When Dr. Ormandi speaks, he sounds almost prophetic. "Then you will know what it means to choose the Light." The old man heaves himself out of the chair, stretching out his legs before approaching Diver. "How is the work coming? Will he be salvageable?"

"I don't know, he's pretty bad." I frown, looking over the pitiful little welds my hand torch made on Diver's knee. It's the size of a Volkswagen, and about as complex. Definitely some ancient, alien-level tech. "This might be more than I can handle. But I'll keep trying."

"I would imagine the Diver is a far more intricate project than Nemo." My little robot speeds toward Dr. Ormandi at the sound of his name, shaking his makeshift toy at the old man. Dr.

Ormandi looks between me and Nemo with confusion.

"He wants to play fetch," I explain. "Just toss that wad of paper for him."

"Ah." Dr. Ormandi winces when he bends to retrieve Nemo's toy, and tosses it deep into the basement lab. Nemo whizzes away, waving his arms joyously. "Speaking of your tiny friend, have you been training him?" Nemo wheels back quick as a flash, clamoring for another fetch. Dr. Ormandi obliges, throwing the paper even farther this time.

"I've been trying, but I can't keep him focused for long." Nemo returns, this time with an ancient, dried up ink pen he found. I flash an enthusiastic thumbs up, and he wheels off, his paper abandoned for the new piece of trash my robot thinks is a toy. "He can pay attention for half-a-second before he's distracted. Plus, he has zero concept of the human need for sleep."

"He will mellow with time and age," Dr. Ormandi assures me.

"Yeah, well, he needs to mellow out massively by December," I mutter to myself. "I'm supposed to present him to my entire robotics class."

"That is a conundrum." Dr. Ormandi obviously doesn't have any good advice for that one. Maybe he's never trained a newborn mech. "And the Light Core? Have your hands been glowing again?"

"My hands are normal, but that's probably because I haven't touched the Light Core in a week." I hop off the Diver and begin unhooking the gas from my torch.

"When you learn to control the physical manifestation of your Light, you will be able to manipulate it at will." Dr. Ormandi returns to his seat in the swivel chair. "As an exercise, practice calling the Light into your hands and then suppressing it."

"Got it. I can do that. I think." I call for Nemo. He instantly appears at my side at the sound of my voice. "I'll see you next week, Dr. Ormandi. Diver."

The giant robot gives me a pat before settling against the wall, his creaky joints relaxing. Dr. Ormandi glances at Diver with a wry grin.

"Yes, a nap sounds like a good idea after an afternoon with an energetic teenager."

"Same, being around a couple old dudes makes an energetic teenager sleepy," I snark. Dr. Ormandi laughs.

"Well played, you're quite witty," he says with a smile. "It reminds me of —"

He stops short, grief overtaking the sheen of his eyes. He doesn't have to finish, because I know what he's going to say. It reminds him of Nate. Not that I intend to bring up the unsettling fact I've been talking to a dead person, but the fact that said dead person is Nate would only cause Dr. Ormandi more pain. Definitely a good idea to keep that secret for now.

"Have a pleasant evening, Callie." Dr. Ormandi shifts gears, repressing the sorrow on his face until it is neutral once more.

"You, too." I glance over my shoulder at Diver, waving at him. "Bye, Diver! Rest that knee, okay?"

Diver nods, creaking his neck in the process. I don't have to tell the old robot to rest — he's glad to do it.

As I make my way to my car up the block, Nate's admonition about Luminauts comes back to me. Sounds like ancient Luminauts were guardians and defenders. They protected people with robots like Diver and their Light powers. And yet, Nate said bad things happen around Luminauts. That there are aspects of the Lore his dad might not tell me. But why? What would Dr. Ormandi have to hide?

Somebody isn't being completely honest with me, and I can't decide who: the ghost with the beguiling smile, or his reclusive father.

CHAPTER TWELVE

ABOVE MY HEAD, the California sun bears down with blazing intensity—no less white-hot and penetrating in autumn than the dead of summer. All around, the deep, blue-green Pacific shimmers, sparkles, glimmers. Diamonds droplets splash over the nose of my board, catching the light. Icy water penetrates the protection offered by my wetsuit, and a delightful shiver runs across my skin. It's an absolutely perfect morning to catch a few waves. Will and I bob on our boards, watching other surfers race across the swells while we wait our turn in the line-up.

"Why are we out here with the dawn patrol?" Will asks, paddling closer so we can chat.

"We aren't with the dawn patrol," I argue. "It's 10:00am."

"Whatever," Will gripes around a grumpy scowl. "It's too early to surf. I should be sleeping right now."

"And miss all the good waves?" I smile, but Will doesn't smile back. He looks even grumpier as he straddles his board.

"Are you kidding? The tide is low. These waves suck."

Will's isn't entirely wrong. Choppy breaks, petering out into foam and spray before anyone manages to really get a satisfying ride.

"They're not that bad." I'm determined to be positive, even if

Will isn't. I paddle out a few yards. "It's my turn. See you on the beach!"

I catch the next wave as it crests, riding it a few yards before bailing into white-water. The waves this morning are remarkably tame, without much power behind them. Normally, I'd skip surfing in waves like these because they aren't worth the effort— not when I could go get coffee in sweatpants and chill. But my afternoon is booked solid, repairing dilapidated old Diver. If I'm going to surf with Will like I'd promised, it's going to be this morning, no matter how much he complains.

I trudge into ankle deep water to wait for Will. He's wobbling on one of the tiniest waves I've ever seen, and a few seconds later, he loses his balance and splashes face-first with a plop. My hand flies to my mouth, stifling a laugh. A moment later, his head bobs out of the water, and he pulls himself and his board into the shallows.

"You were much better that time!" I greet him cheerfully to offset the murderous frown on his face. "You rode that wave for at least eight or nine seconds!"

"Quit lying to make me feel better," he mutters. He shakes the water out of his hair, sending sparkling droplets flying. "Why do I always wipe out?"

"You just haven't found your balance yet." I heave my board out of the surf. Will does the same.

"We've been surfing for years," Will goes on. "You're really good now. I still suck." He breathes the world's most dramatic sigh. "I never do anything right."

"Well, you insist on surfing goofy-foot," I remind him.

Will's shoulders hunch defensively. "It's more comfortable for me."

"You want to surf one more wave, or hit the beach?" I catch Will's eye with my question. "I have to leave by eleven."

"Yeah, I remember." Will looks even more unhappy about my time crunch than his surfing fail. "Let's go chill on the beach. I'm tired of wiping out."

We march through the sugar-fine white sand, dragging our boards behind us, then strip off our wetsuits and flop down on the warm, inviting beach. The sunbeams make luminous our damp, salty skin, and the breeze trips mildly through our hair. It's a perfect day to relax and hang out, and I'd love to spend the rest of the day in this exact spot. But I've made a promise.

"Are you sure you have to leave at eleven?" Will says exactly what I'm thinking.

"I do," I answer. "I'm sorry."

"I thought you got all your homework done Friday because your mom had another wedding she needed you to work," Will goes on, a little pouty. "What do you have to do today that's so important?"

"I have to work on robotics again." It's not exactly a lie. I *am* going to work on a robot. It's just a fifty-foot-tall World Diver.

"Seriously? It's not like you're making something for NASA, it's just a high school elective," Will grumbles. I can't help but bristle, because Will's constant complaining about my life choices is getting old, fast.

"Building a robot is hard work!" Repairing Diver is especially hard. My hand torch isn't making much progress against the rust, damage, and neglect the poor robot has suffered in his basement prison.

Will's mouth opens, a complaint ready, but he's interrupted.

"Hey, Callie!"

Will and I turn toward the voice. Matt and Mark, two local surfers, saunter down the beach with their boards. They're older than us, probably early-thirties, so they work all week, but we see them a lot on the weekends. I wave and smile.

"Hi, guys!"

"Haven't seen you around in a while," Matt tells me, a question lingering in his eyes.

"Yeah, you used to be a permanent fixture out there," Mark adds, pushing his hair away from his forehead. "What's up? You got a new boyfriend?"

"Nothing like that," I laugh. "Just been busy. Life stuff."

"Callie plays volleyball and cares about her grades now," Will interjects woefully.

"No worries," Matt says with a grin. "I was in high school once, too. I get it."

"See you around, Callie, Will." Mark makes his way down to the waves, and Matt follows. Will stares at his hands, quiet.

"Well, *do* you have a new boyfriend?" When he faces me, his glare is suspicious. "Is that why you've been avoiding me?"

"Oh, my gosh, Will, I just told those guys I don't have a boyfriend!" I roll my eyes at his ridiculousness. "And I'm not avoiding you. We hang out at school all the time. And despite my mom running me ragged with fall weddings and appeasing my dad with weekly volleyball games, plus a full plate of schoolwork, I *still* made time to surf with you today."

Will's body tenses, so full of repressed emotion he's like a bomb about to blow. "Izzy said you've been giving Zack Mendes rides home."

My jaw drops, flabbergasted Will could even *think* something is going on between me and Zack. But Will's eyes grow cold, narrowed in a serious stare. I can feel him withdraw from me, the emotional distance between widening by the second.

"I am not giving Zack rides home." I attempt to sound like a calm, centered human being in the face of how in-my-business Will is being—even though I have every right to rip his head off. "Jase, my brother who is on the soccer team with Zack, is giving him rides home while his car is in the shop. It has nothing to do with me. Zack barely acknowledges my presence."

"That's not what Izzy said." Will stubbornly refuses to drop the issue.

I purse my lips, brows knit together. "How does Izzy know anything about it?"

"She said when you get in the car, Zack immediately turns around and starts talking to you." Will's tone vacillates between hurt and accusatory. "And he told Chase Jackson how cool and funny you are."

It is a truth universally acknowledged amongst my friends that I absolutely *hate* high school drama. The fact Will insists on creating some where none exists makes me grit my teeth. "Let me repeat my question: how does Izzy know all this? Especially the Chase part?"

"She's been staying after school to get help with Algebra II, and so has Chase." Will acts like I ought to know this particular detail of Izzy's life. "He's in her class now that she switched. They were talking about you and Zack, and she saw you herself in the parking lot when she got done with tutoring."

I know Izzy switched math classes — she reworked her schedule so she could be in English with me, Will, and Emily. Instead of having Mr. Harmon for Algebra II — who is notoriously easy — she now has Ms. Jimenez, who is probably the hardest math teacher in the whole school.

"Look, none of that means I'm remotely interested in Zack. Because I promise you, I'm not." I fix Will with a stern look. "But I'm *not* particularly happy you and Izzy were gossiping about me."

"I wasn't gossiping!" Will tosses his hands high. "I was complaining that you're so busy I hardly see you, and she told me what Chase told her, and what she saw. It's not gossip if it's true."

"Either way, it's discussing me behind my back, and making assumptions. And I don't like it." Remember how much I abhor drama, Will? Don't go there.

Will hangs his head and rests his elbows on his knees. When he looks up, his big, brown eyes fill with contrition. "It wasn't right of me to talk about you behind your back. I'm sorry."

I touch his shoulder and offer a conciliatory grin. "I forgive you."

"So, um, Zack's not taking you to Homecoming or anything, is he?" Will's question is almost shy.

"Absolutely not." My grin turns into a dry laugh. "I'm sure he's going with one of the popular girls. You know I don't have enough social clout to go to Homecoming with *anyone* in the bonfire crowd."

At that, Will smiles. "Well, maybe I could take you."

I give a start, going completely still. Will? Take me to Homecoming? On a date? I swallow hard, suppressing the urge to throw up in my mouth. I mean, Will is *Will*. Jase and Ryan give me a hard time about Will, but only because they're my irritating brothers and know it'll get a rise out of me. Will is totally not dateable. Not to me, anyway.

I scramble to think of a way out of this that won't hurt Will's feelings. He's still my best friend, after all.

"How about we all go together?" I suggest. "You, me, Izzy, and Emily? You can have three dates instead of one!"

A flicker of disappointment flashes across Will's face, but it's gone so fast I'm not sure I didn't imagine it. "Sounds great! Who wouldn't want three beautiful dates to Homecoming?"

"Awesome!" Total catastrophe avoided.

"Just promise you'll save a dance for me."

Okay, maybe not.

"It's eleven, I've got to go." I hop to my feet, gathering up my board and wetsuit. "I'll see you tomorrow at school, okay?"

Will's on his feet, too, brushing beach sand off his board shorts. "I can help you take your stuff to the car."

So he can finagle a slow dance out of me? Nope. "Thanks, but I've got it."

Will deposits my car keys into my waiting palm, which I asked him to keep in his shorts pocket. "See you tomorrow. I'll text you later."

"Bye, Will!"

"Bye, Callie."

I dash up the beach as fast as I can dragging a surfboard behind me, and ascend the stairs to the parking lot, accidentally bumping a couple middle school kids with the nose of my board (one of the guys makes a lewd comment—punk). By the time I reach the parking lot and load up my things, I'm so distracted I almost forget my route home. Innate sense of direction comes in handy when all I can think about is Will asking me to be his date for Homecoming. And how awkward and gross that will be. Aren't I like a sister to him? What kind of brother would want to take their sister to Homecoming? Jase would literally rather die— pretty sure I would, too.

I'm already thinking about this too much. I need to think about working on Diver instead, and which question I'm going to ask Dr. Ormandi about Luminauts and Seers and all his strange theories.

Once I'm home, I unload my board, sneak to my room to get dressed, and load up Nemo and my robotics supplies in my duffel bag before anybody catches wind of my presence. My family has no idea about my covert visits to Dr. Ormandi, or the fact Nemo is alive. They think I surf with Will all afternoon, and spend an inordinate amount of time working on robotics when I'm at home. But my grades have been good and I'm playing volleyball, which means Dad's off my case, so they complain less about the surfing and self-imposed seclusion.

"Where are you sneaking off to?"

I'm almost out the door when Jase's voice stops me in my tracks. I spin toward the sound. My brother sits on the kitchen counter eating chips straight from the bag, looking at me like he just caught a thief red handed.

"I'm not sneaking anywhere," I reply.

Jase raises a brow. "Then where are you going with that 'I've got a secret' look on your face?"

To see the boogeyman and his enormous, sentient mech. "None of your business."

"Of course it's my business." Jase hops off the counter with his chips and takes a few steps toward me. "You made it your business that I'm failing Civics, and took the car hostage. Mom and Dad think you're at the beach with Will. They wouldn't be happy if they found out you lied to them."

"Just like they wouldn't be happy you've been lying to them about studying with your friends when you're really going to bonfire night?" I put my hands on my hips. "You don't have anything on me, and I've got three years' worth of lies and secrets on you. Don't even try it."

The ice in Jase's eyes could freeze water. "I'm gonna get that car back, Callie. One way or another."

I meet my brother's frosty stare head on. "Is that a threat?"

"I don't know." Passive-aggressive shrug. "You tell me."

"Aren't you supposed to be studying right now?"

"Aren't you supposed to be surfing?"

"Not that you care, really, except to steal the car back, but the reason I'm home is I'm going to work on my robotics project." I gesture to my bag. "I had to run back to get my supplies."

Jase frowns, disappointed he can't catch me in a lie, so he

sneers meanly. "You went from being an all-around loser to a loser geek. Congrats, Callie. What's next, Loser Club President?"

Jase doesn't hit zingers often, but wow, this one hurts. Just beyond the raw wound of his words, fury builds, a physical, almost tangible anger like I've never felt churning deep inside. The sensation rises toward my lips from the pit of my gut until it becomes an overpowering urge to control my brother, to make him get on his knees and swear he'll never insult or demean me again.

Power fills every muscle and nerve like an electrical charge, and a nearly imperceptible Light appears before my eyes just above my brother's heart. A Light within him and without him all at once, one I have never before seen, yet always known was there. The Light in me burns with the need to control the tiny Light in him, as if everything's caught fire around a single target: Jase.

I don't know what this feeling is, but I'm horrified by what it wants me to do. I close my eyes and breathe, repressing the urge, dousing the flame.

"I think you need to look up the definition of loser, Jase," I snap, willing my voice steady. "I'm not the one failing school. Maybe it wouldn't hurt to be more of a geek yourself."

I shoulder my bag, spin around on my heel, and slam the door behind me.

Still, the dangerous spark lingers, a gnawing canker just under my heart. The power wants to be freed, to latch onto a victim and force its will onto them. And next time, I don't know if I'll be able to control it.

Next time, the power might win.

CHAPTER THIRTEEN

DR. ORMANDI SMILES BRIGHTLY when he opens the door, welcoming me inside his house. I've calmed down sufficiently from my confrontation with Jase—a few extra trips around the block took care of things—and the smell of coffee wafting from the kitchen sets me completely at ease. The percolator echoes over the wood floors when I hang my cap and hoodie.

"Callie! Welcome!" The old man greets me.

"Is that coffee? I thought you were more of a tea person." I find Dr. Ormandi's eyes, a question in my own.

Nemo jabs my shoulder blades—his signal to be let out. I crouch, unzipping my backpack, and my little robot tumbles out. We've been working on keeping still in my backpack, because wriggling, punchy backpacks are definitely not a normal occurrence around Verona Beach High, but the sound of Dr. Ormandi's voice always makes him antsy. He's usually pretty amped by the time I let him out. Sure enough, he spins circles, arms flailing excitedly.

"I am a tea person, but you mentioned last time you prefer coffee." I follow Dr. Ormandi into the kitchen. The coffee mug he hands me is chipped and fading, *"I love Dad"* in childlike writing scrawled across the front. A tiny ache fills my heart.

Nate made this. He kept it all this time. Nate hasn't appeared since last week, but next time I see him, I'll tell him about the mug. *If* I see him. Maybe the haunting is over.

Why do I feel kind of sad about that?

"This old machine hasn't been used in years." Dr. Ormandi gives the coffee machine a pat. "I was a bit shocked it still works. Nate always preferred coffee... anyway, I had some delivered in my grocery shipment."

"That's really nice of you." A grin spreads across my lips, and I take a sip. *Way* too strong—I can tell it's been a while since he last brewed a pot. I chug it down anyway.

"It's the least I can do, after all the hard work you're doing on the Diver," the old man replies modestly. "My only rule is no coffee in the lab. I never take tea down there. Too many metals, charts, and maps."

"Got it, no liquids in the science space." I give Dr. Ormandi a thumbs up. "How's Diver?"

"Perfectly old and rusty. He is waiting for you in the usual place."

"Come on, Nemo!" My tiny friend teeters on a stack of scientific journals, dangerously close to knocking them over. "Let's go see Diver."

Nemo sends the journals flying and whizzes after me. I scoop him up in my arms and begin my descent. Diver senses my presence on the stairs, and his lumbering footfalls echo across the cavernous space. By the time I reach the basement, he's standing before me, glowing with contentment. Nemo wheels up to Diver, drums a beat out on his gigantic foot, then rushes off to find a fun new toy. Nemo has the attention span of a gnat.

"Hey, Diver," I greet the old robot. "Ready for the hand torch?"

Diver nods, and lowers himself. It takes tremendous effort for him to sit down, and he loses even more bits and bobs from his joints, leaning against the wall with a thunderous groan. I begin the mundane, time-consuming task of hunting down all the lost nuts, bolts, and screws before I get to work.

"I am coming, just very slowly." Dr. Ormandi begins his climb down the steps.

"Do you want some help?" I call up to him.

"No, don't trouble yourself." He swishes his hand through the air — the one not clinging for dear life to the stair rail. "These knees may be old and arthritic, but they aren't so far gone I can't handle a staircase."

Soon enough, Dr. Ormandi joins me.

"I've been thinking about what I want to ask you today," I shift gears as I scale Diver's foot, making my way toward his corroded knee.

Dr. Ormandi eases himself into his trusty swivel chair. "Fire away."

"Tell me all about Seers. Especially the freaky, glowing-eye thing."

He smirks. "That's not a question."

He's a stickler for grammar, too. Should have guessed. "Fine. Can you please tell me about Seers and their freaky, glowing-eye powers?"

"Very well." Dr. Ormandi settles into his chair until he's comfortable. "Seers are beings with elemental magic, sensitive to the push and pull of people and objects through space, time, and reality. We have special Sight that allows us to see gateways wherever they exist — in the water, in the sky, on land, in thin air. The Luminaut we are bonded with can then pilot the Diver through those gateways to other worlds in the multiverse."

"Sounds pretty cool. Is that all Seers do?" I hammer a bit of the malleable metal with my mallet.

"No, not at all," Dr. Ormandi replies. "We all have a power called Manipulation. It allows us to control the environment and the elements — usually a specific element in particular, called our soul element or Manipulate. It's a power that's also useful in avoiding… unwanted confrontations."

I frown behind my goggles. "What kind of confrontations?"

"Never mind about that." Dismissive hand swish. "Another conversation for another time."

"So how does a Luminaut know when she — or he — has met a Seer?" I go on. "Are the neon eyes the dead giveaway? And what's your soul element?"

The old man grins. "That's rather a lot more than one question, you know."

"Please?" I implore him. "I thought you'd like talking about yourself. Seers, I mean."

"Oh, very well." Dr. Ormandi settles a bit farther into his chair. "The Seer's Eye — what you like to call the 'freaky, glowing-eye thing' — only shows itself when we are in the presence of a Light Core, finding gateways, or using our Elemental Manipulate. My particular Manipulate is fire. Other Seers may be gifted with earth, water, or air. However, we can control all the elements to some minor extent." Dr. Ormandi waits until I'm done with a particularly loud bit of hammering to continue. "A Luminaut and Seer share a bonded connection, a kind of yin and yang counterbalance. Often, a Seer perceives — Sees, technically — the Luminaut they are destined to bond with at the onset of their Sight. Luminauts will be drawn to their Seer as two separate sides of the same coin."

Nemo brings the old man a new toy, a magnet he'd gotten stuck to his hand. Dr. Ormandi takes the magnet and puts it on the top of Nemo's head. My robot wheels off, intensely focused on how to unstick the little annoyance.

"Your wife was a Luminaut." I take a pause in my soldering, and push my goggles to the top of my head. "How did you luck out and meet your Luminaut in San Francisco in a whole world full of billions of people?" I quirk my brow. "Is California some kind of hotbed for making super-humans?"

"Mariasol was not from San Francisco, or California in general." The old man takes his wallet out of his front pocket. "She was from Ensolorada."

"Where's Ensolorada?" It's not a place I've ever heard of.

"Another world."

"*What?*" My eyes bulge. "Your wife was from another world? No way."

"Yes, way," Dr. Ormandi chuckles. He pulls a picture out of his wallet and hands it to me. "Here she is. I keep her close always."

The woman in the picture is stunningly beautiful. Long-limbed, tall, and athletic, with wavy black hair, tawny skin, a wide smile, and amber-colored eyes. It's clear Nate inherited her impressive height and athleticism, as well as her hair and smile. She wears a Cal Track and Field sweater with a skirt and wellies, leaning against a brick building on a college campus. I would have never guessed she was from another world.

"Wow. Definitely not what I expected a Luminaut alien to look like." Dr. Ormandi snorts humorlessly, and I hand him the picture with a smile. "Are Luminauts and Seers always fated to get married? Because I'd kind of like a say in my own love life."

"Mariasol and I had an uncommon Luminaut and Seer relationship—rarely do they become romantic. The bond I described is more of a transcendent dyad... you will understand." Dr. Ormandi puts his wife's picture back in his wallet.

"So she happened to end up on our world with Diver, became your college sweetheart, and you discovered your mutual destiny of hunting Light Cores and trapping sentient robots in your basement," I surmise. "Sounds like an all-American love story."

"We only trapped *one* sentient robot in our basement," Dr. Ormandi reminds me. "And don't take that sarcastic tone when speaking of my late wife."

"I'm sorry, I don't mean to be disrespectful. To you, or to her." I meet Dr. Ormandi's black eyes. "It's just… none of this is very believable, and it's hard to wrap my head around."

"I understand you're feeling overwhelmed," Dr. Ormandi says with a sympathetic smile. "Believe me, when my Sight first manifested, I had just as many questions, and even fewer answers. But, I have something that will help you begin to understand what you are."

The old man rises from his chair and makes his way to the far side of the laboratory table. He opens a drawer and pulls out a stack of books. They aren't textbooks, but small, leather-bound, and stuffed with loose notes. The spines have creased and cracked with age and use, the edges rounded into blunt nubs.

"What are these?" I open one of the books and flip through it. It's filled with chicken-scratchy handwriting that, at first, I can barely read. But, as I look more closely at the page, the words begin to take shape and make sense.

"They are Mariasol's journals." Dr. Ormandi gazes at the little stack of books tenderly, as though they're his wife in the flesh. "She began keeping them during our search for oceanic gateways. I'd like you to have them."

"Really?" I'm uneasy about taking them, and not just because I don't know if I believe this Luminaut stuff in the first place. "Aren't these the only pieces of her you have left?"

"They are a part of her soul she left in my possession, and one she always intended for me to give away." Dr. Ormandi scoots the journals across the table toward me. "Mariasol would want you to have them. She *meant* for future Luminauts and Seers to have them. You wouldn't deny the previous Luminaut her final wishes, would you?"

When he puts it that way, it's almost rude not to take the journals. I pull them toward me, clutching the stack in my arms.

"Once I've read them, I'll give them back," I promise the old man. But he only shakes his head.

"Keep them as long as you need. I insist."

As I hold the journals in my hands, I sense the presence of a shadow, a sinister darkness imbued with emotionless, cruel cold. Nothing like the chill that accompanies Nate, but the icy hand of death itself. The same presence appeared in my room the night I found the Light Core, crept like a malevolent ghost to peer at Nate's baseball pictures over my shoulder. The flash of unfeeling black eyes that spoke my name in the shadow realm. That same sensation of evil and horror, growing stronger by the second, stares at the journals with heart-hammering intensity, worming its way through my blood like poison.

I whirl all around, trying to find the formless source of my fear. But nothing's there.

"Callie?" Dr. Ormandi cocks his head, a strange look I can't read clouding his eyes. "Is everything alright?"

I shudder, and the shadow leaves, a spidery whisper like dead leaves in winter lingering in the air. "*Calliope...*"

"I'm fine," I promise the old man. "I thought I felt something behind me."

"What did you feel?" The old man's frown deepens.

"I don't know..." I shake my head. "It's nothing."

With shaking hands, I load the journals into my duffel bag, along with my hand torch, mallet, and Nemo, who growls at how tightly crammed he is with the journals taking up extra space.

"I'll be back next week." I shoulder my bag, bending slightly under its newfound weight. "Same time, same place."

"We always look forward to it, don't we, Diver?" Dr. Ormandi casts a look toward Diver, who reaches out to touch my back with his gigantic finger. I give his knuckle a pat, and he glows with peaceful contentment. It warms my frigid limbs, still trembling with the coldness of the shadow.

"See you later, Diver! Dr. Ormandi!"

I race up the rest of the stairs and out of the house. My car is just up the block, and I sprint for it before the dark presence can follow, calling my name and manifesting spidery tentacles just behind my shoulder.

"Finally." I toss my backpack into the back seat and lean into the headrest, taking a deep breath. The presence is gone. The shadows and darkness haven't pursued.

And yet, a different kind of chill persists, this one instinctively more familiar.

"Had a long day?"

"Gah!" I jump a mile, whacking my head into the roof of the car and kicking the steering column.

"Careful, you don't want to break your patella," Nate advises from the passenger seat. I rub my knee and head, both of which are smarting.

"Seriously. Pick a less creepy way to make an entrance," I grumble. "I end up with a huge bruise every time I see you."

"You didn't want me in your room, I thought your car might be more acceptable. Besides, I'm a ghost, I think creepy pretty much comes with the territory." Nate glances around, drinking in the houses, street lamps, and rocky cliffs with a reminiscent gleam in his eyes. "Man, the neighborhood hasn't changed a bit. How's Dad?"

"Why don't you go see him yourself?" I put the key in the ignition, gritting my teeth against the pain in my head and knees.

"If you can haunt my car, you can haunt his living room. Then I could drive home without risking a concussion."

"I'd love to have a cup of coffee with my old man, but I think seeing me would give him false hope…" Nate trails off. "I don't want him to believe things can be like they were before."

Speaking of cups of coffee…

"He saved your mug." Nate tilts his chin, perplexed, so I elaborate. "The 'I love Dad' mug."

"He did?" Nate's eyes lose their dark edginess, flooding with something like regret. "I made that when I was seven or eight." A pause, and another glance back at the old man's house. "He misses me. I didn't think… she always said—" The radio blares pop music when I start the engine, and Nate's face wrinkles into a scowl of pure loathing. He turns away from his musings to glare at the speakers. "What *is* this?"

"Music." I mean, duh.

"This is not music. What happened to Morrissey? Sonic Youth? Pavement?" He tsk's his tongue. "At least the stuff on your phone is halfway decent. I mean, kind of reductive, but a catchy hook."

Nate Ormandi is a total hipster. Noted. A flick of the volume dial extinguishes the offensive noise. "Is that better?"

"Much." Nate shifts in his seat, facing me with an inquisitive look in his eyes. They're dark again, and purposeful, as if he'd never reminisced at all. "So, what happened today? Anything interesting?"

"Which part of Haunting 101 dictates I give you a full report every time I visit your dad and Diver?" I glare across the console. "Last time I checked, I wasn't obligated to discuss my personal life with a ghost."

"Of course you aren't obligated, I'm just curious." He leans back, pensive, and crosses his arms behind the headrest. "I don't remember a lot of my human life. Some memories are clear, others are hazy—like I'm remembering them through a fog. But I remember everything about Mom and Dad. He's the only person in my family left alive. I ask because I want to know he's okay."

Well, when he puts it like that... "He's good. Old."

Nate averts his eyes, a faraway look obscuring the piercing black. Yet another small glimpse of strained emotion I don't feel like I'm meant to see. "He was getting old when I went sailing that day. He's probably lived another lifetime since then."

"Do you remember your accident?" A rude question, probably, because Nate's eyes darken again, and the splintering chill around him turns to ice.

"Yeah." He pales, his face stricken—with horror, grief, or anger I can't say. "I remember everything about that, too."

A shudder runs through me—one that has nothing to do with the disquieting cold of his presence.

"I asked your dad about the Lore." A change of subject is a good idea. "I don't understand why you told me bad things happen around Luminauts. They used their Light powers to help others. They were protectors. Guardians."

"Guardians—that's cute." Nate laughs, a steely sound. "It's what Mom and Dad always wanted to believe, but unfortunately, it's not true."

"I'm assuming this is the segue where you tell me your version of the truth?" I cross my arms over my chest, waiting for his speech to commence.

"Not *my version* of anything. The absolute truth," Nate replies. He leans forward in his seat, his unsettling eyes searching mine. They're the same color as Dr. Ormandi's, and yet, they seem darker than the old professor's. I look away, feigning interest in the AC control panel.

"Luminauts were greedy, evil overlords who terrorized those

they were meant to protect." Nate's proclamation is frigid and bleak. "Untold numbers of people were destroyed by the Light. It brings nothing but violence, and leaves total decimation in its wake."

"Why should I believe you?"

And yet... why shouldn't I? The idea that my newfound powers and the Light Core are dangerous has been the thing I've feared most from the beginning. I never felt the dark presence before I found the Light, the specter that feels like pure evil crossing over from the realm of shadow. And yet, Dr. Ormandi says the Light is a gift. Nate is adamant it's a curse.

Who is telling the truth?

"I wanted to believe the stories as much as you." Nate's voice quiets, and I dare to face him. His words and eyes hold the pain of broken trust in once-cherished beliefs. "Most of my childhood was spent in hospitals while Mom went through chemo. She told me tales of ancient Luminauts and Seers to pass the time, stories of adventures with their Divers across the multiverse. But now I know the heroics she believed in were a lie, and I don't want you to get hurt the way countless others have been."

Tension of every kind courses like a current between us. Opposing ideals, uncertain truths, and something else — something like a live wire coiling tight, pulling me into his orbit. The all-consuming need I feel in the presence of the Light Core, the need to reach out and touch it, to have it for my own... that need bears down when his eyes look into mine, wraps around my lungs, makes it hard to breathe.

My phone buzzes in my pocket. A sharp gasp reminds me that, unlike Nate, I'm very much alive, and my central nervous system works remarkably well when startled. I whip my phone out, glancing at the screen. Will. Bad timing, Will.

"What's that?" Nate observes my phone's screen curiously.

"A text," I reply.

"What's a text?" I forget smartphones were lightyears away when he died.

"Instead of calling, we just type messages to each other," I explain.

Nate makes a face. "What's the point of having a phone if you don't call people?"

"It's—never mind." I turn my attention to Will's message.

> Hey, I just texted Em and Izzy about Homecoming and they're stoked. Em suggested Italian for dinner, is that cool with you?

"Homecoming?" Nate grins in a way that makes my heart *kick-thump* against my ribs. "That's a dance—I remember going. It was horrible. Do you have a hot date, or what?"

I snort-laugh. "My best friend, Will. Not exactly hot."

"You've got a guy best friend?" Nate's grin becomes a broad smile. "Let me guess, he's secretly been in love with you since second grade. Your life is totally a movie, isn't it?"

"If it's a movie, it's a horror show," I retort. "Ghosts keep showing up and invading my personal space."

"How rude of those ghosts!" Nate clutches his chest, feigning shock.

"I know, right?" I give him a look. "You'd think somebody would have taught them better manners when they were alive."

"Somebody ought to take it up with afterlife management," Nate agrees with a nod. "New memo—pretty brunettes named Callie only want polite hauntings."

Pretty brunette? *Kick-thump-thud-thud.*

My thumbs move with rapid-fire speed as I text Will back.

Yeah, sounds good! I'm driving home,
TTYL.

"Okay, back to Luminaut business." I stow my phone in my pocket. "Why would I get hurt being a Luminaut? Do you think I'd hurt other people? I'm not dangerous."

"Are you sure? I kinda like danger." Nate's smile softens around the edges and his gaze loses a little of its sharpness, an expression that's almost… fond. A rush of heat warms my cheeks.

"You didn't answer my question." Focus, Callie. Don't get lost in those magnetic eyes. "Why should you care if I get hurt? In the grand scheme of things, I'm nothing to you."

"You aren't nothing to me." The chill surrounding Nate gives way to ember-glows and sparks — or, maybe, I'm confusing something in him with something in me. "You look after Dad and Diver. Besides Mom, they were the two people I loved most when I was alive. You're thoughtful, you're kind. There's so much good in you. Why would you want to corrupt it with Light?"

Light corrupts? Dr. Ormandi said Luminauts falling into corruption was impossible. And yet, Nate is so insistent Light can, and will, ruin me. I wish I knew who was right, and who was lying.

"Also, I might be a little bit into you." Nate's shy admission unleashes a cage of butterflies in the pit of my belly. "You're totally my type, when I was alive. Smart, spunky, sarcastic. You don't do something just because it's popular, you have your own robots-and-surfing thing going on. I like that. It's cool."

"How do you —" my voice constricts, trapped around the breathlessness that's overtaken me — "how do you know all of that? About Luminauts? About Light being corrupt and harmful?"

"Once you cross over to the other side, answers that eluded

you in life become clear." His penetrating stare reaches for my soul until I can't possibly look away. "Please, Callie. Let me help you, before you're in so deep you can't escape."

My phone buzzes in my pocket again. Izzy this time.

> Want to come dress shopping with me and Em next weekend? I am sooooo excited for Homecoming!

"Sorry, I've gotta reply to this," I tell Nate, looking up from my phone. But Nate is already gone.

I don't know how I manage to reply with trembling fingers and a thundering heart, but I do.

> Awesome. I can't wait!

I put the car in gear and speed away, not quite sure which new development I find most distracting: Will and Homecoming, my Light powers and their potential for danger, or Nate's confession I'm just the type of girl a ghost finds attractive, and why that doesn't scare me nearly as much as it should.

CHAPTER FOURTEEN

"READY? One, two, three—say cheese!"

Izzy holds her phone high above our heads to snap a selfie. The screen reflects the fading sunset behind our heads.

"Awesome." Izzy checks the picture and grins. "Looks good. Nobody closed their eyes. I'll post it on social later."

Izzy, Emily, Will, and I have spent the last forty-five minutes taking pictures at Will's house before the Homecoming dance. Balcony view of the ocean and all—it makes for the best photo ops. I won't pretend my girlfriends and I don't take advantage of Will's amazing house when the occasion arises.

"This is so fun." Emily looks between the three of us with a sunny smile.

"Yeah, it's great!" I force a smile to accompany my lie. I rarely get decked out and fancy, or wear a lot of makeup, and I definitely never wear heels. I can't tell if the reason my stomach is in knots is because I'm excited, or incredibly uncomfortable.

"Much better than Homecoming last year," Em adds.

"It wouldn't take much to top last year." Izzy rolls her eyes. "That was beyond stupid."

"What happened last year?" Will asks. He wears a smart, navy suit and purple-patterned tie, and his floppy, dark brown hair is combed neatly across his suntanned brow. I have to admit, he cleans up nice. I'd probably think he was pretty cute if he wasn't, you know, *Will*.

"Emily was dating Sean Pettit last year, remember?" My face twists into a scowl, like I've sucked too hard on a lemon. Will's face does the same.

"Oh, yeah, I forgot about that."

"I wish I could forget about it," Emily laments. "Worst night of my life."

Sean Pettit was a senior last year when we were sophomores, and is a massive tool. Emily dated him for a hot minute before coming to her senses. He ran with Jase's bonfire crowd when he was at VBHS, which ought to give an indication of his moral character. Or lack thereof.

"I still can't believe he ditched you and stole your phone." Izzy puts her phone in her clutch and whips out her lipstick for a refresh. "If some guy ever pressured me into hooking up, and then ditched me when I told him no, I'd kick him in the nuts so hard he'd never be able to hook up with anyone ever again."

"Nobody would ever dream of doing that to you, Izzy," I assure my friend.

"I never thought Sean would do it to me, either." Emily's face crumbles at the memory. "I left my phone in his car, and I had to beg half the people at the dance to let me borrow theirs so I could call my parents to come get me. I had to save for months to buy a new one. It was beyond humiliating."

"We're going to have fun tonight." I put my arm around Emily and squeeze her shoulders. "So much fun you'll forget all about last year."

"I'm a way better date than Sean ever thought about being," Will adds.

"Thanks, guys." Emily grins.

"Alright, kids, it's time to get going!" Will's mom, Cindy, appears in the door to the balcony. "You don't want to miss your dinner reservation."

"Twelve o'clock curfew, Callie," Mom adds, joining Cindy in the doorway.

"Same for you, Isabella!" Juan, Izzy's dad, yells from inside.

Parents. What can you do?

"Hey, Callie," Will speaks up as I wobble my way down to his SUV.

"Yeah?"

"I was gonna ask... would you —"

"Shotgun!" Izzy calls, hopping into the front passenger seat.

"Not fair!" Emily laughs. Her blonde curls bounce in cadence with her voice.

"You snooze, you lose," Izzy jokes. "Come on, Will, let's get this party started."

"You got it, Izzy."

Will hops into the driver's seat, and I sit next to Emily in the back. Whatever Will was going to ask me is forgotten. Although, I'm pretty sure I know what it was. And I know my answer. And I'd *so* rather not deal with that awkwardness.

I've never been to Homecoming. Mom and Dad have strict rules about formal dances, one of which is you can't attend until you're a junior and have your driver's license. Emily's horrible experience last year makes me kind of leery. That, on top of my discomfort with being dressed up—and I'm pretty sure Will is going to ask for a slow dance—makes it hard to eat much at dinner. All I can do is pick at my ravioli.

By the time we get to the dance, my feet hurt from the stupid heels, my stomach is growling and raw, and they're already playing a slow song. I refuse to meet Will's eyes, even though he's hardcore trying to make me look at him.

"Where's the punch?" I scan the room, desperate for an excuse to slip away. "Don't these things have punch?"

"Only in the movies," Izzy laughs.

"Let's go get a table before they're too picked over." I spin away on my heels the best I can. I'm sure literally every woman alive has had this thought, but seriously, there is no way whoever came up with the concept of high heels was female. There's no way we'd design something so difficult to walk in for ourselves.

By the time we scout a table, the slow dance song has—thankfully—ended. A dance-worthy pop song blares instead, although my peers seem far more interested in gossiping about each other in cloistered circles than in dancing. I plop into a chair and kick my shoes off, rubbing at the blisters already forming on my toes. Tension floats between Will and me, and he takes a seat uncomfortably close to my side. He wants to talk. I refuse to look at him.

"Hey, can we sit with you guys?"

Oh, thank you, vaguely familiar voice behind my shoulder! What excellent distraction skills you have! I find the source of the voice in an instant. It's Chase Jackson, Izzy's Algebra tutoring partner. And next to him is Zack Mendes.

"Hi, Chase!"

Izzy lights up like Fourth of July fireworks at the sight of Chase, and Chase looks just as excited to see her. He pulls his chair close, and they're instantly deep in conversation, like they're the only two people in the room.

Izzy and Chase are crushing on each other? What have I missed being so busy with Nemo and Diver all these weeks? Chase is a nice guy. He plays football, so he's on the fringes of the bonfire crowd, but he's also on the mock trial team and really involved with Habitat for Humanity, two things which exclude him from being fully accepted by the popular clique. I approve of him for Izzy.

Why Zack, who is 100% popular, is with him right now, apparently dateless, is beyond me.

"Is this seat taken?" Zack gestures toward the seat next to me.

"It is now." Did I just flirt with Zack Mendes? I must have, because Will bristles like a porcupine next to me.

"Sweet." Zack sits next to me, completely ignoring Will and the nasty glower Will is wearing.

"You look really nice," Zack tells me. Is he flirting, too? No, can't be. He's just being polite.

"So do you." His crisp gray suit and blue tie accentuate his hazel-gray eyes. "Where's your date?" I look around for the gorgeous popular girl I'm sure Zack came with.

"I don't have one. I didn't really want to come to Homecoming this year," Zack confesses. "But Chase wanted to see Izzy, so I guess that makes me his wingman. What about you?"

Zack notices Will for the first time and nods his chin. My best friend nods back, but barely. If looks could kill, Zack Mendes would be stone dead.

"We all came as a group," I explain. "Me, Izzy, Emily, and Will."

"That's tight," Zack replies, sounding almost relieved. "We're going down to the beach later for a bonfire. You should come."

"Really?" Zack Mendes wants to be seen with me—in public—at bonfire night? I must be making a weird face, because Zack grins reassuringly.

"Yeah, it's fun. Jase goes all the time. I'm surprised you're never there with him."

I hate to break it to Zack, but I know all about what his crowd does at bonfire night, and Jase has informed me on more than one occasion that I am nowhere near cool enough to join him.

"Hey, Zack!"

Jase waves Zack over to the popular kid table from across the dance floor, completely ignoring me. Not even so much as a chin nod of acknowledgement for your little sister, Jase? At least one person in my life is perfectly predictable.

A sardonic grin parts my lips. "You're being summoned, Zack."

"I'll be back," he assures me. "Keep that seat warm." He makes his way through the throngs of closely-gathered teenagers, drawing the eye of every girl he passes before disappearing into the popular clique's raucous crowd in the corner.

"I'm glad he left," Will mutters. I whip around to face him.

"He was just trying to be friendly. Zack's a nice guy."

"Yeah, and Emily thought Sean Pettit was nice, too." Will crosses his arms over his chest, glaring like I ought to know better. "Those popular guys are all the same. Huge egos. You know what they're like—Jase treats you like a loser. He always has."

"Zack is infinitely more civil than Jase." A rabid badger is more civil than Jase.

"Only because he wants something from you." Will's sneer twists his face. "When you don't measure up, you'll be back in Loserville with the rest of us."

That stings. "What are you trying to say, Will? Because I feel like there's a point, and you're dancing all around it."

"My point is, Zack's not the 'nice guy' you think he is," Will concludes. "The bonfire kids won't let me hang out with them, despite how rich my parents are. Why would they let you hang out? Jase clearly hasn't done you any favors in the popularity department."

"Wow. Just—wow." I shake my head, slow-clapping right in Will's face. "Of all the rude and insensitive things you've ever said to me, that one wins the grand prize."

Will pushes my hands away from the tip of his nose with a

huff. "I'm just looking out for you."

"It's not your job to look out for me," I retort. "That's ridiculously patronizing. And after your last speech, the optics are especially gross."

"Callie, I didn't mean—"

"Uh-huh. Sure. You didn't mean to sound like a huge jerk, and I'm making a big deal out of nothing, and you're not wrong for telling me the truth. Save it, Will." I stand, holding my chin high as I regard him frostily. "I'm going to find the punch."

"There's no punch," Will reminds me.

"Whatever." I wave my fingers through the air, like Dr. Ormandi when he's dismissing something ridiculous I just said. "See you later."

"Callie!"

I refuse to look over my shoulder when I spin and storm away.

Izzy and Will aren't wrong about the no-punch thing. Maybe the big punch bowl that gets spiked by the class trickster is just a thing that happens in movies. The only refreshments are a couple coolers filled with water bottles sitting in the far corner. I open one, snatch a bottle, and twist the cap. But the plastic is cheap, and water gushes down my front, the bottle crinkling like dead leaves in my hand.

"Oh, great." If the very noticeable wet streak right down the middle of my dress isn't a complete vibe-killer, I don't know what is. Note to self—next time, don't wear pale turquoise. A huge water stain trailing down my chest to my hem isn't going to attract unwanted attention at all.

Needless to say, this night is not going well for me.

"I thought I saw you over here."

I leap, coming face to face with Zack right behind me. Izzy and Chase are at his side, looking every bit a trendy, hot couple in matching black (something tells me they planned it). And here I am, water bottle in hand, wetness covering my whole front, caught like a deer in headlights.

"Is everything okay?" Zack eyes the water stain on my dress with a scowl.

"I, um, spilled." Thanks for nothing, cheap plastic bottle.

"Oh, sorry." Zack doesn't seem all that sorry, but whatever. "We're bailing to go to the beach, want to come?"

"To bonfire night?" I look toward Izzy. She gives an almost imperceptible nod.

"Emily and Will can come, too." Zack must sense my hesitation. "I think I saw them over there."

I cast a glance over my shoulder. Emily grins and chats animatedly with Will on the dance floor, but scurries over when she catches my eye. Will lags behind, glaring.

"What's up, guys?" she asks.

"Izzy and I are thinking of going down to the beach with Chase and Zack," I tell my friends. "Do you guys want to come?"

"Sure!"

"No."

Emily and Will answer in unison. My eyes dart between the two of them.

"You're our ride, Will," I remind my obstinate best friend. He shrugs, completely unmoved.

"So?"

"No worries, I'll take you all home," Chase offers. Izzy beams like Chase is her gallant knight in shining armor, riding in on his Chrysler-shaped stallion to save the day.

"You're really going to bonfire night, Callie?" Will stares in dismay.

I shouldn't go. Underage drinking, smoking, and partying are most definitely *not* my scene. But I'm also pretty miffed with Will for insinuating I'm too much of a loser to be seen at bonfire night with the popular crowd. My current desire to shove his words back in his face is stronger than my desire to avoid any awkward social interactions.

"Yeah, I'm gonna go."

"Whatever." Will takes his keys out of his pocket and jangles them at me and my girlfriends. "Have fun. I'm going home."

As I watch Will sulk away, it's all I can do not to run him down and slap the drama out of him.

"What's with Will?" Zack asks.

"He's just grumpy tonight." There is a one thousand percent chance I will be giving Will Avila a piece of my mind before he even *thinks* about surfing with me again.

As soon as we pull up to the beach for the bonfire, I immediately regret my decision to come. Tons of cars line the parking lot beside the dunes, from junkers like Chase's Pacifica to snazzy sports rigs and raised trucks. Every single popular kid at my school is here. Jase and his senior friends, juniors from our class, plus some freshman and sophomores. And, I notice, a few kids who graduated a year or two ago that go to Verona Beach State. They're all gathered in groups around a blazing bonfire lit inside a barbecue pit, wearing their formal clothes. Somebody's car bumps music from a cheap subwoofer, and a couple of kids meander around the parking lot, smoking and drinking from cans I know are not soda.

Yeah, this really isn't my thing.

"You want my jacket?" Zack asks. I forgot mine in Will's SUV.

"Um, yeah. Thanks," I reply.

Izzy's wearing Chase's sport coat. What does this mean? Are Zack and I here together, the way Izzy and Chase obviously are? Am I cool with that? Or is it really weird and uncomfortable?

I slip my arms in the sleeve of Zack's jacket, clutch my heels at my side, and make my way down to the sand. The fine, slippery grains beneath my feet put me at ease. I'm in my element on the beach, despite how out-of-place I am with the popular clique at the bonfire. I gaze toward the crashing waves, longing swelling in my chest. They're beautiful tonight. Billowy white and navy blue, silhouetted against the starry sky.

"I wish I had my board right now." I don't realize I've spoken aloud, but Zack hears every word.

"That's cool you surf," Zack says. "I've always wanted to learn." Flirty grin—I think. "Maybe you can teach me sometime."

He's got a cute grin. I mean, not as cute as Nate's. But then, Nate's grin is just… so… I mean, it's indescribably hot. Same with the biceps. *Swoon.* Too bad he's dead, because if he were alive, he'd totally be—

Wait, why am I thinking about Nate Ormandi and his dead-guy biceps right now? I'm at bonfire night with Zack Mendes, the most popular junior at my school, who gave me his jacket and is maybe-totally flirting with me. Plus he's also, like, alive.

Leave my thoughts, Nate. Shoo. Go away.

I smile at Zack. "Uh, yeah. Sure. I can teach you to surf. For sure."

I said 'sure' twice. Yikes-and-a-half. Not smooth.

"Hey, Callie." Jase's voice reaches my ears, and I find his eyes in an instant. I move away from Zack, meeting my brother on neutral ground.

"Hi, Jase, nice of you to acknowledge my presence." I smirk. "Can't speak to me at the dance, but once I'm invading your turf you remember we're related?"

Jase ignores my not-so-thinly veiled sarcasm. "Do Mom and Dad know you're here?"

I arch a brow. "Do they know *you're* here?"

Jase presses his lips in a thin line. Ratting me out would rat him out, too—his worst nightmare. My brother narrows his eyes. "Just don't embarrass me."

"Likewise."

Jase stalks away, and Izzy rushes to my side. The look on her face is grave.

"What's wrong, Iz?" I ask with a frown.

"Sean Pettit is here."

All good feelings gone.

"Where?" I try to catch sight of him through the crush of bodies and haze of smoke. He's instantly recognizable in the oversized LA Kings cap he always wears. "Does Emily know?"

"No, I don't think so." Izzy looks over her shoulder at our cheery friend, talking with Chase and Zack. "We need to bail."

"Agreed."

"I'll tell Chase we need to go home because of… girl stuff," Izzy suggests. I nod my agreement.

"Good plan. I'll try to get Emily into the car before Sean sees her."

"Emily Sawyer!"

Too late.

Sean's obnoxious voice draws the attention of the entire bonfire crowd. He's got a beer in his hand, and his cheeks are flushed like he's already had more than two or three. He leers down his nose at Emily. My heart sinks to my toes as the sunshine leaves her eyes.

"Sean." She can barely squeak out a whisper.

"Hey, you left your phone in my car." Sean approaches us slowly, because he can't walk in a straight line. More and more people stop what they're doing to watch Sean and Emily.

"Please, go away," Emily murmurs.

"Huh? What's that?" Sean cups his palm around his ear. "You wanna talk a little louder so we can all hear?"

Emily's eyes brim with tears, and Izzy and I rush to flank her, planting our feet firmly in the sand beside our friend.

"Come on, let's go." Between Izzy and I, we turn Emily away from the scene Sean's created, plodding our way toward Chase's car.

"Hey! I'm not done talking to you!" Sean calls after us.

"Yes, you are. She asked you to go away." I shoot a black look at Sean over my shoulder. He stares a tic, trying to place my face. At last, recognition dawns on his features.

"Hey, I 'member you!" He points his finger. "You're Jase James's little sister. Calliope, right?"

A hushed fit of whispers flitters through the crowd. Nobody at school knows my full given name, except Jase and Will. Even Izzy and Emily don't know my name is actually Calliope. It's been written on every single teacher placement card since the beginning of kindergarten to "call her Callie OR ELSE." Ice shards crackle through my veins as Sean regards me.

"How do you know my name?"

A very drunk hiccup-laugh. "My mom's the registrar."

Crap. I forgot about that.

"What kind of a freak name is 'Calliope,' anyway?" Sean jeers.

"It's my great-grandmother's freak name," I announce.

"Calliope. Sounds like something out of a bad Western movie." He laughs again, nearly spilling his beer. "Tarnation, Calliope, rustle us up some prairie dog! Yee-haw! Rootin'-tootin' cowgirl, Calliope James!"

Nobody moves as Sean cackles at his own idiotic joke. Zack cowers behind Chase, looking embarrassed enough to die. Jase glares at Sean like he wants to punch him but cares too much about his reputation to defend me, which is all at once shocking and not the least bit surprising. Tears course down Emily's face, smearing her mascara and eyeliner down her cheeks, and Izzy's eyes burn with rage. And yet, no one makes a sound.

The pop and snap of the bonfire mingling with Sean's insidious laughter are the only sounds I can hear over the softly crashing waves in the distance.

I'm angry. No—angry isn't the right word. There is no word for the furious power surging through my body—every nerve, every muscle, every last fiber of my being. The same power that bubbled and churned when Jase confronted me in the kitchen is no longer a vague inclination I can easily suppress. This power is raw, engulfing my heart and soul with luminous fire as it takes over every sense I have.

Sean is going to pay for this. He's going to pay for hurting Emily. For belittling me. For thinking he's better than another human being and can get away with treating them however he wants.

The power fills me, crackling like lightning. When I open my eyes, I can see tiny Lights above the hearts of every person around the bonfire, flickering like a hundred candles in the ocean breeze. But only one flame matters.

I lock my eyes onto Sean's, the Light in me latching onto the Light in him, ready and willing to bend to my will.

"Shut up, Sean Pettit!"

Instantly, Sean goes still and quiet. His eyes glaze over, as though in a trance. I couldn't care less that every single popular kid at my school is staring at me, and that my reputation will never live this down.

"Drop your beer. You've had enough," I command. Sean obeys, his half-empty bottle crashing to the sand with a thunk.

"You will *never* speak to Emily again." My voice is hard as diamonds, frigid as Arctic snow. It hardly sounds like my own when it rings in my ears. "You won't look at us again. Do you understand?"

"Yes." Sean's reply is flat, hypnotic. He darts his eyes downward and turns his head so he can't look at us. The Light above his heart sways, as hypnotized by my voice as Sean is.

"Get out of here," I say. "Go home."

"I can't drive, I'm drunk."

That's definitely a problem. I almost tell him to call his mommy, the blabbermouth registrar, to come get him, but a better idea strikes. Payback time. Humiliation for humiliation.

"Then go take a swim and sober up."

Sean wordlessly jogs toward the waves.

"Hey, Sean!" He stops at the sound of my voice, still as a statue. A wicked grin parts my lips. "You don't want to get your clothes all wet, do you? Better take them off."

Sean strips down until he's wearing nothing but his tighty-whiteys, then runs headlong into the rolling surf.

The silence surrounding me is oppressively heavy. Slowly, the power fades, leaving me cold, trembling. The Lights in my classmates fade and my teeth rattle like stones, limbs wiggling as though my bones have turned into jellyfish. I keep my eyes on my bare feet sinking into the sugary beach sand, unable to stomach the reaction of my stunned schoolmates.

I'm done for. My reputation is ruined. I'll be—

To my surprise, a couple of kids begin to laugh. Nervously at first—because who would dare laugh at Sean Pettit? But even more join in, until almost everyone at the bonfire doubles over in laughter at the sight of Sean frolicking through the sea in his undies. A couple rounds of brief applause mingle with the chuckles, giggles, and snorts, and people pull their phones out to get pictures and video of Sean making a complete fool of himself.

"Thank you, Callie." Emily takes my hand and squeezes it gratefully.

"Come on, let's get out of here before he realizes what

happened," I tell my friends. "We'll take my car, Izzy. Don't ask Chase."

When I finish pushing my way to my brother, all he can do is stare, completely dumbstruck. "Callie, what the —"

"I need your keys, I'm taking the car," I interrupt. "Emily needs to get out of here."

"Then how am I getting home?" my brother protests. "And what did you do to Sean?"

Jase's girlfriend, Jen, appears at his side. She glances at me with a look of understanding in her eyes. Maybe Jen is cooler than I assumed. Or Sean's burned her, too, like so many other girls.

"I'll drive you home, babe," she tells Jase.

"Thanks, Jen." She and I exchange a nod, and I lock eyes with my brother. "Keys, Jase. Please."

Jase doesn't argue, with me or with Jen. He just drops the keys in my waiting palm, staring at me like he isn't quite sure I'm the same little sister he schemes to steal the car from — the one he teases, the one who makes him coffee when he's nice.

If that's the way Jase is looking at me, Zack must think I'm the biggest reject alive. I refuse to look at him when I hand him his jacket.

"I'm sorry, I have to go." I glue my eyes to my feet. "Thank you for letting me wear this."

Zack doesn't say a word. He just turns on his heel and walks away.

I dash to my car as quickly as possible. Izzy, Em, and I climb in without a word, and drive off into the night.

"Homecoming totally sucks." Emily slumps in the back seat. I can hear the lump forming in her throat as she speaks, choking her words. "I can't believe Sean was there. It was so stupid to go down to the bonfire. I should have known. That's his crowd."

"You couldn't have known," Izzy consoles her. "None of us

did."

"Thank you both for standing up to him," Emily places a hand on each of our shoulders. "I don't know how you did that, Callie, making him take his clothes off and jump in the ocean like that, but things could have gotten a lot worse if you hadn't stepped in."

She's right—things could have gotten a lot worse. Just not in the way Em imagines. Because making Sean strip and go for a swim was the least I could have made him do...

"And can we talk about Sean wearing the world's smallest chonies?" Izzy roars with laughter. Emily bursts out laughing, too. I wish I could laugh. But nothing about what happened feels funny—not even the sight of Sean's teeny-weeny underwear.

I drop off Emily first. She looks a little better when she waves goodbye and retreats into the safety of her house.

"Okay, you've gotta come clean." Izzy crosses her arms. "How did you pull that off with Sean?"

"I—I don't know."

How can I explain something I don't understand myself? All I know is the Light inside me caught fire—its power took over, trapped the Light inside of Sean like a vise, and I could have made him do whatever I wanted. I *controlled* him with my voice. And everything about it was terrifying.

Is this what Nate means when he says Light is corrupt? That ancient Luminauts were power-crazed maniacs who did nothing but destroy? Because the way I spoke to Sean certainly didn't feel like I was protecting my friend the way a Luminaut would.

It felt like revenge. And I liked it. A lot.

"I was just so mad..." I try to think of a lie that will make sense to Izzy, one that doesn't sound like I'm losing my grip on reality— even though that's exactly how it feels. "I think he was too drunk to realize what was going on. He'd have probably turned into a chicken if I said I wanted nuggets."

Izzy ignores my attempt at a joke. She's uneasy—no, *scared* of me. As afraid of me as I am of myself. "You spoke to him like he was a bug you wanted to step on." She shudders. "I've never heard you speak to anybody like that."

"I didn't know what I was doing." I want to plead with Izzy, to make her believe everything will be back to normal by Monday. But the truth is, it won't, and both of us know it. After tonight, I don't think things will ever be normal again.

"Hey, it's cool. You did what you did for Em," Izzy tells me. "And it's not like Sean didn't have it coming."

She does her best to smile, to pretend that everything's fine, but the massive distance spanning the space between us grows larger, more cavernous. By the time I drop Izzy off at her house, the cupholders between our seats feel miles wide.

"I'll see you Monday," I tell my friend. She grins, but won't meet my eyes.

"See ya, Callie."

Tears pour down my face as soon as Izzy turns her back to me. I sob the rest of the way home.

Homecoming most definitely sucks.

CHAPTER FIFTEEN

"GOOD AFTERNOON, CALLIE! I hope the Homecoming dance was pleasant."

As soon as Dr. Ormandi says the word *Homecoming*, I collapse on his loveseat, spewing a fresh flood of tears and verbal diarrhea.

"My best friend won't talk to me and everybody at school probably hates me and I'm the biggest disaster-show in the world because I made Sean Pettit jump in the ocean in his underwear!"

Dr. Ormandi just stands there, staring at me for a solid minute. Emotionally compromised sixteen-year-old girls are clearly way out of his comfort zone. At last, he says, "I'll put some coffee on for you."

"Th-thank you!" I blubber around my sobs. Nemo wriggles out of my bag, and my little buddy crawls into my lap, petting my shoulder as I hug him tight. Dr. Ormandi disappears into the kitchen, returning a few minutes later with a mug of creamy, sweet coffee.

"Alright, let's try to make sense of the mess you're in." Dr. Ormandi lowers himself into his creaky leather recliner. "Would you tell me again why you are so upset? Slowly?"

I wipe tears from my soggy, wet-streaked cheeks and take a deep breath.

"Okay, so Homecoming started out great. Except my best friend, Will, was going to ask me to slow dance, which would be, like, no way. But that didn't happen, because Zack Mendes—this guy from my school who's really popular—came and asked me to go to bonfire night. And that made Will get all jealous and rude, to which I made some pithy retorts that weren't all that nice and I kind of regret. So after that, my friends and I went down to the beach to the bonfire, except Will didn't go because he still wasn't over the Zack issue."

"I see." Dr. Ormandi looks like defending his Ph.D. dissertation was easier than keeping up with my high school drama.

"When we got to the beach, this skeevy dirtbag named Sean Pettit was there," I ramble, "and he was really drunk and obstinate. He started harassing me and my friend Emily, who's his ex—Emily, not me, I'd never date him—and I got angry. More angry than I've ever been in my life. This... *power* took over everything. Like I was on fire with power. When I talked to Sean, I could see a tiny Light hovering over his heart, and when I commanded him, he obeyed. I humiliated him in front of everyone. And now, nobody will speak to me ever again."

Dr. Ormandi allows me to pause for breath. "And what was that you said about some boy jumping in the ocean in his underwear?"

"Oh, yeah. That. Remember how I said I told Sean what to do, and he obeyed me?" When Dr. Ormandi nods, I go on. "Well, I told him to take his clothes off and go jump in the ocean."

The edges of Dr. Ormandi's mouth twitch. His eyes shine with repressed mirth.

"You want to laugh, don't you? It was the worst night of my life, and you want to laugh." I hang my head, and Nemo runs his robot claw over my hair soothingly.

"I'm sorry, Callie." Dr. Ormandi can hardly keep a lid on holding back a laugh. "But when you described making that boy strip to his underwear and jump in the surf…"

He loses it. A gigantic laugh breaks free from his lips. And despite how horrifying it all was, and the rawness of the wound the power ripped wide, I finally let myself laugh, too. Because Sean leaping about in the waves like a mermaid mated with a gazelle, wearing nothing but a pair of tiny, white briefs, was honestly one of the funniest things I've ever seen.

"Dr. Ormandi, what's happening to me?" I ask once our laughter dies down. "Ever since I found the Light Core, my life has been a train wreck."

"I can't speak to the generally disastrous nature of your current circumstances, but I can shed some light on the young man taking a dip in his unmentionables," Dr. Ormandi tells me with a grin. "It appears as though you used what is called Persuasion on that boy, Sean Pettit."

"Huh?" I cock my head and scowl.

"Do you recall how I explained that Seers have a special power called Manipulation, which allows us to control, or manipulate, the elements around us?" I nod, so Dr. Ormandi continues. "In addition to bending, harnessing, and physically manifesting Light, Luminauts have a special power called Persuasion. They can see the Light within another's being and control it, thereby 'Persuading' others to do specific things, or divulge information. It's a most helpful skill in the hunt for Light Cores."

"Luminauts can control people with their voice?" When Dr. Ormandi doesn't counter my question, I almost start crying all over again—what bursts from my lips is a strangled bark of dry laughter mixed with a sob. I stretch myself out on the loveseat like a psychiatrist's couch. "Nobody will trust me again, because they won't know if I'm making them do something, or if they're doing it because they want to. Mind control has got to be the worst superpower ever." I crank my neck around, giving Dr. Ormandi a withering look. "Have you seen any movies lately? It's always the villain who has mind control powers."

"If it makes you feel better, Luminauts rarely need to use their Persuasion," Dr. Ormandi offers. "I can count on one hand the number of times Mariasol used hers, and they were all with the Cal admissions office." His voice is calm, like he really is playing the wise-but-put-upon therapist in this scenario. "A sharp wit and adaptability are far more practical skills, and you have both of those in abundance."

"Thanks. Still doesn't take away the movie-villain mind control thing."

"I firmly believe you will only use your powers for good." Dr. Ormandi smiles. "You used your Persuasion last night to help a friend. That's honorable."

I didn't exactly use Persuasion to help a friend. I used it to publicly humiliate Sean Pettit in front of my peers. One could argue he deserved it, and in the moment, it felt satisfying. But nothing about what happened makes mind control honorable. The fact I so willingly used it to be cruel and malicious makes it all the more petrifying.

"Besides, people do not realize they are being Persuaded most of the time," Dr. Ormandi adds, swishing his hand for emphasis. "And Seers are immune."

I blow a raspberry through my lips. "I can't Persuade you to do anything—that's good, I guess. What will Sean think happened last night? He went for a swim in his skivvies because he was drunk as a skunk?"

"It's a reasonable assumption," Dr. Ormandi agrees. "Especially if he was as intoxicated as you say."

"So, let's recap the dumpster fire we just explored: Luminauts can control people with their voice, physically manifest Light and use it to—I don't know, do stuff—and travel the multiverse with Diver." I list the things Luminauts can do on my fingers. Nemo mimics counting on his claw-hands, too. "Anything else? Shape-shifting? Force lightning from my fingertips?"

Dr. Ormandi narrows his eyes. "Had you been reading Mariasol's journals, as I suggested, you would—"

"Please, don't lecture me about everything I should have done in the first place," I interrupt the old man. "I get that enough from my parents. I just want you to tell me the truth."

The whole truth. Nothing but the truth. Especially since Nate suggested his dad might not be entirely forthcoming.

"Luminauts always possess an excellent sense of direction, and perfect night vision. It helps them to be drawn toward the Light, wherever it is hiding. In fact, these are the subtle ways in which the Light power first begins to show itself." Dr. Ormandi leans back in his recliner, a smug smirk playing about his lips. "I suspect these two talents are very near and dear to you, and have been for some time."

"That's me, Callie James, the human GPS," I deadpan.

"The fact you were able to see the Light in that boy's being last night confirms what I've told you from the beginning," Dr. Ormandi concludes. "You are a wielder of Light, the most power-ful and ancient magic the multiverse has ever known, and it would be in your best interest to accept this and stop living in denial of what you truly are."

If I'd doubted I was a Luminaut before, there is no trace of disbelief left now. Maybe I've known the truth all along despite my valiant efforts to reject it, even in the face of all that's hap-pened to me. Except, there's no denying it anymore. Not after last night and the Big Scary Power Trip that could have ended with somebody getting terribly hurt—all at my bidding. Tears prick my eyes, and my throat grows thick with a rapidly forming lump.

"I wish I wasn't a Luminaut. I wish I could get rid of the Light Core." My voice cracks, almost breaking. "If I'd never found it, none of this would have happened."

"Your Luminaut powers would have begun to manifest regardless of the Light Core falling into your possession." Dr. Ormandi's tone is measured as he regards me, grave seriousness filling his black eyes. "Even if you were to bury the Light Core in the deepest pit you could dig in the farthest corner of the darkest cave, your power would continue to grow until it overwhelmed and consumed you. You *need* to begin reading Mariasol's journals. They are your only connection to another Luminaut. I will help you as much as I can, but I cannot teach you what you truly need to know."

I hold Nemo close, letting the old man's words sink deep inside my heart and mind. My power would *consume* me. I'd become lost to myself. The fire that wrapped tight to my bones last night would come back, stronger than ever, and burn me up from the inside out until I'm nothing but a husk of a human. It would be a fate worse than death.

There's only one choice: learn to control the Light inside me, or be destroyed by my own untamed, raw power.

I stand and load a very surprised, instantly irritated Nemo into my bag. Dr. Ormandi looks me up and down, confused.

"Are you not going to work on the Diver?"

"Nope." I shake my head. "Give my regards to the big guy, but I can't stay. Not today."

"Where will you go?" Dr. Ormandi grins like he already knows the answer.

"Home." I shoulder my bag and pop my sunglasses over my eyes. "If I'm going to train as a Luminaut, I've got a lot of reading to do."

CHAPTER
SIXTEEN

"OKAY, MARIASOL. Let's start Luminaut training."

The sound of my voice springs Nemo into action. He climbs the blankets onto my bed and wheels over to perch on top of my shoulder, inspecting the journal with a tilt of his head.

"Are you going to learn to be a Luminaut, too, Nemo?"

My robot glances at me, blinks once, and then turns his attention to the book in my hands.

"I'll take that as a yes."

The leather spine cracks pleasantly when I open the journal and begin to read.

> My name is Mariasol Zaira. If you are reading this, I am dead, and you are the last Luminaut in existence.

Mariasol's already a huge downer. This should be loads of fun.

> I am keeping these journals at the urging of my Seer, Richard Ormandi, in case one or both of us should perish before we discover you. If we are both dead, the likelihood you will ever find these journals or the World Diver is very slim. All of our

> Lore will die with us. The wisdom of our predecessors will be lost to the ravages of time, vulnerable to the evils of Darkness.
>
> I explained this to Richard, but he doesn't always listen to me. He is a man, after all.

Okay, that was a good line.

> I shall begin at the most logical place. If my journals have come into your possession, you have most likely met the World Diver and my husband. You will have started to manifest Luminaut powers, otherwise Richard would not have seen fit to gift you my life's work. I will also go so far as to say you haven't the faintest notion about how to control and manipulate the Light inside you.

Wow. It's like she *knows* me.

> The first thing you must learn, if you are to be a Luminaut, is how to communicate with a mech.

I glance at Nemo, still perched on my shoulder.

"What do you think? I communicate pretty well with you, don't I, buddy?"

As if driving home my complete incompetence with any and all forms of mech communication, Nemo wheels away. He finds the rubber bouncy ball I bought him a few weeks ago and begins tossing it against the wall.

"Hey, not so loud," I caution my robot. He looks at me in a way that reminds me of Olivia's three-year-old defiance, then returns to the ball tossing.

Learning how to communicate with a mech is a skill I could use some work on.

> As a Luminaut, you will be bonded with the Diver for the rest of your life. The World Diver will have an affinity for you right away, and you will be able to sense his emotions, but communicating with him in order to effectively Dive through gateways will require skill and practice.
>
> Concentrate very hard on the Diver's mind. He has one, although not like yours and mine. The Light which long ago animated him resides in his psyche, as it does in you. It is what allows you to connect to him, to sense his feelings, and, eventually, to command him. You must reach out with your inner Light—with your feelings and soul.

I chuckle. "Use the Force, Callie."

> Once you have latched onto the Diver's mind, you will need to concentrate on what it is you want him to do. You must then will the action into being. For example, if you want him to move a certain direction, you must focus on willing his movement in that direction.

Fantastic—the only way to get Diver to do what I want is to mind-meld with him. I've got to mind-meld with a fifty-foot-tall, sentient robot. I see zero ways in which that could go wrong.

> The Diver will respond to your desire and your will, so it is best to try and keep a calm composure while communicating with him. Becoming highly emotional can compromise your

connection, and a schism will have disastrous consequences. Theoretically, you could end up Diving through the wrong gateway, or cause the Light Core to become unstable, which could shatter the Diver's Prism and injure or kill yourself and your Seer.

No pressure, Mariasol. Thanks.

Once you have mastered communicating with the Diver, he will respond to any command you give him. It will become intuitive, almost second nature. Practice makes perfect in this area, so you should begin working with the Diver as soon, and as often, as possible.

End of entry one. I set the journal aside. Diver obviously isn't in my room to practice the whole mind-meld thing, but Nemo is. I stare at him, trying to force my mind to find the Light in his mind. Narrowing my eyes on the tiny robot, I concentrate so hard I get a headache. But I can't latch onto anything. All I can sense is a feeling like a pinball being tossed around the machine—contained, but just barely, and zipping from one thing to the next so rapidly I can't keep up.

"Maybe it doesn't work on baby mechs." Or Nemo's mind is a pinball machine. I'd say there's an equal chance of both being the case.

Nemo tires of throwing his bouncy ball against the wall and shimmies down the bedpost to the floor, searching for something new. He finds a stack of textbooks and my English homework, a paper on Maya Angelou.

"No, Nemo! Bad robot! Put that down!" I leap off the bed pointing my index finger at Nemo. I've got an A in English for the first time since eighth grade, and I'm not going to blow it because my robot-dog ate my homework.

Nemo hangs his head like I just crushed his little spirit, and the essay drops from his hands. I wince, a guilty pang in my chest. Nemo might be a pinball machine, but he's only curious. He doesn't mean to be destructive.

But hey—he listened to me. We communicated.

Maybe the trick to communicating with mechs is pointing and scolding just like Mom. It certainly seems to do the trick for Nemo. I'll try it with Diver next time I see him. Listen, Diver, get your metal butt in gear and go left! Now turn right, mister, or you're grounded!

"It's okay, Nemo." I ease myself onto the floor so Nemo can crawl in my lap. "You aren't bad. I didn't mean it. You just can't eat my homework."

Nemo wraps his skinny robot arms around my elbow, and I pet his head. He purrs softly, a sure sign all is forgiven, then wheels away, returning a blink later with a blank notebook.

"You want some paper to shred?" I concentrate with all my might on Nemo's mind, and somewhere out of the chaos comes a flicker of Light, and an answer. Yes, he wants to shred the paper.

"Alright, fine, just do it quietly." I rip a few pages and hold them out for Nemo, who rakes his arms in a greedy gimme-gimme motion. As soon as the paper leaves my hands, bits of it fly through the air.

"Nemo, I wish I was happy about anything the way you're happy about shredding notebook paper," I laugh.

Nemo is so blissed out he spins, twirls, and does his herky-jerky robot dance as he shreds and shreds. The joy bubbling from his tiny being is contagious.

"HA! I knew it!"

My bedroom door flies open, and I leap over Nemo

protectively, shielding him with my body. Will stands at the threshold, glaring at me like he just caught me committing a crime and the jig is up. Both of us stare at each other as bits of paper fall softly to the floor like autumn leaves.

My eyes pop. So do Will's. Nemo wiggles free of my grasp and rushes toward Will, growling like the world's fiercest metal chihuahua before I pounce on him again. Will stares at Nemo and pales. He is silent.

"Okay, I know what this probably looks like, but I can explain."

"AAAAHHHHH!"

I'm on my feet in an instant, racing down the hall after Will. As fast as he bolts away from Nemo, he could be the star of the track team. But I'm a hair faster, and before he can reach the safety of the living room, I tackle him to the ground.

"Let me go! Let me go!" Will hasn't stopped screaming. "You've got a — a —"

"Shut up!" I clap my hand over his mouth. "Somebody's going to hear you. Get in my room. *Now.*"

"No way! Not with that thing in there!" Will's so frightened I think he might pass out. Seriously, who would be *that* scared of Nemo? He's the size of a teacup poodle.

Then again, I was terrified of Nemo the first time I saw him. But I also didn't scream loud enough to alert the whole neighborhood there's a living robot in my bedroom. Not cool, Will.

"That *thing* is not going to do anything, except maybe scratch your ankle," I hiss. "Get in my room. I'll explain everything."

Will's face has gone completely ashen. I stand, helping him to his feet, and follow close behind, fingers wedged between his shoulder blades. He's a flight risk; I'm not taking chances. Nemo stands guard at the door, whirring his wheels and growling in a way I'm sure he thinks is very fierce. It sounds a lot like a blender.

I have to forcibly push Will past the threshold.

"What — what the — that's — "

"That's Nemo," I say, locking the door behind me. There's no way I'm risking another interruption. "Nemo, meet Will."

Nemo growls the most menacing growl a robot his size can muster. Will presses himself so far into the wall I'm pretty sure he's trying to become one with the paint.

"Nemo, that's rude." I sound too much like Mom for my own comfort. "Come over here and say hi."

Nemo begrudgingly wheels toward Will, looking up and up at his face. Will regards my robot with a mixture of horror and burgeoning curiosity.

"You can say hi, he understands you," I inform Will. He looks at me, then at Nemo, then back at me.

"Callie, I swear, this is — "

"Just say hi, Will."

"H-h-hi."

Nemo blinks, beady eyes flashing twice, then returns his gnat-like attention to shredding notebook papers — Will and his terror long forgotten. My best friend slumps to the floor.

"What is happening?" he mumbles to no one in particular. "How is this real? That robot's alive." Will whips his head in my direction. "He *is* alive, right? You aren't the world's most genius robot builder and programmed him to be that way?"

"He's alive." Will looks like I just confirmed his worst nightmare.

"How? What happened to him?"

"It's a long story." I slip to the floor, too, sitting beside Will in silence, watching Nemo shred paper into confetti. "What are you doing here, anyway?"

"I ... I came to confront you," Will confesses.

"About what?" I narrow my eyes.

"Zack Mendes." A muscle ticks in Will's jaw. "I thought you'd be with him today, after you guys ditched me for the bonfire last night." He pauses, hesitates, and then blurts, "I thought I'd walk in and find you making out."

I allow myself a very satisfying eye-roll. They almost tumble out of my head and crash to the floor.

"Really, Will?" I shoot him the most acerbic scowl I've got in my arsenal of dirty looks. "That is the most asinine bunch of nonsense I've ever heard. Zack does *not* like me like that, nor do I like him like that. And he's not going to want *anything* to do with me after last night."

"Oh, yeah, the Sean Pettit thing," Will says with a half-grin.

My scowl deepens. "How do you know about the Sean Pettit thing?"

"Dude, it's viral." Will's grin becomes an impish smile. "Haven't you looked at your phone? Everybody's posting it on social. You're tagged in at least a hundred videos."

"What?!" Panic buzzes like an anxious bee around my brain, and Will whips out his phone. I haven't looked at mine all day — I've been way too worried about what I'd see. For good reason.

Sure enough, I'm the first video that pops up on Will's screen: shaky, muffled footage of me telling Sean to take off his clothes and go jump in the ocean before he strips to his teensy undies and pirouettes a gazelle-ballet in the waves. Whoever filmed it starts laughing so hard they drop their phone. The screen goes dark as the laughter continues.

"This is my personal favorite." Will pulls up another video captioned CALLIE JAMES IS A TOTAL BAD@$$!!! It's got a boomerang loop of Sean stripping and prancing, and my words have been auto-tuned over "These Boots Are Made For Walking."

"That's it." My face falls into my waiting hands. "My life is over. I'm dead."

"Are you kidding?" Will smiles far too enthusiastically about my imminent social demise. "It's the most awesome thing I've ever seen in my life!"

"It was horrible, Will." Tears of rage, hurt, and desperation spring to my eyes. What looks funny on video can't capture how terrible Persuasion power feels — what it was like to have that all-consuming fire scorching my insides, and not be able to contain the burn. Guilt and anger bleed throughout my body, raw and tender — a scabbing wound the videos rip wide open.

"You were right." I lean my head against Will's shoulder, grasping my middle. "I never should have gone to bonfire night. And now I'm internet famous for humiliating one of the most popular former students all the bonfire kids admire. *Maybe* by Prom people will forget what I did to Sean."

"If people hate you for that, I have no faith in humanity." Will drapes his arm around my shoulders with a reassuring squeeze. For the briefest of moments, he turns his face toward my hair — a weirdly intimate thing for Will, but maybe his nose itched?

"Sean is a terrible human being. To say he had well-deserved payback coming is an understatement." Will eases away, resuming a neutral stance. "And if Zack or anybody else won't talk to you because you defended Em from her jerk ex-boyfriend, they're all just as bad as Sean."

"Thank you." I smile at Will. He smiles back. Whatever residual frustration either of us might have felt after our fight floats toward the ceiling and out of sight.

Nemo busily wheels past — fresh out of paper to shred, he begins building a tower of my rubber flip-flops instead.

"Forget about Sean Pettit." Will nods his chin toward Nemo. "Tell me how you have a robot-dog living in your bedroom."

I sigh wearily. "Where do I even begin?"

Words gush out of me like a wave barreling toward the shore.

Finding the Light Core. The bizarre things it does. Dr. Ormandi's book. The whirlpool. Nemo coming to life. Glowing hands. The World Diver. My secret Sunday post-surf visits to the old man and his robot all these weeks. Being a Luminaut. Other worlds. The Persuasion I used on Sean Pettit. I tell Will everything—everything except about Nate Ormandi's ghost, the phantoms of venom and ice creeping over my shoulder, and crossing over to the shadow world. For some reason, those parts I want to keep hidden.

By the time I'm finished, prickling tears well in my eyes, and I've never felt more exhausted. I didn't realize the emotional and physical toll it was taking to keep my secrets, but my eyes are so heavy and my bones so droopy I want to curl up in a ball and sleep for weeks.

"Wow, Callie." Awe and wonder flood Will's face when I finally finish my tale. "I thought you were sneaking away to hang out with Zack all these weeks."

"In all fairness, I *was* ditching you for another guy. Two, actually." I draw on my fading energy reserves to wad some paper into a ball for Nemo—he switched from flip-flops back to paper about halfway through my story. "They just happen to be a reclusive ex-scientist and his gigantic, sentient, portal-cruising robot."

Will shakes his head, amazed. "That's incredible."

"No, it's not." I snort humorlessly. "It's... I don't have a word for what it is."

"You have superpowers!" Will looks at me like he can't understand how I'm not just as stoked about this as he is.

"I don't feel very super," I mutter. "So far, everything about being a Luminaut feels like a curse."

"Have you ever done it to me?" Will glances at me out of the corner of his eye. "The Persuasion thing?"

"No." I shake my head fiercely. "Absolutely not. The only person I ever used it on is Sean. I promise."

"When you found the Light Core, why did you take it to the boogeyman? I don't get that part." Will takes a turn tossing the paper to Nemo.

"First, don't call him the boogeyman anymore. Second, you don't think googling was the first thing I did?" I arch my brow. "Do you know what kind of websites pop up when you google 'glowing rod?' People do some lewd stuff with photoshop."

Will laughs. "I think I can imagine."

"I read dozens of books and articles on oceanic phenomena, and totally struck out," I add. "Going to Dr. Ormandi in person was my last resort."

Plus, Nate Ormandi's ghost told me I should. But Will doesn't need to know that. Because reasons.

"Well, at least your paper got an A+. Mr. Evans thought you were a genius." Will looks all around my room. "Where are you hiding it? Can I see it?"

"The Light Core?" I press my lips. "I don't think that's a good idea. Whenever I hold it, bad things happen."

"I'll hold it," Will suggests. "You said it won't do anything if somebody who's not a Luminaut holds it, right?"

"That's what Dr. Ormandi told me, anyway." Might as well see if the old man was right. I go to my closet, rooting through my stacks of clothes and discarded robot parts, and kick the shoebox hiding the Light Core toward Will. "Just keep it away from me. And put it back really fast."

Will pulls the Light Core from my shoebox, his eyes wide and shimmering in the ethereal, almost magical glow. Dr. Ormandi was right—when Will holds the Light Core, it's little more than a glow stick. A particularly beautiful glow stick, but benign. I, on the other hand, do not feel benign. As soon as I catch sight of the

Light Core, the need to hold it, to connect to its Light overtakes my senses. I force my body to remain perfectly still—not to draw breath. But the Light calls to me, floats from the Light Core toward me. Against all reason, I reach, my hand glowing gold and manifesting tendrils of perfect, sparkling Light.

"Whoa, Callie! Your hands!" Will drops the Light Core, leaping to his feet. He comes close, staring at my blazing fingertips with even more awe and wonder.

Stop glowing. Stop, please.

Light zips away from my hands with blinding speed, racing through my veins before screeching to a halt just under my heart. The jarring sensation takes my breath away. But, my hands are back to normal. I shove them into my pockets, clenched tight to ease the shaking left by the power surge.

"Put it back now." I inch the shoebox toward Will with my toe.

Will does as I ask, burying the Core in the folds of clothing and piles of shoes before shutting my closet tight. Once the Light Core is safely hidden, the urge to connect myself to it vanishes. I can breathe again.

Will grasps my wrists, searching for any residual glow. "What happened with your hands just now? That was some amazing superhero flex! Is the glow some kind of special energy? Can you shoot light beams like Captain Marvel?"

"I don't really know what the glowing does, other than—you know, glow." I give a shrug. Will remains unconvinced.

"There's got to be a purpose to all of it," he says. "Maybe there's a supervillain you'll have to fight. One that wants to take over the multiverse, and only you can stop him—or her—with your magic light fingers."

"I'm not going to fight any supervillains, because I'm not a superhero." Light sucking tentacle phantoms aren't villainous, right? No, definitely not. "That's not what Luminauts and Seers do."

Except, I don't really know what Luminauts and Seers do. Nobody has ever explained what, precisely, Luminauts and Seers need to use their powers for... Mental note: next time, ask Dr. Ormandi what I'm supposed to actually *do* with the glowing hands. Because if Will's right, lurking supervillains kind of need to be on my immediate radar.

"Dr. Ormandi is a Seer, right? He can see all the other worlds in the multiverse?" When I nod, Will continues his summary. "And Luminauts like you pilot a giant robot through space wormholes to other worlds using the magic light power inside the Light Core. But you don't fight villains, or save the world — despite totally sounding like every comic book version of a superhero."

"Drop the superhero thing, okay, Will?" I crumble up another paper ball for Nemo. He's shredded the first one into microscopic bits.

"Can I be a Seer?" Will grins eagerly. "I want to go to other worlds with you."

"Sure," I deadpan. "Have you ever seen any gateways to Alienville just chilling in midair? Noticed your eyes glowing weird colors at random? Elements obeying your unspoken command?"

"No." Will tosses the paper ball for Nemo.

"Then you might be out of luck."

"Maybe I can come along as a helper," Will suggests. "You need a guy to carry equipment and make wisecracks, don't you? I'll be the Chewbacca to your Han Solo."

"That's what a Seer is. You'd be more like the C-3PO."

Will wrinkles his nose. "No thanks."

"Anyway, I'm nowhere close to being ready to Dive off and

explore other worlds — with or without superhero powers." I toss the paper ball for Nemo again. "I have to master this mind-meld communication thing with Diver first. And I have no clue how to do that."

"So you're grounded." Will takes his turn tossing the paper ball.

"Basically." Nemo wheels up to me, the wad of gnarled paper in his hand, and a brilliant idea strikes. "Actually, if you want to help, I *really* need someone to help train Nemo."

"Seriously?" Will plays keep away with Nemo and the paper for a second before tossing the ball into the corner of my room. "Why do you have to train him? It's not like he's gonna poop on the carpet."

"Not that kind of training." I take the paper ball from Nemo, hiding it behind my back. Nemo starts hunting for it, but gives up easily. "He's got to pass for a normal robot at my robotics final in seven weeks. And he's still, like, well…"

Nemo picks up a stray pencil and bangs it against the side of his head. Again. And again and again and again. I snatch the pencil away and hand him a loose sock, a much quieter distraction. Immediately, he manages to get his arm stuck inside and starts spinning around the room, trying to shake the sock away. I shoot Will a humorless look.

"I see what you mean," he concedes.

"So will you help me? Please?" I bat my eyes a few times for good measure. "You're the only person who knows about Nemo. About… *everything* I just told you."

Will smiles, his chest puffing like a proud peacock. "I'll help, Callie. You can count on me."

"You've got to promise you won't tell anyone," I go on. Will nods.

"I promise."

"On pain of me never surfing with you again." I jab my index finger into the fleshy part of his shoulder. "And I mean it this time."

"Ow, geez." Will rubs his shoulder, scowling. "I swear, I won't let it slip to anyone about your robot-dog-thing. Happy now?"

"Yes, very." I grin, relieved. "Thank you, Will."

Will smiles a genuine, happy-go-lucky, Will smile. "So, what's the first thing we need to teach him? How to get the sock off his arm?"

I smile, too. "That's a great place to start."

CHAPTER
SEVENTEEN

IT'S SUNDAY, and it's raining. I hate rain with the fire of a thousand burning suns.

The silver lining here is pounding rain means I can go see Diver earlier than normal, and I'm anxious to visit the old robot to start my real-life application of what I'm learning in Mariasol's journals. Jase tried to sneak the car out from under my nose because he knows I can't surf or go to the beach in the rain, but I averted his subterfuge and took the car without an issue. Dropping the word 'Civics' in front of Mom is all it takes to get him off my back.

"Good morning, Callie." Dr. Ormandi looks surprised to see me, but he smiles wide and lets me in. "You're here earlier than I expected—I'm afraid I haven't put the coffee on quite yet. How has school been since your Homecoming disaster? Does the student body despise you as much as you anticipated?"

"No, not really," I reply with a grin. "I guess Sean Pettit is more universally hated than I thought."

"And the boy you claimed will never speak to you again? I believe you called him Zack Mendes."

That one stings a little more. "He's said hi once or twice. But other than that…"

Zack's gone back to acting like I don't exist. It sucks to think he's as shallow as Will claimed, but he obviously values his reputation with the bonfire crowd and Sean Pettit above anything else.

Would Nate have cared that I humiliated Sean Pettit?

There I go letting Nate creep into my thoughts again…

"I am sorry about that," Dr. Ormandi says, and retreats to the kitchen to make me some coffee.

"The attention was flattering, but Zack could have majorly complicated my sentient-robots-and-superpowers secret identity," I quip. Plus, I never had a crush on Zack the way I might-maybe have a crush on—

Seriously, Nate, *go away.*

Dr. Ormandi barks a dry laugh. "That is very true."

"If anything, it's because of Zack I went to that dumb bonfire, and used my Persuasion, and accepted that I'm a Luminaut once and for all." I take the coffee Dr. Ormandi hands me. "I guess I should thank him."

The old man's grin turns wry. "Perhaps you should hold off on that thanks," he advises. "You've got a lot of hard work ahead of you."

"Yes. I do." I take a sip of the coffee—too weak this time—and call Nemo to my side. "On that note, I'd better get down there and start Luminaut-ing."

Diver practically glows at the sight of me descending the basement stairs. His warmth is tangible, and almost bursting with happiness. It makes me smile.

"Hi, Diver," I tell the robot. Nemo leaps out of my arms, anxious for a new plaything to distract him, and I face the gigantic World Diver. "Let's try to understand each other today, okay?"

Diver can't talk, but I sense his agreement. Maybe communicating with him and getting him to move with my will won't be as hard as Mariasol cracks it up to be.

"I didn't see the bag with your hand torch today," Dr. Ormandi observes, slowly tackling the stairs. "Just your backpack with Nemo."

"I'm going to try piloting Diver today," I reply over my shoulder.

"Ah! You've been reading Mariasol's journals!" Dr. Ormandi beams.

"Yeah, I've been going through them. She's been really informative about Diver and how being a Luminaut works." More informative than Dr. Ormandi, at any rate, but Dr. Ormandi is a Seer—he probably doesn't know the Luminaut fine print.

"You don't have the Light Core hidden in that backpack, do you?" A small amount of panic overtakes Dr. Ormandi's features. "You're in no way ready to Dive, or even attempt it."

"No," I assure the old man. "The glow stick of doom is at home. I just want to see if I can move the Diver around this basement lab."

"You had me worried." Dr. Ormandi releases a breath, and his shoulders ease. "Very well, that is an excellent starting point."

I gesture at Diver. "So, do I just stand here and issue commands, or what?"

Dr. Ormandi scowls, peeved at my question. "I thought you said you'd been reading Mariasol's journals."

"I have!" I throw my hands up in defense. "She goes on and on about the mind-meld thing I've got to practice, but never said where I have to stand to do it."

"Ah, I see what you're getting at." Dr. Ormandi grins. "To begin, you'll need to be in the Crow's Nest."

"Crow's Nest?" I repeat, raising my eyebrows. "That sounds like something on a pirate ship. I thought you said Diver was ancient."

Dr. Ormandi chuckles to himself. "My particular name for this room was the Crow's Nest, much to Mariasol's annoyance. Come, I'll show you. Ask the Diver to pick us up."

"Why don't I have to mind-meld with him to get him to pick us up?"

"It is an extremely simple command, and one he wants to perform," Dr. Ormandi explains. "Fully controlling his movements to prepare for a Dive is rather more complex."

"Gotcha." I turn toward Diver. "Pick us up, please."

The robot lowers his hand so Dr. Ormandi and I can step onto his palm, then up we fly until we're parallel with the Diver's electric, glowing eyes. Dr. Ormandi's iron grip finds my shoulder as we come to a jarring halt.

"I'd forgotten how quickly he does that," the old man mumbles, releasing my shoulder. "Now, tell him you want to go up to the Prism."

"Diver, I want to go up to the Prism."

The Diver moves his hand toward his shoulder, coming to a more gentle stop. There's a small door like a ship's hatch near his neck. I step onto the robot's shoulder ahead of Dr. Ormandi.

"This might be a far-reaching assumption," I say, "but I'm supposed to open the door, right?"

Dr. Ormandi laughs. "Yes, indeed. Go on up. The lack of light will not bother you. I'll be along as soon as my joints cooperate."

It takes me a minute to get the door open; it's rusty and corroded, like everything else about Diver. But when I do, a set of stairs leading up to a dark room materializes.

"Paging Starship Enterprise…" I mutter. This 'Crow's Nest,' as Dr. Ormandi called it, looks more like the inside of a spaceship, if a spaceship and a steampunk robot could have a baby together. I can't make out all the details without any light, but I can tell this place is full of tech. My geeky heart thumps aflutter.

"Hey, Dr. Ormandi, how do I get a little light in here?" I call to the old man, who growls and snarks about his knees as he climbs the narrow stairs.

"There's a small lever beside the Prism," Dr. Ormandi replies. "Do you see it?"

"Is the enormous glass thing in the center of the room a Prism?"

"Yes." Dr. Ormandi rounds the top steps.

"Then I see it." I pull the aforementioned lever, and the metal casing around the top of the Diver's head retracts away, revealing a 360-degree view through a glass-like enclosure of my surroundings.

"Amazing."

The Crow's Nest is part cozy apartment, part Millennium Falcon, part *20,000 Leagues Under The Sea*. A sofa and some chairs are arranged around a low table in a far corner, with a large storage trunk and a bookshelf along the wall. The setup looks comfy enough to spend the night — which I may have to do, if I'm out exploring a world and away from civilization. Next to me is the giant Prism, sparkling with every color of light, and in front of that, closest to the windows surrounding the Diver's head, twin chairs like pilot seats. Everything has been constructed of bronze, glass, leather, and crystal — intricately delicate and mechanized all at once.

"Ah, memories." Dr. Ormandi looks around with a fond smile. "It has been many years since I've been inside the Crow's Nest."

"Mariasol said I've got to use the Force to mind-meld with the Diver," I cut right to the chase. Dr. Ormandi blinks, very confused. "I mean, reach out with my feelings to communicate with him."

"Ah, I understand." The old man makes his way to the little sitting and sleeping area, sinking into a chair with a contented sigh. "I'm afraid you will not find a Seer like me to be of much help."

"You're just going to sit there and do nothing?" I glare, hands on my hips.

"I'm not doing nothing. I'm sitting, and enjoying relaxing in this chair." Dr. Ormandi grins. "You're the Luminaut who wanted to practice the finer points of mech communication, which—as I have mentioned several times—is not my area of expertise."

Why do old people have to develop a snarky sense of humor at the worst possible times? So irritating.

Guess this is all on me. Great. I plop myself into one of the chairs at the front of the Diver's head, running my fingers along the smooth, buttery leather. There's a harness attached to the chair. Padded leather straps, bronze buckles. I fiddle with them, adjusting the fit to my shoulders and waist.

"For particularly rough Dives," Dr. Ormandi tells me. "No need to buckle up now. Focus on the task at hand."

Okay—right. Task at hand. I have to reach out with my feelings. Use my inner Light to find the Light within Diver. I face forward, close my eyes, and concentrate. Nothing.

"You were squinting rather hard," Dr. Ormandi observes. "Perhaps don't close your eyes."

Yes. Eyes open. I focus on trying to find Diver, to hunt down his mind. I grit my teeth and strain to feel something, *anything* like Diver—like the feelings I sense from him when I walk into the basement, or give him pats, or fix his mangled joints.

"Don't tense your face and neck," Dr. Ormandi offers yet another suggestion. "You look as though you're trying to give yourself an aneurysm."

"I thought you said you weren't going to be very helpful?" I fix him with a pointed look. The old man smiles.

"I'm merely warning you of impending injury."

"Uh-huh. Sure."

I slump into the chair, hissing a frustrated puff of breath through my nose. I wish Mariasol was here to tell me what to do. I wish Diver would just pop into my brain and tell me himself. I close my eyes, rubbing my aching temples. Maybe I should call it a day. Maybe I'm not ready for this.

Diver, where are you?

Out of the darkness comes a tiny spark of awareness and Light, a small flame flickering in and out of my consciousness.

Here.

I bolt like a rocket in my chair.

Diver, it's me, Callie. Can you hear me?

Silence. Maybe he can't hear me after all. I focus on the tiny flame, holding it tight, letting it warm my mind and heart.

Yes, Luminaut.

He heard me! I think about the command I want to give him. I raise my left arm, focusing on willing the movement, just like Mariasol said.

Left.

There's a jolt, a sudden force of powerful movement as Diver stands and begins a slow, stiff, shuffling walk in the direction I gave him.

"I did it!" I spin around and smile at Dr. Ormandi. "I told him what to do! He listened!"

"Callie, you may not want to break your connection with the Diver." Dr. Ormandi looks fearfully at a point beyond my shoulders. I crank my neck around, finding the source of his worry.

We're about to hit a wall. Like, an actual wall.

"Stop!" I yell.

Diver keeps going.

"STOP! STOP! STOP!" Panic rises into my throat. Still, Diver continues. He even picks up speed. Like he's making fun of me, or something. Jerk robot.

I frantically force myself to reach out with my feelings, even though Mariasol had said to keep a calm, cool composure. Sorry, Mariasol.

Diver, stop!

Diver hears me this time. Except, we're too late. We crash into the farthest wall of Dr. Ormandi's basement lab. There's a sickening crunch of bending, twisting metal, a tinkling of loose gears, cogs, nuts, and bolts hitting the ground, and at last, a deafening boom as Diver falls into a seated position. The air around us fills with dust, like fine smoke clouding my vision.

"Dr. Ormandi, are you okay?"

The old man white-knuckles his chair, and his black eyes bulge in his pale face. He blinks hard, clearing his vision, and faces me.

"That was… riveting."

"I'm so sorry!" I help him stand. "Are you hurt?"

"No, no, just startled," Dr. Ormandi assures me. "The Diver is in far worse shape than me, I'm afraid. We'd better go assess the damage."

Once on the ground, we both walk a circle around Diver. The rusted knee joint I spent weeks repairing looks like a train slammed head first into an oncoming car — completely mangled and ripped to shreds. I groan when I see it, crestfallen that poor Diver had to suffer even more horrific damage because of me.

"On the bright side, Nemo is unharmed, and as energetic as ever." Dr. Ormandi comes around the back side of Diver with Nemo on his heels. My tiny friend instantly perks at the sight of me. I slide off Diver's leg and pick him up.

"This sucks," I grumble. "The casing on his knee is wrecked worse than it was before. I don't know if my hand torch is going to even touch this mess."

"We'll find a way to repair the Diver. I'm sure this isn't the worst injury he's suffered over his many long eons." Dr Ormandi offers a reassuring grin. "Don't be too hard on yourself, Callie."

"I could have tried harder to stop him." I lean my forehead against Diver's leg. My shoulders slump, leaden and dejected, and my robot reaches down to give me a comforting pat. The specter of being a complete disappointment never seems to leave.

"Perhaps that's true, but it was only your first attempt," Dr. Ormandi replies, and we walk over to his worktable. "You will have many more opportunities over the course of your life as a Luminaut."

My life as a Luminaut. Life. Except, I'm only sixteen. Life is a long time. And eventually, my life will extend beyond this basement — beyond Verona Beach. How does being a Luminaut fit into what comes next? What part do Diver and the Light Core and Light powers play in my future? And if they *are* my future — as Dr. Ormandi suggests — what is the purpose of said future?

"Can I ask you something?" I sit on the stool beside the worktable, crumpling a paper ball for Nemo to toss around.

"Certainly." Dr. Ormandi swivels his chair toward me.

"What's the point of all this?" I spin a stray pen in a circle on the tabletop. "Luminauts and Seers. Going to other worlds with Diver. Hunting Light Cores. Why should I devote my entire life to it?"

"You *would* pick the day I had just gone on the equivalent of a roller coaster ride to ask me the most important question," Dr. Ormandi observes wearily.

"I have really good timing."

"Yes, quite." Dr. Ormandi sinks into the depths of his leather chair, his skin falling heavily over his eyes until he appears as old and run down as Diver. "We hunt for the missing Light Cores to restore the Lightbridge. To reconnect the multiverse."

Hold the phone. Reconnect the who-now? The pen comes to a standstill, same as my hands in midair. "What did you say?"

"Our world and the others were once connected," Dr. Ormandi elaborates. "There were no separate realities. All was one and whole. Light connected us to each other."

"In a Lightbridge?" I repeat. "That sounds like a bad fantasy cliché."

"Well, not an actual bridge, mind you, but it's the best equivalent concept." Dr. Ormandi folds his hands in his lap. "In ancient times, it was called many different things by ancient people. In our Lore, as Luminauts and Seers, the Lightbridge was the central, connecting unit, that which we used to travel between worlds. The upkeep of the Lightbridge and the welfare of the people living within its boundaries were their purpose and mission. And the Light must be restored."

"Okay, but why?" I meet Dr. Ormandi's eyes, probing as deep as I can. Something about the darkness in them shrouds important secrets he doesn't want to tell me. The weight of them fills the basement air, obscuring facts when I desperately need the truth. "Why do the worlds need to be connected? Our world is pretty crappy, in case you haven't paid attention for the last, like, literally forever. Aren't the other worlds better off without us?"

"But perhaps we aren't better off without them?" Dr. Ormandi lets me digest the question. "You see, when all was connected by Light, the multiverse was peaceful. Prosperous. When Darkness destroyed the Lightbridge, peace became nothing but a memory. Wars broke out. Ignorance and hate tore people apart. Some shut themselves up in their villages and caverns, behind walls of wood and stone. Some sought to preserve the knowledge of Light in our Lore, to keep hope however they could. Hope Mariasol clung to — hope I cling to as well." A smile parts his lips. "Until you showed up on my doorstep with Earth's Light Core in your backpack, hope was as fleeting as a dream. And now, it stirs. Light has returned. Hope will be saved."

Not the best time for a philosophical pep talk, Dr. Ormandi.

"So you want me to go to all the other worlds in the multiverse," I surmise, "treasure hunt the missing Light Cores, and then magically connect them to form a bridge. A Lightbridge. Let's just toss wrangling unicorns and killing a troll or two in that list for good measure."

"Very simplistic, but you have the idea. And there are no such things as trolls and unicorns." Dr. Ormandi didn't pick up on my sarcasm, I guess. Subtleties have never been his strong suit.

"No trolls and unicorns, but a magic Lightbridge only I can connect is going to save all the hope in the multiverse? Save it from what, exactly? Since, you know, trolls are apparently not a threat. How about man-eating giants? Werewolves? Zombies, maybe?" I make a face, regarding him with more than a little incredulity. "I haven't even taken my SATs. What you want me to do will alter the course of human history."

"Great destinies such as yours take lifetimes to attain," Dr. Ormandi assures me. "Focus on fixing the damage done to the Diver today, and learning how to properly pilot him. We'll cross the next bridge when we come to it."

"Speaking of bridges…" I purse my lips. "What did you mean when you said Darkness destroyed the Lightbridge?" I stare into the distance, mulling his words in my brain.

Darkness—the thing that destroyed the Lightbridge and unleashed hate, ignorance, and violence. The phantoms. The icy presence that creeps and crawls just over my shoulder. All the things I'd felt at the cemetery, the terrifying suspension between one reality and another—is it the Darkness he's referring to? The evil that severed the Light?

What if Will is right—what if there really *is* a supervillain I have to defeat with my powers?

Dr. Ormandi's eyes darken further, veiling any emotion, any thought from my sight. "You have reached your limit of questions for today." When he speaks, his voice sounds deadened, hollow — and horrified.

"Does Darkness still exist? Can it hurt me?" I have to know that much.

Dr. Ormandi shakes his head and turns away. "There is nothing for you to worry about, Callie."

And yet, he won't look in my eyes. He grips the arm of his chair so tight his knuckles turn gray, and I'm not sure I trust his promise not to worry—he doesn't seem to trust himself. I don't like the vibe I'm getting here at all. There's something he's not telling me. Something sinister, something dangerous. Something about Darkness that might make me give up everything—the Light Core, Diver, and hope for the multiverse—right here and now. Bit by bit, the secrets he keeps in the depths of his eyes are surfacing, and I don't like what I see.

I've got a dreadful suspicion Nate might be right after all.

CHAPTER EIGHTEEN

IT'S STILL RAINING OUTSIDE, and harder than before. Because if my day is going to suck, it's going to suck in every way possible.

I run up the block, wind and stinging rain attacking me from every angle until I reach the safety of my car. Heavy droplets pound a rat-a-tat beat on the roof when I slip inside, letting the motor run as the heater dries my damp, frizzy hair and warms my soaked skin. But I can't seem to get warm, no matter what I do. Everywhere and all around, a chill lingers...

"You're there, aren't you?" Sure enough, when I look to the passenger side, Nate's reclining in the seat, his feet propped on the dash.

"Congrats, you're getting far more perceptive about ghostly apparitions," Nate replies with a smile.

"Where have you been all this time?" I ask, rubbing my palms together in front of the blasting heat vent. No luck. Still freezing.

"All this time?" Nate seems inordinately confused. "How long has it been? You're not twenty-one and in college, are you?"

It takes me a moment to realize he isn't joking. "No, but it's been weeks. Is there a reason you stayed away?"

Something like relief washes over Nate's face, the familiar curve of his smile on his lips once more. "No reason, except the fact there's no concept of time beyond the — well, where I go when I'm not here, haunting you."

"Not Heaven?" I raise a brow. His smile turns dark and deeply sardonic, almost a leering grimace. A shudder runs through me at the sight of it, one that has nothing to do with cold.

"Not exactly."

I rub my hands harder, willing warmth and life to flow. "You didn't make the cut, huh?"

"I think God might be a Dodger fan," Nate quips, his good humor returning. "And I bleed Giants' black and orange." He notices me trying to heat my icicle fingers, and knits his brows. "You seem really stressed out. Are you okay?"

"No." I clasp my hands together in a ball, twisting my fingers so hard they might snap. "I'm not okay."

"Don't do that." Nate reaches for me, gently pulling my hands apart. "You'll pop a knuckle. Trust me, that hurts."

It's the first time he's touched me, the first time I've felt the skin of his hands. They're ice cold, as I'd expect any dead person's hands to be. But beneath the icy surface, there's something else — something flowing, creeping, crawling toward me. A need — no, a want. A connection with another person like I've never felt, living or dead.

Our eyes meet across the expanse of the console. Does he feel it, too?

Also, he's surprisingly solid. His fingers don't pass through my skin. I thought ghosts were supposed to be intangible… you know what, I'm gonna just go with it.

"What happened to upset you?" Nate asks, releasing my hands.

"It's just—" I breathe deep, willing my lungs to expand. To take in air and release it. "I'm starting to think you're right. Being a Luminaut isn't for me. I don't know if I can handle the pressure."

"Did Dad drop a bomb on you, or what?" The look on Nate's face says he already knows the answer.

"Not just a bomb—I, Calliope MaryJean James, am the sole hope of returning Light to the multiverse." I gulp down the nausea accompanying that statement. "My life's purpose is to restore the Lightbridge and save the multiverse from—I don't know, some elusive evil he didn't want to talk about. I exist to alter time, space, and reality forever."

"Wow." Nate whistles in amazement. "And I thought he was hardcore when he was pressuring me to make up my mind about Cal or USC."

"Trust me, I wish that was the only choice I had to make." I lean against the headrest. "Ever since I can remember, somebody or something else has been in control of my future. Don't want to fix the broken multiverse? Too bad, says fate—here's a bunch of superpowers and a massive destiny you're in no way equipped to handle." I puff air through my lips. "Learning how to control my Light and connect with Diver is one thing. Even piloting him to other worlds sounds pretty cool. But it's all starting to feel too big for me. Beyond what I'm capable of."

"What do you—Callie—want to do?" Nate arches a brow. "Not my dad, not anybody else. Just you."

A sigh. "Honestly? I don't know. I've always felt like there was *something* I was supposed to be doing. Something I could never figure out. All I knew was it had nothing to do with my grades, sports, and college, so I slacked off instead of figuring things out. Now, I don't have an option. I'm a Luminaut. The end."

"I know how you feel," Nate murmurs. "Like you're lost, always searching for something just out of reach. Truth is the only thing you want, but the one thing you can never have."

"Exactly. It's like the answer is hidden in plain sight, but for some reason, I can't find it." A tiny grin quirks the corners of my lips. "I think you're the first person to ever *get it*, you know?"

Nate's smile steals my heartbeat, skips it like a stone across the waves. "That's why we fit."

His fingers trail over mine, slipping across the chipped polish on my nails. It's a strange sensation, being touched by a ghost. Tingly. Cold. A shuddering thrill runs through my body, electric current crackling through my veins and manifesting the physical spark that's always existed between us. Everything is intense, overwhelming. I can't tell if I like it far too much, or wish he'd disappear so my bones would feel less rattled.

"Being a Luminaut doesn't have to be the end. You have a choice. And Light is the most terrible choice you can make." Nate inches closer. "Mom chose Light—to live her life in the unknown, hunting it. She ended up dying of a disease her world could easily heal, but our world can't. She chose Light, and chose her death." He laces our fingers together, the warmth of life and chill of death stitched together, entwined as one. "Do you really want your future to be death and destruction? Because I don't."

I hold tight to his hand, surpassing the urge to stroke his knuckle with the pad of my thumb. "Who says my Light will cause death and destruction? Is the Lightbridge really all that bad?"

"Is it all that bad?" Nate scoffs. "You think you can put no less than five other worlds—and those were the ones Mom and Dad knew about—on a collision course with each other and *not* expect violence?" He shakes his head just like Dr. Ormandi when I'm not seeing the big picture. "There are powers other than Light, Callie. Horrors you can't imagine lurking in the shadows. Creatures hunting Light, same as you. Believe me when I say they'll do anything to get it. They'll take what they want, and leave ashes in their wake."

The tentacle phantoms, the icy presence, the shadow world. Darkness.

I chew my cheek, watching raindrops drip down the window-pane, weaving a tapestry of streams in ever-changing patterns along the glass. Is Darkness waiting in the wings, biding its time for the opportunity to attack a naive, unsuspecting Luminaut? To destroy the Light once and for all?

"Let me help you," Nate goes on. "Give me your Light Core. I'll make it so Light can't harm you, or those you love. Ever."

My blood stills to a slow, painful crawl in my veins. I take my hands from his, backing away. "What did you say?"

"Your Light Core. I'll take it from you, and—"

"Why do you want my Light?" The thought of giving up my Light Core makes me feel empty, hollowed out, like a piece of myself is being cut away. My *destiny*—or whatever—can go shoot itself in the foot, but my Light? My Light is just as much a part of me as I'm a part of it. A terrifying, out-of-control, wild part of me, but still mine.

"I'm sure Dad told you I died hunting the Light Core," Nate says, "but Light wasn't what I was after. I just wanted the truth— to know if everything Mom believed in and died for was real." His eyes cloud with memory while he traces the patterns of raindrops with his finger. "Finding the truth about Light cost my life. I don't want Light to cost yours, too. Light isn't your destiny just because somebody says it is. You can choose to give it up— before it's too late."

"What if the truth is Light is a part of me no matter my choice?" I search him, hoping to find more transparency in their dark depths than I find in his father. "I'd still have Light, with or without the Light Core and the massive destiny. I can't give it up."

I hold out my hands, palms open, toward Nate. Closing my

eyes, I search for the Light, willing it into my fingertips. To flow from my soul and manifest.

A flame ignites in my inmost recesses, growing stronger until a blaze rushes through every cell, every molecule, culminating in my hands. When I open my eyes, my hands glow gold, bursting with tendrils of Light and color. It reflects off the windows, the mirrors, the smudged metal keys on my keyring, and bounces all around Nate's eyes—blacker-than-black. The look inside them when he stares at my hands is as ferocious as it is awestruck.

"Incredible…" he half-whispers, greedily drinking in the Light like a drowning man gulps air. "I didn't realize you were already this powerful."

When I snap my hands into fists, the Light retreats, swirling backward through my arteries and veins until it rests safely inside, leaving me shaken and breathless.

"Be careful who you trust with your power." Nate puts his hands over my quaking fists, wrapping his icy fingers around mine until they are entwined in a way that feels like flying and falling at the same time. "You don't want the wrong person to know how strong you've become. The consequences would be deadly."

"I'm not strong, Nate."

It's the first time I've breathed his name aloud. He lurches forward, as though his own name is a shock, a lightning bolt to his heart. For a fleeting moment, his eyes lose a little of their piercing darkness, and he feels almost human.

"Callie…" One word: my name, softly spoken. He holds me tighter—an act of safekeeping, or control?

With a blink, the overwhelming chill returns, and I tremble at the ominous tone in his next proclamation. "You're stronger than you give yourself credit for. And one day, you're going to meet someone who knows exactly who you are, and what you're capable of."

The look in his eyes slices through my skin, striking my heart, and it beats furiously against my ribs. Am I afraid of him? Or is this feeling something else entirely?

"You mean someone like you?"

"Someone *exactly* like me." A soft smile turns Nate's lips, and he combs his fingertips into my hair. "If only you could see what I see in you—how frighteningly beautiful you are."

The paper-thin suspension between life and death floats between us as we hold each other as close, yet remain worlds apart. His eyes that hypnotize pull me farther out to sea, promising dangerous freedom in their depths. When he steals a glance at my lips, I allow myself a fleeting glimpse of his. Shapely and perfect, a tiny white scar in the corner.

What does it feel like to kiss a ghost? Heart-stopping? Terrifying? Entirely wonderful and amazing? Why do I want so badly to find out?

"Please, Callie," Nate whispers. "Let me protect you."

I bite my lip too hard. Acrid blood blooms against my tongue. "I… I don't know…"

"Your Light Core can't hurt me anymore." His lips are so close they're practically kissing me with every word. "Let me keep you safe."

"Please… Nate." I tilt my head, on fire with every subtle move of his mouth near mine. But the kiss I crave doesn't come. I turn my face from him, sense returning as the heady sensation of his closeness fades. "Don't make me choose."

Nate's fingertips brush my cheek, tucking my hair behind my ear. With one last look of longing, he releases me. "Tell me when you've made up your mind. I just hope you decide before it's too late."

He's gone in a blink, and I'm left alone.

CHAPTER NINETEEN

> Today, I'll discuss the physical manifestation of Light and how to accomplish this.

Awesome, physically manifesting Light. Other than, you know, the glowing-hands thing I've got going on. Maybe this won't be as difficult as mind-melding with Diver. Because clearly, I've got some work to do with that. I have no clue how I'm going to fix his knee that I wrecked, but I'll figure it out. With any luck, I can get it fixed before I graduate—college, that is.

> Physically manifesting Light requires concentration and practice, much like all other aspects of being a Luminaut. If you have any kind of contact with a Light Core, its Light will become part of you, and you can recall it at will.

Yes, Mariasol, I've got the call-and-recall Light trick mastered. Glowing hands, normal hands. Just like I demonstrated for Nate in my car, when he held me close and looked in my eyes in a way that made it hard for me to breathe—

No thoughts of Nate and what happened in my car. I'm training as a Luminaut with his mom via her journals. Which isn't in any way weird or complicated. People use their dead crush's equally dead mother as a tutor for mastering their superpowers all the time, right?

I wonder what Nate would say if he knew I had his mom's journals...

Ugh, there I go again. Nate, Nate, Nate. I place my hands on the journal in my lap, forcing myself to concentrate on the words and not the ghost I almost kissed.

> I will explain how to create an orb with your Light.

Orbs are cool. I like orbs. Kind of how I also like Nate, and the way he—Stop it. Now.

> Concentrate on calling Light into your hands, and on lifting the Light away from your body. When enough Light has manifested, you should be able to move your hands in a circular motion to create an orb.

I set the journal aside and stretch my hands in front of me, willing the Light into my fingers and palms—an easy, second-nature occurrence now. My hands start to glow, fingertip to wrist, with glimmering, golden Light tendrils. The Light rests, waiting, and I focus on willing it to leave my body, to occupy the space surrounding me. Concentrating with all my might, I move my hands in a circle, just like Mariasol said, and a wispy, spectral orb begins to take shape.

Out of the corner of my eye, I spot movement, and a tiny click of robotic claws straining to touch my Light.

"Aren't you supposed to be in robot mode?"

'Robot mode' is Nemo's cue to be still and silent, and only

move when and how I tell him. Will and I have spent every waking moment we can spare teaching Nemo 'robot mode' and all the commands he needs to know for my final. He's been in robot mode for an hour now, but any distraction and he's done for. Light orbs are very distracting for baby robots.

Nemo ignores me, whizzing toward my bed to shimmy up my comforter and play with my Light.

"Robot mode," I command. "I mean it."

Nemo growl-grumbles at me, but falls to the floor, resuming his statue-like stance.

"Yeah, that's what I thought," I murmur to myself, and focus my attention on the shimmering ball of Light hovering above my palm.

Spinning my fingers around, the orb twirls and dances, responding to the movement of my unspoken will. I give the Light a toss, and up floats the orb toward my ceiling. A few flicks of my finger, and the orb moves this way and that, gracefully gliding through the air whichever direction I want it to go. I form another orb and send it free-floating into the air, too, making the twin orbs play tag.

"This is awesome." At least I'm not a total disaster at *something* Luminaut-related. Although, I have no idea what Light orbs are meant to do, despite how cool they look. I check the journal to see if Mariasol gives any indication of the purpose behind my new magic trick, but the entry is over, and she's on to the next topic.

Maybe Nate or Dr. Ormandi would know... although, between the two of them, I don't know who I can trust to tell the truth. Light orbs are meant to protect the multiverse from Darkness, or Light orbs are meant to destroy everyone and everything you love forever. Flip a coin to see which Ormandi is right.

Knock-knock-knock.

The Light grows erratic, nerves kickstarting my heart until it beats hard and fast. The sparkling tendrils that were so ethereal take on the look of live wires, writhing around each other with sharp, pulsating twitches, and the orbs zoom and whiz like untamed comets on a collision course with anything in their path. One of the orbs careens into my fan and knocks the blade, marring it black, before the other ricochets into my jewelry box on my desk. Exploded beads, destroyed bracelets, and earrings tarnished and marred by Light fly everywhere.

Remain calm, almost emotionless. That's what Mariasol said. Kinda get it now, Mariasol.

My eyes dart to Nemo, assessing his ability to remain in robot mode with a plethora of new distractions surrounding him. He's still.

"Who's there?" I call to my door.

"It's just me," a familiar voice says from the other side.

Will. Whew. The anxious hunch works itself out of my shoulders, and the Light calms, becoming gently glowing, hovering orbs once more. I recall them back into my hands and turn to Nemo. "You can relax, buddy. It's safe."

Nemo rushes the door the moment Will opens it, and my friend scoops my robot up in his arms. "Hey, little dude!" Will greets Nemo, giving him a toss. Nemo whirs his wheels with glee. "Were you being good, or being a pest?"

"I had him in robot mode about an hour before you came." I hop off my bed, taking the bag of school supplies Will's carrying on his arm.

"That's great!" Will pats Nemo's head. "I'm proud of you. So much better than that time we took you to Starbucks and the barista thought you were a cat stuffed in a handbag."

"I don't think anything could be worse than that disaster," I say with a laugh. "Thanks for bringing the supplies."

"No problem." Will lets Nemo loose on the floor, and my

robot climbs the bedpost in a flash, rooting through the bag of pencils, notebooks, binders, and pens.

"Robot mode," I command. Nemo radiates frustration, but becomes stationary.

"Wow, Callie, he's really getting good," Will observes, clearly impressed.

"He's improving." I'll give my robot that small credit. "But today we're doing the Locker Test, and that's a big one."

"It'll be fine." Will likes to feign optimism about Nemo's ability to hold it together, but he's usually wrong. "And if it's not, we'll just have to spend more time together working on training."

He puts his arm around my shoulder and smiles the boy-likes-girl smile that makes my stomach burst with butterflies when it's Nate, but swim with nausea when it's Will. I mean, *it's Will.* Just, no.

I slip away from his grasp and move for my closet, retrieving the makeshift locker Will and I constructed out of discarded Amazon boxes. Inside go a few notebooks, some pencils, a binder, and pens from the bag Will brought.

"Hey, what happened to your fan and your jewelry?" Will asks, easing himself onto the floor to survey the damage caused by my Light.

"Luminaut stuff," is my vague reply. I don't really want to talk about how out of control my Light became after only a teensy flare of nerves. It gives me a bad feeling that Nate might be the Ormandi telling the truth: that Light can be destructive. Dangerous, even.

"Did your glowing hands do all that?" Will frowns, his gaze lingering on the black streak smearing my fan blade. Thanks for reiterating my worries with your face, Will.

"I'm not really interested in talking about it." So take a hint and drop the questions.

Will does the opposite of take a hint. He reaches for my hands instead, holding them tight in his own. "That's some pretty serious damage. You can tell me what happened. I can help you fix it."

I extricate myself as fast as I possibly can. "I don't need you to fix it. I'm just—learning." I swear, if one more teenage boy offers to fix my problems for me, I'm going to blow a gasket, no matter how good their intentions. And if Will touches my hands again, he's going to find himself slapped with these same hands.

I scoop my ruined jewelry into a drawer, and pray nobody notices my fan before I can attempt to wipe the black mark off the blade. In the meantime, I've got robot training. Locker Test time. A snap of my fingers gets Nemo's attention, the signal that he can break robot mode.

"Okay, buddy," I announce. "Hold robot mode for at least fifteen minutes in there, and we'll let you destroy something. Deal?"

Nemo plops onto the floor, wheeling up to the box to inspect it. A tilt of his head back and forth as he takes in the duct tape on the sides, the floppy door, and the cramped inside before he shakes it no vehemently.

"Come on, you're going to have to be in a metal box for hours the day of my final," I argue. "Cardboard is not that bad."

If Nemo had a nose, he'd stick it high in the air. He wheels away with what can only be described as a robot-huff.

"Come on, Nemo." Will rips a page from one of the notebooks and crumples it into a ball. Nemo perks at the sound, wheeling up to Will with palpable eagerness and toddler-like greed. "If you go in the box, you can have this."

Will tosses the paper ball into the box, and Nemo whizzes in after it. Quick as a flash, I close the cardboard "door" and secure it with duct tape. "Nice move," I congratulate my friend. "Why didn't I think of that?"

"My mom's owned small, yappy dogs my whole life," Will says with a shrug. "I know how to get them to do what I want."

Hmm. Interesting. Mom is allergic to dogs and cats, so we've never had pets. Little did I suspect it would put me at a disadvantage when training a baby mech with an attitude. "Well, I'm glad you're around to try all the tricks I don't know."

"I'm always glad to help you." Will's voice goes all soft and boyfriend-ish, and his eyes widen a little when he smiles, leaning in close to my face for some strange reason.

Go sit at a respectable best-friend distance, Will.

Knock. "Cal!"

Perfect timing, Dad. "What is it?"

Dad pokes his head in. "I need your help at the marina. Open season is winding down, and the boat needs to be cleaned up."

"I'm doing robotics stuff for my final."

"I don't see a robot, I just see Will," Dad counters, nodding his chin Will's direction.

"Hi, Mr. James." Will has known Dad for eleven years and still won't call him Ted.

"The robot is in the box." I gesture to the simulation locker. "We're, um, practicing getting him to break it open for, uh, final presentation day."

"Jase is at soccer, Ryan is at science olympiad, and Tyler is at viola lessons, so you're it," Dad says. Did he miss the part where I told I was working on a class project? *Take school seriously and get good grades, but also, your classes aren't as important as dropping everything to help me clean up the boat.* Way to be super clear with your messaging, Dad.

"I'll pick up here, Callie, don't worry," Will assures me.

"Thanks, Will." I throw a hoodie over my tee shirt and step into flip-flops, grab my bag, and follow Dad out the front to his truck. Before I've even buckled up, my cell buzzes with a text.

He shredded everything, even the pens.
I didn't know you could shred pens. The
box is wrecked. Locker Test is a fail.

Crap-and-a-half, Nemo.

Dad and I drive in awkward silence for a while, him concentrating on the weekend tourist traffic clogging up the highway, me slouching in the passenger side with my arms crossed.

"I'm glad you were free to help me on the boat," Dad attempts to converse.

I wasn't free, Dad, I was training my mech to be a normal robot so I don't get expelled for cheating after my robotics final. But I guess I'm only busy if it's something that's important to Dad.

"I feel like I hardly see you anymore," Dad goes on. "You're always gone nowadays. Not home from sports until late, and then shut up in your room with homework on the weekends. Or, surfing."

"You wanted me to be involved." Suddenly Dad's gonna forget all the years he spent harping on me to get my act together and try at *something* just because he misses my face glued to my phone at home? Fat chance.

"I'm happy you're making an effort this year." Dad smiles. We pull into the marina complex, driving onto the dock. "Mom and I both are."

"Uh-huh. Cool."

A frustrated wrinkle creases Dad's nose. "Even if you're a bit distracted nowadays."

Can he blame me for being distracted? I've been trying to fix a fifty-foot-tall, ancient, corroded, rusty bucket of bolts—otherwise called a World Diver—with a hand torch. Oh, and emotionally process a massive crush on a literal ghost, come to terms with a big, scary, out-of-my-league destiny, and train my robot-dog-cat to be a normal robot. And now, Will might have a crush on me, too.

"Are you still getting all As?" Dad parks next to his boat, killing the engine.

A swift nod. "I have a B in US History, but I think I can bring it up."

I might have an F in robotics if Nemo can't behave himself for my final. But Dad has no idea that Nemo is sentient, just like he doesn't know about Nate's ghost, my Light powers, or my visits to Dr. Ormandi and Diver. As far as I'm concerned, it can stay that way. My family would *so* not understand anything about my current situation — well, even less than they typically understand what's going on with me.

Dad and I hop out of the truck, and he sets up the gangplank down to the boat deck. "See what happens when you put in the least amount of effort?"

Which in Dad-speak means, 'that C-average crap you pulled the last two years was your own lazy fault.' One slip up, one low grade, and I'll be back in the doghouse.

"Uh-huh." It's the most noncommittal agreement I can muster.

Dad flashes a broad grin under his cap and sunglasses. "If you keep this up, you can write your ticket to any college you like."

College. *Ugh.* Dad can't spend fifteen minutes in my company without bringing up my grades and college. How about reconnecting all the worlds in the multiverse, Dad? Would what make you just as proud as me getting into college?

Dad starts to root through the fishing gear in the boat's supply cabinet, so I pitch in, organizing lures in tackle boxes while he sorts through all the different types of lines and rods. After a minute, he pokes his head out of the closet.

"Can you head up to the dock shop and get a few things for me?"

"The shoppette or the marina supply store?" There's a small snack shop next to a huge marina retailer at the far end of the dock. It's never a good idea to confuse the two. Fish food can mean two very different things, depending on the shop: ice cream, or bloodworms and sardines.

"Marina supply," Dad clarifies. "I need some rust remover and buffing cloths, three more five-gallon buckets, and two new lifejackets. Can you handle all that?"

"Yeah, sure." Not a hard list. Mom has forgotten her entire grocery list before, and I've helped her get a week's worth of basics without forgetting much.

Dad hands me his credit card. "Tell Gus to put it on my tab."

"Got it." I ramble across the gangplank and head for the shop.

Gus—the store manager, according to his name tag—sits behind the counter at the front of the store when the bell dings, announcing my entrance. He glances at me with a puzzled frown. Teenage girls strolling in on a random Saturday must not be a common sight.

"Can I help you?" he asks.

"I can find what I need, thanks." I've got a perfect sense of direction. Didn't you know, Gus? I'm a Luminaut. I always find what I set out to look for. It's because I have magical Light superpowers.

I check the aisle markers, gather the supplies Dad needs, and head back to the counter quick as a flash so Gus can ring me up.

"Name on the account," he drones. I hand him Dad's credit card.

"Ted James."

Gus glances up and down my frame, searching for even a slight resemblance to Dad. He won't find any. All of my siblings favor Mom except for Ryan, who looks just like Dad. Medieros genes for the win—although, Dad says I'm the exact same height and build as my Grammy Jean. Mom's side is petite and curvy. I'm lanky, lean, and taller than average.

"You're really Ted's kid?" Rude, Gus. He doesn't even bother to hide his surprise when I nod.

"One of five." Gus looks even more surprised, if that's possible.

"Five kids, wow," Gus mutters to himself, his eyebrows grazing his receding hairline. He swipes Dad's card and hands it back to me, then cuts the price tags from my items while I take in my surroundings in more detail.

This marina supply store is packed floor to ceiling with anything a fisherman or boating enthusiast could want. Coast Guard requirements like oars, ropes, life jackets, and fire extinguishers are nestled beside fishing rods, lines, and bait, as well as boat repair and maintenance supplies—it's more stocked than a private fishing pond.

Hmm... boat repair and maintenance... Diver is kind of like a boat. I mean, he's made of metal. And he's embarrassingly busted, thanks to slamming into a dirt wall at full speed...

"We also need a welder. Do you have one we can rent?"

Gus sets his scissors aside and gives me a skeptical glance. "Ted knows how to weld?"

"Yeah, sure." If 'yeah, sure' secretly means 'no, my dad can't weld, but it's not for him.'

Gus makes a clicking noise with his tongue like he doesn't believe me, but he turns around, pulls up a screen on his computer, and opens a spreadsheet.

"Oxyacetylene or MIG?"

"Oxyacetylene." It's just a bigger version of my hand torch, right?

"It's checked out until the end of the day," Gus informs me. "He can come get it tomorrow."

"That's fine." Perfect, actually. Tomorrow is Sunday, and Sunday is my day to work on Diver. Plus, I won't have to explain to Dad why I snuck a couple huge fuel tanks into the back of his truck while I was supposed to be buying him buckets and lifejackets. Win-win.

"We open at eleven on Sunday," Gus goes on. "And it'll be a hundred dollar deposit. Card only."

"A hundred bucks?" I hurriedly scrape my jaw off the floor. Dad's going to notice a one-hundred dollar charge on his card that he didn't make. I planned to pay for the rental with my saved up money from serving at Mom's weddings. My cover will be totally blown. "Can't he pay cash?"

"The deposit reserves the welder and covers any damage it accrues when it's in his possession," Gus explains. "He can pay the rental fee any way he likes, and the deposit will go back on the card once the welder gets checked in."

I conceal my sigh of relief. "Sweet. I'll come get it tomorrow morning."

Gus shoots me a stern look. "Only adults over eighteen are allowed to rent the welder."

"It's for my dad," I argue. Gus is unmoved.

"Then he can pick it up."

"He's going to be busy working on the boat all day."

"On his lunch break."

"But I'm eighteen."

Gus seems to believe it even less than he believed the one about Dad knowing how to weld. Please, Gus, don't make me use my Persuasion powers on you. Just go along with it.

"You're eighteen." He snorts incredulously. "Let me see some ID."

"I left my wallet in my backpack, and my backpack is on my dad's boat," I counter. "Next time you see him, ask him if one of his kids is eighteen. He'll tell you."

True, Jase is the one who's eighteen, not me. But this Gus guy doesn't need to be bothered with minor details. He gives me one more look over, like maybe I'm the type that's older than I appear — or eighteen-year-olds look exceptionally young these days — and shrugs.

"Whatever. Ted's an honest guy." He enters Dad's information on the spreadsheet for the welder rental. "How long does he need it?"

"A week or two," I estimate.

"I'll put him down for two weeks." Gus clickety-clacks on the keyboard. "He can return things early. No penalty." Gus finishes up on the computer, and I hand him Dad's card for the deposit. "Is his boat pretty banged up?"

"Just some routine maintenance stuff," I answer. Gus nods and scans the card.

"Lots of guys have been in here getting maintenance supplies." Gus hands me the receipt. "Tomorrow after eleven."

"Tomorrow after eleven," I repeat. "Thanks."

I carry the supplies for Dad out of the shop and down the dock, where Dad waits on the boat. He grins when he sees me.

"Good work, Cal." I hand him the items across the space between the dock and his deck. "And you got the rust remover and buffing cloths?"

"They're in one of the buckets," I answer dutifully.

"Gus didn't give you a hard time, did he?" Dad loads the new lifejackets in the supply closet.

"Nope. Not at all."

"Good." Dad locks up and scales the gangplank to the dock. "That didn't take as much time as I thought it would. Let's pack it up and get some lunch. What do you think? Tacos? Burgers? Fish and chips?"

"All three, I'm starving."

Dad laughs, and we hop in his truck, driving down the highway into the beautiful California sun.

See you tomorrow, secret-and-possibly-illegally-rented welder.

CHAPTER TWENTY

"OH, GREAT."

Not great, actually. Opposite of great. All I can do is stare at the welder in dismay. Gus left me at the back of the marina supply store after I assured him up, down, and sideways I didn't need help getting the welder loaded into the back of my car.

Except, I've got no clue how I'm actually going to load the welder in the back of my car. It's *way* bigger than I thought it would be. The dolly alone would take up my entire trunk, not to mention the fuel tanks. And my Camry is not exactly the epitome of cargo space.

"Okay, Callie, you can do this."

I'll start with the fuel tanks first. I pop the trunk and heave them inside. As I'm squeezing the tanks between all the empty soda bottles, fast food bags, dirty gym clothes, and old surf wax canisters Jase and I keep in the back, I decide one of us needs to be semi-clean and organized. The tanks look like a couple sausages stuffed into a corset, but, at last, they're in.

"Finally." I push the trunk down. It won't close.

A low growl emits from my throat as I try again. It still won't click shut.

Desperate times call for desperate measures, and my car

already has half a dozen sizable dents, so what's another, right? I hop onto the trunk and jump on it with my full weight. There's a very satisfying click this time.

"Time for the dolly." Which is also huge.

Backseat is too narrow. Fantastic. Will has an SUV, maybe I should text him. He's been helping with Nemo and I know he wouldn't mind helping with this, too. But a part of me doesn't want to give up so easily.

"No, Callie, get this done," I mutter to myself. Texting Will is a last resort. Wear the Luminaut pants. Get the dolly in the Camry.

I lower the front passenger seat and push and shove until, at last, the dolly is inside my car.

"Finally, geez!" I dust my hands on my jeans, pretty pleased with myself, then take my seat on the driver side and shut the door.

Click-thump.

The trunk pops open.

This is going to be a very long day.

I'm pretty sure Dr. Ormandi hears me heaving, grunting, and dragging the welder up the sidewalk to his house well before I approach his door. Come to think of it, his entire block can probably hear all the ugly, labored noises spewing from my mouth. Sure enough, the old man darts onto his front step with a book in his hand and looks up and down the street, wearing the world's most perplexed frown.

"Callie?" Dr. Ormandi catches sight of me and hustles up the block with surprising speed for a man his age. "What are you doing? What is this thing? You're about to give yourself a hernia."

"It's not my fault you live by the stupid hilly cliffs," I retort through gritted teeth.

"Let me help you." Dr. Ormandi shoves the book under his arm and moves around to push the dolly while I pull.

I shake my head. "No way, you're, like, ninety-something."

Dr. Ormandi straightens, glaring. "I am not a day over seventy-nine, thank you very much."

"Either way, if I throw my back out, I'll be fine by Tuesday," I counter. "You'll take months to recover."

Dr. Ormandi's in the middle of opening his mouth to make some snappy retort when a car drives by. He seems to know the occupants, because he waves. Dr. Ormandi knows real, actual people? This is news.

The immaculate car pulls into the house next door, and a man and woman in their sixties step out. A gaudy, Hawaiian print scarf is tied around the woman's neck, and she wears a bejeweled ring on each finger of her left hand. In her arms cowers a shaking little dog in a pink sweater, one I'm pretty sure Nemo could beat up in a fight. The man, by contrast, is entirely square-shaped, wearing a gray driving cap over his gray hair, and a gray jacket and trousers. He wipes a tiny smudge from the hood of the car with his index finger, inspecting the contents with a disapproving scowl. They look at Dr. Ormandi, and then at me.

"Afternoon, Rick," the woman calls.

Rick? Dr. Ormandi is *so* not a Rick. I bite my tongue to keep from cackling.

"Hello, Barb," Dr. Ormandi replies, forcing a tight-lipped smile.

"You got company, Rick?" The square, gray man shoots a suspicious look my way.

"My great-niece," Dr. Ormandi lies. Good thinking. Old man, unknown teenage girl, industrial equipment for no apparent reason... not a good look. "Her family just moved to town, and she's taken pity on an elderly uncle."

"Why's she dragging a welder up the block?" the man continues.

"My oceanography interests, nothing I want to bore you with." Dr. Ormandi waves his hand dismissively through the air. "Needless to say, it requires a bit of welding." His eyes dart toward me, and he smirks. "She was nice enough to go pick up my supplies this afternoon and bring them by, seeing as I'm so frail and infirm."

The woman, Barb, laughs. The man grunts and heads into the house, griping about having to buff the car for the third time this week.

"Nice seeing you, Rick." Barb raises her jewel-encrusted hand in farewell. "And it was nice to meet you — well, actually, I didn't catch your name."

"Mary. Jean. Erm, MaryJean." I give the woman my middle name, just in case she knows anybody relevant to my social life. "You can call me MJ."

"MJ, I like that," Barb says to herself, then grins at me. "Nice to meet you, MJ!"

"You, too, Barb." I turn to Dr. Ormandi. "Go hold the door for me, Uncle Rick."

Dr. Ormandi's stare narrows. I'm certain he's going to murder me for calling him 'Uncle Rick,' but he goes and holds his door anyway. I finish hauling the welder up the step and through the threshold, and Dr. Ormandi shuts the door firmly.

"Rick? Is she for real?" Laughter I've been holding back since the syrupy woman and her microscopic dog stepped out of the car tears from my lips. Dr. Ormandi folds his arms, nonplussed, waiting until my giggle-fit subsides.

"Are you finished?" He raises a brow.

"I think so," I reply. "But that's going to be funny for a solid week." A pause settles between us while I wipe tears of mirth from my eyes. "I didn't know you knew your neighbors."

"Why wouldn't I know them?" Dr. Ormandi's unamused scowl deepens.

"Aren't you a hermit?"

"Of course not!" The old man's face tightens, indignation and peevish anger pressing his mouth into a hard line. "I am intro-verted, and something of a reclusive homebody, but I go on a walk every morning for at least two miles down the cliffs, to the beach, and back, during which I go bird watching with Father Gabe Escobar — although, he prefers the term ornithologist. I also frequent the library. Carla Espinoza, the librarian, is a good friend."

"Yikes, don't bite my head off!" I hold up my hands. "I've just never seen you leave your house, and your car doesn't look like it's been driven in twenty years. Plus you said you get your groceries delivered, so…"

"The station wagon in the carport was Nate's. I don't care for driving." Dr. Ormandi places the book he's been carrying on his bookshelf. "I was born and raised in San Francisco. I took public transportation almost exclusively until I received my Ph.D. and moved down here, and even then preferred to walk or bike. That doesn't make me a hermit."

"Okay, point taken," I concede. "I won't make any more assumptions about you."

"Actually, I believe I saw you at the library once," Dr. Ormandi admits. "You were looking for reference books on oceanography, correct? I thought I recognized your face when you showed up on my doorstep."

"Yeah, that was me…" The old guy in the library wearing the sunglasses and ball cap was Dr. Ormandi? Who'd have thought?

"That's where I found your book. And then... you know the rest."

A wry grin tugs the corners of his mouth. "Are you suggesting this is all my fault?"

"A thousand percent all your fault." I lug the welder across the living room into the kitchen, depositing it by the basement door. "I've got to go back for the face mask and gloves. I'll just be a minute."

"You never answered my question about why you've brought a sixty pound welder into my home," Dr. Ormandi reminds me.

"Isn't it obvious? To fix Diver."

As I stare down the staircase into the darkness of the basement, I want to cry. It required a feat of strength just to get the fuel tanks out of my car and into Dr. Ormandi's house. Maneuvering them down these rickety, narrow stairs will prove nothing short of impossible. Why did I think this was a good idea?

Okay, Callie, focus. The best way to do this is get the whole contraption down to the initial landing, and then... regroup. I breathe deep, steeling myself, and heave the tanks on the dolly down the first step. *Thud.* Second step. *Thud.*

"Please don't break my stairs," Dr. Ormandi calls.

"You're worried about your stairs?" *Thud.* "I'm going to break myself!"

"Oh, you'll be fine. You've assured me whatever injuries you suffer will be miraculously healed by Tuesday."

Dr. Ormandi has picked a crappy time to be sassy.

I thud down the rest of the flight to the landing. The next set of stairs are the rickety metal switchbacks, and there is a very high likelihood of me losing my balance and breaking my neck, or being crushed by the weight of the welding tanks. There's no way I'm recovering from that by Tuesday.

"What am I going to do?"

Diver reacts to the sound of my voice. His eyes spring to life, and he cranes his neck to see me. His familiar contentment and excitement float through the emptiness of the lab, settling inside the Light under my heart. I look across the basement, meeting his glowing eyes.

"Hi, Diver."

A faint spark shines across the cavernous dark, calling out to me. I close my eyes, letting it wrap itself around my mind and heart. It beats through my veins, slowly at first, but then quicker, more urgent.

Diver, come to me.

Diver rises awkwardly, almost toppling over when he tries to put any weight on his mangled knee. He limps badly, dragging his leg behind him, but he obeys. With a groan and a crunch, he comes to a stop before me, expectant.

Yes, Luminaut.

The tiny spark becomes a glowing warmth, an ember coal catching fire. I face Diver head on, more confident than I've ever felt.

Diver, I need help. Take this equipment. Put it on the ground.

Yes, Luminaut.

Diver holds his palm level with the landing. I easily push the welder through the metal rails onto Diver's hand. He places the welder gently on the floor and straightens himself, awaiting my next request.

"Wait right here." I turn to climb the stairs. "I'll be back."

Yes, Luminaut.

Racing up the stairs, I grab the torch gun, hookups, face mask, and gloves from the living room, then race back through the kitchen. Dr. Ormandi is rinsing a teacup in the sink, but lifts his head when I dash to and fro.

"That was fast," he observes. "How did you —"

"Can't talk, bye!" I call over my shoulder, already down the first two steps. A few more hops and I reach the landing.

"Okay, Diver," I square my shoulders. "Take me down. Please."

Yes, Luminaut.

Diver's hand stops before the landing one more time, my own personal elevator. A second later, I'm on the floor of Dr. Ormandi's basement.

"So much faster than taking those stairs." I grin. "Nice work, Diver." I hold my hand up for a high-five, but Diver simply stares.

We do not understand, Luminaut.

"You don't do high-fives, huh?" Diver shakes his head. "It's okay, I'll teach you later."

"Callie? How did you manage the stairs with that heavy equipment so quickly? And without crushing every bone in your body?" Dr. Ormandi appears on the landing high above me.

"The Diver and I are totally mind-melded now." I turn to my robot. "Help the doctor, please."

Yes, Luminaut. Diver holds his hand up for Dr. Ormandi to step onto. The old man wears the world's smuggest grin as he's carefully lowered to the ground.

"So, communicating is going well," he surmises.

"It's not hard once you figure out how to find his inner Light," I answer. "Right, Diver?"

Luminaut is with us. We are with Luminaut. I give Diver's foot a fond pat and begin setting up the welder.

"You never told me you were familiar with metallurgy." Dr. Ormandi watches me hook up the fuel tanks to the torch gun with mild interest.

"Oh, I'm not. I mean, technically."

"Excuse me?" Dr. Ormandi's eyes pop. He stares, a muscle ticking near his eye as the vein in his neck visibly pulses. I can't decide if he wants to bail in case I light his basement on fire, or scream at me.

"What possessed you to bring a piece of industrial equipment into my basement if you have no idea how to use it?!"

He chose the second option.

"Chill out, I've got this." I slip the mask over my face. "I watched, like, thirty YouTube videos on welding last night."

The old man's stare narrows. "What is YouTube?"

"The internet. It's an app on my phone, see?" I hold up the screen for Dr. Ormandi to inspect. "You seriously need to get with twenty-first century technology."

"You think watching videos on the internet makes you a competent welder?!" Dr. Ormandi's voice has risen several octaves too high. I fight the urge to roll my eyes.

"Don't give yourself an aneurysm," I chide. "Isn't that what you like to tell me? Besides, it's not like it's *that* much different than my hand torch."

"You have to have permits for these things!" Dr. Ormandi ignores me, lost in his dad-mode lecture. "You're sixteen! There's no way any shop owner worth their salt would rent a welder to a teenager who has no idea how to use it."

"First of all, the rental is under my dad's name." I adjust the mask and pull on the gloves. "And second, I'm almost seventeen."

"Wonderful." Dr. Ormandi drips sarcasm. "An *almost* seventeen-year-old who learned industrial welding from the internet is responsible for two highly combustible gas tanks and a torch gun."

"It's not like I'm going to burn your lab down." I fire up the torch gun, and a giant blue flame bursts forth, shooting at least three feet through the air. "Okay, so, I'm *probably* not going to burn your lab down. But I really think the odds are in my favor."

Dr. Ormandi pinches the bridge of his nose, so infuriated he could pop. "Never in my life have I been more grateful to be a Fire Manipulator than I am at this moment."

After a couple misfires, which nearly give Dr. Ormandi a heart attack, I figure out the basics of using the welder. I was wrong—it's radically different from my hand torch. But machinery and I have always gotten along, and the videos taught me a bit about troubleshooting (take that, Dr. Ormandi). Soon, I'm cruising. Repairing Diver's knee goes much faster with more firepower, and Diver very helpfully points out which parts need additional adjusting.

"No laboratory fires, see? I told you everything would be fine." I smile triumphantly at Dr. Ormandi when I finish. He's still tensed, shoulders hunched beside his ears like a cat on a fence-post, but relaxes when I shut the gas off and unhook the fuel tanks from the torch.

"How long is this monstrosity going to remain in my basement?" he asks, blunt as a two-by-four.

"Depends." I take off my goggles and mask. "Diver, how's that knee?"

My robot stands, testing the joint. He still limps, and it's unsteady. But he's no longer dragging his leg as dead weight behind him like before.

"One more week. Maybe less. I'll try to come finish the job this week after school, since I know it freaks you out to have a kind-of-illegal welder in your basement."

"Kind of illegal?" Dr. Ormandi's silvery brows touch his hair-line. "I'm fascinated to hear your definition of legality. Please, elaborate."

"Can I listen to the record player while I work?" I change the subject to avoid answering the old man's query. "I saw one in the corner a while ago."

"It was Nate's." Dr. Ormandi's voice constricts around itself until it becomes hollow and tinny.

"Sorry, I didn't know…" I could have guessed, considering how often Nate's talked about his preference for vinyl. But for some reason, I didn't put two and two together.

Dr. Ormandi straightens himself, blinking back the all-too-familiar grief. "You can listen to music, if you can hear it over the noise that hideous welder makes."

"Really?" I search his face. "You don't mind?"

"No, I don't." Dr. Ormandi manages a grin. "Nate used to bring his homework down here and play records while he kept the Diver company. He would appreciate that someone else enjoys his musical tastes. I know I never did."

A plastic crate of vinyl records sits next to the record player, a fine layer of dust gathering over otherwise mint condition albums. Flipping through them is like taking a trip through the world's coolest record store. Nineties classics fly past, the ultimate rock playlist: Bad Religion, Nirvana, Sublime, Weezer, Pixies, Radiohead, and Mazzy Star, followed by indie stuff like Sonic Youth and Pavement. Next come punk albums from the seventies and eighties—The Replacements, Ramones, and Dead Kennedys, all sandwiched between mainstream classics like Bruce Springsteen, Bon Jovi, and U2.

"This is amazing. Nate had some awesome stuff." I'll have to tell him the next time I see him—whenever I see him. Ghosts in real life are remarkably finicky compared to how they're portrayed in movies. Aren't hauntings supposed to be a little more… consistent?

"Some of those belonged to Mariasol," Dr. Ormandi says with a soft grin. "She and Nate used to sing so many songs… Part of me misses music in the house. Although, I never cared for the 'grunge.' I believe that's what Nate called it."

"He's got grunge, punk, alternative, ska… I'm impressed." I

choose The Replacements, place the album on the spindle, and set the needle. "Alex Chilton" echoes and reverberates off the decaying walls, bringing the place to life. I do a little shuffle dance to the beat.

"Let's put the terrifying, reunite-the-multiverse destiny on hold for a sec and talk about practice Diving—taking Diver through a gateway to test my skills, see how he and I work together. I think we're almost ready to try, don't you?" I stop mid-shuffle to gauge Dr. Ormandi's reaction. The old man's face drains of color as he regards me.

"Absolutely not."

I frown. "Why not? Diver and I are synced, plus I've got Earth's Light Core. The Core is the mechanism that opens gateways, isn't it? Besides, Diving doesn't sound that complicated. Mariasol says I've got to stand in the Crow's Nest and put the Light Core in the Prism. Then I use some cheesy catch phrase so Diver knows we're going through the gateway. Bam, he Dives. Done."

"Callie." Dr. Ormandi sighs, rubbing his eyes. "Turn the music off, please."

I switch the record player off, the silence between us instantly tangible.

"You're not ready." Dr. Ormandi's tone allows no room for argument. "You have no idea how to survive on other worlds. If you're lucky, the gateway you open will lead to a friendly world familiar with our Lore. Without luck, you'll land on an inhospitable world where the people and environment are adversarial at best. You could be killed."

"But you're a Seer," I remind the old man. "Can't you find us a gateway that isn't going to lead to a total crapshoot? Isn't that the whole point of a Seer?"

"I could, but I would not be Diving with you." Dr. Ormandi

fixes me with a measured look, one that says I'd be wise to heed him. "The likelihood of you opening the correct gateway without a Seer in the Crow's Nest is slim. These cliffs are rife with gateways. Dozens exist within a half-mile radius alone."

"Why won't you Dive with me?" I cock my head, perplexed. "I get it, you're not *my* Seer, but Diving to another world for an hour or two for experimental purposes is—"

"Diving carries a high likelihood of miscalculation—and, therefore, death. Surviving a Dive with a novice Luminaut at the helm is not likely for a Seer my age." Dr. Ormandi shakes his head firmly—I will not be able to change his mind, no matter what I say.

"I refuse to die in the middle of the unknown, separated forever from my family," he goes on. "I want to live out the remainder of my life on this world before my ashes are scattered at sea, reunited with my wife and son. I will not come with you. If you Dive now, you will be Diving alone."

"Well, if I'm not ready to practice Diving, *when* will I be ready?" I cross my arms over my chest. "When you say I am? When I've scoured the world and maybe, miraculously, found a Seer? Then will I be allowed to make decisions for myself?"

It's clear this is the very last topic Dr. Ormandi wants to talk about—his entire body coils around itself, like a spring ready to burst. I should quit while I'm ahead. Drop it and leave for the day, none the worse for the wear. But I can't stifle my frustration.

"You don't need my approval to do anything, Callie." The old man's tone is as delicately sharp as the blade of a knife. "All I can do is advise what's safe and what's not. Diving is not safe. You need more practice. More training. It takes years in order to—"

"How many years did it take *you*?" I interrupt. "How long before you and Mariasol were Diving?"

"We were academics," Dr. Ormandi answers carefully. "We

spent many years researching gateways and the location of the Earth's Light Core, building a solid foundation of Lore and mythos around modern scientific understanding."

"That doesn't answer my question. *When* did you make your first Dive together?" He doesn't like me pressing, and shifts uncomfortably in his chair, his jaw ticking.

"In truth, we did not," Dr. Ormandi admits at last.

My mouth falls off the hinges, rage filling me to my core. Too bad Persuasion doesn't work on Seers, because I'd make him slap himself senseless. His inner Light burns like the fire he can Manipulate, but I can't touch it, can't break through the barrier separating me from his Light to make him explain himself and his omission. Instead, I clench my fists at my side, shaking with the effort of containing the bomb of fury ticking inside.

"Are you telling me I've been taking life-changing, history-altering advice about Diving from a guy who never left California?" My voice rises closer to a shout with every syllable. "You've been trying to sway my destiny, convince me I'm the Luminaut who will reunite the entire multiverse, and you never made a Dive yourself? Everything you told me could be a lie!"

"It is *not* a lie. We did not have the Light Core. You cannot Dive without a Light Core." Dr. Ormandi's eyes spark with the blackest black lightning. "We researched, and planned, and hunted every corner of the ocean we could, yet we never found it. Mariasol Dove here with the Diver under extreme and unique circumstances. We never dreamed it would take as long as it did to track down Earth's Light." He takes a rattled breath and turns away from me. "When you showed up that day with the Light Core you happened to stumble across in the shallows, it was—"

"It was an insult." I can feel the anger in his soul as clear as my own. "I'm nothing but a blow to Mariasol, and all the decades she spent searching with nothing to show for it. I rendered her life's work meaningless. Go ahead, say it."

Dr. Ormandi's face drains of blood until it is gray, ashen, and drawn. Simmering emotions—nothing I can pinpoint, but everything I can feel—bubble into his eyes all at once. "Mariasol left her world and everything she'd ever known to hunt the Light and restore the multiverse to glory. In that, she failed. But that isn't the part that has hurt me most."

"What is, then?"

"Nate—my only child, the last family I had in this world—died trying to find the Light. I lost my wife and son to the thing you've been so flippantly sarcastic toward since the moment I met you." A grimace of disappointment and sorrow lingers on his downturned lips. "Your Light Core is the source of my greatest heartbreak twice over, and yet you stuffed it in your closet and tried to throw it away like a plaything you've outgrown. Now you want to Dive into the unknown as though it's little more than an afternoon excursion before dinner? People I loved more than anything have died for this, yet you *still* treat every word, every piece of advice with indifference."

Uncomfortable, cagey, stunned silence follows. Dr. Ormandi won't look at me. I don't want to look at him. I can't decide if I'm immensely guilty and sorry for all the things I've done wrong, or if I'm furious with him for dismissing me, for belittling me, for treating me as though I'm nothing more than an indignity whose presence he's been forced to bear.

I'm an affront to his losses—to his wife, his son, and their sacrifices for the Light. He tolerated me because I gave him hope, maybe. But that hope was vague and faint, and now, almost thoroughly broken.

"I'll see you later, Dr. Ormandi."

I run up the stairs and through the house—as far away from him as possible.

As I cross the threshold to the front step, a pair of black eyes watches me. But when I spin around, no one is there. Just a ghostly shadow resting over the house, materializing like a tangible, swirling mist. If I didn't know any better, I'd swear the penetrating black eyes of the nameless phantom were following me as I dash away down the street. At long last I reach my car, and the cold, spidery tentacles grasping at my shoulders fade away.

"Nate?" I call his name into nothingness. "Are you there?"

No answer.

"Are you messing with me? Trying to spook me again? I'll pretend to be scared, I promise."

Silence.

"Please, Nate." I close my eyes, awash with longing—for what, I can't find words. I only know one thing for certain: a plea I whisper, hoping he'll hear. "You said you'd come when I needed you. I need you now."

But Nate doesn't come. All is quiet. Still. Just a trace of swirling shadow over the old man's house, one that makes the back of my neck itch with an impending sense of dread I can't quite place.

"I swear, Ormandi males make me want to pull my hair out," I mutter to myself, swallowing a lump of disappointment, shame, and defeat. "Forget both of you."

I slam my foot to the gas, and peel away.

CHAPTER
TWENTY-ONE

"OKAY. This is it. Deep breaths. You can do this."

"What are you muttering about?"

Jase shoots me a look from the driver's side as we pull into the school parking lot. I clutched my backpack tight against my chest, hoping to comfort myself—and keep Nemo from squirming. Mostly the latter.

"Today is my robotics final," I tell my brother. "Well, the practical portion. The applied exam is next week."

The day has come. *The* day. The day all my hard work training Nemo will pay off, or blow up in my face. There are only two possible outcomes: either I succeed in passing Nemo off as a normal robot, or end up with an F in robotics and a suspension (or expulsion, let's be honest) for cheating. So, no pressure at all. None whatsoever.

"Oh, yeah, you gotta do the robot thing in the parking lot." Jase puts the car in park. "Well, good luck, I guess. Don't screw up."

"You're bursting with the power of encouragement," I snark. Jase shoulders his backpack and shuts the door, leaving me alone in the car.

The second the driver-side door slams, Nemo begins punching at my backpack, growling to be let out. I groan and roll my eyes.

"Hey, knock it off." I poke my backpack. "You can be as irritating as you want after today, but today, you've got to do me a solid. Robot mode."

As of this morning, Nemo is about 75% proficient with robot mode, and can hold still for several hours if there are no distractions. But today is a regular six-and-a-half-hour school day, and Nemo will have to follow every detail of our presentation performance. It's not a practice session with Will and I watching his every move like a hawk. One slip-up and we're doomed.

Nemo punches the backpack one last time, then goes stationary.

Will rushes to my side the second I step out of the car. His brown eyes are as round as a pair of sand dollars in his face, and he rubs his sweaty palms against his shorts.

"Cold sweats already?" I ask with a laugh. "I'm the one with the final, not you."

"Hey, I've got a lot at stake today, too," Will quips as we head for our lockers. "My future career as a robot trainer is riding on your success."

"I just want it all to be over," I confess. "I didn't sleep last night, and I'd have thrown up breakfast if I'd been able to stomach anything."

"We worked hard." Will puts a reassuring hand on my shoulder. "We did the best we could. Besides, Nemo's been doing much better these past few days."

"Much better isn't what I need." I breathe in and out, trying to dislodge the tightly wound knot of nerves wedged in the pit of my stomach. "I need one hundred percent proficiency. I can't afford to fail."

"Nemo will pass, Cal, you'll see." Will gives my shoulder a

squeeze.

"Says the guy who's sweating bullets," I retort.

"It's going to be fine," Will reiterates. "I know it."

I wish I knew it.

Izzy, Emily, and Chase wait by our lockers, chatting amiably. They brighten at the sight of Will and I approaching.

"It's robot day!" Izzy announces, tossing her hands in the air. "The day your robot steals the answer key for the chemistry final and we all get As!"

"Sorry, I didn't quite get that far with programming." Training Nemo to become a ninja test thief wasn't really on my to-do list, either.

"It's okay, next semester," Izzy replies with an easy grin.

"Where is it? Can we see it?" Emily clamors up to me, and I unzip my backpack with shaking hands. Nemo, do *not* fail me.

"Awww!" Izzy and Emily gush as I pull Nemo from my backpack. He's still as a statue, just like I need him to be. I exhale a silent sigh of relief. Next to me, Will does the same.

"Oh my gosh, Callie, it's *the cutest thing ever!*" Izzy squeals, taking Nemo before I can protest. She inspects his claw-hands and neck-motor — which would earn her a pinch and a smack from my robot if Nemo weren't valiantly holding robot mode.

"Look at his little arms! And his beady eyes!" Emily points out Nemo's features. "That's the most adorable robot I've ever seen in my life!"

"This is really cool, Callie," Chase adds, smiling at Nemo as he fiddles with my robot's wheelbase. "You built the whole thing yourself?"

"Yep." With help from a magic Light Core that makes robots come to life.

"Callie is really smart with science and engineering stuff," Izzy informs her boyfriend. "She's going to work for NASA one day."

"That's awesome." Chase returns Nemo to my waiting arms. My robot has never had so many different people hold him in quick succession, and I'm shocked he's not growling and swatting them away. The sooner I hide him, the better.

"When is your final?" Emily asks. "Are spectators allowed?"

The decoy remote control I built for the sake of duping my class goes into my locker next to my history book. "Fourth period. There's an arena set up in the parking lot. Anyone can come watch, you just have to have permission and a note."

"That would be so cool." Izzy puts her English notebook into her backpack. "I have math fourth period, and you know I'll do pretty much anything to get out of math. Ms. Jimenez probably won't let me, though."

"I'll be there for sure," Will promises. I smile.

"I know."

The bell for first period rings, and I slip Nemo into my locker. Izzy and Chase wander off to take every last second saying goodbye, and Emily and Will rush to put their things away before heading to the humanities wing. The second he's in my dark, crammed locker, Nemo breaks robot mode, whipping his head around. His eyes blink greedily at all the loose papers and notebooks, and he goes right for an old volleyball schedule, shredding the corner into bits.

"Nemo!" I hiss. "Stop it! Put that down! Robot mode!"

Nemo growls angrily, batting my hand away when I try to snatch the schedule. I narrow my eyes and point my finger at him.

"Don't you growl at me, mister, or you're gonna get it!" My gosh, I sound just like Mom.

"Callie?" Emily, Izzy, and Will are waiting for me to walk with them to English. My girlfriends probably wonder why I've got my head poked into my locker whilst tiny bits of paper fall to the ground like snowflakes from the open door. Will's drawn face contains nothing but dread.

"Yeah, sorry, I'm coming." I glare at Nemo one last time. "I'm serious. Robot mode."

Nemo growls—a very begrudging, whiny sound—before going still. I slam my locker and join my friends before we're late for English.

There's no way I'm able to concentrate in any of my classes, which is a real bummer because so many of my teachers are reviewing for finals next week. All I can think about is what will happen if Nemo wrecks his performance. What if he spots somebody waving a loose bunch of papers? What if the temptation is too great for him to resist? What if he wheels off and climbs that person's leg to steal the papers? What if that person has a heart attack and dies? Will I be held responsible if my robot is the one who caused the heart attack? Will I be locked up in prison for life? Is manslaughter-by-robot even a thing?

By the time the bell rings ending third period, I can't focus on anything other than how nauseated I am. If I had any food in my stomach, I'd have puked at least twice, but my insides can only gnaw around themselves, hollow and raw. Will practically carries me to my locker to retrieve Nemo, because my legs are too weak and wobbly to function.

"You'll be fine. Everything will be fine."

"I feel like I'm going to my execution," I murmur.

"Nobody's going to kill you if Nemo breaks robot mode and runs amuck," Will promises.

"No, but they'll probably expel me for cheating," I gulp. "My future is over."

"You're going to be a portal-jumping robot pilot, you don't need college," Will teases. I give him a black look.

"Tell that to my mom and dad."

We've arrived at my locker, and Will and I face each other. He grasps my forearm.

"I gotta go. The parking lot demos start at 11:30, right?"

"Yeah, 11:30. We've got to do an oral presentation on our projects first."

The warning bell rings, and Will smiles. "I'll see you then."

Will dashes away, and I open my locker, steeling myself for the worst. Sure enough, a pile of confetti—the remains of my dearly departed chemistry notebook—land at my feet.

"I wasn't going to study that or anything," I grumble at Nemo. Thank goodness I have chemistry with Will and can study his notes. My tiny robot reaches his arms toward me, begging to be freed from my locker, and the bedraggled notebook is instantly forgotten.

"This is it," I tell Nemo, patting his head as he nuzzles my side affectionately. "You've got to do everything I tell you, exactly as I tell you, for an hour. Can you handle it?"

Nemo looks up at me and blinks, nodding his head. Who am I kidding? This is as much about my ability to train a mech as it is Nemo's ability to learn and follow directions. It's a big test of both of our skills.

"Let's do this." I give him a squeeze. "Robot mode."

Nemo goes completely quiet, a regular robot in my arms. I swallow the bile threatening to rise into my throat, and march toward my robotics class.

My fellow robot geeks flit around the room, abuzz with excitement when I enter. This is the day we've all been working toward. A bunch of kids gather in the front of the class, showing off their creations to each other before the presentations officially commence, while just as many busy themselves with last minute adjustments and tweaks at their desks—heads bent, screwdrivers twirling furiously.

On a typical day, I love robotics class. Nobody calls me a nerd or a geek here, except as a compliment, and I'm surrounded by peers who share my interest. But not today — today I'm praying a tsunami will come and take out the parking lot in the next twenty minutes.

As inconspicuous as possible, I slip into a desk at the back of the class, stowing Nemo under the seat.

"Okay, nerdlings, simmer down!" my teacher, Mr. Barnes, announces. He adjusts his bowtie and black-rimmed glasses — which he wears without a trace of irony — and flashes a broad smile. "Let's get this show on the road!"

This is it.

"Who wants to go first?" Mr. Barnes scans the room as almost all my classmates shoot their hands sky high. For some reason, his gaze lands on me. Even though I'm trying to squish myself as far into my seat as possible and turn invisible.

"Callie James! Come on down!"

Fan-freaking-tastic.

My mouth is parched, and my heartbeat hammering like a jackhammer in my ears as I shuffle toward the front of the class, holding Nemo tight. My face must betray my nerves, because Mr. Barnes grins and gives me an encouraging thumbs up. He's an awesome teacher, and I really like him. I'm just not his biggest fan at this exact moment.

"This is Nemo." I set my robot on the table at the front of the classroom that's been set up for our oral presentations. "He's a four-wheeled, rover-type, mini-robot. He has functional arms, which are programmed to move up and down independently of one another, and can grasp and lift small objects, carry them a short distance, and deposit them. His neck is mounted with an internal motor which allows him to turn his head in a 360-degree rotation. His wheelbase allows him to move in any direction, and is remotely controlled with a toggle. His eyes are internally mounted LED's and programmed to turn on, off, and blink with a signal from my remote control. Nemo enjoys long walks on the beach, rainbows, and unicorns, and wants to be R2-D2 when he grows up. Thank you."

That draws a laugh from my class, and they erupt in enthusiastic applause. I let loose a huge sigh. Nemo hasn't moved an inch. One potential disaster averted.

"Nice presentation, Callie," Mr. Barnes says. "Very cool robot. I can't wait to see it in action!"

You and me both, Mr. Barnes.

"Okay, next victim—Marco Sandoval!"

I retreat to my seat with Nemo, and Marco takes my place at the presentation table. Once I've got Nemo safely stowed under my seat, I allow myself a brief moment to release some stress. But not all of it. Because while Nemo may not have totally blown it this round, all he had to do was sit still on a table while I talked about him. He didn't have to follow any commands while otherwise staying in robot mode.

Marco proudly talks about his robot's functions, and I'm trying to listen, but a wiggling under my seat makes my blood run cold. I dart my head under the desk only to see Nemo inching a loose paper from my unzipped backpack. I give him a small kick, and he whirls on me with a growl.

"No paper!" I hiss. "Robot mode."

Sometimes I'm glad I never gave Nemo a more expressive face, because I don't want to know the kind of dirty looks he'd give me. Now is definitely one of those times. He just stares at me, his eyes dimming in a way that means he's glaring, then drops the paper and goes still.

"Stupid mech," I mutter. Luckily, my class is enthralled with the presentation, and nobody pays attention to me. I clap as Marco wraps up and returns to his seat, and Mr. Barnes calls out the next student.

A few more presentations fly by, and soon, half my class has taken their turn. Before long, it will be time for us to head out to the parking lot.

The wiggling under my seat starts up. Nemo's claw hands root through my backpack for his paper prize. I give him a little shove with my foot.

"Stop it," I whisper.

Nemo ignores me. He reaches his whole arm and half his body inside to pull the paper free. Narrowing my eyes, I give him a swift kick before ducking my head under the desk.

"For the last time, robot mode!" I threaten through gritted teeth.

"Callie?"

When I look up, Mr. Barnes and literally every single one of my classmates is staring at me. They saw Nemo move. They must have.

"Y-yes?" I stammer.

"Are you alright back there?" Mr. Barnes asks. He sounds a little annoyed, but nobody seems to have noticed Nemo. Whew.

"I'm fine. Sorry. Just, um, a leg spasm."

Mr. Barnes motions for the presenting student to continue, and my class forgets all about me. Nemo and I dodged a bullet—but if he pulls these shenanigans in the parking lot, there will be no place to hide.

As much as I'd like to pause time and go back a solid month to give Nemo more training, I don't have that option. At 11:30 sharp we take our robots to the parking lot to show off their functions in real life.

"Oh, great."

Half the school is gathered around the small arena we've built, buzzing like a swarm of over-excited bees. I had no idea the robotics class presentations were so popular. The principal, vice-principal, and a couple of teachers on prep showed up. Will and Emily are here, and Izzy and Chase, too. I guess they managed to slip through the iron clutches of Ms. Jimenez. They all wave at me, smiling and encouraging me with shouts of "Go, Callie!" and "You've got this!"

Even Jase hangs at the back of the crowd, with his sunglasses covering his face and his arms crossed over his chest like he's too cool to be seen with all the nerds and geeks and obviously only came because I'm his little sister.

I manage a half-hearted wave at my friends and brother, and an even less enthusiastic grin. All I can think of is how badly I want to vomit, or pass out. And, preferably, never wake up.

"Thanks for coming out to our robotics class presentations!" Mr. Barnes announces to the gathered crowd. "I hope you enjoy the hard work my nerdlings have put into their projects this semester. First up, Carter Dixon!"

At least I'm not the first this time. I hang back while Carter steps into the ring, clutching Nemo tightly in my arms. It's a lot easier to keep him in robot mode if I'm holding him. After Carter's presentation, Mr. Barnes calls another student. Not me. Then another. Also not me.

"Callie James! You're up!"

It couldn't be not-me forever, I guess. I gulp hard, even though my throat is completely dry, and trudge on leaden feet into the middle of the arena with Nemo. My friends cheer for me, and Jase manages to clap a couple times.

Will catches my eye and smiles. "It's going to be okay," he mouths. I can only pray he's right.

With a dip of my head toward Nemo, I whisper to him one

last time. "Please, buddy, don't mess this up. I'm counting on you."

Whether Nemo's inner Light sensed my desperation over the noise of the crowd remains to be seen. I set my robot on the ground, pull the decoy remote from my back pocket, and face the gathering of students. *Just keep it together for ten minutes.*

"This is my robot, Nemo, and I'm going to demonstrate all of his programmed functions." My voice shakes like a withered, winter leaf. "Right now, he's in robot mode," I go on. "But using this remote, I can make him go forward—"

I hold my breath, pleading and hoping against all hope that Nemo will remember all his commands. Nemo wheels forward a couple feet, and comes to a halt. The crowd claps. One down.

"He can spin around in a circle." Nemo spins in a circle.

"And wheel backward." Nemo goes backward. Three for three.

"Nemo's eyes are also controlled with a switch on my remote, and they turn on…" Check. "Turn off…" Check. "And blink." Check. The crowd claps again. "He can turn his head left and right." Nemo turns his head left and right. So far so good.

"Nemo's arms are functional, too. He can wave one arm… And then the other arm… and both at the same time." More polite clapping for me and my robot.

Now, the big test. I take a tennis ball from my hoodie pocket, and place it on the far side of the arena. Nemo has performed all the actions I've taught him flawlessly, but losing his cool with the ball has always been his biggest downfall. Will and I have tried for weeks to perfect this trick, and he's only done it once successfully. I close my eyes, willing myself to connect to the pinball of Light in Nemo's scattered mind the way I connect with Diver.

Please, Nemo, please please please…

"Lastly, Nemo can go get the ball I've placed in the arena." Nemo does this. "Pick it up." Nemo obeys. "And bring it to me." Nemo whizzes beautifully across the concrete with the ball in his arms. "Before dropping it at my feet."

Nemo hesitates, but just for a moment. Nobody but me would notice the internal struggle my robot is battling. After the tensest half-second of my life, the ball drops from his arms and lands on my toe.

"Wave goodbye, Nemo!"

Nemo wheels to the edge of the arena, faces the crowd, and waves his arm up and down. The crowd loses it. I'm engulfed in screams, claps, and whistles as I rush toward Nemo and pick him up.

"Thank you, buddy," I whisper. "You were perfect."

Nemo gives me a quick nuzzle before I put him in robot mode. Mr. Barnes beams as he approaches me, and gives me a pat on the shoulder.

"Amazing work, Callie! You've got a future with NASA for sure!"

"Thanks, Mr. Barnes."

My friends rush the arena, and I'm swamped in hugs and congratulations from my girlfriends, and applause from Chase. Jase joins them, too, and throws his arm around my shoulder— briefly, in case somebody sees.

"I knew you wouldn't screw it up," he tells me with a half-grin of approval—Jase's equivalent of showing pride in something other than himself.

"Thanks for coming, Jase." I really mean it, too.

"Yeah, well, don't think this means I'm over you swiping the car on Sundays," Jase replies.

"Pass your Civics final next week and we'll negotiate car rights."

Jase smirks. "Count on it." He turns and saunters away.

I face Will at last, throwing my arms around him in gratitude and relief. He holds onto me, and finally, I can relax. It's over. Nemo and I passed.

"We did it," I tell my best friend.

"I knew you would." Will pulls away, meeting my eyes. "I didn't doubt you for a second."

"I would have failed, if not for you." I give him another huge hug. "Thank you."

Will squeezes me tight, his arms lingering around my waist a bit longer than I would normally be cool with, but I'm so happy I overlook it. Will's been as anxious about today as I have. Maybe he needs a second to gather himself, too.

"Let's celebrate this weekend," Will suggests, finally releasing me. "We deserve a day to surf and pig out." He's totally friend-zone in tone and demeanor, and when I look at him, his smile is easy and bright. I must have imagined the lingering hug.

"Sounds awesome," I agree.

It's the first time I've smiled all day.

CHAPTER
TWENTY-TWO

"I'VE GOT A BAD feeling about this."

A cluster of thunderclouds roll in from the northwest just beyond the cliffs, black as midnight. They settle in over Verona Beach and block the late afternoon sun like an omen of wintry doom. Aggressive gusts of icy wind rip through my hair, beating against the side of my surfboard in my arms and threatening to rip that away, too. Every minute that passes, the potential for downpour grows tenfold. Our little nook along the California coast isn't prone to storms and bad weather, but this year certainly seems to be an exception. First the storm in August, now again today.

"I don't think we should surf in this, Will," I caution my best friend.

"But look how awesome the waves are!" Will gestures toward the enormous, crashing waves, spraying us with foam and mist even in the ankle-deep shallows. I clutch my board close to my side.

"I don't know, it looks dangerous."

I've been so busy these past few weeks I haven't had time to surf at all, and I desperately want to feel the rush of a wave under my board. This is supposed to be my celebration day — Nemo and

I passed our final with flying colors. But there won't be any celebrating if Will and I drown because we made an impulsive decision to surf in treacherous waters. Dad always says a careless sailor is a dead sailor. Same goes for surfers.

"Most of the people we know are out of the water." I sweep my arm across the expanse of abandoned waves. "Even Matt and Mark are heading back to the parking lot."

Will and I wave to our fellow local surfers, who wave in reply. But Will doesn't look deterred.

"This is nothing. You surfed in worse weather last August." Will hefts his board and wades out deeper. "I've still never ridden a wave more than a couple seconds without bailing. Today is my day. I can feel it."

I don't feel it—in fact, I don't feel good at all. A few droplets of water drip down the bridge of my nose and tangle into my hair, and I look skyward. A drop hits my cheek. And another. The gray-black clouds open up, assaulting the beach with a violent torrent of rain to rival the ferocity of the waves just offshore.

"Will!" I cry. My best friend trudges knee-deep in the choppy surf, about to fling himself across his board deck and paddle out. "This isn't safe! I'm not surfing today!"

"Come on!" Will calls over the roaring, thunderous crash of water and wind. "The surf looks great!"

The surf in question does *not* look great. The ocean rises to frightening heights, filled with monstrous waves the darkest shade of blue-black, rolling hills and valleys of fifteen-foot crests before crashing into each other like gnashing teeth. That's it—I'm not going to risk this, not today. I want a surfing session with Will, but I don't want to end up like Nate Ormandi—dead as a doornail at the bottom of the sea, lost forever because of a crappy teenage decision, my only contact with the living world haunting people who've spied on my grave.

"Will, I'm not surfing today." I stick the tail of my board in the muddy silt, propping it at my side. "Let's go get changed, and find some food."

Will glowers, as angry as the waves facing down the impending rainstorm.

"Fine. Whatever." He plods through the water toward me, his expression darker than the sky. "I can't believe you're going to let a little rain and wind scare you off."

It's not just "a little rain and wind." The downpour beats down steadily, and shrieking gales whip through my hair, turning it into wet, stinging coils that shred my cheeks and the nape of my neck.

"Things will blow out soon," I assure him. "We'll come back tomorrow."

Will doesn't reply. He just glares, dragging his board through the sand next to mine, leaving twin trails from the sea to the boardwalk steps. When I look back over my shoulder, the rain has already washed them out.

All the restaurants, hotels, and shops we meander past along the Verona Beach Boardwalk have been decorated to the nines for Christmas. Colorful lights are sprinkled through the evergreen wreaths in windows, and wrapped like spools of twinkling thread around palm trees, reflecting off the silvery pavement. Loudspeakers and radios blare Christmas music from open doors, and lifeguards, locals, and tourists alike walk up and down the Verona Beach Pier, taking in the sights and sounds of the season reflected against the violent sea. Umbrellas pop open, restaurant workers hastily erect tarps over patio dining spaces, and life goes on as usual—as if the perilous ocean wreaking havoc yards away from Christmas lights and 'Jingle Bells' is a minor inconvenience, not a highly disconcerting backdrop for holiday cheer.

"What's Nemo doing to celebrate passing your final?" Will

asks as we maneuver our way through the Christmas season crowds. Even in December, Verona Beach gets a ton of weekend tourists.

"I bought him a couple dozen ten-cent notebooks and about fifty bouncy balls. He's making the world's biggest mess in my room, but he's happy."

"I can only imagine what your room will look like when he's done with it," Will laughs. He's in a better mood since we changed out of our wetsuits and committed to dinner. "What do you want to eat? I'm buying."

"Hmm…" I consider my friend's question. "I'm down for anything. Fish and chips is always good, but I heard the new burrito truck on the corner is amazing."

"Yeah, their guac is supposed to be — "

"MJ! Oh, MJ!"

It takes me a second to realize the woman calling 'MJ' from across the boardwalk is speaking to me. MJ. MaryJean. My middle name. The name I gave Dr. Ormandi's neighbors.

I whip my head around and sure enough, Barb, her shaking little dog, and her square-headed husband stroll casually nearby, carrying the world's most contrasting umbrellas. Pink and purple floral for her, solid gray for him. I'm starting to sense a pattern with these people.

"How are you, MJ?" Barb, the woman, approaches me. "Have you been to see your Uncle Rick lately?"

Nosy much, Barb? "Yeah, last weekend."

Barb looks about ready to impart something gossipy I probably don't want to know, but she notices Will, and smiles her syrupy smile. "Oh, hello, Will!"

Will looks between Barb and me, very confused about why this woman would be calling me MJ and referring to an Uncle Rick I do not have. The only uncle I have is called Manny, Mom's brother, and he lives in Chula Vista. Dad is an only child.

"Um, hi, Mrs. DeLuca," Will says. Guess he doesn't call her Barb. How does he even *know* Barb?

"I didn't know you knew MJ!" Barb's dog shakes so hard in its sweater I feel like it's going to lose consciousness. Maybe you should pay more attention to your pet than to me, Barb.

"Uh—MJ is my friend." Will glances at me, an expression in his eyes says I owe him a huge explanation. "How do you know her?"

"MJ is my neighbor, Rick's, niece," Barb replies, spilling words so rapidly I can hardly keep up. "Such a nice man, but lives alone since his wife and son died. Oh, it was tragic, especially when the son died. His wife had been sick for years, but his son... so young, so unexpected. They say a rogue wave capsized his skiff, and—poor boy!—they could never find his body! Just the old boat, upside down and abandoned. He was a month shy of eighteen, bound for Cal, or the MLB. Star ballplayer, you know. Rick was so proud of that boy. Had to hold the memorial with an empty casket, can you imagine the indignity? Oh, but I'm telling you things you already know, MJ."

Yeah, I know the story of how Nate died—how that's Barb's business to share with two random teenagers is beyond me.

"Barb!" Square-Head barks. "We've got reservations at five."

"Coming!" Barb waves her bejeweled hand, then gives Will and me one last smile. "Goodbye, Will. See you tomorrow at Mass. It was nice to see you, too, MJ!"

"Bye, Mrs. DeLuca." Will waves as Barb joins her gruff, gray husband, and they walk into a nearby restaurant. My best friend faces me, a smile playing about the corners of his mouth.

"So... how do you know Mrs. DeLuca, and why does she think your name is MJ and you have an Uncle Rick?"

"Did you miss the part where Dr. Ormandi is her neighbor?"

I keep my voice down. Will's eyebrows arch and he makes an 'oh' with his mouth.

"I didn't put it together he was the person she was talking about." Will quirks a brow. "Is his name seriously Rick?"

"No, it's Richard," I snort. "I've never heard anybody call him Rick, except for Barb."

"Sounds like something Mrs. DeLuca would come up with." Will rolls his eyes. "I thought Dr. Ormandi was a total hermit?"

"Another false rumor." Will and I make our way toward the burrito truck on the corner. "He takes walks on the beach and goes to the library all the time. He and Father Escobar go bird watching together."

"Who knew?" Will says, slightly stunned. "We could have seen him around town and never known. A boogeyman in plain sight."

"I told you not to call him a boogeyman anymore." I give Will a smack on the arm. "It's rude. Anyway, Barb saw me at Dr. Ormandi's house one day and asked who I was. He said I was a niece, as a cover to get her off my back, and I told her my name was MaryJean." We get in line for the burrito truck, and I turn to face Will. "How do *you* know Barb?"

"Mrs. DeLuca?" Will uses Barb's last name. "She goes to our church and is in Bible studies with my mom. She's really gossipy."

"I picked up on that." Wonderful. Will's family attend St. Francis of Assisi, where Father Escobar is the priest. The degree of separation between Dr. Ormandi's world and my personal life keeps shrinking.

"It's smart you gave her a false name," Will goes on. "And you guys don't go to St. Francis. She probably doesn't know anybody you know."

"I gave her my middle name," I remind Will. "It's not exactly false."

"Not many people know your middle name, besides me and your family," Will counters. "If she starts going off about you, nobody is going to assume you're the MJ she's talking about."

"Not yet, anyway." I kick a pebble back and forth between my feet. "But sooner or later, all this lying and living a double life is going to catch up with me."

"You don't have to lie to me." Will's voice and eyes go strangely soft—like boyfriend soft. He reaches for my hand, the tips of his fingers grazing mine just before I snatch them away and cross my arms over my chest.

"It's cold tonight, huh?" I shiver a little despite the fact I'm wearing my winter jacket. "But at least the rain stopped, and we're next to order. I think I'm gonna have the carne asada with extra guac. What about you?"

Even if the stormy weather killed my surfing session dead on arrival, at least the hype surrounding the new burrito truck is real. I snarf my burrito like I haven't eaten in days, and afterward we hit the corner bakery up the block for a cupcake. I keep my one hand stuffed in my pocket, the other balancing my cupcake as we wander the boardwalk. I don't want any more sneaky hand-holding nonsense from Will this evening.

"You know what we haven't done in forever?" Will asks around a mouthful of coconut cupcake.

"What's that?" I lick some stray cream cheese frosting off my finger.

"Walk the pier."

I make a face. "Yeah, because it's super touristy."

"Come on, it's fun!" Will nudges me with his elbow. "Plus, everything's all decorated for Christmas. The Pier Club set up the tree walk."

Will knows I adore Christmas lights and decorations—my birthday is Christmas Eve, so Christmas decor always reminds me birthday cake is imminent. Plus the ocean has calmed a bit since the rain blew out. Less likely to take down part of the pier, anyway.

"Okay, fine," I agree. "Let's pretend to be tourists."

Every year the Verona Beach Pier Restoration Club, one of our local civic organizations, sets up The Wave of Trees on the pier and auctions them off for charity. Before the auction, the public can come 'Ride the Christmas Wave,' which is the Pier Club's cheesy marketing line for walking around and taking pictures. Twelve-foot Christmas trees flank the sides of the well-worn planks, each of them decorated by local businesses. Classic silver and gold, candy canes and sweets, Santa and his reindeer, snowflakes and glittery pinecones, starfish and mermaids, and Verona Beach State regalia grace the branches of the trees, offset by thousands of strands of twinkling lights.

"I'm glad the storm didn't take all the trees out to sea," Will observes, watching the Pier Club members remove protective tarps and pick up stray ornaments blown off by the wind.

"We used to walk Wave of Trees every year when I was a kid." I reminisce on less complicated times, when I wasn't balancing my normal teenage existence with two sentient robots and the multiverse fantasy world of Luminauts and Seers—when words like "destiny" and "only hope" weren't thrown in my face as though I've got no choice in any of it.

"My parents never brought me down here. They think this kind of stuff is kitschy." Will finishes his cupcake. "When I have kids, I'm definitely bringing them to Wave of Trees."

"Me, too." I lick the last bits of frosting and red velvet crumbs off my fingers and toss my cupcake wrapper. "I mean, if I'm still in Verona Beach."

"Why wouldn't you be?" Will frowns, tilting his chin.

"Remember the giant robot and Diving to other worlds? The

superpowers? Light magic?" Come on, Will, you've seen my powers for yourself.

Glittering incandescent lights and sparkling trees give way to wide planks surrounded by dark, raging waters as we wander toward the end of the pier—the famous lookout point where tourists like to crowd during whale-watching season. But there are no whales to watch this time of year, and Will and I are the only people out this far. All alone, except for water below, and creeping shadows overhead.

"Well, yeah, I get the questing thing. But I mean, you'll come back home, right?" Will glances my way. I lean against the worn, weathered railing, willing my body to go even further out toward the sea. Will leans on the rails next to me. "Eventually you're going to hunt Light Cores on other worlds, but that's not for a long time. Right?"

"Not for years, according to Dr. Ormandi." I huff through my nose. Neither of us has mentioned our blow-up fight, but the elephant remains in the room. It's been awkward and tense between us. Luckily, I've been too busy welding to talk.

"That's a relief." Will catches my eye and grins. "I want to keep you close for a while."

Will grasps my hand before I can snatch it away and holds it tight. His eyes stray to my lips, and he leans in, his own parting as he inches closer to mine.

This is *not* happening.

"Will!" I wrench my hand free and leap away from him. "What are you doing?!"

Will blinks hard, giving his head a shake as if to clear it. "I— I thought…"

"Thought what—that I want you to kiss me?" I curl my arms tight around my middle to protect my damaged heart.

Will is my best friend. *Best. Friend.* But this… my best friend would never try to kiss me. Has he forgotten who we are? Wanting to slow dance at Homecoming is one thing. Putting his arm around me or trying to hold my hand crosses a line, but it's still forgivable. But kissing me…

"I should have asked," Will gazes down at his feet awkwardly. My mind reels, breath rattling in my throat, shallow and tight. My ears buzz so loudly I can hardly make out his words.

"Yes. You should have." But please, Will, don't. My head and heart want to bolt, yet my feet are planted in place. Will looks to me, searching for a glimmer of hope.

"Can I kiss you?"

I'd wanted to puke during my final with Nemo, but it takes every ounce of willpower I have not to lose my cupcake and burrito on Will's shoes. Not that Will is vile, because he's not. He's a nice guy, and I know some girls at school think he's really cute, with his mop of surfer hair and big brown eyes. But kissing the boy who's been closer than a brother since I was five goes against every ounce of reason and sense.

Besides, the insidious thought creeps into my brain, *if I'm going to kiss anybody, it's going to be Nate.*

"Absolutely not." My voice trembles when I exhale. "I don't know what I said or did to give you the impression I have those kinds of feelings for you, but I don't. I never have."

Will falls silent, and I can see his heart being torn in two before my eyes. He swallows, his Adam's apple bobbing, but still, he doesn't speak. We're frozen in time, two statues locked in a moment of tense emotion for spectators to dissect and analyze, yet unable to move or speak for ourselves.

"Callie," Will whispers at last. "I've loved you so long."

I shut my eyes. In my heart, I know it. I've always known it. And yet, it was easier to close myself off from it, to pretend everything wasn't changing before my eyes. What I have to say will rip his already broken heart out of his chest. But there can be no lingering questions and doubts. No maybe or what-if.

"I don't love you the way you love me." Tears well in my eyes. "You're my best friend and I *do* love you. But not like that."

"Why?" Will wipes his eyes with the back of his hand, his voice thick and muffled. I can't bear it. "What's wrong with me?"

"Oh, Will." My heart breaks, too, with every tear that slips down my cheek. "Nothing is wrong with you. You're great. Wonderful. You know I care about you. I just can't force myself to feel something I don't."

"Is it some other guy?" Will's tone takes a bitter turn. "Is there somebody else?"

"There's nobody else." Total lie. Because I am startlingly enamored with a literal ghost. Why can't I fall for normal, kind, *living* guys like Will? Why does every good thing my life have to come with a catch? Why can't I just… stop being weird?

All I know is I have no idea what happens now. Where do Will and I go from here? What happens tomorrow? Monday? How about the days, weeks, and months that will follow? Will we heal? *Can* we heal? Or will nothing be the same, no matter how hard we try?

What will happen to my best friend and surfing partner? My confidant? My steady, constant companion, the person I can always count on to come through for me in a scrape? The one who laughs with me, plots with me, and is always a text away?

Will, why did you have to ruin everything?

And why did I have to ruin everything by not loving him back?

Lights begin to flicker all around, and not just the Christmas trees blinking like a strobe—it's every light on the pier. At first, it's faint, almost a slight electrical interference. A couple of laughs float over the crowd, jokes about the Christmas decorations taking too much wattage. But there's a sense of darkness approaching. A sinister presence I've felt before, but only in glimpses. One that makes my shattered heart kickstart in my chest, reminding me I'm still alive, and can very much feel fear.

BOOM

A sound like a subwoofer dropping all the way down, and a deep *zumm* of power loss as all the current is sucked away in an instant. The pier goes black.

A sensation like a fish hook snares the base of my spine, a sharp prick of pain pulling me away from the pier and drawing me down, down, down into the dark, away from my world. Through the invisible gateway into the void, like Alice falling into the rabbit hole—except, this drop into the unknown offers no wonder on the other side.

Miles from where I land, people start to panic. Cries and screams from far away reach my ears. I look all around, but the world above has gone dark. I can barely make out Will's features—faded and blurry, like I'm staring at him through a blackened mirror covered in funereal gauze. He panics, searching for me, but I'm gone, just out of reach.

There are no moon and stars in this land of shadows. No pier. No crowd. No Christmas trees. Just darkness.

"Will?" I can no longer hear him, or feel his presence. I can't feel anything human.

What I do feel is anger. Hate. Cold, calculating fury. Everything moves in slow motion, as though I'm underwater, sinking further and further beneath the surface until I'm gasping for air around constricted breaths. Power and ambition swirl through the air like sparks, and the temptation to reach out and touch them crackles through my veins. I'm caught in the veil once again, stuck between my world and the darkness that possesses me so wholly it's as if the shadows and I are one.

I try to find the familiar warmth of Light in my soul, to burn away the chill of death and decay. But I can't feel it. The Light is shoved down, repressed, dying in this world of darkness.

"Calliope…"

That voice. The one I heard months ago at the cemetery, the day the shadows stole the Light from my world and drew me into their horror. That frighteningly sinister whisper that crawls across my skin like spider venom, sending a chill racing down my spine.

"Who's there?"

Spinning wildly around, I hunt for the source of the voice. I can't find it. It isn't in front of me, behind me, on either side. All I see are wispy, floating strands of snow-white hair surrounding a face. I can see nothing to pinpoint if it might be male or female. The only features I can make out clearly are immense, black-and-red eyes, staring at me in a way that makes me tremble with terror. Like this creature, whatever it is, can and will destroy everything I love and want to protect—my Light included.

Again, the voice speaks, reverberating through my consciousness as if it has wormed its way into my brain. "Hello, Luminaut."

Then, I am yanked back, my feet finding solid ground on the well-worn planks of the Verona Beach pier. But the dark horrors from beyond the portal have followed. A different voice—yet no less petrifying—speaks a malevolent purr into my ear as the darkness takes on the splintered sensation of confusion, despair, and vengeful anger.

"I can see you, Callie…"

From the inky, churning ocean below rise a thousand phantoms, shapeless and yet formed, a fog and yet solid. Untold numbers of tentacles climb the posts of the disembodied, nightmarish pier, emerging from the depths like a sea monster of legend as they threaten to consume me. Terrible, featureless faces of phantoms turn upwards, their jaws gaping, opened wide enough to suck me into the abyss.

I try to scream. No sound comes out.

Black tentacles inch closer and closer, ripping the pier apart. Panic erupts all around. People run and scream, trying to get away from the heaving, trembling pier. I grab Will's arm, forcing him to look at me and not the horrible creatures below.

"Will, go! Now!"

Will and I run through the crowd, pushing and fighting our way to safety. The boardwalk is in sight—just have a few more yards until we're safe, until the horror on the pier is behind us, and we land on solid ground.

Almost there. A few more steps…

As quick as the phantoms came, they disappear. The lights on the Christmas trees and pier posts spark to life, and speakers blare with spirited carols once again. Will and I stop running. The crowd instantly calms. It's as if the darkness, the shaking pier, the phantoms rising from the deep never happened.

Was I imagining everything?

"What was that? Something rocked the end of the pier and took the power out," a man close to me wonders. "A rogue wave, maybe?"

"Whatever it was scared the daylights out of everyone!" another adds.

"It was probably just an earthquake," a woman rationalizes. "This is California, after all."

Will and I turn to each other. His face has gone bone white, and I know mine is identical. Every petrifying second was real.

We bolt to Will's car and lock ourselves inside as the skies open up and rain spills across the windshield.

"What just happened?" Will breathes. Terror fills his eyes when he looks at me. "You know the answer, don't you?"

"I've seen *something* like this before." I gather myself the best

I can. "But not on this scale. Not this powerful."

"What were those—*things* climbing the pier?" Will shudders. "They were going to eat us alive."

"I don't know what they are." It's the truth. But Will only scoffs, shaking his head like he doesn't believe a word.

"It's Luminaut stuff. It has to be." He sounds almost accusatory, as if I was the one who made the phantoms attack the pier. "You disappeared. I couldn't find you. And the second you came back, something said your name. It called to you."

I bury my face in my hands, wanting to cry and scream and bang my fists against the dash. All I can do is shake my head, unable to speak around the trembling.

"Callie, look at me." Will takes my face in his palms and turns me toward him. There is nothing comforting in his touch. "What happened back there could have killed us, and a whole lot of innocent people. Those things… they were coming for *you*. What if this is a warning that something worse is going to happen? You have to put a stop to it. All of it."

Will's right—this did seem like a warning. A small test of power. Whoever—whatever—controls the phantoms was showing off what it could do. And next time, it wouldn't hesitate to finish what it started.

And yet, I don't know how to defeat it.

"I can't." My voice is barely a whisper.

"Can't, or won't?" Will's eyes light with fear and fury as he pleads with me, begs me to see reason. "The next time those things come back, you might not be able to escape. Do you realize what that means?" He sits back, watching me cautiously, as though I'm a brand new human he's never met in his life. "What did those creatures want with you?"

"I don't know."

Don't I know?

"Yes, you do." Will turns away. "You just won't admit it."

Will watches heavy drops of rain streak down the window. He's quiet, and for a moment I fear he's forgotten how to speak. I wish he'd say something—even something as awful as declaring his love for me. But he's silent as the grave.

"I can't do this, Callie." When Will's voice finally cuts the tension between us, he's cold, distant. "I can't help you anymore. I can't be around you. Not if you're going to throw your life away for this Luminaut fantasy." A resigned sigh loosens itself from his pressed lips. "I thought I knew who you were—but I'm starting to wonder if I ever did."

My tongue can't form a reply. All I can do is stare at my hands in my lap and weep.

Will puts the car in gear and drives me home without another word. When he drops me and my surfboard off at the curb, he won't tell me goodbye. He doesn't even look back when he peels away, headlight fading out of sight with stunning finality.

Will and I have become perfect strangers.

CHAPTER
TWENTY-THREE

"WHAT ARE *YOU* DOING HOME? Aren't you supposed to be on a hot date with Will Avila?"

Ryan and Tyler engross and engorge themselves playing video games on the couch, since their normal gaming spot on the floor is occupied by the Christmas tree. They've got no less than three bags of chips, five packets of Skittles, a box of Christmas cookies, and a two liter of soda in the narrow space between them. Ryan dumps the aforementioned candy into his mouth and gives me a quizzical look.

"Shut up, Ryan," I mutter. Ryan's snark is the absolute last thing I want to deal with right now. Can't he see I'm barely holding it together? My arms and legs are shaking so furiously I struggle to stay standing. I'm a mental, physical, and emotional wreck.

"Did he break up with you or something?" Ryan asks around his mouthful of Skittles. He looks me over with a scowl, taking in my disheveled hair, trembling hands, pale skin. A slightly more perceptive response than I'd have gotten from Jase.

"You'd better work it out, I've got big plans for that Mexican beach condo." And Ryan is back.

"Forget the condo, I'd rather have the Porsches," Tyler cuts in.

I flee the scene as Ryan and Tyler debate which Avila amenity they'd rather be able to access at the drop of a hat.

Sobs shake my entire body when I reach my room, and I crumple to the floor in a heap. Nemo immediately drops the remnants of a mangled notebook and rushes toward me, patting my cheek and hair as I quake with tears so overwhelming I can't breathe. My body tries to cough, cry, and puke all at once, and what comes out of my throat is a strangled, gagging dry-heave. I drop Nemo, crawling on my knees over a mound of shredded confetti notebook paper toward the corner. I curl myself into a miserable ball and lean against the wall, trembling so uncontrollably my teeth begin to chatter.

"What's with all the shredded paper?" A much-welcome voice reaches my ears. "Are you taking up decoupage in a major way?"

"Nate!"

Leaping to my feet, I rush for his arms, falling into him as I sob and sob. He pulls me close, holding me until the pain begins to subside, fear and peace mingling together like twin vapors inside my lungs, fighting for control.

"Hey, hey, it's okay." His fingers tangle deep into my hair, and the top of my head slides perfectly under the crook of his chin, my cheek pressed to the spot his heart should beat. "Everything's going to be okay."

"You were right." My voice is thick around the lingering lump in my throat. "Everything is so messed up."

"What happened?" He pulls back, taking in my terror-stricken face.

"My best friend and I almost died tonight. Something attacked us at the pier. It could have killed us. It could have killed everyone." My breath sticks in my lungs, raspy and unsteady. "I don't understand what's happening to me. Even worse, I don't know how to stop it." I squeeze my eyes against a flood of tears threatening to break free.

"Who attacked you?" Nate comes closer, lifting my chin until the tips of our noses brush.

"Tentacle phantoms."

Nate's mouth twitches and he purses his lips, a bright spark of laughter shining in his eyes. A move Dr. Ormandi has pulled on me before.

"You want to laugh, don't you?" I accuse.

"You're going to have to be a little more descriptive than tentacle phantoms, because the mental picture I'm getting, is, well…" He's holding back a major laugh.

"Why do both you and your dad make fun of me when my life is the absolute worst?"

"An Ormandi trait."

Clearly, Nate.

From his hiding spot in the corner, Nemo rushes us, whirling his arms and growling fiercely as he attacks Nate's shoe. Nate looks down at him with a smirk.

"Somebody doesn't like the ghosty-ghost putting the moves on his mom," he observes.

"Nemo, stop." I wipe my eyes and snatch my robot off the ground. He's shaking his head fiercely, blinking wildly in Nate's direction. "I know, he's a spooky old ghost, but it's fine, really." Nemo isn't convinced. He swats at Nate with all his might.

"Knock it off, or you're going in the backpack," I threaten. Nemo is deaf to the warning, snarling at Nate like a rabid Yorkie with a vendetta.

"I'm sorry," I finish zipping Nemo away in my backpack and turn to Nate. "He's not usually like this…" He's *never* been so ill-behaved around Will.

Maybe because Will isn't a ghost who leaves me utterly

bewitched.

"So, tentacle phantoms," Nate motions for me to go on.

"They were swirling black *things*, with horrifying mouths like gaping voids in the middle of their... faces. If you can call whatever that was a face." I shudder. "They were all darkness, hate, anger, and death. And power. There was so much power in them. It would have snuffed every last bit of Light inside me if they'd gotten close enough. My Light would be gone forever."

"This is exactly what I knew would happen." Nate's handsome face falls, and his jaw clenches hard and serious. "Didn't I tell you there were powers that would do whatever they could to steal your Light? You're lucky you're not as dead as me right now."

Bad things happen to Luminauts. Because of Luminauts. My grand destiny is nothing but a curse. I hang my head, sobs threatening to overtake me again.

"These attacks—the phantoms chasing you. This is just the beginning. It's only going to get worse." Nate's proclamation quakes through my petrified insides.

"I know." The whisper is faint on my lips, so soft it barely registers in my ears.

"Please, Callie. Let me take the Light from you." Nate's arms slip around my waist, pulling me into him. "I can protect you from them. I'll be the one they haunt."

"What kind of demon can haunt a ghost?" The thought fills me with as much terror as the feeling of Nate's embrace fills me with eerily cold fire. It's not safe, none of it, and yet... I want it. I want to feel every inch of his strong arms around me, feel his lips finally pressed to mine.

"I'd find out if it would keep you safe." Nate's vow is firm, resolute.

"I won't let you put yourself in danger for me." I give my head a shake. "I don't know if there's such a thing as a second death, but those things would destroy you however they could."

"I'm not in danger from them. I'm in danger from you." Nate cups my face in his frigid palms. "I am completely infatuated with you." His words make my bones ache. "I can't stop thinking about you no matter how hard I try. Fighting it only makes things worse. I know I shouldn't feel this way. You're human, I'm not. Love stories like ours don't have happy endings. But I can't deny how I feel."

A breath flies from my lungs. He catches it, consumes it.

"Please, Callie. Let me save you from the hideous Light, before I lose you to it for good."

For the briefest of moments our eyes meet, a look of understanding passing between us. His eyes are black as moon-less midnight, a shadow of insatiable hunger clouding them. The terrible need filling the space between us scorches through me, until it stops my heart mid-beat.

I am not just going to touch this. I'm going to lose myself in it.

Our lips crash into each other, hands and fingers grasping, twisting, twirling around hair, arms, shoulders, skin. He is strong, powerful, holding my body and parting his lips against mine with a force that walks the line between love and hate. And I rise to meet it, drinking him in with desperation, like an addict far too long denied their drug of choice.

"Give me your Light Core." Nate's whisper is silken, smooth, almost sinister.

He kisses me again, demanding all that I can possibly offer until I'm bled dry, a withered husk of myself lost to his eyes, his smile, his mouth pressed to mine.

This isn't right—love shouldn't feel like losing myself. My mind and my soul scream against my body and heart as I tilt my head, deepening the kiss, falling further away.

Air is thin here, and I'm drowning. Darkness I cannot name but feel within every inch of me swirls around my Light. A few seconds more and it will be extinguished completely, so battered and torn there will be no hope of saving it.

No—this can't go on. I wrench myself away, gasping. A searing pain, like a layer of skin being torn from my flesh, rips through me, and yet, I can breathe again. The Light returns, glowing steadily in my soul.

"Nate, I—no."

"No what?" His eyes narrow as I back further away.

"No. I refuse to give you my Light Core." A rattled breath escapes my constricted chest. "What happens if I give it to you? You'll take it away, wherever you go when you're not here with me. But the Light will be with me, always, because the Light is in me as much as it's in the Core. Nothing can change it."

"It will change, Callie, I promise." Nate reaches for me, grasping my wrist and winding me into his web yet again.

"How can you promise something like that?" I take his face in my hands, holding it firmly in place before he can kiss me again and change my mind. "Do you really want to protect me? Keep me safe? Then help me fight this darkness. Help me figure out what to do with my Light instead of trying to take it from me."

"I don't think you understand." A chill creeps into Nate's voice, ice as hard as a diamond freezing every syllable. "Giving up your Light Core and turning your back on Luminauts is the only way to make this go away."

"It doesn't matter how many Light Cores I have or don't." My hands move over the frosty skin of his cheeks, his neck. "I can't just make my Light go away. Neither can you."

"You have the power to choose the life you want. Destiny isn't something decided for us. It's what we make it. Truth outweighs fate, and the truth is you're in danger. As long as you choose the

Light, you always will be." Nate speaks his slippery words, their irresistible purr snaking into my ears, worming around my brain. I fight hard, swimming against their power.

The urge to encircle him with my arms, to mirror the way he moves to hold me, is so powerful I slip. Just a little. A little is all Nate needs. He kisses me again before trailing his lips across my chin, my jaw, my cheek, making his way toward my ear.

"You want to get rid of it. You're terrified by the Light, the phantoms, your own raw power. You have no clue what kind of damage you could do if you wanted to. How many people you could hurt—or kill." His whisper is a truth I can hardly deny. "You can be safe. You can be free to never worry about your destiny, or Luminauts, or the danger of your powers again. But you have to make your choice, and decide the life you want."

The life I want…

Is *this* what I really want? To get rid of my Light for good? To never again feel that wild rush or power and warmth, to never know what it really is, and what it's for? And is this only what I want right now, in a moment of vulnerability? Am I reacting to adrenaline and fear? Do I really, truly want to walk away and forget everything that's happened since I found the Light Core, and turn my back on what might be my destiny, without knowing the whole truth?

The life I want…

I want to figure out my destiny on my own terms. *That's* the life I want. Not a life stuffing down everything about myself, fighting a battle I can't win trying to make Mom and Dad proud. Not a life hellbent on finishing a quest Dr. Ormandi and Mariasol never could. Not a life worrying whether or not Will can be my best friend if I can't love him back. Not a life without Light that Nate convinced me to give up forever because I was too afraid to find the answers to my questions.

"Nate, I can't. I'm not giving you the Light Core. Don't ask me again."

The pause between us is ominous.

"So, this is your decision." Nate's eyes are blacker than I've ever seen them. "You choose the Light. Luminauts. The destruction and death of countless people. That's the life you want—the destiny you choose."

Nate frees himself from my grasp and steps back, an expression like I've never seen filling the depths of his black eyes: pure and utter disgust mingling with the agony of a deep, horrible wound laid bare. I've betrayed his offer of protection, denied his version of the truth, and become something entirely unknown and loathsome. A creature worthy of revulsion, one who exists to be conquered and destroyed.

Menacing darkness overtakes his expression as he awaits my reply.

I can scarcely gather my reeling thoughts to form words, but somehow, I do. "Yes. This is my decision. I'm going to find my destiny and the truth about Light for myself. Not what you or anybody else says it is."

"You're making the biggest mistake of your life." He turns, giving me one last look of pain and contempt over his shoulder. "Goodbye, Callie."

He disappears from sight as tears appear in my eyes, falling down my face as ferociously as the pounding rain outside my window.

CHAPTER
TWENTY-FOUR

"OH, CALLIE, you're up early."

I didn't sleep, Mom. That's what happens when your best friend ruins a decade-long partnership by falling in love with you, and abandons you after killer black phantoms emerge from the depths to eat your faces. Oh, and then spend the rest of a seriously terrifying evening making out with a ghost before he breaks your heart into a million pieces, too.

"I just felt like getting up."

Mom grins and sets Olivia on the floor, handing my sister a breakfast biscuit before filling a kid-sized cup with milk. Livvy shouts a bright "Thanks, Mommy!" before skipping up to the table to join me, spilling half her milk in the process.

"How about some coffee?" Mom asks.

I've already had a whole pot, Mom.

"Coffee would be great."

Mom fills the carafe with water and takes a bag of beans out of the cabinet. "Did you eat breakfast?"

If I eat I'll puke, Mom. I could have died last night. Will won't ever speak to me again, and Nate's gone for good. How do you expect me to eat?

"No, I didn't. Not yet."

"I'll make you scrambled eggs," Mom says with a smile. "Sound good?"

No, eggs sound horrible.

"Sure, thanks."

Mom whisks some eggs in a bowl, melting a pad of butter in a frying pan on the stove. The smell of it permeates every corner of the kitchen, threatening to gag me. I force my revulsion down my throat.

Olivia abandons her booster seat, holding her arms toward me to be picked up.

"No, Mommy, I feed sissy bwekfist," she says with all the audacious confidence of a three-year-old who has absolutely zero worries.

"Thanks for taking care of me, Livvy." I set her in my lap, and my little sister pretends to feed me her biscuit while I wait for my eggs.

Oh, to be a preschooler again. No stupid teenage boys (living or dead), no major, life-altering decisions to wrestle with, no phantoms trying to kill you. Stay little, Livvy. As long as you can. Trust big sissy on this one.

"You aren't surfing this morning, are you?" Mom asks. I glance out the kitchen window. The sky above our backyard garden is gray, and heavy with clouds. Rain seems inevitable.

Besides, it's not like Will's going to surf with me ever again after last night…

"I wasn't planning on it. Why?"

Mom moves a spatula around the egg pan. "We've got the luncheon at the Chamber of Commerce for the businesses that participated in Wave of Trees."

Oh, right. The Christmas tree lunch. Trees aren't going to be auctioned until next Friday, and the Pier Club always hosts a luncheon to thank the participants the Sunday before. Mom caters it every year.

"I forgot that was today, sorry." Mom brings me a plate of eggs, and Olivia steals a bite before crawling out of my lap. "What time?"

"We need to be there by eleven to start setting up," Mom reminds me. "Service starts at noon. Red sweater, black dress pants, black pumps."

I shovel eggs into my mouth and swallow them before I can register the texture or the taste. "I was going to get coffee with Izzy and Em, but I won't be late," I say, taking my plate to the sink.

Mom pins me with a threatening glare and a wag of her infamous finger. "You'd better not be. This is one of my most important networking opportunities of the year. All the other wedding vendors in the area will be there."

"Yeah, it's a big deal, got it."

"Eleven o'clock *sharp*, Calliope MaryJean James."

My full name seems like overkill.

"Eleven o'clock." I give Mom a quick thumbs up. "I'll be back. It's just coffee."

Coffee, and confronting Dr. Ormandi about the phantoms that have been haunting me since I discovered the Light Core. Oh, and Nate's ghost. Might as well come clean about that, too.

When I arrive at the old man's house, he's not there, but it's not even eight o'clock. He's probably out on his morning walk, and besides, he has no reason to expect me this early. Most teenagers wouldn't dream of waking up before eight on the weekend. Nothing else to do except sit on the front step and wait.

I check for the DeLucas' car in their driveway, just to make sure Barb and Square-Head aren't home. No car, no sign of her garish scarves and jewelry, or her shaking little dog. Does she take her dog to Mass? Wouldn't surprise me. Either way, I don't have to worry she's going to pop up and ask intrusive questions. I let Nemo out to play.

Then, the rain comes. A soft clap of thunder breaks the relative quiet, and a sheet of water unfurls from the sky.

"Nemo!" I call my robot, who's been happily exploring in the flower beds, and zip him away in my backpack. The last thing I need is my little buddy rusting.

But humans don't rust—although we do get soggy. Soon, I'm soaked to the bone. My hair is plastered to my head like a stringy brown blanket, and my hoodie and jeans cling to my skin, leaving me shivering, water-logged, and freezing. I'm debating hiking back up the block to take shelter in my car when I catch sight of Dr. Ormandi coming up the path that meanders down the cliff face to the beach.

"Callie?" Dr. Ormandi whips off his sunglasses. His brow furrows under his beat-up Cal Bears cap, and he rushes toward me with that surprising speed I never expect a man his age to possess. "You're wet as a drowned cat!" He takes off his water-proof windbreaker and drapes it over my shoulders. "Come inside, immediately."

Dr. Ormandi rushes me into his warm, dry house, but my teeth won't stop rattling. He tosses a few logs and some kindling into his wood stove and lights it, giving his wrist a little flick. The tiny spark roars to a full blaze instantly—crackling and popping with delicious warmth.

Fire Manipulation is very useful in certain scenarios.

"Sit," Dr. Ormandi instructs. "I'll make you coffee and find a spare blanket."

The old man disappears down the hallway and returns moments later with a patchwork knitted throw before marching into the kitchen. I wrap the throw around my shoulders, and scoot his coffee table close to the stove, perching on the ledge. Wringing my fingers in and out of each other's grasp, I rub my hands in front of the fire, and comb through my sopping hair. Nemo wants out of my backpack, so I unzip it for him. Even though the canvas got wet, he's relatively dry. At least one of us is.

"May I ask what you're doing at my house so early? Had I known you'd be coming, I'd have left the key for you." Dr. Ormandi hands me a steaming cup of coffee. "How long were you sitting in the rain?"

"A while." I take a sip.

"Given the state of your hair and clothes, that much is obvious." Dr. Ormandi hangs his windbreaker and cap on a hook by the door. "You're very pale. You should go home. The Diver is in a relative state of repair now that the blasted welder is gone, and it won't hinder your training if you don't practice with him today."

"I can't go home." I take another sip of coffee around chattering teeth.

"Why?" Dr. Ormandi sinks into his rocker. He rests his elbows on his knees, leaning forward to search me. "Are you in some kind of trouble?"

"Yes."

I look down at the mug I'm holding. Coffee sloshes over the rim as my hands continue to shake, brown splotches dotting my jeans. Nemo climbs into my lap to comfort me, but it doesn't help. I have no idea how Dr. Ormandi will take this, what he'll say about my deception, but I have to come clean.

"I haven't been honest with you. I haven't told you everything."

Dr. Ormandi frowns and cocks his head. "What do you mean?"

"I've been haunted." My shudder has nothing to do with the cold. "By Nate."

The old man doesn't move. He won't even blink. Not a sound escapes his lips, and for a moment I don't think he's breathing.

At long last, Dr. Ormandi speaks. "What did you say?"

"I've been seeing Nate, as real as you or me," I go on, daring to glance at him. He hasn't moved.

"That is impossible." Dr. Ormandi gives his head a violent shake, as though to clear it of the glimmer of impossible hope my words imply.

"Yeah, I thought so too, trust me," I deadpan. "But hold your horses, I haven't even gotten to the best part."

"Which is?"

"Nate isn't the only thing haunting me." I tremble, visions of phantasmic horror flashing through my mind. "There are these… phantoms. They're so angry, so terrifying and hateful. There's power in them, same as there is power in the Light Core, but this power is all fear, greed, and corruption."

Dr. Ormandi's face draws tight, his skin ashen as he regards me. "How long has all this been going on? When did it first begin?"

I steel myself for his reaction. "Since I visited Nate's grave."

Dr. Ormandi becomes a stone statue in his armchair. "Why did you visit my son's grave?"

"It was before I met you." I turn away, concentrating on the swirling wisps of cream in my half-finished coffee. "After I read your book, trying to figure out what the Light Core really was, I saw your 'about the author' picture, and it mentioned Nate. And then, I found out he'd died."

Dr. Ormandi remains still and motionless, growing more horrified by the second as words tumble from my lips.

"I don't know what came over me, but I had this urge to go to the cemetery and visit his headstone. When I was there, I touched his grave, and I—crossed over for a second. I was trapped in a dark realm with the phantoms, and *something* called my name. After that, the phantoms began following me, and Nate started appearing." I purse my lips, turning my head away. "It was wrong not to tell you. I'm sorry."

Now it's Dr. Ormandi's turn to start shaking. He leans back in his recliner and covers his mouth with his hand, his face paler-than-pale—almost deathly gray.

"How often have they appeared to you since?" he murmurs. "Both my son and the phantoms?"

"I don't know the exact number of times, but it's happened… frequently. Last night was the most terrifying experience I've ever had. I could have died. And it was in public. Around a huge crowd of people."

"Excuse me?" Dr. Ormandi can barely whisper.

"My friend, Will, and I were walking on the pier last night, when all of a sudden, the lights went out." I close my eyes and force myself to recall the memory, even though it's the last thing I want to do. "Everything was dark, full of shadows and dis-embodied—like I was pulled away from Verona Beach into another world where the phantoms live. I saw a creature, a white-haired monster, one that knew I was a Luminaut. And then, I was brought back to our world, and the creature was gone. Instead, I saw phantoms climbing the pier posts like tentacles. Those mouths…. I've never seen mouths like that. All of them gaping open, decaying and putrid and rotten. And they were *hungry*. They could have killed me and my friend. And then—" I choke, hardly able to speak.

"Then what?" I open my eyes, finding Dr. Ormandi's. His are fearful, sharp as a razor blade.

"Whatever, or whoever, controlling the phantoms *said my name*." I tremble uncontrollably. "It knew who I was. It said it could see me."

For a while, all I can hear is the clock ticking in the kitchen—*tick-tock tick-tock* filling the deafening silence until Dr. Ormandi finds his voice. "There are witnesses to this event?"

"My friend, Will, is the only other person who saw the phantoms, but everyone on the pier saw it shaking as they climbed the posts." I pause, sipping coffee to wet my cracked, dry mouth and lips. "When I got home, Nate was there, in my room. He offered to take the Light Core so the phantoms would stop haunting me, but—"

"My son tried to take your Light Core?" Dr. Ormandi's sharply punctuated words come out stiff and pained, yet tainted with shock and more than a trace of fear. "Please, tell me you didn't give it to him."

Why would giving my Light Core to a ghost matter all that much? And yet, I've never seen Dr. Ormandi look more terrified. "No, it's still hidden," I promise.

Definitely leaving out the part where Nate and I made out and had a thing for each other. I don't want to kill poor Dr. Ormandi, and that particular bit of information would give him a heart attack. Besides, it's not like I'm going to see Nate again. He made it clear it's over. Whatever "it" was.

I gain some semblance of control over my body, enough to ease the tremors in my limbs. When I face the old man, he looks as petrified by my revelations as I am.

"Dr. Ormandi, what's happening? Do you know what those phantoms are?"

"You and your Light Core are being hunted by a Shadowmancer." The words chill the blood in my veins as he speaks them.

"I'm going to assume that's something that can kill me." When Dr. Ormandi nods, he confirms my worst fear.

"Yes."

All I can hear, all my brain can process is the sound of rain pattering against the window panes. The rest of me has gone numb with shock and horror.

"For every Luminaut with the power of Light, there is the potential for their equal to exist in Darkness." Dr. Ormandi can't stop shaking. I've never seen his skin so ghostly white—even paler than Nate's. "That equal is a Shadowmancer, beings with the ability to control Darkness—the entities you call 'tentacle phantoms.' They are filled with hate, greed, anger, manipulative to a fault, and deceitful. All the dark forces you felt at the cemetery… that is the life-blood of a Shadowmancer."

"Are they demons?" A real-life demon is not something I want to anger, or face.

"Shadowmancers are human, relatively speaking." Even scared spitless, Dr. Ormandi can channel professor lecture-mode. "They can take human form and walk among us, sowing seeds of discord and fear. A single Shadowmancer will exist for eons, made undead by Darkness, and the phantoms are an extension of a Shadowmancer's emotions and consciousness, craving power however they can attain it. Murder and chaos will do just fine, but what creatures of Darkness desire most is to destroy Light."

"Murder and chaos." Real-life horror movie stuff. Right on.

"They can rip through a living body, reducing the physical remains to ash in a matter of seconds." Dr. Ormandi shudders, horrified. "I've sensed Darkness in my Sight for months now, but it was little more than a vague suspicion. Nothing I wanted to worry you about."

"Nothing you wanted to worry me about?" I straighten, blinking hard, and lean forward, fixing him with my fiercest glare. "A murderous, undead phantom-sorcerer who turns people to literal ash isn't something you 'wanted to worry me about?' I've got a supervillain coming for me, maybe even trying to kill me.

And you don't think that particular tidbit of information is something I should have known, like, *yesterday?!*"

"You stalked my late son at his grave, have been seeing, and — I assume, interacting with him—for months, all while Darkness has been hunting you, and *you* didn't think that was information *I* should have known yesterday?" Dr. Ormandi's eyes flash, and his lip twitches, a barely-contained half-snarl forming.

"Okay, fine." I sit back. "We both omitted critical information, and kept secrets. Let's deal with what we know, now that it's all out in the open: there's a Shadowmancer after me. How do I stop them?"

"Light drives out Darkness," Dr. Ormandi's cryptic answer floats over the pounding rain and crackling fire.

"I have to battle this Shadowmancer and their tentacle phantoms with my Light? Is that what that means?" Shadow sorcerers seem like an awesome enemy for me to contend with. Why not a sea monster, or a killer dinosaur? At least you can torpedo those. "Any clue how I go about doing that? I can barely keep my Light contained within my body half the time. The one time I tried making orbs, I almost destroyed my bedroom. Forget controlling it to the point I could use it to fight off someone trying to kill me."

"I can't answer that question." Dr. Ormandi pinches the bridge of his nose, looking weary. "Neither Mariasol or I faced the Darkness. It was a far-away threat relegated to our Lore, not something imminently attacking us."

"Maybe I should have focused on reading the Lore, then, instead of repairing Diver all those weeks." Hindsight is twenty-twenty, as they say. Except, in this case, hindsight happens to include murder-phantoms.

"Diver…" Dr. Ormandi trails off thoughtfully. "Yes, perhaps the Diver can help…"

"How?" I told my chin.

"Mariasol said the Diver contains memories of all his previous Luminauts," the old man says. "Theoretically, if you access them, you might be able to learn the necessary techniques for fighting Shadowmancers. If the Diver remembers his ancient Luminauts and Seers, he surely remembers their battles with ancient Shadowmancers."

"Ancient Shadowmancers." A horrific thought crosses my mind. "Are all those Shadowmancers still around? Is there an army of undead, eons-old villains trying to kill me? Or are we talking single-serving bad guys?"

"I don't know," Dr. Ormandi replies. I can see no lie, no concealment in his eyes.

I recall the creature in the shadow world, the one with floating white hair. How different that monster felt from the shadow tentacles attacking the pier, like two separate entities working apart. Or, maybe, together.

One evil baddie, or two? Does it even matter in the end?

"I guess I'd better find a superhero cape and come up with a codename, since I'm basically the living embodiment of a comic book. Lightgirl has a ring to it, don't you think?"

"This isn't a joke, Calliope." Dr. Ormandi gives me a stern glare. I give him one right back.

"Considering a whole pack of phantoms tried to kill me and my friend last night, trust me, I know this is not a joke." I set my coffee down. "Would they have killed everyone else on the pier, too?"

The old man doesn't even blink. "Probably."

This story keeps getting better.

"Anything else I should know, since we're finally acknowledging the arch-nemesis I'm going to have to face down?" I ask. "What does the Lore say about them, since you've clearly read it?"

"According to the Lore, the first Shadowmancer was a power-ful Luminaut." Dr. Ormandi's back in lecture mode. He seems to channel it remarkably well when he's nervous—I don't know if that makes me feel better, or worse. "She was the first human to harness the power of Darkness, and used it to destroy the Lightbridge. The Queen Beyond The Stars, she was called. She's said to have been the most powerful human being that ever existed. It is because of her the worlds are separated to this day."

"A Luminaut turned Dark-side and tried to destroy the multiverse." Fabulous. "Is she the one coming after me?"

I don't really like the odds of a novice Luminaut facing down an ancient, all-powerful Shadowmancer commanding an army of killer phantoms. I definitely wouldn't bet on me.

"As per the Lore, she was defeated," Dr. Ormandi answers. Kind of vague, but right now, I'll go with vague. "I don't believe— no, she no longer exists. It is not possible. She disappeared from the Lore thousands of years ago. It cannot be..." We've gone from vague to questioning—not positive. Dr. Ormandi straightens himself, and goes on. "This is likely a young rogue with a pen-chant for the theatrical. Hence attacking you in public, and toying with you so many months before making a move."

I allow myself a sardonic smirk. "Yeah, they can definitely put on a show." I blow a defeated sigh through pursed lips. "What happens now?"

"You must constantly be on guard for danger. Protect the Light Core at all cost."

Protect the Light? How about protecting me? "What if I'm attacked head on?"

"Then you will have to Dive." Dr. Ormandi fixes me with his flinty stare. "If you value the safety of everyone and everything you care about, the only way to protect them from Darkness may be to escape this world entirely."

Escape this world entirely. The magnitude of his words stun me like a punch in the face.

"I'd have to Dive without a Seer." The big, fat, not-survivable scenario. "If I even make it through a gateway alive, how will I get back home?"

"You might never return home." Dr. Ormandi's eyes bore into me, his words piercing my heart.

Never return home. I can't comprehend, can't fathom the consequence of such a choice—or the fact I might be forced to make it. Soon.

"I have the SAT in January." I reel for an excuse, all of which fall short even as I list them. "I have to play varsity volleyball. I have to apply for college, and scholarships. I have... plans and stuff."

"The Shadowmancer stalking you doesn't care about your plans." Dr. Ormandi stares me down with a fierceness in his eyes I've never seen before. "You were not destined for the mediocrity of mundane plans, or life in this small town. You are a Luminaut, Callie. The only one in existence."

There he goes, talking about my destiny like he doesn't know how terrible a hero I'd make. I'm not the type of person anyone would pick to fight villains and reunite the broken multiverse. I'm a robotics geek who surfs. The only thing I'm known for is my lack of ambition. I've heard it all my life, a broken record played over and over until it's become my truth. *If only you applied yourself... How a girl as smart as you can care so little about your future is beyond me... Grow up, Callie, and start taking life seriously...*

And yet—despite my vast and numerous failings— the Light Core chose me. I command the last World Diver, a mech so ancient he defies time and space. Light magic resides deep inside my soul, living under my heart, bursting from my hands until my whole world begins to glow. I *am* a Luminaut. There is no denying that truth — because of it, I lost Will. I lost Nate.

And now, I might have to lose everything else I love, too.

"What if — by some miracle — I escape, and the Shadowmancer follows me to another world?" Maybe this answer won't be as absolutely atrocious as all the other answers have been.

"Then you would have to use all your cunning, resource-fulness, and wit, and pray you find a Seer to open an escape gateway before this Shadowmancer finds you." Never mind, equally atrocious. Should have guessed. Dr. Ormandi runs his fingers through his hair, shaking his head. "You're not ready for this. I wish we'd had more time." Then, he laughs, a dry, brittle sound. "Well, Callie, you wanted to Dive. You may get your chance after all."

A pause as I steel myself ask the most difficult question of all. The one that throbs with the rawest kind of pain. "And what about Nate? His ghost? Why would he want to take my Light Core from me?"

Dr. Ormandi's expression falls, emotions and feelings of every sort mingling together until he becomes almost unreadable. The only thing I can decipher is the sheer terror in his eyes. "I cannot even begin to tell you what I think that means...."

There's an angry buzz in my pocket, like a bee got trapped inside my jeans. I pull it in front of my face, skimming the text notification on the screen. It's Ryan, which makes me scowl. Ryan never texts, except to ask me to pick up his favorite snacks on my way home from school.

> Where are you? Mom is going to call the police and have them arrest you for corporate malfeasance and conspiracy to tank her business ventures.

It's 11:15. Holy crap, I'm dead.

"I have to go. Right now." I knock my mug onto the floor in my rush to leave, spilling coffee and cream everywhere. The patchwork throw gets tossed aside, and I shove Nemo roughly into my backpack, earning me a growl and a pinch.

"What's happened?" Dr. Ormandi leaps from his chair, facing me with a look of dread.

"If this Shadowmancer doesn't kill me, my mom definitely will." I swing my backpack over my shoulder. "I'm supposed to cater a luncheon with her at noon. I should have been home half an hour ago."

Without another word, or a pause to hear his reply, I throw open the front door and sprint into the pounding rain.

CHAPTER
TWENTY-FIVE

WHEN I PULL INTO the driveway five minutes later at 11:20, Ryan is waiting for me on the porch, an obnoxious smirk on his lips. Tyler hops around at his side, grinning, with a smug this-is-going-to-be-good look on his face.

"Mom says to start planning your funeral," Ryan informs me. "I'm going to be taking over your room. I hope you don't mind if I start painting before you're actually dead. Coral and teal aren't really my thing."

"Get out of my way." I shove my brothers aside and sweep into the house.

Jase sits at the kitchen table, ready to go in his red polo shirt and black slacks. Dad is next to him, his face hard and jaw set. Mom stalks between the stove and the pantry, hackles raised like a caged lion. Her head bursts into flames when she sees me.

Okay, not literally, but I've never seen Mom so mad.

"You're grounded! Forever!" I'm pretty sure our neighbors a couple blocks away can hear Mom screaming.

"I figured." I avert my eyes from the lightning bolts of fury in Mom's. "I've got to get ready."

"Where were you?" Mom snags my arm and drags me back into the kitchen before I can slink away. "Why are you soaked? I told you *explicitly* we had to be at the Chamber of Commerce at eleven. Because of you, I'm late, we're going to be late setting up and serving, and my business looks extremely unprofessional. I could lose my contract for this job! I could lose future clients!"

"I'm sorry I'm late. I was out for coffee, and lost track of time." I dare to look at Mom. Even though she's about five inches shorter than me, she's never not intimidating when she's angry. And right now, she is absolutely incensed with rage.

"You got that wet at coffee?" Mom's blazing eyes narrow on me. "Where did you go, some underwater mermaid cafe?"

I got wet sitting on Dr. Ormandi's front step in the rain for over an hour, Mom. But instead of telling her the truth, I dig my heels in harder.

"I'm not lying, you can smell my breath, I had coffee." It's the truth. I did have coffee. At Dr. Ormandi's house.

Mom's grip tightens until she's practically wringing the skin from my arm. "Do *not* give me sass, Calliope."

"You'll be lucky if we don't strip every single privilege you have," Dad threatens. "This is serious. Tell us where you were, and why you're soaked through your clothes and late."

"She was probably surfing with Will Avila."

Jase smirks, a self-satisfied look of triumph in his eyes. I whirl on him, my lip curled ferociously.

"I was *not* surfing." Anger begins to buzz in my ears. I can feel Persuasion rising into my chest, swirling and slithering into my throat toward my tongue as I glare at my brother.

Mom and Dad look at each other, then at me. I can't tell if they're shocked, betrayed, or disappointed.

"Is that what you were doing?" Mom squares her hips, facing me head on. "Did you lie to me?"

"No. I wasn't surfing," I promise. "I wouldn't surf in my clothes, anyway."

"Whatever, you surf with him every Sunday," Jase persists. "You probably just left your clothes on the beach like a moron, and they got wet in the rain."

I'm *this close* to slaughtering Jase right now.

I give him a warning look. "Stop it."

My Persuasion begs me to take him down a peg, to take control of his inner Light and humiliate him the way I did Sean Pettit. I can see it flickering around his heart, calling to me. But Jase is my brother. As stuck-up, entitled, and petty as he might be, he's *my brother*.

Although, the way he's looking at me with that repulsive little "I won" smile, planning all the ways he's going to use the car now that he's the only one with access to it, is anything but brotherly.

"You're constantly sneaking around," Jase goes on. Mom and Dad's confused faces look from me, toward Jase, then back again.

"So are you." I can't believe Jase is going to pull this, after all the dirt I've got on him. But he doesn't stop.

"You've been saying for months you're working on robotics stuff when you're secretly going surfing," Jase argues. Dad whirls on me, his eyes steely.

"Is this true, Callie?"

"Yes, I surf on Sundays with Will, but only in the morning," I admit. "I spend my afternoons working on robotics." Except, that robot is the World Diver. Minor detail.

"Did you surf today?" Mom takes my chin and forces me to look at her. "Answer me, Callie."

"No, I didn't."

Her grip tightens. "Then tell me how you got so wet, and why you're late."

My tongue ties into knots, and I can't speak. Tears well in my eyes. As much as I want to tell Mom the truth, there's no way she'd understand, or even believe it.

"I'm telling you, she was surfing!" Jase pipes up. "She's lying!"

Okay, that's it. Jase has done it now. I wrench myself free from Mom's grasp and stare Jase down. The look in my brother's eyes as I glare at him is instantly panicked. He crossed the line, and he knows it.

"You want to talk about lying?" I snarl. "Tell Mom and Dad about bonfire night, and how you're failing Civics."

"What?"

"Excuse me?"

Mom and Dad's ire switches from me to Jase. My brother gulps like a criminal during cross-examination whose web of deceit is laid bare, exposed for the jury to see.

"You're failing Civics!" Mom spins around, glaring at Jase, and Dad's eyes go wide, completely aghast.

"What is bonfire night?" Dad's tone grows suspicious. "It better not mean the same thing it did when I was in high school."

Now, it's my turn to smirk. "It means instead of spending his Friday and Saturday nights going to study groups, like he told you, Jase has been going to the beach to get wasted with all his friends."

"Jason Estevao James!" Mom's face pales, and she claps her hands to her mouth. Dad groans, resting his forehead on his fist.

"I'm not getting wasted." It's the only defense Jase has. "I don't drink. Other kids do, but I don't. I swear."

"But you lied to us for months!" Mom starts crying, tears pouring down her cheeks. "You told us you were studying to get your grades back up!"

"You can kiss your chance at a soccer scholarship goodbye," Dad growls hotly. "No college is going to care how talented you are if you fail classes your senior year."

"Hey, I'm not the one who ruined Mom's lunch thing because

I lied about surfing," Jase snaps.

"*I. Did. Not. Go. Surfing.*" I'm shrieking as loud as Mom now.

"Uh-huh. Yeah, right. Your hair and clothes are all wet because you were at coffee." Jase rolls his eyes. "You're just as much of a liar as I am, and you know it."

Something inside me snaps. Maybe it's because I know I'm grounded for life. Maybe it's because I'm fed up with Jase's manipulative crap, and on top of Will hating me and Nate leaving, I'm so sick of teenage boys and their drama I could scream. Maybe it's because Dr. Ormandi told me not even an hour ago that a Shadowmancer is hunting me, and won't think twice to kill me to get my Light Core. Maybe it's because I might have to leave California behind forever. Maybe it's because I just don't care anymore.

In the blink of an eye, Persuasion breaks free, latching onto Jase's Light as tight as a vise.

"Shut up and listen, Jase!"

My brother's eyes glaze over, locked in my Persuasion trance. Mom and Dad stare between me and Jase, too terrified to move.

"I am *done* with you acting like I'm some loser, like you're so much better than me. You're the one who's the loser. Say it."

"I'm a loser," Jase murmurs.

Ryan and Tyler laugh, cheer, and high-five from their hiding spot in the foyer. Livvy marches up, demanding to know what's so funny. I ignore all of it. All I can see is Jase, all I can feel is fury scorching my bones and malice pulsing through my veins.

"Now, get out of my sight," I command my brother. "You're the most selfish, egotistical person I've ever met. I hate you."

Even through my Persuasion, the suffering in Jase's eyes is palpable. When he gets up and goes to his bedroom in the basement, my Persuasion breaks. I sink to the floor, shaking like a leaf on the wind as the tears flow freely across my cheeks, over the edge of my chin.

Mom and Dad just stare at me, like their daughter has vanished and a complete stranger is sitting on their floor weeping uncontrollably. "How could you say that to your brother?" Mom whispers. There is no mistaking the heartbreak on her face.

Heartbreak for Jase, of course. Even though he lied, sneaked, and played them for a fool. Who cares about Callie and the fact her life is falling apart?

"Is that really all you care about? That Jase's ego got bruised?" I look at Mom, blind to the mess I'm making. Rising to my feet, I face my parents, words rushing from my tongue like a roll of unstoppable thunder, building momentum until the inevitable crash.

"I'm doing everything you ever expected of me. Straight As — check. Sports — check. Now I've got to be Jase's best friend, too? Fine. I'll go to the basement and apologize. But it won't fix anything. You guys will just find some other way I don't measure up. You want me to be just like Jase, or Ryan, or Tyler, or anybody else but *me*. I've never been good enough for you, and nothing I do ever will be!" I glance at the clock. It's 11:40. "May I be excused? I've got to get ready for the luncheon."

Mom nods, too stunned to speak. An anguished grimace lines Dad's weatherbeaten face. Before either of them can form a thought or counter-argument, I turn sharply on my heel and march toward my room.

"Hello, and welcome to the Jase James Haters' Club." Ryan pops out of his bedroom, Tyler right behind him. "I'm Ryan Emmanuel James, Esq. — President and Founder. This is Tyler George James, Vice President and Member At Large."

"Leave me alone!" I roar in their faces.

Ryan and Tyler dissolve in a fit of riotous laughter as I slam the door to my room. Well, mine until Mom and Dad kick me out to the garage for my performance in the kitchen. Might as well start calling it Ryan's room.

I let Nemo out of my backpack and change, quick as a flash, into my red sweater and black slacks. It takes no time to throw my damp hair into a neat bun, and I return to the kitchen less than two minutes later. Jase came back up, too, but I refuse to look at him. Or Mom and Dad. I keep my eyes glued to an indistinct spot on the wall.

"Pablo is coming over to boot the car while you're gone," Dad informs my brother and me. A boot? Seriously? Dad being friends with Police Chief Navarro completely sucks.

"And you're handing over your cell phones." Mom adds. "Right now."

Jase and I deposit our phones into Mom's waiting palm without a word.

"You're restricted to school and sports," Dad goes on. "Absolutely no other activities. No surfing, no bonfires. Is that clear?"

Which also means no Diver, right when I need to see him the most—trying to access his past memories to learn about fighting and defeating Shadowmancers is sort of critical for me at the moment.

"Yes." Jase and I answer in unison.

"Good." Mom slips her purse over her shoulder and motions for us to get going. "You are both beyond lucky I made the food and took it to the Chamber kitchen yesterday. All we've got to do is set up for service. We'll be a little late, but we'll manage."

Jase tries to catch my eye as we follow Mom into the garage, but I turn away. We don't say a word to each other the entire drive.

It's a mad dash in the Chamber of Commerce kitchen to get the appetizers on trays and hot dishes in the ovens to warm, but we manage to start service by 12:15. None of the VIPs and city council members in attendance seem to care that much, because they're all walking around with cocktails and glasses of wine, chattering with nervous energy. The topic of conversation on everyone's lips: the events at the pier last night.

"An earthquake, I heard." A man takes a cheese palmier off my tray, and his companion nods, agreeing.

"Only explanation," the other man says.

"Most everyone thinks it was a rogue wave, but my daughter and her family were there, and they didn't see a wave big enough to rattle the whole pier." A woman brushes around me, sipping her drink while she gossips to a friend.

A couple stroll past, munching on Mom's famous profiteroles. "As dark as it was with the power outage, we may never know the truth," one of them says.

Except I know the truth. The silent, doe-eyed girl standing in the corner holding an appetizer tray is the reason for the horror and mayhem that nobody can stop talking about. The phantoms that attacked my town landmark could pop up any second, massacre everyone at the luncheon, and all of it would be my fault.

Maybe Dr. Ormandi is right. The best way to protect everyone from the nightmare on my heels is to Dive—leave for good, and never come back. Guilt gnaws at me, eating me up from the inside out. I can't focus on anything, let alone serving up plates of cabernet-braised short ribs and sweet potato gratin. All I can think about are Shadowmancers, malevolent phantoms, and threats waiting for me around the edge of dark corners.

"Callie, weren't you and Will down by the pier last night?"

Mom is letting Jase and I have a quick plate of lunch during our fifteen-minute break between main service and dessert. We still aren't speaking to each other, but we both look up when she asks her question.

"Yeah, for a bit," I answer cautiously. "We went to the burrito truck and the cupcake place."

"Everyone says there was an earthquake, or a rogue wave or something." Mom opens a bottle of water and leans against the stainless steel countertop. "It caused a major power outage, and rocked the whole pier. Did you see anything?"

"No." I didn't need to 'see' it. I lived every horrifying second of it.

"That's a relief." Mom takes a quick sip, then screws the cap on her bottle and sets it aside. "Okay, let's plate dessert. Jase, can you take the coffee pots out and get them brewing?"

Mom flits away to get the mille-feuille out of the fridge. Any trace of the rogue wave-earthquake rumors—or the fact I could be boldfaced lying about my involvement—are forgotten in favor of work and precision. Typical Mom.

Jase darts a glance my way. I keep mine on my picked-over plate. I don't think I've eaten more than two bites. My brother looks at the hardly-touched food, then at me.

"Did you *really* not see anything last night?" he asks quietly.

"I thought Mom told you to brew the coffee." I set my plate in the sink and turn my back. We finish service, clean up, and tear down without looking each other in the eye.

This is the worst weekend of my entire life.

CHAPTER
TWENTY-SIX

> Today, I'll discuss Diving without a Seer. This is a scenario
> that should never be undertaken, except in the most extreme
> of emergency circumstances.

Is a Shadowmancer stalking me an extreme emergency, Mariasol? Maybe you've got some better advice than your husband did about using my Light to fight off Darkness. Any pearls of wisdom on surviving being grounded indefinitely, making my best friend not hate me, and getting over my ghost crush? Because I could really use some help there, too.

> This manner of Diving is an endeavor that must only be
> undertaken when the probability of death is likely in either
> scenario—just more likely in one versus the other. For the
> love of Light, future Luminaut, please don't Dive without a
> Seer. End of story.

Yes, got it, Mariasol. It's super dangerous, and I would probably die. But how do I actually do it?

> If, for some horrific reason, you must Dive without the aid of a
> Seer, water is the best medium to open a gateway. If you are
> not near the water, the air is the next best medium, although
> it is far less stable. You will need to activate the Light Core
> with your powers, place it in the Prism, then allow the gateway
> to open naturally before you. These gateways will remain open
> only seconds without a Seer's power to focus the elements
> around them, so do not waste time. Dive immediately, and
> pray to whatever deity you believe in the gateway remains
> open long enough for you to complete your Dive without
> slicing the Diver (or yourself) in half.

Okay, seems simple enough. Other than, you know, not cutting myself and Diver in half when an unstable gateway closes
mid-Dive. The entry tapers off strangely, picking up a few inches
down the page, toward the bottom.

> I grow weary, Luminaut. The sickness I once defeated has
> returned, with such ferocity I'm certain I do not have long to
> live. Though I did not impart to you all I wished to say, I want
> to spend the last days of my life on Earth with those I love
> most. And so, I must bid these journals, and you, an early
> farewell. If you need further instruction, I have transferred as
> many memories as I can to the Diver, as did his other
> Luminauts before me. Should you need us, we are always with
> you.
>
> Goodbye, and good luck. And remember to seek the Light,
> even in the Darkest places.
>
> Mariasol Zaira-Ormandi

The last entry in the last journal. Her words and advice are gone, just like she is. Looks like I'll be facing down the looming Darkness alone, even though I could really use the guidance of another Luminaut now more than ever. Mariasol had bigger things to worry about than the crap-show I've gotten myself into. Like, you know, dying. It makes my problems seem selfish, and small by comparison.

I have transferred as many memories as I can to the Diver... we are always with you.

"Callie!" Dad taps on the door.

"Robot mode," I whisper to Nemo. He goes still, a lifeless toy robot as soon as Dad pokes his head in my room.

"Ready to go to your game?" Dad gives me a once-over. I'm in my uniform, warm-ups pulled over the stretchy volleyball shorts.

"Yeah." I tuck Mariasol's journal under my pillow and snatch my duffel bag off the floor.

"What were you doing?" Dad tries to make small talk. I haven't been in the mood for talking lately. Too busy looking over my shoulder for a Shadowmancer and their minions trying to kill me.

"Journaling." True, I wasn't writing the journal, I was reading a long-dead Luminaut's last words, but Dad really doesn't care about the fine print.

"I didn't know you journaled."

There's a lot you don't know about me, Dad.

"Are you excited about your first varsity game?" Dad goes on, a little awkwardly, since I never responded to his last statement about the journal.

"We're just playing alumni for the athletic booster fund-raiser," I reply with a shrug. The volleyball season ended two weeks ago and tonight's game is only for fun, but the girls slated for varsity next year were invited to play with the team tonight. In Dad's eyes, that makes this an official 'varsity' game.

"Sorry I can't stay to watch you play," Dad continues as we hop into his truck. My car is still booted, because Mom and Dad haven't forgiven me and Jase for being lying liars who lie.

"It's fine. You guys have other stuff, I get it."

For people who pressured me to play sports in the first place, my parents aren't making a huge effort to support me tonight. But honestly, I don't want them there. They have no idea about the danger that's haunting me, that could hurt them — or even kill them — to get my Light Core.

"Tyler's Christmas recital is tonight, and Mom needs to stay with Olivia while she's sick." Dad explains this like he's justifying his actions. Or inactions.

"I just told you I understood." I'm more snippy than I mean to be, but it's hard to concentrate on anything Dad says and keep my eyes peeled for murder-phantoms.

Dad goes quiet. He wants to chew me out, I can tell by the way his eyes strain at the crow's feet. Instead, he takes a deep breath and forces a grin.

"Well, I'm sure Will Avila will be there to support you."

I swallow hard, gulping down a lump threatening to form in my throat. Will won't be there. He won't speak to me, won't read my texts, won't acknowledge my presence. But Dad doesn't know Will hates me, and telling him would lead to a whole bunch of questions with answers he won't understand: Luminauts, Dr. Ormandi, Diver, Nemo. The Darkness.

"Yeah, he will." Lies, lies, lies. I hate lying. It makes my mouth feel bitter and dirty.

"When is your game over?" Dad pulls into the gym parking lot and parks by the main doors. Athletic booster signs have been duct-taped to the walls, and a wilting balloon-arch is draped over the doors. People slowly trickle in with donations.

"Eight-thirty." I shoulder my duffel bag.

"Hey, hold on a sec." Dad puts a hand on my elbow, stopping me. I face him, expectant.

"Yeah?"

"Has everything been okay lately?" His hazel eyes search me carefully. "You've been out of sorts since last weekend." When I don't reply, Dad squirms in his seat. "You can tell me what's wrong. Is it friend trouble? Some boy being a jerk?"

You have no idea, Dad.

"I'm going to be late." I open the door to hop to the curb, but Dad reaches across me, catching the handle.

"Listen, I just wanted to say—" Dad takes a deep breath. "I know I've been pressuring you about your grades and being more involved in school this year. But it's only because I care about your future. I'm really proud of you for stepping up. Mom and I both are. You're going to accomplish great things, Cal. I know it."

Dad's proud, but only because I followed orders. I fit into a predetermined mold of high school success like a square peg being forced into a round hole. If I didn't think it would make things worse, I might cry. I know Dad means well, but this pep talk—or, lack thereof—is the absolute last thing I need on top of everything that's lurking over my shoulder. It only makes me feel more alone.

Dad leans over to give me a hug, and I half-heartedly drape my arms around him.

"See you later, Dad."

"Good luck, kiddo." Dad smiles when I step to the curb. "Have fun!"

I manage a half-grin before I shut the door, and Dad's face disappears from my sight.

My teammates fill the locker room with excited chatter and

laughter, the sound of their voices floating through the air like the twitter of birds in the morning. Tomorrow is the last final before winter break, and a couple girls next to me talk excitedly about their vacation plans, what they want from their boyfriends for Christmas. I'm not acknowledged, nor do I feel like discussing the suck-fest otherwise known as Callie's life. I make myself as small and obscure as possible as I take off my warm-ups and put my duffel bag in a locker.

"Hey, Callie showed up!"

Julia Olsen, who's in my US History class, approaches me with a smile. She's a junior, like me, but has played varsity volleyball since she was a freshman. She's tall and graceful, and looks like a Viking warrior princess.

"Hi, Jules." I force an upbeat, peppy tone.

"Nervous for your varsity initiation?" Jules sits on the bench next to me while I tie blue and white ribbons into my ponytail— our school colors. Ribbons like mine weave through her long, golden French braid.

"Nah, I'm good." Jules grins at my reply.

"This game is all about throwing a bone to the booster club. The alumni always suck," she confides under her breath. A few of the girls have parents or siblings on the alumni team; retaliation would be swift if she were overheard.

"Don't let them score on me, is basically what you're implying."

"It's not that big a deal if you do, we'll just never let you live it down." Jules winks. I make myself chuckle at her joke. Be normal, Callie. As normal as you can be in a public setting with the shadow of an enemy stalking your every move.

"Do you have anything going on over winter break?" Jules asks.

"My birthday is Christmas Eve."

My seventeenth birthday. Nate was seventeen when he died. The thought creeps up my spine and makes me shiver.

"Seriously?" Jules's blond eyebrows shoot sky high. "Dude, that's lame. I mean, no offense, it's your birthday. I'd just hate it if my birthday was Christmas Eve."

"No, I love sharing a birthday with Jesus and Santa Claus," I deadpan. "My parents never overlook it, like, ever."

"Do they do the thing where they say, 'This present is for your birthday *and* Christmas?'" Jules goes on. I smirk.

"Every. Single. Year."

Jules seems about to reply, but our coach claps her hands loudly. We cease whatever conversations we were having and turn, facing her expectantly.

"Time to line up, ladies," she announces.

"Game time, Callie." Jules hops to her feet. "You got any family and friends here? Your parents are in the athletic boosters, right?"

"Yeah, but they're busy. My friends are busy, too." Emily's family left to go on their annual holiday vacation last weekend, and Izzy is going with Chase to his little sister's Christmas play. Oh, and Will hates my guts.

"It's a busy time of year. My mom and dad couldn't come, either," Jules confides. "Whose bright idea was it to hold a fundraiser game in December when everyone is broke from buying presents and a million other things are going on?"

"Not the most brilliant booster crayon in the box," I snark. Jules snorts a laugh, and we line up by the locker room door. The announcer has just called out the alumni team, and we're next.

"And now, the home team, your Lady Makos varsity volleyball!"

The team surges out of the locker room, running onto the court as music blares and the student section cheers. It's sparsely populated, to say the least. Mostly kids in student leadership class who were required to be here for their participation grade—all bored to death. Thanks for the disingenuous support, fellow peers. The alumni section has a few more spectators, but not many. At least they don't look like they need a caffeine drip to function.

I'm going to guess a lot of boosters mailed in their donations this year.

"Serving for the home team, number 14, Julia Olsen," the announcer's voice floats over the gym, signaling the start of the game.

Jules takes her place at the back of the court to serve and I ready myself to set when the ball comes over the net from the alumni side. The ball goes flying before volleying back to our side of the net, and our middle blocker bumps it gently my way. I rush to get under the ball and set it, and our spiker sends it flying into the face of the alumni blocker.

"Home team scores!"

We give each other a quick round of high fives before getting into position again. For the most part, we dominate the alumni. One of their players graduated two years ago and plays for Verona Beach State, but she can't carry the whole team, and soon it's game point.

"Okay, ladies, let's finish this up!" Jules announces.

Yes, finish it up so I can get out of here. A Shadowmancer already scared half the town at the pier. I don't need trouble at a volleyball game. We give each other one last round of encouragement before taking our positions.

As Jules goes to serve, the lights begin to flicker.

Oh no.

My pulse kick starts and panic takes over, and my ears buzz as I search the gym for shadows, for a trace of the phantoms. My worst nightmare can't be happening. *Please, no. Not here. Not now.*

Jules pauses her serve to look up at fluorescent lights in the ceiling. All the girls do. But as soon as the flickering starts, it's over.

"Hey, somebody in the booster club want to tell the janitorial staff not to turn the lights out?" the announcer jokes. "We've got a game going on!"

The titter of laughter ripples through the crowd, and I take a few deep breaths. It was obviously a small electrical malfunction. Nothing more.

Jules serves, and as the ball flies over the net, the gym goes black.

A sound like a whoosh of violent wind courses through the rafters as all the electricity and light is instantaneously sucked away. The gym is so dark I can't see my hand in front of my face. All I can hear is my pulse hammering in my ears around the faint, muffled shouts of a crowd in panic.

"Everyone remain calm!" the announcer blares. "This is a random power outage. We'll get it fixed shortly."

Except it's not a random power outage. I know exactly what this is — and it's far, far worse than anyone can imagine. A familiar chill of dread fills the gym, and the air around me grows stale and sour. Anger, despair, and fear swirl all around, from my ankles to the tendrils of my hair. Peering into the darkness, I hunt for any sight of *them* – the phantasmic source of the impenetrable black permeating the space.

"Look up there!"

I don't know who screamed, but I instantly know why. Ashes fall from the heights above our heads. Where the gym roof once covered us, sheltering us from the starry night, there's nothing. It's being eaten away before our eyes, dissolved by black tentacles wrapping themselves around the building.

"Get out!"

"Go! Run!"

Everyone in the gym begins to sprint away, a mad dash toward the doors. They pour out like fish swimming upstream, trying to push past each other, tripping over themselves in their furious race to escape.

I stand alone, unmoved, in the middle of the volleyball court. If this nightmare has come for me, I will face it. Nobody else deserves to get hurt.

The gym begins to quiet, save for the hideous, unearthly crunching and gnawing as phantoms continue to tear the gym to shreds. I tense, every muscle and nerve on edge as I wait in the silence for the monster to show itself at last—to come face to face with the source of my terror.

"Hey there, beautiful." A voice behind me, spectral and ominous. And yet, as familiar to me now as my own.

Slowly, I turn. My body falters, lurches, forgets to breathe.

"N-Nate?"

No. No, this can't be. It's impossible. This isn't really Nate—not the one I know. This Nate is a demonic specter from my worst nightmare.

In some ways, he's himself. His dark, wavy hair tumbles across his forehead, his lips turn up in a self-confident smirk. But the eyes... they are fearsome and terrible. Black as a grave, no whites to be seen beyond the oversized midnight-and-crimson irises, and rimmed in purple gray. In place of his jeans and hoodie he is garbed in forbidding black, and his handsome face, the one I held in my hands and kissed, menaces as he stares, unblinking.

"Miss me, Callie?" His lips part. This smile is nothing like the smile I know. The charm and humor are gone. Horror takes their place.

"What—what are you—"

"Doing here?" Nate finishes for me. "Just popped by to try for that Light Core one last time, since doing things the easy way wasn't as effective as I'd hoped." His voice is hollow, inhuman. Nothing like the voice I'd come to know—and yet, everything like it all at once.

"You—you're a—"

"Shadowmancer." His smile stretches wide, a leering taunt. "Are you going to make me finish all your sentences tonight?"

"You—you lied to me."

"Technically, no. I mean, I lied about the ghost thing. But really, I just omitted certain facts." He spreads his hands wide, like a kid caught red-handed pulling a prank. It's not very humorous. "Surprise! Are you shocked?"

Shocked, horrified, betrayed. Thousands of swirling emotions steal my breath, my reason. I can hardly form coherent thoughts as everything I thought about who Nate was and what he meant to me comes crashing down, as ashen and dead as the gym roof.

"Were you always…"

"A Shadowmancer? Since I met you, yes. But always, no. I was as human as you." Nate's once-alluring smile is a darkly horrible expression in his current state. "Now's the part where I give my movie-villain monologue about how I became all dark and undead and scary, right? I was drowning—literally—when Darkness called to me in the storm. I had a choice. Darkness, and the truth I'd been desperate to learn, or death—never knowing if everything I believed about Light was real, or a lie. And because I chose the truth, I know I'm not really the bad guy here."

"You sure look like one." The black eyes with blood-red irises, the corpse-like shadows under them, bone-white skin. He is a monster.

"Oh, you mean—" Nate snaps his fingers, and the phantoms swirl around him, revealing his heart-stopping, handsome, human form.

My Nate. The one I cared about. My heart breaks all over again.

"You like me better like this, don't you?" He cocks his head. "A lie is always a lot prettier than the truth, isn't it? I'm not as powerful in this form, and I can't sense the Light. But it does make moving around the human world easier."

Another snap and the horrifying visage returns.

My head spins with the depths of Nate's betrayal, fury and fire filling my veins. "You're the one who attacked me and Will at the pier that night. And then you came to me, comforted me and kissed me. You tried to take advantage of me when I was the most vulnerable I've ever been."

"Nice deduction. I always knew you were smart. Just not smart enough to listen when I warned you what would happen if you didn't give up the Light." Nate's minions come to him, swirling all around like a thousand snakes slithering up the legs of their master.

The conflicting feeling of dread mingling with my crush, the shadowy hint of danger and heartache that always lurked around the edges of Nate's smile and darkened his penetrating eyes—I thought it was the fact he was a ghost that frightened me.

But it was Darkness. His Darkness trying to destroy my Light.

My heart shatters, crumbling into a thousand aching pieces at my feet. And yet, somehow, it still beats. In place of the feelings I once had for Nate, a new sensation begins to fester, growing more powerful with every passing second: rage. A horrible, hateful blaze of Light scorches across my skin, and I face him, newly fearless.

From deep inside, power and Light and wild, untamed magic race through blood and bone, culminating in my hands. Without control, without thought, I raise my hands toward Nate and the power flies away, a streak of pure Light slashing through the Darkness. Nate disappears into the Dark, reappearing a half-second later well away from the Light's unstable path.

BOOM

Light crashes into the wall, blowing a hole straight through the VBHS trophy case on the other side. Cups and plaques crash to the floor, along with a thousand tinkling shards of glass. I hold my shaking hands to my face, unsure how — or what — I just did.

"Impressive. A couple of those were mine, you know." Nate glances at the hole my Light blew in the far wall, more than a little disconcerted. "She always said you'd try to kill me if you got the chance."

"*She* always said?" I struggle to form words as the massive surge of power drains away. "Who is she?"

"Somebody you just proved right about everything I was told about Luminauts." Nate's eyes darken — a phenomenon I didn't think was possible.

"It doesn't matter who said what. Everything you tell me is a lie." I cannot consider what his ominous *she* means — for all I care, it's yet another layer of deceit to peel away from my blinded eyes. "You said you wanted my Light Core to protect me. That was a lie, too, wasn't it?"

"I *was* trying to protect you from *this*," Nate argues, his wicked eyes, nightmare face, and swirling phantoms overwhelming my senses. "You think I wanted it to come to this? I told you to give up your Light Core and your power. I warned you to be careful — and what would happen if you weren't."

Be careful who you trust with your power… the consequences could be deadly…

It never occurred to me Nate was talking about himself.

"It's not too late, you know." His burning red eyes sear my soul. "It doesn't have to be like this. We don't have to be enemies.

Change your mind. Give me your Light Core. Put an end to everything, right here and now."

"No." For all the questions I have, for all the confusion and hurt and quaking fear, that answer rings true.

"You have no idea what Light truly is." Nate takes a step toward me. I back away instinctively. "You don't know the danger you're putting millions—no, billions—of people in with your Light."

"I'm the dangerous one?" A bleak laugh threatens to escape. I choke it down. "I'm not the one with the army of murder-phantoms that just destroyed a high school gym."

"Listen—violence, murder, mayhem, they're not really my thing. But I'll do what I have to do to make sure you don't bring about the death and destruction of millions." Nate's malevolent glower freezes the blood in my veins. "You know what my friends are capable of. What *I'm* capable of in this form. Don't force my hand."

"You mean killing me and everyone I care about?" I shoot him the fiercest glare I can muster. "Yeah, I know what you're capable of, you monster."

I can't be sure, but for a split second, it looks like Nate winces—just a little—when I call him a monster.

"Then you understand why it's in your best interest to give me the Light Core." Nate jerks a nod, and a looming cloud of fearsome phantoms burst forth. Their gaping, grasping mouths lunge right for me. "I have no problem letting my friends have their way with your family. Is that really what you want? To risk everyone you love for Light?"

Mom, Dad, my brothers, little Livvy… my mind seizes with the horrific vision of their unblinking eyes turned toward Nate's gruesome phantoms while our blackened house crumbles to ash. And it would be my fault.

I'm caught between the impossible, and the unthinkable: I can't give up the Light Core. But I can't let anything happen to my family, either. I feel as if my soul is ripped in two as I stand before Nate, hardly able to comprehend the way he led me on, played with my heart, and betrayed me to my very core—let alone consider what he just threatened to do.

"Don't hurt my family," I plead, willing myself not to reveal the throbbing hurt taking over my every feeling and thought. "I don't have the Light Core. I have it hidden. In secret."

"Yeah, I figured that out." Nate's smirk returns, and he snaps his minions into thin air. "It wasn't stashed in Dad's basement with Diver like I expected."

My gut drops, a leaden weight pulling me off my feet, and my mouth goes dry. I lose my balance, stumbling, and fall to my knees. Shallow gasps escape my lips, and my spinning vision struggles to find focus.

He was at Dr. Ormandi's house, looking for the Light Core. That means...

"You didn't—you wouldn't."

"Wouldn't what?" Nate's smirk becomes a terrifying sneer once more. "Kill Dad to find a Light Core I thought you hid in his house?"

"You aren't that heartless." I shake my head, unable to believe his words. Dr. Ormandi can't be dead. Please, no.

"That's questionable. I mean, I did just threaten to let my friends annihilate everything you've ever cared about, so—" Nate shrugs nonchalantly. As though murdering his own father is just a boring, mundane nuisance, like cutting your toenails or shaving.

This person—this *creature*—is the worst thing in existence. He's a terror. The embodiment of Darkness. And I have never hated anything more in my entire life than I hate Nate Ormandi at this moment.

I leap to my feet, racing toward what remains of the gym doors. Nate's voice stops me cold.

"Callie." I whip around, facing him. His terrible eyes meet mine. "Before you run away with good intentions to save my old man, you owe me a Light Core." He's unforgiving as death as he regards me. "You have an hour."

"That's not enough time." I think fast. "If your dad needs an ambulance, I have to call one. Plus, I'm grounded without a car, so I have to walk back home. It's five miles, at least."

Nate's black eyes narrow at the edges, and he pinches the bridge of his nose.

"Ugh, fine," he mutters. "Two hours, then. Until ten o'clock."

"Swear to me you won't hurt my family while I'm gone." I fix him with the most severe look I have. "If you even think about touching them, you'll never see the Light Core. I'll make sure of it."

"We Shadowmancers always keep our promises, unlike you Luminauts. I swear I won't hurt your family, so long as you hold up your end of the deal." He holds his hand out for me to shake. "Agreed?"

This could all be a trick, another lie. It's clear he doesn't trust me, and I don't trust him one bit. But at this point, I have no other choice, not if I want to get out of here with any hope of keeping my loved ones safe. Two hours buys me time to come up with a plan, time I didn't have before, and won't have again if I don't at least play along.

I grasp Nate's cold, undead fingers. "Agreed."

"Meet me by the pier with the Light Core at ten o'clock sharp." Nate releases my hand. "You know what will happen if you're late." Another ice-cold smile stops my heart. "I'm so glad we had this talk, Callie. I knew you'd see the truth, especially in light of the consequences." A bark-like chuckle. "Light, get it?"

Punny, Nate. Know any jokes that don't imply killing people?

He backs away, eyes locked on mine, and for one terrible moment, we face each other in complete truth. Phantoms twist and swirl around his form, enveloping him in Darkness like a puff of tentacled smoke.

As quick as he came, he's gone. I'm alone in the shell of what was once my high school gym. Just me, and the deafening silence.

Sirens outside alert me to my mission. First things first: I have to find Dr. Ormandi. I have to make sure he and Diver are okay, and that Nate's threats were only a bluff.

I slip out the back exit as the firefighters begin pouring in from the front, and race toward the old professor's house by the cliffs.

I only hope I'm not too late.

CHAPTER
TWENTY-SEVEN

I'VE NEVER RUN TWO MILES faster in my life. The distance between Dr. Ormandi's house and the high school isn't great, but I'm not much of a runner. Tonight, I could qualify for all-state track. Cars honk angrily as I sprint across streets, swerving to miss me. I'm blind to danger. All I can think to do is pray Nate was lying, and I don't walk into the old man's house to be greeted by the shell of a broken Diver, and a corpse.

Dr. Ormandi's quiet street is forbiddingly dark. Every street lamp has burned out, and a creeping sense of menace lingers in the air. There's no doubt in my mind Nate paid his father a visit, and I sprint the length of the street to the house. The burning in my lungs is nothing compared to the sorrow bleeding through my heart.

"Dr. Ormandi!" I bang on his door. I can't hear anything—no sound of footsteps, no locks being clicked. But I smell something clear as day.

Smoke.

"Dr. Ormandi!"

I shove my entire weight against the door once, twice, three times. It doesn't budge.

The smell grows stronger, permeating the air. I think fast,

trying to remember the layout of the old man's house. The front window has bars, so that's a bust, but there's a small window in the kitchen, above the sink. I rush around to the side of the house, behind the carport and the ancient station wagon covered in cobwebs.

"Come on, where's a crowbar, a two-by-four?" I scan my surroundings in the dark, never more thankful for excellent night vision. Except Dr. Ormandi has zero in the way of useful, window breaking stuff. The only option is a garden rake.

"Okay. Rake it is." I slam the metal head of the rake into the glass. It cracks. The second time, it shatters. Glass sprays everywhere, and I hold my arms in front of my face to fend off the shards.

Instantly, I'm engulfed in angry black smoke, spilling from the window. It chokes me as I fumble around the broken glass for the window lock, and completely fills my throat when I lift the window high.

"Dr. Ormandi!" I call out the old professor's name around violent coughs, and pull myself into the kitchen. My arms and hands are bleeding profusely, cut to bits by the window glass, but I don't care.

I can't see any flames—just clouds of putrid smoke surrounding the gas stove, floating toward the ceiling. I toss some damp dish towels on top of the range to smother the rest of the smoke plumes, then stumble through the inky house, desperate for signs of life.

"Callie?"

Dr. Ormandi's voice sounds weak, hoarse—and injured. I rush toward the sound of it. He lies on the floor, his body crumpled and cracked like a winter leaf.

"Dr. Ormandi!"

I'm at his side in a blink, checking him over for injuries. There isn't any blood. At least, not his. My hands and arms drip purple-red rivers from several deep gashes, but Dr. Ormandi isn't bleeding. Not that I can see, anyway.

"You have no idea how relieved I am to see you're safe." He manages to take hold of my hand. I try to help him up, but he cries out in pain. "No, no, none of that. I can't move. Cracked a few ribs."

"I have to get you out of this smoke," I say, trying again to lift him. But he waves me off.

"Smoke doesn't bother me. Fire Manipulator, remember?" He winces. "What's far more concerning is the fact I might have given myself a concussion." He manages a wry grin through his obvious pain. "As I'm sure you're aware, I had quite a surprising revelation tonight."

"Did you know?" I hold onto his hand, for his comfort as well as my own.

"That Nate is a Shadowmancer?" Dr. Ormandi murmurs the question in my heart. "No. I suspected something the day you told me you'd crossed into the Shadow Plain at his grave, and had been hunted by phantoms ever since. But I did not realize the truth until tonight."

Well, that makes two of us, Dr. Ormandi.

"What did he do to you?" I look him over in the dim light of the moon streaming through the curtains.

"My injuries are all my doing. I took a fall in a state of confusion and shock." He finds my eyes, fear in his own. "He was here for your Light Core—to destroy it. When he realized he'd made a mistake, he lit a fire in my kitchen and left to hunt you down. I thought surely you'd be dead."

Nate lit a fire... does he know his dad is a Fire Manipulator? That fire can't harm him? Why light a fire, in that case? Was it all a bluff? Or is he ignorant of his Dad's power, and hoped to burn him alive while he lay there—injured and immobile—on the floor? So many questions, and so little makes sense. Even worse, there's no time to find answers. Only one word rings clear. A siren piercing my muddled, petrified, furious thoughts. *Why.*

"I'm so sorry." Tears fill my eyes that have nothing to do with the smoke. "Your own son... a Shadowmancer." The word squeezes my heart in the most painful way. It can only be half of what Dr. Ormandi is feeling.

"The person who was my son—my Nate—is dead. He was loyal, brave, thoughtful, kind. The best person I've ever known." With a shake of his silver head, Dr. Ormandi squeezes his eyes. "The hateful creature inhabiting his form means nothing. I do not know that monster. I never will." The old man's voice remains firm—and yet, the wavering doubt behind his words is painfully obvious.

"But, Dr. Ormandi—"

"You have to take the Light Core as far from here as possible," he interrupts. "You must lure Nate and his Darkness away from this world altogether, if you have any hope of evading him."

"So, Diving without a Seer." I gulp. "Except, you and Mariasol both harped on me about how dangerous that is, and how I could die, and basically should never do it."

"If you Dive alone, there is a chance you will die in the world awaiting you." Dr. Ormandi's breaths are labored around his words. "If you remain here, you *know* what Darkness can do."

"Yeah, Nate made it pretty clear." I shudder at the thought of the horrible fate awaiting my clueless family.

"Then stop wasting time with me." Dr. Ormandi's eyes lock onto my own. "I am old. Useless."

"You aren't useless to me." Tears fall down my cheeks as I squeeze his hand. "You're my friend."

Dr. Ormandi squeezes my hand back. "I am the past. Your

future is ahead of you." His fingers are frail, nothing but withered skin and bird-bones. "However you can, go to Ensolorada with the Diver. There are people there who knew Mariasol, and our Lore. Serai Eradah—she's the one you must find. She will help you."

"Ensolorada. Serai Eradah." I commit the name and place to memory. "I'll find her."

"Above all, you must fight the Darkness, and keep safe the Light." A rattled cough escapes his quaking frame. "If Darkness is allowed to rise, the multiverse will not survive. Now go. You don't have much time."

"I'm not going to leave you." I shake my head. "We have to get you to the hospital. Your broken ribs could have punctured a lung. You might have internal hemorrhaging."

"No, Callie, you have to leave now," Dr. Ormandi counters. "Use the Diver's strength to break through the tunnel Mariasol began in the cliffs. Make your way out to sea—there are so many oceanic gateways you will not miss. And whatever you do, don't come back until you've found the Light Core on each world and restored the Lightbridge. Promise me."

"Dr. Ormandi." I struggle to hold back a sob, and give voice to my deepest fear. "I—I don't know if I can do this. I don't know if I'm strong enough. I don't want this destiny. How am I the Luminaut who can reunite the worlds with Light?"

"Fate never asks what we want, and what we don't. You might be young and unprepared, but the Light chose you, and you are all the worlds have." Dr. Ormandi coughs again. "You are the last Luminaut—the only hope."

The only hope.

My family's only hope.

My family...

Time is running out.

I undo the locks on the front door, flinging it open. Fresh air busts into the house, scattering the smoke, and I drag a groaning, swearing, struggling Dr. Ormandi across the step, laying him down under the blanket of starry night. He cries out in pain, but quiets when I fix him on the sidewalk.

"I'm going to call 911 for an ambulance," I tell him. "And I'm going to steal your car. Sorry."

"Committing grand theft auto is the least of my concerns regarding you, Luminaut." Dr. Ormandi's eyelids flutter, and he exhales a deep, resigned sigh. "Goodbye and good luck, Calliope James."

"This isn't goodbye." I bend down, planting a swift kiss on his silver-gray hair. "I'll see you later, Dr. Ormandi."

A quick trip through the house, and I find the old man's keys. And his phone. A rotary landline. How do you even dial one of these old-school contraptions? What's wrong with a cell phone? Why did Mom and Dad have to confiscate mine at literally the worst possible time?

I pick up the receiver and hear a dial tone. Sweet. At least the fire didn't destroy the phone line. The wheel spins around with my finger — 9, 1, 1. Hopefully, I didn't screw this up. A tense pause as nothing happens, and I hold my breath. But after an eternity that's probably a couple seconds, ringing.

"911, what's your emergency?" the dispatcher answers.

"My uncle's house had a fire, and he's hurt," I rattle anxiously. "I don't know how bad, but he can't walk. The fire is out, he's just laying on the sidewalk and not moving."

"Calm down, miss," the dispatcher tells me. "What's your uncle's address?"

"1256 Shore Cliff Dive," I give her Dr. Ormandi's house number. "Please, hurry!"

"The fire department and EMTs will be there very shortly.

Stay on the line."

"I can't, I'm sorry, I have to make sure he's okay."

"Miss, do not hang up, please—"

"I'm sorry."

I slam the receiver back on the dock and rush out the door with the old man's keys. Dr. Ormandi lies still and silent, his heavily-lidded black eyes staring straight forward, unblinking, as though he's completely lost in the depths of grief. I swallow the lump forming in my throat and drink him in one last time, my unexpected mentor and friend rendered invalid and broken.

"Please, be okay." My whisper disappears into the breeze, floating over the cliffs and out to sea.

This nineties hunk-of-junk station wagon better be operational. I don't have all night to fiddle around trying to get it started. Judging by the amount of cobwebs and dust covering the windows and dashboard, my chances of successfully driving this thing are slim.

Finding the right key (Subaru, easy-peasy), I unlock the creaky, rusted door and slip into the driver's seat. The old key crunches in the ignition, fighting against me when I turn it over. The starter rumbles, wheezes, then dies.

"Come on, piece-of-trash old car," I mutter, turning the key over again. "Start!"

I channel all my Luminaut power over ancient, corroded machines and will the stupid engine to spring to life. It gives a massive start, like a zombie resurrected from the dead, and settles into a contented, purring rumble.

"Yes!"

I put the station wagon in reverse, back out of the car port, and drive toward the corner. Sirens from the approaching ambulance and firetruck reach my ears, their bright, flashing lights filling my vision as they speed up the street toward Dr. Ormandi and his burned out house.

When I pull up to the curb at home, Mom's SUV isn't there. Neither is Dad's truck. The house is completely dark, save the Christmas lights lining the gutters and tossed into the bushes along the porch. My poor, booted Camry keeps a lonely vigil in the driveway.

Nobody's home. Perfect. Although, how Jase managed to escape despite being grounded is a feat. But whatever.

I jiggle the front door handle. Unlocked. Which is unusual, but not out of the ordinary. Once inside, I creep down the darkened hall to my room. Nemo rushes to greet me, and I pick him up.

"We're taking a trip, buddy," I tell him. "Ready to go somewhere new?"

Nemo whirs his wheels excitedly, and I rush to pack an overnight bag and my backpack. My sports duffel would be better, but I forgot it in the locker room. Or, what's left of the locker room. Mariasol's journals, the Light Core, some changes of clothes, and my heavy jacket, plus a beanie cap — in case I end up in a world whose winter is far colder than California. There, that should be good enough for a voyage into the unknown. I change out of my volleyball uniform into jeans, a tee shirt, and my winter boots, then wrap some ace bandages from volleyball around my cuts as makeshift first aid. A hoodie pulled over the top hides the evidence.

"Okay, Nemo, keep the Light Core safe for me." My little buddy blinks in affirmation, and I zip him up in my backpack. Time to bail.

As I stalk through the silent house toward the door, a light springs to life in the kitchen. Guess I'm not as alone as I thought.

"Callie?"

Jase runs toward me at a pace that's unusual for Jase when he's not on the soccer field. He looks relieved. Happy, even. A smile parts his lips, and he hugs me—actually hugs me.

"Who are you, and what have you done with my brother?" My voice is muffled against his chest. Jase releases me, his smile only growing.

"You're okay!" We haven't spoken more than two words to each other since our fight, and barely exchange glances. Now he's all smiles. This is weird.

"Yeah, I'm fine, why wouldn't I—"

And then, I remember the gym. How the roof was reduced to ash by Darkness at my volleyball game. The firefighters breaking down the front doors as I escaped. The sirens and panicked screams.

"Mom and Dad got the call you were the only player unaccounted for after the accident, and everyone rushed to the school to find you," Jase explains. "I stayed home in case you got back and there was a mix-up. What happened? Everyone's saying there was a fire or something. It's all over the news. I was watching it downstairs on Mom's computer."

"Jase, I—" How can I tell my brother, in the few short seconds I have with him, the truth? I find his eyes, and the look in mine erases all the good feelings in his. "I can't stay."

"Why?" Jase places his hands on my shoulders. "What's going on, Callie? Are you in trouble?"

"Yes."

Jase notices my backpack, my overnight bag. Thankfully, my hoodie and ace bandages hide the tracks of dried blood on my arms, or else he'd really freak out.

"You're going somewhere?" It's a statement more than a question.

Deep breath, in and out. I will myself to remain collected and cool. I don't have time for this, and yet, Jase looks so scared. It's the most emotion Jase has shown in a long time—especially toward me.

"Look, you guys are going to hear things, see things. Things that won't make any sense…" I shake my head. "I can't explain it right now, but tell Mom and Dad I'm okay. That I'll see them again one day."

Probably. Hopefully. Maybe not.

Fear and panic cloud Jase's brown eyes. He grips me tighter, as though he's afraid I'll disappear if he lets me out of his sight.

"Listen, whatever happened at the school, we'll figure it out. You'll be okay. We can fix it." He starts shaking, words crashing all around his lips, barely making sense. "I know I was a huge jerk to you about the car, about why you were sneaking around on Sundays, but I didn't think you were dealing with anything that would make you want to run away. If somebody's threatening you, or trying to hurt you, I'll protect you. I promise."

I bite down hard on the inside of my cheek. There's no way Jase can fix this. No way he can protect me. I'm the one who can fix it—the one who can protect them. But fixing it will break everyone's heart.

I look at the Christmas tree in the living room, decorated with Mom's favorite ornaments that we've made for her over the years. The Santa and gingerbread men I crafted in elementary school are front and center. A few of the presents underneath it are for me. Mom already bought all the ingredients for my favorite birthday cake—vanilla with chocolate frosting. Dad is not-so-secretly planning to take me fishing.

I think of Ryan and Tyler teasing me as badly as I tease them, of Olivia's happy, smiling little face, of Mom and Dad and their well-meaning, if constant, pestering about college, my future, and figuring out who I am. And then there's Jase, stoic Mr. Popular, standing in front of me with a look of horror that he might lose his little sister for good.

I may never see any of them again. But I have to go—to save them from a terrible fate they have no idea exists. Tears start to fall before I can stop them.

"I'm sorry, Jase." I throw my arms around him. "I'm sorry we got into that dumb fight. I'm sorry I humiliated you. I don't hate you, and I never did. You're my big brother. I love you."

Jase holds me tight. "Callie, please, don't."

I wrestle myself away from his grasp, and face him head on.

"I have to go." If not, you'll die, Jase. I grasp the doorknob. One step between my past, and my maybe. "Tell Mom and Dad I love them. And Ryan, and Tyler, and Livvy. Tell them I'm sorry."

"I'm not letting you leave." Jase grabs my arm desperately. I put my hand on his wrist, wiggling my fingers under his to break his grip.

"Don't make me force you, Jase."

Recollection of my Persuasion, and the terrifying effect it had, flitters across Jase's face. I can see his internal struggle as the muscles in his jaw twitch, his eyes darkened by uncertainty. But he releases me. Tears continue to slip down my cheeks as I turn away from my brother, and shut the door behind me.

There is one more thing I have to do before I can meet Nate at the pier.

I have to tell Will goodbye.

Will's house stands out from the rest of the block in the strangest way. All his neighbors have obnoxious, festive lights and yard decorations bedazzling their mansions, but Will's is dim, austere, set back from the others as though it can't be bothered to participate in joy and festivities. The only sign it's Christmastime is a single, slim tree in a front window, covered in white lights, but no ornaments.

Mr. and Mrs. Avila are kind of weird sometimes.

Will's car is parked by the four-car garage—his parents' cars are nowhere in sight. At least we'll have privacy. Hopefully, Will doesn't slam the door in my face as soon as he sees me.

When Will answers, he gives a start. My friend stands with his arms crossed over his chest like a bouncer, blocking the threshold to keep me out and away from his personal sphere. He tries to look tough and emotionless, but I can see the hurt in his eyes.

"Hi." I approach. He stiffens.

"Hi." His voice is tight.

"I know I'm the last person you want to see right now."

Will doesn't answer. He glances over my shoulder instead, and his scowl deepens. "What's with the station wagon?"

"It's Dr. Ormandi's. I kind of stole it."

"You steal cars now?" Will's eyebrows shoot sky-high. "Every time I see you, even more secrets come out. Anything else you want to tell me?"

"Yes. Goodbye."

"Goodbye?" Will's arms drop to his sides, instantly less defensive. "Where are you going? Why are you leaving? Is that blood on your fingernails? What happened?"

"Remember how Dr. Ormandi had a son—Nate—who died?" Will nods, and I go on. "Well, he's not quite dead—technically. At first, I thought he was this super hot ghost, and I had, like, a really intense crush, and we made out. But he's actually an undead Shadowmancer, and he's the reason the phantoms attacked us at the pier. And he and the phantoms just destroyed the high school gym at the booster fundraiser."

"Seriously?" Will's eyes pop, his tension and anger replaced by alarm. "I thought you had a thing for Zack Mendes, but this is way worse."

"Yeah. No joke." Let's not dwell on this particular embarrassment, okay, Will?

"Are Shadowmancers good kissers? What's it like to French kiss with a phantom sorcerer? I mean, wasn't the fact you could kiss him a dead giveaway he wasn't a ghost? You can't touch a ghost, they're translucent."

"The word you want is intangible. Focus, Will." I snap my fingers in front of his face. "He's after my Light Core, and he's threatening to hurt my family if I don't give it to him. I only came to say goodbye before Diver and I left."

"No, Callie, wait." Will grasps my elbow as I turn to go. "Come inside. Let's talk about this reasonably."

"I don't have time." I yank my arm away. "I have to get Diver and be at the pier at ten sharp."

"So you're actually giving him your Light Core?" Will looks incredulous. Shocked, even. "After all you went through for it, you're just going to give it away?"

"Of course I'm not going to give it to him." I snort impatiently. "I'm going to pretend I am, and then... I won't. I'll run away, or something."

"You expect to run away from the phantoms when he realizes what's up?" Will shakes his head. "Those things are killer, Callie. You can't wing this. You have to have a plan."

"Right. So let me finish saying goodbye, and I'll come up with one."

"I'll help you." Will pulls me inside the house, and shuts the door. "We have to have a distraction. Like, a decoy Light Core."

I blink, stunned. "Wait. Back up. Are you seriously going to help me? I thought you'd be happy I was leaving for good."

Will faces me, squaring his shoulders like a determined soldier.

"I'm helping you." He takes a deep breath. "I—I've been

awful to you. If you didn't love me, I didn't want anything to do with you, even though you didn't do anything wrong. You let me down as gently as you could. You even saved my life that night on the pier. And I was a selfish brat." He locks his puppy-dog eyes onto mine, his long lashes casting shadows over his cheeks in the dim light.

"I still love you, and a part of me always will. But if you're leaving tonight and never coming back, I'd rather part ways knowing we were best friends than nothing at all. Do you forgive me?"

"I forgive you." Relief forms a smile on my lips, and I give him the biggest hug. "I missed you, Will."

"I missed you, too." Will hugs me back in the best friend way he always hugs me before letting me go. "Okay, for real, you needed a plan to get past the bad guy five minutes ago."

"No kidding." I purse my lips, tapping them with my finger. "I like your decoy idea, but I don't know anything that makes the kind of light the Light Core does."

"When I held it, the light was really dim, remember? It didn't look like anything special at all." I can see the wheels spinning in Will's mind. "How about a bunch of glow sticks tied together? You always joke about it being a killer glow stick."

"Where are we going to get glow sticks in December?" I make a face. "That's kind of a Halloween thing."

"My mom has a bunch in the garage," Will offers excitedly. "She buys them as trick-or-treats for kids with peanut allergies."

"Okay, how's this: I'll be inside Diver with the real Light Core hidden in my backpack. Then, you paddle out on your surfboard with the decoy, and lure Nate and his phantoms away from me." Yes, this plan might—sort of, theoretically—work. Given Nate doesn't see through it straight away. But let's not dwell on the negative, right? "You could carve up some waves while I use the real Light Core to open a gateway. Then, when the gateway opens, you'll surf to shore, and Nate will follow me through the gateway while you get away."

"That could totally work." Will nods resolutely. "Let me get my wetsuit, and find those glow sticks."

"And I'll load your board into the station wagon."

Time to outsmart a Shadowmancer, save my family, and Dive into the unknown.

But, really, it's time to hopefully not die.

CHAPTER
TWENTY-EIGHT

"THIS IS DEPRESSING."

Will's dry observation is not inaccurate.

The fire department is just leaving Dr. Ormandi's house when we round the corner onto his street, one last engine heading up the street toward the fire station. When I pull up to the curb in front of the old man's house, the place is dark, abandoned, eerily like a haunted house on Halloween. The entire property has been cordoned off with caution tape, and the smell of charred wood, leaking natural gas, and singed wires hangs in the hazy air.

None of this feels as depressing as finding my friend enveloped in smoke, choking on a broken heart and writhing in a broken body. But yeah, the sight of the burned-out house is also pretty depressing.

"Come on, we've got to get Diver," I say instead. "Don't make any noise. Gossipy Barb is his neighbor, remember? She's the last person I want to see right now."

"Yeah, she'd interrogate you like a hardened FBI agent," Will agrees.

We shut the car doors as quietly as we can, lest Barb or Square-Head hears. Will pulls his surfboard from the back hatch, and I shoulder my backpack and overnight bag. The front door of the house remains still unlocked, and I hang Dr. Ormandi's keys on the hook. I say a silent prayer that he'll be home soon to find them.

"Dude, this place is wrecked." Will looks all around, blinking in the dim light. "How did the fire start?"

"Nate." The name is like poison to me now. It gags me to speak it. "He started it in the kitchen. I had to break the window to get in and air out the smoke. That's how my arms got all cut up."

"He torched his dad's house?" Will looks aghast. "That's messed up."

I want to tell Will the burned-up kitchen isn't even the worst of it. But we don't have time. We're on a mission.

"Diver is this way." I motion for Will to follow me through the dark. "Don't scream when you see him."

"Why would I scream?" Will is defensive.

"You screamed when you saw Nemo," I retort, "and he's the size of a chihuahua. Diver is three stories tall."

"I didn't scream at Nemo," Will mutters.

"You screamed. Totally screamed."

After a few minutes spent prying open the blackened basement door, we begin our descent. Will hefts his surfboard and follows me into the pitch dark. He sticks so close, the nose of the board jabs my shoulder blades.

"Diver!" I call into the impenetrable gloom. "It's Callie! I'm here!"

Crunching, creaking metal reverberates and echoes all around the cavernous space, and Diver's heavy footfalls reach my ears. Will starts breathing very hard behind me.

"Don't hyperventilate, and don't scream," I remind him.

A moment later, Diver's glowing eyes crackle to life about ten feet away. Will screams.

"I told you not to scream," I chide.

"But he's staring at me!" Will's voice hasn't been this high or pitchy since pre-puberty.

"He's looking at me," I assure my reactive friend. "He doesn't care about you."

"Are you sure it's not an evil robot? Because I'm not gonna lie, the eyes look pretty malevolent." Will tries to whisper, but what comes out is a squeak. "Like, he's just waiting to militarize all the other robots and become humanity's mechanical overlord. Maybe Dr. Ormandi was keeping him down here for the good of our species."

"No." Even though it's dark, I roll my eyes. Hard. "Diver is an old, lovable, rust bucket who wouldn't hurt a fly."

Luminaut. There is sadness. For the first time, Diver reaches out without waiting for me to command him. He bleeds grief from every cog, joint, and gear. It makes my insides ache.

The old Seer was injured. Darkness came. The son betrayed us. A Shadowmancer.

"I know, Diver," I whisper. "I'm sad, too."

"What was that?" Will whispers back.

"Nothing, I wasn't talking to you." Mental note: communicate nonverbally with Diver around Will. I don't have time to explain myself twice.

Diver, we're leaving. We're going to escape this basement and Dive.
Yes, Luminaut.

Take my friend and me to the Prism.

Diver lifts his hand to transport Will and me, and I guide my friend onto my robot's palm. Will grips my arm tight enough to cut off my circulation as we whoosh through the air toward Diver's head.

"Okay, so it's pitch black down here and I can't really see anything, but I can tell this place is absolutely massive." Will fumbles with his board as I guide him across Diver's narrow shoulder. "What is it?"

"Dr. Ormandi's basement lab."

Will whistles in amazement. "Is his lab as big as a football stadium, or what? How did he dig this place out? Did you help? What do you do down here? Where's the extra dirt from this massive hole? How far are we underground? Is a hole this big even legal?"

"If I wasn't on a time crunch with the fate of my entire family at stake, I'd be happy to have that discussion with you." Of all the times I've needed Will to just go with it, now is the most critical time.

After a bit of fumbling trying to open the hatch door, I lead Will by the hand to the Crow's Nest. Will's surfboard bumps and bangs the entire way, and he trips and almost falls in the dark, umph-ing and ow-ing every step. I'm glad one of us has good night vision.

"Just sit here." I lead Will to the sitting area, and help him ease himself and his surfboard onto the sofa. "Do you have your cell phone?"

"Uh, I'm in my wetsuit."

No pockets. Right.

"Never mind. I'll be doing this in the dark, I guess."

I trust my night vision, so far my most useful Luminaut power—because, let's face it, mind control is morally gray at best—and find my way to the lever by the Prism. A sharp tug is all it takes for the metal casings surrounding the Diver's head to retract with a swoosh.

"That sounded cool," Will says.

Diver, we need to get out of this basement. We need to finish the tunnel you started in the cliff wall with Mariasol. Can you do it?

It will require maximum effort.

I believe in you, Diver. Let's do it.

Diver surges with purpose and confidence, and begins moving toward the tunnel he and Mariasol worked on decades ago. Will sucks in a sharp breath at the sudden movement.

"Where are we going? Is there some kind of a door out?"

"Nope." I take a seat in the Luminaut pilot's chair, and buckle up in the straps. "You might want to hold onto something."

"What's that supposed to mean?" Will sounds nervous again.

"We're going to bust through the side of the cliff into the ocean." It's kind of unnerving how calmly I can say that.

"What!" Will shrieks. He's going to pop my eardrums before this night is over. "The basement will flood! We'll be underwater!"

"Yeah, that's the point." Flooded basement. Underwater... all the decades of work Dr. Ormandi and Mariasol did will be lost. "Diver! Stop!" I unbuckle from my seat and rush toward the Crow's Nest door. "Wait here, Will. I'll be right back."

"You're leaving me alone in the head of a gigantic, sentient robot in the dark!" Yikes, Will, the screaming is getting old.

"Calm down, I'll just be a minute."

Will does not calm down, and shouts threats and obscenities at me as I ride Diver's hand to the floor.

Rushing over to Dr. Ormandi's workstation, I grab his maps with gateway markers, his notebooks on oceanic currents, as well as some other random books, charts, and graphs — all of the work he and Mariasol did together — from the drawers of his desk. I deposit them in Diver's waiting palm, and hesitate.

Nate's vinyls.

It would be such a shame to lose all those awesome albums forever. They're mint condition, too. Nate is a Shadowmancer, he doesn't have any use for them. But I do. I've got to have some kind of entertainment on these other worlds I'll be visiting — a reminder of my home world and its culture. Besides, broken hearts are messy, and sneaky, lying, phantom sorcerers don't always get their albums back.

Sorry, Nate. Finders-keepers.

I load the record player and the crate of vinyl into Diver's palm, too, then ride up to the Crow's Nest with my treasures.

"Okay," I tell Will, hauling my prizes inside before I lock the door tight. "Now we're ready to bust through the cliff."

"Oh, yippee," Will deadpans.

"Hopefully my welds hold up," I add under my breath.

"Wait, welds?" Will sounds intrigued. "I didn't know you could weld."

"Yeah, I learned on YouTube."

"Dude, that's tight!" Then Will goes quiet. "Wait, what did you weld? Not something necessary for our rock-wall-busting, underwater survival, right?"

Um... "Don't worry about it, okay, Will?"

Diver, let's go.

Diver rushes into the tunnel, full speed. I steel myself to break through the wall into the ocean, to go from the pitch black of the basement to the murky, swirling waters near the cliffs.

This is it. We're going to do it. We—

We hit a wall. Diver smacks into the rocks and falls backward onto his seat. Will flies across the Crow's Nest, his surfboard skidding across the floor until it bumps into my seat up front.

"Geez, Callie!" my friend cries out. "Are you trying to kill me?"

"Sorry. I don't have the best track record with Diver and running into walls." I straighten myself in my chair. "Let's try this again."

Diver, dig out. Blast through the rocks until you're in the water.

Yes, Luminaut.

Diver stands, pounding the rocks with his fists. Once. Twice. A small spray of water hits the glass dome. Three times. Even more water.

"Something's happening," Will's jittery voice reaches my ears.

Four times. Rocks fall away, and water begins to flood the tunnel. Five times. Six times.

We're practically underwater now, violent gushes swirling around Diver, pulling him toward the sea. There's a sizable hole, big enough for Diver to slip through.

Diver, swim. Go through the hole.

Yes, Luminaut.

Diver pushes himself through the hole into the sea. We're instantly battered by rough, churning water slamming into the sides of the cliffs. The dark scatters, and wan moonlight shines through the water. It's eerily blue-black, inky yet clear, and pulling and pushing against Diver as violent waves crash into the cliffs above. We're stuck, floating, suspended in the melee like a half-sunk ship, or a very weirdly shaped submarine. One tip of the scale could send us to the surface and safety, or toward death at the bottom.

"We're in the ocean! We're going to drown! We're underwater!"

"Can you calm down for five seconds?" I snap. Will's freak-outs are getting old, fast.

Diver, go to shore. Swim, if you can.

Yes, Luminaut.

Diver float-bounces through the water, which I'm guessing is his version of robot-swimming, until his feet hit the seabed. He sloshes and plunges through the waves until the top of his head is exposed. Then his neck. Then chest. Seconds later, we're standing on the beach.

Diver, stop. I need to get my bearings.

Diver comes to a jarring halt. I unbuckle myself and rush to Will's side. He's white-knuckling the couch, and his surfboard has slid across the floor, along with my backpack, overnight bag, Dr. Ormandi's scientific charts and books, and Nate's record player. But so far, everything survived intact. Including Will.

"We made it," I assure my friend. "You can breathe now."

"I'm glad you're the Luminaut and not me," Will observes. "I *never* want to do that again."

"Danger and the high probability of death are part of the job description." I help Will to his feet, steadying him while he balances on his jellyfish legs. "Are you going to be okay?"

"Yeah, I'm cool." Color returns to Will's face, and he takes a few deep breaths. "Any sign of Nate Ormandi and his phantoms?"

Good question. From Diver's 360-degree windows, I look all around the beach. The night sky is clear, with a full, bright moon casting pale blue light over the silvery sand. Pillowy soft waves, like fluffy white clouds, gently roll toward the shore to kiss the beach before slipping back to sea. It's a gorgeous night. And yet, the entire strip of beach is deserted.

I'm going to wager a guess it has something to do with the high school gym crumbling to a pile of ash.

"I don't see him," I say. "But I'm sure he's here somewhere, lurking like an evil lurker."

"Where's the decoy Light Core?" Will grasps his surfboard tight at his side.

"My backpack." I find my pack in the mess created by Diver's cliff-busting moves, and get the glow sticks. There are five total, fastened together with clear packing tape. Will constructed it on the drive to Dr. Ormandi's house. I wouldn't exactly call it a close approximation to the Light Core. It's smaller, thinner, weirdly plastic-looking even from a distance, and glows neon greenish-yellow. But, hopefully, it'll pass.

"Stay inside, Nemo," I tell my little buddy, who clamors to hop out and explore. "We didn't Dive yet. We just broke Diver out of robot jail."

"I want to say goodbye to Nemo," Will says. "I mean, I'm his co-trainer."

Nemo pulls himself out of my backpack and whizzes up to Will, waving his little arms wildly. Will picks him up and gives him an affectionate pat. "I'm glad I got to meet you, little dude. Don't forget me, okay?"

Nemo purrs, hugging Will's arm. My friend gives Nemo one last pet, then deposits him in my backpack. I zip my tiny robot away.

Time is rapidly running out. Now or never.

"This is it." I swallow hard. Will does, too.

"We can do it, Callie."

"It's not too late to change your mind," I remind him. "You could die doing this. Tentacle phantoms could overtake you while I'm opening the gateway. Or the gateway could open and start to pull you under before you're safely on shore. There are literally a million things that could go wrong."

Will remains determined. "I promised I'd help you."

"I guess dying while surfing is better than drowning in a giant robot by the cliffs," I say with a smile.

Will smiles, too. "Totally."

"Speaking of surfing," I add delicately, "this may not be the best time to bring up the fact you suck at surfing, but… you suck at surfing, and I kind of need you not to suck."

"This is the night." Will smiles confidently. "I'm going to ride that wave for you. I'll make it all the way down the break. And if I don't, it'll be one heck of a last ride."

I'd rather go out riding a wave of glory, but I'm stuck in the head of a giant robot. Who knows if I'll ever surf again? Who knows if I'll ever come back to California? This could be my last time on this beach, looking at these waves, with my hometown pier forming the backdrop of the starry California night.

This part of my life will be gone in a matter of minutes. My family, my school, my future—or lack thereof—my beach, my home.

My best friend. My Will.

Our eyes meet, and I throw my arms around him. We don't need words. We know what's at stake. We know what happens if we fail.

Even worse, we know what happens if we succeed.

"I'll miss you so much," I whisper. "You're the best friend I ever had, Will Avila."

Will holds me tight, squeezing me until it's hard to draw air into my lungs. "Remember me while you're off hunting Light Cores and exploring other worlds, okay? Maybe come back and say hi sometime."

"Sure—pending I don't die." I blink against the pinpricks stinging my eyes. "I'll never forget you."

"I'll never forget you, either." Will steps back and grins. "My best friend, Calliope James, the famous Luminaut. I'm going to make a killing writing a memoir of your childhood."

A laugh bubbles out of me. "Don't use my full name," I tease him for old times' sake. "You know I hate it."

Will smiles, his eyes going soft, almost sad. There's a twinge of regret behind them, and longing. He wants me to stay—wants things to be different than they are. For time to turn backward and give us both a chance to make a different choice, to arrive at a different crossroad.

"Listen, Callie, we both know it won't mean anything, but..."

He trails off, shifting on his feet awkwardly. "Just once, can I kiss you goodbye?"

The corners of my mouth inch upward, and I nod. "Yes, you can kiss me goodbye."

Will leans in, brushing his lips against mine. He lingers a moment, his breath fluttering against my cheek, before pulling away. It's sweet, ultra-chaste, and full of love—not romantic, boyfriend and girlfriend love, and nothing like the heady intensity of the way I'd kissed Nate. Will's kiss is the love of friendship and memories, and a lifetime of caring about each other.

Will is wrong to say it doesn't mean anything. If this is quite possibly my last kiss, I'm glad it came from my best friend.

"Okay, this is it." Will hides the decoy Light Core in his wetsuit and picks up his surfboard. "Good luck, Callie."

"Good luck, Will."

My best friend leaves the Crow's Nest, and I command Diver to put him on the sand. Then, he darts out of sight, waiting until Nate shows his face to make our move.

Where is Nate, anyway? He made a huge show of taking out the gym with Darkness and threatening me and everyone I love, all to reiterate what would happen if I was late. Well, I'm here. Not late. I mean, I think I'm not. I don't have my cell phone.

What if I *am* late? What if it's after ten? Maybe Will and I should go check on my family. I pace the Crow's Nest, chewing on my bottom lip as I debate my options.

A black fog descends on the beach, rolling in like an ominous vapor from the clouds, the sea, the earth. It obscures the hotels and boardwalk from my sight, turning the beach ghostly, sinister. The cliffs and the pier are lost in darkness. Chill crawls over my skin, and the all-too-familiar combination of fury and terror swells in my chest.

From the fog, he appears.

Nate.

I step out onto Diver's shoulder to face him, rage, sorrow, and terror burning in my heart like an unquenchable blaze. He leers up at me from the sand.

"Hey, you're early. That's surprising. And well-armored, which is less surprising." The leer quickly turns into a threat. "You aren't planning on Diving away with that Light Core, are you?"

"I don't know how to Dive." It's not a lie, because technically, I've only read about how to do it. Does Nate need to know the fine print? Absolutely not.

"Oh, good." The wicked smile returns. "Because trying to trick me would be immensely stupid of you."

"As you've mentioned." I cross my arms over my chest. "I need an intimidating bodyguard to protect me from heartless monsters like you."

"Bodyguard. Cute. As if *you're* not the one who tried to kill me with a Light blast in the gym." Nate's glower could turn water to ice. "Let's cut to the chase. Breaking human hearts isn't very fun for me, and you've probably got raw cookie dough to eat and sad movies to cry over, so give me the Light Core, and we'll both move on."

"I'm waiting on my friend to bring it."

"Your friend? Are you joking?" Nate's mouth strains at the edges until it turns downwards into the most horrifying grimace I've ever seen.

Okay, Will, now would be a super awesome time for you to show up.

"Hey! Over here, you stupid jerk!"

Will appears out in the middle of the swells, straddling his surfboard and holding the decoy Light Core high above his head.

Nate whips around, and tentacle phantoms spring like a visible manifestation of his anger into the air around him.

"Looking for this?" Will swings the decoy around. "Come and get it!"

Nate's phantoms race toward my friend, mouths gaping, sucking, reaching. Will catches the next wave, carving it up and seriously going off like a legit pro. It's the best I've ever seen Will surf, and I itch to be down in the waves with him, cheering him on.

But if I do, I'll lose my chance to escape. Nate vanished with his phantoms, probably using all his power to command them to chase Will and the fake Light Core. If I have any hope of getting out of here alive with the real Light Core, I have to bail. Now.

Diver, let's go. Into the water.

Diver wades into the waves—far from where Will is surfing the heck out of the swells, keeping the tentacle phantoms on their toes as they give him chase—and I pull the real Light Core out of my backpack.

The moment my old beach towel falls to the floor, the Light seeps through my skin and invades my nerves, my blood, my heart and soul. The Light Core hums in my hands, louder and louder until it becomes a whirring pulse. Light floods the Crow's Nest, pierces the windows, reaches for the sky. I can feel it in me and around, filling every fiber, every atom.

Diver, halt.

Below us, the ocean spins like a top mere inches from the Diver's toes. A gigantic whirlpool, big enough to swallow a cruise ship and ask for seconds, forms in an instant.

Nate's phantoms abandon their swirling search of the waves for Will and the fake Light Core, materializing in thin air around the Crow's Nest. Nate is suspended in the midst of them, held aloft by his dark minions. His furious black and red eyes lock onto mine as he realizes he's been played the same way he played me.

I didn't lie—not technically. I just omitted certain facts. Surprise, Nate. Are you shocked?

Will reaches the shallows just as the whirlpool takes shape, sprinting to shore and safety with his board.

The Light Core hangs in midair high above my head, a beacon that blazes for miles. I stand, surrounded by Light, its power flowing inside and out. I am one with the Light, the sea, the sky. My body trembles with the raw strength of the magic. This is it. Time to—

Whup-whup-whup.

Seriously? What now?

A Coast Guard chopper buzzes into view, swarming around the Diver's head like an irritating little bee.

Fabulous. A Coast Guard chopper. The authorities are the absolute last thing I need right now. Can't they *see* the black phantoms materializing like Cthulhu in thin air? The three-stories-tall robot and the ginormous whirlpool?

Go away, Coast Guard chopper.

"Move away from the whirlpool. Return your... uh, watercraft to port immediately." The pilot yells at me over the loudspeaker just as the tentacle phantoms begin swirling around Diver's limbs. "I repeat, move away from the whirlpool. Return to port."

I *really* do not have time for this.

"Go away!" I shout as loud as I can, hoping the chopper pilot can hear me through Diver's thick glass dome and the thundering boom of the rotor blades. "Get out of here before the murder-phantoms get you!"

"Move away from the whirlpool! Your watercraft will be cited and fined. Return to port immediately."

Guess he couldn't hear me.

I ignore the poor Coast Guard pilot—who's probably taking videos of this to post online as soon as he gets off duty—and place the Light Core in Diver's Prism. Light narrows into laser-like focus on the whirlpool, then bursts from the sea in a column of space-shattering brilliance. It stretches from the farthest depths to the heights of the stars and beyond.

My door to another world.

Time to see if Dr. Ormandi was right—if a broken multiverse lies waiting for me on the other side.

If he's wrong, I'll die. But my family will be safe.

Plus, no SAT in a couple weeks. Score.

Tentacle phantoms climb Diver's chest, scratching and clawing at the thick metal casing, desperately hungry to reach me and my Light.

They're unable to pierce it. Can they pierce it? I don't want to find out.

Nate hovers inches from Diver's head, his stare narrowed as we regard one another. A twinge of regret and fear fills his eyes that I'm the enemy he's made for himself. I just might be the most stubbornly difficult adversary he'll face, and he knows it. If he wants me and my Light Core, he's going to have to bring his A-game. I'm certainly bringing mine.

One last glance over my shoulder toward my beloved beach. Will is safely ashore, his arm high over his head in a farewell wave. It's the first time Will has ever surfed a wave. He did it for me when I needed him. His last act as my best friend.

"Goodbye, Will."

I buckle into the Luminaut's chair, steeling myself for the unknown.

Goodbye, Dr. Ormandi. Goodbye, Mom, Dad, my siblings and friends. Goodbye, Verona Beach. California. Earth. Home.

This is it. The first moment of my terrifying, unwanted

destiny.

"Diver, let's go."

Nate's phantoms encircle themselves around Diver, surrounding my robot's form as he leans over the edge of the precipice. Wherever we're Diving, they're coming with us. Away from my family, friends, and home. For better or worse.

Light consumes every sense I have. Time, space, and reality are suspended in the power of Light, juxtaposed to the violence of Darkness creeping up my robot's limbs.

We only have seconds to Dive before the gateway becomes unstable. Before I lose my chance.

From the depths of my fear and uncertainty comes a small voice, the long-dead spirits of Luminauts past urging me to embrace what I am. To be the Light. To seek it even in the darkest places.

We are always with you.

Trust it. Breathe. Dive.

I spread my arms wide and let myself fall.

The adventure continues in

LIGHT HUNTER!

Callie James crash-lands the World Diver into an alternate dimension. She kind of needed a Seer to help with piloting. Too bad she was busy escaping evil hottie Nate Ormandi to worry about that.

Now she's stuck on Tremurheim, a mysterious world of tree-vikings and soul-sucking mist monsters.

But somewhere on the planet a Light Core calls to her. Now she just has to find it as part of her quest to unite the multiverse. A quest she'll complete no matter what stands in her way.

The only local who will help is Toran Rykjiersen, who's basically a jerk. But he's also desperate to get his little sister Heike off Tremurheim—even if that means aiding a dangerous "skyfire sorceress" like Callie.

Meanwhile, evil dude Nate must capture the Light Core of the world Ictari. As an undead Shadowmancer, finding Light isn't his forte, but if he fails, his master will end him the rest of the way. Permanently.

As Luminaut and Shadowmancer race to find the Light Cores, the line between hero and villain blurs. And the quest that Callie holds dear might lead to the very evil she hopes to prevent.

ACKNOWLEDGEMENTS

This list of people who have supported me in relaunching my first trilogy back into the world is so long I am sure I will forget somebody, but I'll try my best.

To my editors, Katie Phillips and Amy Williams: your expertise and knowledge helped make this book even better than I thought it could be. In case you don't hear it enough, you're amazing.

To my lovely critique swap partner, Margaret McGriff: thank you for your honesty and enthusiasm, even when reading my dumpster fire zero drafts. That early feedback is so appreciated, and you're a rockstar.

To my Realmie Roomies, Liz, Michelle, and Kaitlyn: thanks for the laughs and emotional support the summer after I received the devastating news of my former publisher's closure. It meant more than you know.

To every beta reader I've ever had, please know that I've appreciated your feedback at whatever stage of writing we encountered each other. All of you rock!

To my fantastic character artist Kristen Hildebrand and cover designer Emilie Haney: you captured the spirit of the books and characters in a way I never thought possible, and I'm forever amazed by your skill and artistry.

Thanks to everyone who has supported my books and writing adventures over the years: my readers who have hyped and loved my characters, my fellow writers in mastermind groups and advanced writing and marketing classes, all of my editors, teachers, and friends. I literally could not have done this without you. There are far too many of you to name without forgetting anyone, so please know that if you supported me even in a very minuscule way, it didn't go unnoticed, and I'm so very grateful.

Last but not least, to my family: my parents, my sisters, literally countless aunts, uncles, and cousins, and my own little unit—Ty, Aaron, and Evie. I can't say I love you enough, or express how grateful I am to have your support all these years. You're simply the best.

ABOUT THE AUTHOR

Haylie Hanson is an author, teacher, and disability educator who loves everything geeky. When she isn't dreaming of adventures in a galaxy far, far away, Haylie can be found drinking too much coffee and writing stories about kids with superpowers, a love of STEM, and snarky humor. Haylie lives with her family in Colorado.